Keelie was finding it hard [...] Michael's mouth. How had sh[...] much it made her want to kiss [...]

He looked even better than when he'd been dressed in scrubs. He was wearing cowboy boots, jeans, and a henley shirt with a dark green wool shirt over it that set off his eyes. She had to stop staring at his eyes; they were deadly.

"So tell me this story about Rip."

She loved the way he listened to her, his face still, his eyes never leaving hers. It was like he really heard her. Sometimes he smiled a little at the things she said.

Don't think of the smile . . . don't look at the eyes . . .

She stood up too quickly and got a head rush, which made her sway a little. He stood, too, and reached out to steady her.

"I . . . um . . ." Her vision swam, because his face seemed awfully close, and then he did it. He kissed her. Her body leaned into his as her mind emptied of everything except the warmth of his lips. The slightly minty taste of his tongue. The way his face scratched against hers. The smell and feel of him. She'd known she hadn't been the only one who felt the attraction . . .

BOOK YOUR PLACE ON OUR WEBSITE AND MAKE THE READING CONNECTION!

We've created a customized website just for our very special readers, where you can get the inside scoop on everything that's going on with Zebra, Pinnacle and Kensington books.

When you come online, you'll have the exciting opportunity to:

- View covers of upcoming books
- Read sample chapters
- Learn about our future publishing schedule (listed by publication month *and author*)
- Find out when your favorite authors will be visiting a city near you
- Search for and order backlist books from our online catalog
- Check out author bios and background information
- Send e-mail to your favorite authors
- Meet the Kensington staff online
- Join us in weekly chats with authors, readers and other guests
- Get writing guidelines
- AND MUCH MORE!

**Visit our website at
http://www.kensingtonbooks.com**

A Coventry
Christmas

Becky Cochrane

ZEBRA BOOKS
Kensington Publishing Corp.
www.kensingtonbooks.com

ZEBRA BOOKS are published by

Kensington Publishing Corp.
850 Third Avenue
New York, NY 10022

All Kensington titles, imprints, and distributed lines are available
at special quantity discounts for bulk purchases for sales promo-
tion, premiums, fund-raising, educational, or institutional use.

Special book excerpts or customized printings can also be created to fit specific needs. For details, write or phone the office
of the Kensington Special Sales Manager: Attn. Special Sales
Department. Kensington Publishing Corp., 850 Third Avenue,
New York, NY 10022. Phone: 1-800-221-2647.

Zebra and the Z logo Reg. U.S. Pat. & TM Off.

ISBN 0-8217-8042-5

First Printing: October 2006
10 9 8 7 6 5 4 3 2 1

Printed in the United States of America

Acknowledgments

I couldn't do what I love without my editor, John Scognamiglio, the people at Kensington including Cara Muller, and my agent, Alison J. Picard.

With thanks to the women who've inspired and supported me along the way: my mother Dorothy, Amanda, Amy, Audrey, Carreme, Christine, Clara, two Debbies, Debby, Denece, Elnora, Geraldine, Gina, Heather, Janet, Kathy, Katie, Laura, Lil, Lindsey, three Lisas, Lynn, Lynne, Marika, Marla, Mary, Michelle, Nan, Nancy, Nora, Pat, Rhonda, Robin, Sarah, Sarena, Shannon, Shanon, Sharon, Shawn, Star, Susan, Tandy, Tara, Tay, two Terris, Trish, Vicki, and Wendy.

And to the men: my husband Tom, Aaron, Alan, Alex, Bobby, Craig, Daniel, two Davids, Dean, Don, two Geralds, Greg, James, Jason (not an ex), three Jeffs, Jess, Jim, Joe, two Johns, Josh, Larry, Richard, Riley, Rob, two Rons, Stephen, two Steves, four Timothys, and Tracy.

Thank you to all my online friends, especially Sheila, who has not only encouraged me, but whose niece gave me Destiny's name.

Bless you, 249 Animal Clinic, West Alabama Animal Clinic, and Sunset Boulevard Animal Clinic, for taking such wonderful care of those who've taken good care of me and the people I love.

River: Rip is your gift to me.

Chapter 1

"I *hate* Christmas," Keelie Cannon said, flinging herself into a chair at the table in Bennigan's where she'd agreed to meet her friends. She blew her ash-blond bangs out of her blue eyes and reached under the table to rub her ankles, looking around at the noisy restaurant. She'd have preferred a quieter place, but because of her schedule, she'd chosen convenience over atmosphere.

"How can you hate Christmas?" Evan asked, signaling their server, who hurried over to take Keelie's drink order.

"It's the most wonderful time of the year," Holly agreed. "It's also my birthday."

"Vodka martini," Keelie muttered. "Two olives. I don't care what brand of vodka as long as it gets here fast." As the server turned away, Keelie yelped, "Wait!" The woman turned back with a puzzled look. "I can't drink. I have to go back to work in an hour. Just bring me a Coke, please." The server nodded and again tried to walk away, but Keelie said, "No, wait. I don't need the calories."

"Or the caffeine," Holly said.

"Just water," Keelie said. "I'm sorry. I'm as bad as my customers. I promise not to bitch about my food. And I'll leave a good tip."

"Don't worry," the server said. "I've never spat in anyone's food yet."

"Bring her the martini," Evan said firmly. After the server walked away without further protest from Keelie, Evan continued his pep talk. "I'm all about Christmas spirit. Tinsel, mistletoe, Christmas carols. Exchanging presents. Chestnuts roasting on an—"

"You two should join a choir," Keelie said. "Walk a mall in my shoes. Which reminds me. I'm sorry I had to make you come to the Galleria. I'm sure parking was awful."

"It's okay," Holly assured her. She pointed toward the restaurant windows that overlooked the indoor ice rink and said, "I brought the boys with me. They're skating with their sitter, and she's taking them to the food court for Happy Meals after. They're thrilled to have a McNight, so it was the perfect choice."

"You know I'm all about the shopping," Evan said. "Since I'm always off on Monday, I spent the whole day buying presents. I'll be ready for Christmas way early."

"I won't," Keelie said. "Everybody can count on books from me this year, because I'll never get enough time away from that damn bookstore to shop for gifts."

"I suppose if Buy The Book is really busy, it's a good sign for the economy," Holly said.

"Do you *always* look on the bright side?" Keelie smiled, as much at the martini that was set in front of her as to take the sting out of her words.

"Are you guys ready to order?"

"We're waiting for one more person," Holly said. When they were alone again, she said, "You know Ivy will be late. These days, she never seems to leave the office on time."

"She's probably stuck in traffic," Evan said.

"If she's too late, I'll miss her," Keelie said. "Charlotte wasn't happy about staying longer so I could come to dinner."

"Tell us about your awful customers and why they have you drinking on your dinner break," Evan said.

"A preschooler climbed a pyramid of books on Egypt and brought it crashing down on top of her. Two boys turned themselves into Jedi knights by using rolled maps for light sabers. We had an upchucker in Children's. I had to explain repeatedly that we are *not* Houston's renowned bookstore, Murder By The Book. Although I've had maps printed up for their store, which saves me a lot of time giving directions. All in all, a typical day. Just before I came to meet y'all, I got stuck with a real winner. Nothing pleased her. 'The associates weren't *helpful,*'" Keelie mimicked the customer's tone, "so she demanded to see a manager. Charlotte was still cleaning up puke, so I took the customer, who bitched because I'm only an *assistant* manager. I gave her Rodney's card if she wants to call him tomorrow. But get this. The problem was that she doesn't like dust jackets. 'They're *tacky* and *cheap looking.* Don't you have any leather-bound books? I can't give *these* as gifts.' So I explained that we're a chain store; we don't carry those kinds of books. I told her about all the wonderful specialty bookshops in Houston where she might find gifts that would suit her. I even offered to write down their names and addresses. When she realized that one of them is a collectible book dealer, she shrieked that she couldn't give her friends used books. She thinks of first editions and rare books as used!"

"What an idiot," Evan commiserated.

"She probably *will* call Rodney, and he'll act like it was all my fault and give me another lecture on customer service, as if I haven't been doing this job without his guidance for six years." Keelie sighed. "Remember when I used to like my job?"

"You still do," Evan said. "It's just that evil Rodney."

"And that you're tired," Holly added.

"Rodney's all worked up because some shrinkage guy is coming from Corporate in New York. Apparently, shoplifting is on the rise in our store. Corporate thinks it's employee theft. Right. Like anyone who works there has time to figure out what books they'd like to steal. Instead, do you think maybe Rodney shouldn't have ignored my warning not to put the art books right by the exit? The most expensive books in the store. And our loss prevention system is a big fraud—those sensors don't really do anything. The cameras in the ceiling? Connected to nothing. It's all just for show. A *deterrent,* they call it. We're too understaffed and busy to watch that section constantly, so it's the easiest thing in the world to walk out the door with a two-hundred-dollar coffee-table book."

"I know where I'm doing the rest of my Christmas shopping," Evan said.

"Me, too," Holly said brightly.

Keelie sighed again and said, "You'd better hurry before there's nothing left to steal except books on drawing caricatures or whittling."

"My shopping list is full of people who are all about working with wood," Evan said.

"You should have been made manager, Keelie," Holly

said. "It's so unfair. The employees respect you, you've worked your way up, and you've been devoted to Buy The Book for all these years."

"Can I use you for a reference when Rodney fires me?"

"He wouldn't dare," Evan said. "You're bulletproof, like me. Cleo can never fire me from the salon because I know where all the bodies are buried."

"The salon," Keelie moaned. "I wish I had time to come in for a cut. Look at my bangs!"

"I've been trying not to," Evan said sympathetically.

"I know. They're awful. I'll stop bitching any hour now. At least I have Christmas Eve to look forward to."

"Why? Did Rodney give you time off? Are you going home?" Holly asked.

"No way would he give me enough time off to get to Georgia and back. The days after Christmas are just as busy with returns and exchanges. No, I love Christmas Eve because it's not only a short workday, but that's when we get the desperate shoppers. Especially the husbands. They'll buy anything, and they're thrilled just to find it. Last year, one of my coworkers gave me a stuffed pig that snorted 'Jingle Bells.' I kept it with me when I reassured the customers standing in line that they'd be out of there in ten minutes. You wouldn't believe how many people offered to buy that pig and for how much."

"Sounds like a good way to pick up extra cash," Evan said.

"No shit. I could just fill the office with crap from my apartment, take it on the floor one item at a time, and make more on Christmas Eve than the store pays me in a week!" Keelie turned to Holly and said, "Subject change. Why did you want to get together? It sounded important."

"I don't know if it's important," Holly said. "I just want some backup because I have to tell Ivy—"

"Shhh," Evan warned. "Here she comes."

Keelie and Evan laughed as Ivy stopped short at their table and stared at Holly with dismay. They were both wearing black slacks, black sweaters, and a single gold necklace. Both of them had their auburn hair brushed back into ponytails, and they were wearing identical black boots.

"Oops, you did it again," Keelie said.

"After so many years of refusing to dress alike, why do we always end up in the same outfit now?" Ivy asked, shaking her head at Holly.

"Just that twin connection, I guess," Holly said. "But you look great!"

Ivy took the empty chair and said, "We look like Robert Palmer's backup singers."

"If Holly would let me highlight her hair like yours—"

"No!" both women simultaneously interrupted Evan.

"We have to have something that's different," Ivy said. "Everyone promised we'd look less alike as we got older, but they lied."

"Anyway, I don't need high-maintenance hair," Holly said. "Moms don't have time for that."

"I saw the boys skating," Ivy said. "They looked so adorable. Who's with them?"

"The most responsible babysitter in Pearland," Holly said. "Melissa."

"Have y'all ordered?"

"We were waiting for you," Evan said.

After their server came back, took their orders, then brought Ivy a Guinness, Keelie said, "I think Holly was just about to tell us something." When Holly frowned at her, she quickly said, "Or maybe not."

Evan launched into one of his you'll-never-believe-what-happened-at-the-salon stories, and Keelie sat back and sipped her martini while she studied him.

Although Evan Hammett was thirty-five, he didn't look seven years older than Keelie. His blond hair was styled in a faux hawk, a style Keelie had never really understood, but it worked for Evan. At six feet, Evan was too tall to be waifish, but he was thin. Keelie thought it suited him, especially his angular face. When he smiled, deep lines formed on either side of his mouth. Evan said they were wrinkles in training and swore he was going to start Botoxing, but Keelie knew he wouldn't. Evan was only too aware that everyone loved his smile lines.

It was chance that had brought Keelie and Evan together, but it was Evan's extroverted personality that made them friends. Keelie had always been a little bashful about meeting new people. More than three years before, on a rare Saturday off of work, she'd gone alone into Houston's artsy Montrose district and wandered in and out of antique shops on Westheimer. The July heat had been unbearable. On a whim, she walked into a salon and asked the first stylist she saw to shave her head, only half kidding.

Evan had said, "Girl, you do not need new hair. You need new air. Sit in front of the AC until I finish these lowlights, then we'll talk."

They began a conversation that was still going years later. Evan had a way of turning anything into an occasion, whether it was a trip to the grocery store or an impromptu pizza party. He made Keelie feel funnier than she was, but he also had a serious side. She could talk to him about anything, and on the rare occasions when he was in a funk, it made her feel good to be an equally sympathetic listener for him.

Keelie snapped out of her reverie when she heard Ivy ask, "What was Keelie saying that you wanted to talk about?"

"Just everybody's Christmas plans," Holly said casually. "I really should book time at the salon, Evan. I need an overhaul. Hair cut, legs waxed—"

"Eyebrows waxed," Evan said.

Holly picked up her knife, tried to see her reflection, and asked, "Are they terrible?"

"I didn't really notice until I saw Ivy's," Evan said.

"That's just Ivy," Keelie said. "She even looks good in August, and nobody manages that in Houston."

"It's not the heat; it's the humidity," the other three intoned on cue.

"You're like our long lost triplet," Ivy said to Evan. "I think we could all use a day of beauty. A Christmas treat for ourselves."

"Not unless Evan can work on me at the bookstore," Keelie said. "Oh, God, will January ever get here?"

"Poor lamb," Ivy said. "Is it awful?"

"I've already bored them with my tragic retail dramas," Keelie said. "Be thankful you missed it."

"Even though you can't be home with your family, you can spend Christmas with the Johnsons, like last year," Ivy said. "Mom will just happen to remember a box of ornaments in the attic, so we'll all get our chance to finish trimming the tree. Granny will be there driving Mom crazy. Holly's boys will get way too many presents, and Evan will make a pig of himself at dinner."

"But it won't be like last year," Holly said. They all looked at her, hearing the sadness in her voice. "Everything's different."

"It's your first Christmas without your father," Keelie said. "That's got to be hard."

"And Dave's stuck in Scotland alone, instead of being with me and our sons. And last year, Mark was with us."

"That last one is no great loss," Ivy said crisply. She always cut off any discussion of her ex-fiancé. "It'll be hardest on Mom. We'll have to put on our happy holiday faces. As much as I miss Daddy, I know it's worse for her."

Holly winced and said, "That's sort of why I wanted us to get together tonight." When none of them said anything, she went on. "Scotty and Carla want Mom to visit them in Hawaii for the holidays."

Keelie closed her eyes, trying to envision Christmas where there was more high tide than yule tide. As she pictured hot surfers and men sizzling on the beach, she knew she could enjoy a Hawaiian Christmas in a whole different way than Mrs. Johnson would with her son, daughter-in-law, and grandchild.

"Mom will never go to Hawaii at Christmas," Ivy said, as if it were settled. There was a lull in conversation when their food arrived. After Ivy took a few bites of salad, she realized that Holly was watching her. She finished chewing, swallowed, and asked, "Why are you staring at me?"

"Although I want to spend Christmas with Mom, especially since Dave's away, I think it might be good for her to make the trip," Holly said. "She always sees us, and she's spent every Christmas with my boys. If she goes to Hawaii, she'll get to see her new granddaughter, and Scotty and Carla would love to have Christmas with her since they're so far away from home. Plus, I think Christmas will be really sad for her without Daddy here."

"No matter where she is, Christmas will be rough,"

Ivy agreed. "But if she's here, at least she'll have the comfort of knowing that our traditions will go on. And we have so many memories we can share. Keelie and Evan will understand if we all get a little emotional." Ivy glanced at Keelie, who nodded. "Sometimes keeping up our routines helps us deal with grief."

Holly bit her lip, then looked at Evan and asked, "What do you think?"

"Do you always need a man's opinion?" Ivy asked sharply. "Just drop it, Holly. Mom will be with us at Christmas like always."

Keelie and Evan exchanged an uncomfortable look, and Evan said, "I think you both should let your mother do whatever she wants and support her decision."

The twins glowered at each other, but any possibility of further conversation was cut off when half of the Bennigan's staff began clapping their way through the restaurant, stopping at a nearby booth to sing "Happy Birthday" to a little girl who looked completely humiliated. Keelie watched in silent sympathy—she hated that kind of fanfare, too—then groaned when the girl's face took on a greenish tinge.

"Another upchucker," she said as the girl's mother grabbed her hand and led her toward the bathroom. "I can't believe she didn't wait to do that in my store."

On her bus ride home after finishing her shift and closing Buy The Book, Keelie thought about the strain between Holly and Ivy. Since Ivy's breakup with Mark, she'd kept her distance from the rest of them, citing long hours at work or plans she'd made with other friends. Even when she was with them, she never seemed like herself. But in all the time Keelie had known the sisters, she'd never heard them argue. She'd assumed it was because they were twins. Keelie and her own sister, who was two years younger, frequently had big emotional blowouts with each other, but they both knew they'd always make up.

Her bus stop was only a half block from her landlords' driveway, and as tired as she was, it still lifted Keelie's spirits to walk past the Atwells' flower beds to her apartment. Although it was December, because of Houston's climate, the roses, bougainvillea, firecracker ferns, and alyssum were all in bloom. Fat blossoms dotted the camellia trees. She broke off a sprig of rosemary and crushed it between her fingers, inhaling its pungent aroma.

She'd been lucky to find such a great apartment the year before. The Atwells owned one of the more modest River Oaks mansions, but their garage apartment was spacious and pretty, with hardwood floors and lots of windows. They didn't charge her much because they didn't really need the rental income; they just liked having the apartment occupied so that it wouldn't get musty and mildewed from the humidity. Since she was so close to the bus stop, she didn't have to worry about the expense of car payments, upkeep, and insurance. And the Atwells were ideal landlords: there if she needed them, but never snooping into her life.

Not that I have much of a life, she thought as she climbed the stairs and unlocked the door. Working at the bookstore. Occasional nights out at a bar, the movies, or dinner with friends. No boyfriend on the horizon. Her family nearly a thousand miles away.

She dropped her bag inside the door, slid her aching feet out of her shoes, and turned on lights as she walked to Hamlet's cage. The wheel squeaked as the dwarf hamster ran with excitement at her homecoming.

"Hey, buddy," Keelie said. She took Hamlet out of the cage, rubbed his head, and crooned over him, her heart stupid with love for this mini bundle of fur who seemed to love her back. After a few minutes, she put him in his plastic ball so he could follow her through the apartment while she changed into sweat pants and a T-shirt.

She'd never intended to get an animal companion. The long hours she worked made a dog out of the question, and she'd never been a fan of cats. She'd also never been attracted to anything in the rodent family before the night she impulsively went into a pet store while walking through the mall. The way the hamster had watched her from his case and pawed at the glass whenever she talked to him won her over. She'd bought Hamlet, his cage, and the hamster ball that night. Over time, she'd added his metal wheel, Habitrail, and all kinds of toys to keep him busy. She even got a plastic case designed for traveling, and when Joyce was still the store manager, Keelie occasionally took Hamlet to work, where he had a second home in an old aquarium in the stockroom.

The store's associates had turned him into their little Buy The Book mascot. They made up a "Hamlet's Picks" newsletter for book recommendations, wrote silly limericks about him on the dry erase board in the staff room, and had his picture printed on T-shirts that they wore during after-hours inventory and shelving parties.

Maybe that had just been their way of sucking up to her, because they knew Hamlet was her soft spot, but she didn't think so. Hamlet bonded them and built morale. But it had all come to an end when Joyce was transferred and Rodney took over the store. Rodney didn't believe in Take Your Hamster to Work Day.

She put Hamlet back in his cage, filled his bottle with fresh water, and topped off his food while thinking of Holly's words: *You should have been made manager.* She'd been tempted to quit when Jimmy, their Regional Manager, passed her over. He explained that they rarely let assistant managers take over the stores where they'd trained, and Keelie wasn't willing to relocate. Although it might be nice to work in a store closer to her family, she didn't want to start over somewhere else. She'd been through that six years before, when she and Jason, her college boyfriend, moved from Georgia after they graduated and he got a job in Houston with a marketing firm.

She hadn't been as lucky in finding a way to use her degree in English. The bookstore was supposed to have been a temporary job while she was looking for something else. When Jason's company promoted him to their Baltimore office, it forced the couple to admit that their relationship had outlived its appeal. After Jason left, Keelie appreciated the stability of the bookstore, where she'd made friends among the staff. Somehow she just never got around to looking for a new job. Or a new boyfriend.

She noticed the green light blinking on her phone and dialed into Call Notes, groaning as she heard the message.

Keelie? It's your grandmother. I didn't want to bother you at work. Please call me tomorrow. It's important.

Keelie knew it wouldn't be important at all. It would be something her mother had done that had gotten her grandmother into a dither. She didn't know why Gram tried to draw her into their arguments, because Keelie

had been taking her mother's side for twenty years—
since she first became aware of the tension between the
two of them.

When Keelie was eight, and her sister, Misty, was six,
their father was killed when his car veered off the road
and into a ravine. Apparently he'd fallen asleep at the
wheel, which wasn't surprising considering the hours he
kept at the hospital. His dedication to his patients was
the reason Keelie was secretly far less affected by his
death than everyone seemed to believe she should be.
She barely knew him.

They were by no means wealthy; doctors, like everyone else, lived beyond their means. But her father had
substantial insurance, which Polly, Keelie's mother, had
put into a trust for her daughters' education. Polly had
sold their large house in an affluent suburb of Columbus to move them into a smaller house with a less pres-
tigious address.

Having a doctor as a son-in-law had been a dream
come true for Gram, and she approved of nothing her
daughter did after his death. She thought Polly should
use some of the insurance money and keep the house,
staying within the same social circle until she snagged
another doctor, at which time the girls' education would
be a given even without the insurance money. When she
found out that Polly intended to work, Gram was horrified. Having been left with a comfortable income after
Keelie's grandfather died, Gram thought women
worked if they had to, not because they wanted to.
Polly's argument that she had to didn't hold water with
Gram. Nonetheless, Gram didn't offer to help support
them. As far as Keelie knew, her grandmother still had
the first dollar she'd ever inherited.

Gram was slightly mollified when Polly took a position as a legal secretary, believing that her daughter's real motive was to catch a rich lawyer. A lawyer was almost as good as a doctor. But Polly had no intention of marrying for money. She was working to put food on the table and provide a decent life for her girls.

Looking back, Keelie understood how hard it must have been on her mother to have a full-time job, prepare a meal every night, help her and Misty with their homework, and make sure they got to and from after-school activities, all while being subjected to constant criticism from Gram and having no real social life of her own.

Keelie remembered those years as good ones, though. On Saturdays, she and Misty would wake up to Rimsky-Korsakov or Rachmaninoff on the stereo. After breakfast, her mother would put on show tunes, and Keelie and her sister would sing all the words to *The Sound of Music, South Pacific,* or *The King and I* while they dusted, vacuumed, and cleaned the bathrooms. In the afternoons, the three of them might go to a movie. Or they had their friends over for slumber parties and cookouts. On Sunday mornings, they went to services at a nearby Episcopal church. Sunday afternoons were lazy times when they all read or watched old movies on TV.

She was twelve before she finally realized how exhausted her mother was. It was Thanksgiving week, and she and Misty were sitting at the kitchen table doing homework that was due before the holiday. Her mother was trying to get a jump on Thanksgiving dinner by preparing some of the meal ahead of time. She was taking a large bowl of chicken broth from one counter to another when she dropped it. Broth splattered the walls and ceiling, and her mother dropped to the kitchen stool, covered her face, and wailed, "I'm so tired. I need a wife!"

Keelie looked at Misty, who had rivulets of broth streaming down her face, and her sister said, "Get one! But I want to pick her."

Polly looked at her younger daughter with something like despair in her eyes, handed her a dish towel to wipe her face, and said, "Why? Do you want a different mother?"

"Nope. I think it would be cool if there were two of you. One to do all the crappy junk while you do fun stuff with us."

"Don't say crappy," Polly answered automatically.

"I think that's called a housekeeper," Keelie said. "But we can't afford one. Can we?"

"No," Polly said, but she looked thoughtful. "What I need is someone who could do just *some* of the crappy junk."

"You say crappy. Why can't I?" Misty complained.

"So get a part-time wife," Keelie said.

That was the beginning of her mother's great idea. Four months later, having taken out a loan against her daughters' education fund, Polly opened It's a Wonderful Wife. She networked ceaselessly, building up a clientele from the mothers of her daughters' friends or women at church. By the mid-eighties, a lot of women who'd entered the workforce in the seventies were wondering if they could really have it all. Wonderful Wife answered their question, provided they were willing to pay for the services the company offered. Polly's business thrived thanks to word of mouth. An ever-expanding group of women was thrilled to find "Wives" who could get kids to ballgames, buy groceries, clean closets, pick up dry cleaning, or do all the planning and legwork necessary for family vacations or parties.

Her mother was invited to speak to women's groups,

college students, and organizations for entrepreneurs. There was even an article written about her in *People* magazine. Polly's success muted Gram for a while, but it came at a price. Helping organize other women's lives took a lot more time and energy than Polly's secretarial job had, and sometimes Keelie threatened to schedule an appointment with Wonderful Wife just so she could see her mother.

It was around then that Huck came into their lives. He'd been laid off, and he applied for a job as a Wife out of desperation to make money until he could find another welding job. He was Polly's first male employee, and somehow that made Wonderful Wife even more newsworthy. Polly received an award from a national feminist organization for breaking down gender barriers.

The first time Keelie met Huck, he'd come to their house to bring order to the files that threatened to overtake Polly's home office. Keelie was sitting at the kitchen table, grimacing at her algebra homework, and Huck looked over her shoulder and explained what she'd done wrong. When Polly came home from work, she found Huck peeling potatoes and telling her daughters funny stories about his childhood.

Sometimes it seemed like he never really left after that night. The only thing more appalling to Gram than finding out her daughter was dating an unemployed welder was when Polly decided to make a house-husband out of him.

After all these years, Keelie and Misty still adored their stepfather. He'd not only been there for every event of their high school years, but he'd gently eased Polly into delegating some of her responsibilities at

Wonderful Wife. Plus he found ways to buffer Polly whenever Gram went on one of her tirades.

Misty had dropped out of the University of Georgia after her freshman year to marry her high school boyfriend and start a family. Later, she became her mother's business partner. The two couples had done an amazing job of expanding the business into several Southeastern cities. All of them learned to practice what Keelie's mother called the "Three Count Rule." Whenever Gram dished out her disapproval of their lives in hurtful comments, Polly silently counted to three to stop herself from reacting.

Keelie thought that if anyone in the family hadn't lived up to her potential, it was Polly's older daughter. She looked over at Hamlet and said, "So I'm not the store manager. Big deal. Like Evan said, I still like my job."

She hadn't felt too bad about using her English degree to sell books—there was a logical connection—until Evan introduced her to Ivy Johnson. Evan thought his two clients had a lot in common. Like Keelie, Ivy had majored in English. Only two years apart in age, they were both avid readers, had a similar sense of humor, and were crazy about Evan, the last being what he thought was their best shared trait.

Keelie had been a little daunted on first meeting Ivy. For one thing, Ivy was drop-dead gorgeous, whereas Keelie would never be described as anything more than cute, even on her best days. Ivy made a lot of money as a technical editor, and she had an expensive if somewhat conservative wardrobe. She lived alone in a Montrose townhouse, and at the time they met, Keelie was living with two other girls in a drab apartment near the

Galleria. She couldn't think of any reason why Ivy would want to be her friend.

Then on a second night out with Evan, they discovered they were both fierce pool players who could beat just about anyone when they teamed up. A few tequila shots later, Ivy dropped her normal reserve, Keelie overcame her shyness, and their real friendship began. Before long, Keelie had met Holly and Holly's husband Dave Sadler, and eventually she was absorbed into the entire Johnson family. She loved their kid brother Scotty and was a bridesmaid in his wedding to Carla. When Mr. Johnson had his heart attack in February, Keelie's Wonderful Wife gene kicked in. She rented a car and braved Houston traffic so she could do errands for the Johnsons and spend hours with them at the hospital. She and Evan even sat with the family at Mr. Johnson's funeral.

The Johnsons helped ease her homesickness at living so far from her own family. But lately, she'd felt almost as far away from Ivy. It wasn't just Mr. Johnson's death. Ivy had broken off her engagement to Mark Page in April, giving no one, not even Holly, an explanation. Keelie's attempts to get Ivy to talk about it had been rebuffed, and she saw less of her friend, which made the absence of a potential boyfriend even more noticeable.

"It's a little sad that you're the only man in my life," she said to Hamlet, who pretended he wasn't listening. "Other than Evan. And he's gay. For all I know, you are, too. When's the last time *you* had a date, huh?"

Hamlet began running inside his wheel, as if he didn't have a care in the world. Keelie got a Coke and stretched out on the sofa.

"If you would read, like I tell you to," she went on, "you'd know this is the point in my life when a relative

I never knew I had dies. He leaves me his fortune and his castle in Austria. When I get there, I meet a handsome stranger who wants the castle for himself, and eventually our dispute turns to passion."

Hamlet began digging into his bedding like he wanted to bury himself.

"Right. Our family's not from Austria. Then this must be the point when I stumble over a corpse, and the handsome police detective investigating the case is a little too attentive to me. I think I'm his prime suspect, but really I'm his love interest."

Hamlet twitched at her, then started filling his cheek pouches with food, ignoring her altogether.

"Fine. I'm not built for adventure and should go the more conventional route. Meet cute and live happily ever after with someone else who works at the Galleria. There's that blond guy at Armani Exchange. I think he's straight, but he'll always have a better wardrobe than me. The new guy in Nordstrom with the earring is totally cute, but he's a big flirt. Probably not good boyfriend material. But do I want a boyfriend? Or just someone to date occasionally? Or just great sex? Or even just sex? It's been so long, I might not know the difference. I am talking to a hamster. I am officially the most pathetic woman in Houston. I am tired, and I'm going to bed."

As she brushed her teeth, she tried to remember when the shrinkage guy from Corporate was coming. Had Rodney said tomorrow or in two days? He could have said next week. Recently her mind had started to wander whenever Rodney was talking to her.

She indulged herself in a fantasy that Shrinkage Guy would be as handsome and suave as her imaginary Austrian or detective. Shrinkage Guy was sort of a detective, after all. He would think her views on where to shelve the art books were so brilliantly theft-proof that he'd fall madly in love with her and whisk her—and Hamlet—away to Manhattan.

"Pathetic," she reminded herself, drooling toothpaste down her chin. Then she frowned at her reflection. Evan was right. Her bangs deserved nothing but averted eyes and whispered insults.

Chapter 2

Keelie always liked the opening shift at Buy The Book, even when it meant working a turnaround. Mornings were filled with the hushed strains of classical music coming from the store's speakers. The employees left her alone so she could do the prior day's paperwork and get the bank deposit ready. Early shoppers were usually quieter than the ones who came later. Best of all, she had four Rodney-free hours.

Unfortunately, she was on a ladder replacing a burned-out bulb during one of the high points of the morning shift: the arrival of Jake, the armored truck guy. Jake had beautiful blue eyes set off by his closely shaved dark hair, and he didn't wear a wedding ring. Even though their encounters were brief—armored guards couldn't really linger and make small talk—Jake made her teeth sweat, a phrase she'd learned from her sister. Their mother called it lust, and Gram warned that it wouldn't put bread on the table.

"I don't need the extra carbs anyway," Misty had declared when she married Matt, who'd been making her teeth sweat since they were in high school.

Although Keelie hated climbing up and down ladders, she never asked her employees to do any job she wouldn't do herself, so she watched sadly as Kenny, her supervisor, walked with Jake through the stockroom doors to get the deposit from the office. She held the new bulb in her hand, her eyes glazing over as she imagined life with Jake. She'd never dated a man as solidly built as he was. She wasn't thrilled by the gun he wore, so she usually focused on his bulging biceps and powerful thighs. Plus he had a great ass. She wondered if she'd ever have the nerve to look at Jake and say, *I'd love to take you out of that uniform and have my way with you.*

"I'll do it," she heard a voice say.

She glanced down to see Kenny staring up at her. How had he known what she was thinking? And why hadn't she realized that Kenny was gay?

"You will?" she asked.

"It's easier for me. I'm taller."

"Huh?" She saw his outstretched hand and realized that he was talking about replacing the light bulb. She had to curtail this tendency to fantasize about men at work. "It's no big deal," she said.

When Kenny went to put the ladder away for her, she walked up and down the aisles, checking for stray books, facing out fast-selling titles, and watching for customers who needed help. She was usually low-key about approaching them. Customers who wanted assistance asked for it. Most just wanted to browse and take their time finding something to read.

Since it was store policy that a manager always had to be available, Keelie couldn't leave until Rodney arrived, and by the time he got there, she was starving. These were her worst moments with him. She usually had to pee or needed to eat, but he always made her wait while he checked her paperwork. It didn't matter that after six years, she could do it in her sleep. He micromanaged her and Charlotte to the point of lunacy.

It was annoying that he was younger than her and had less experience. And that she'd been well trained by two of the chain's best managers, who'd basically treated her like an equal after she proved herself. Rodney seemed to regard her as just another employee, and he resented the way the staff always came to her for guidance. She could have told him that he wasn't making any allies with his condescending attitude toward her or his brusque treatment of everyone else. But Rodney thought he knew everything.

She tried not to glare at him as he scrutinized the daily report, hating the part in his floppy hair, his ugly tie, and his scuffed shoes. By the time he finally seemed about to let her go, there were two employees eating in the breakroom outside the office. The smell of their food was making her stomach growl.

The phone speaker squawked and Kenny said, "Keelie? Are you back there?"

"I'm here," Rodney said, sounding annoyed.

"Keelie has a call on line two," Kenny said.

Rodney pointed toward the phone with a resigned look.

It was Ivy, who said, "What time do you get off?"

"Around five," Keelie said.

"I thought I might pick up dinner for us and bring it to your place. If you don't have plans."

"I'm free," Keelie said.

"Is Greek okay?"

"Niko Nikos?" Keelie asked hopefully.

"Sure. I'll be there by seven."

"See you then," Keelie said, her spirits lifting because she wouldn't be spending another night whining to Hamlet about her problems.

When she hung up, Rodney said, "You weren't on your break yet."

"What?" Keelie asked, confused.

"That was a personal call, wasn't it?"

Dumbfounded, Keelie stared at him. In the first place, she never took breaks except to eat, which he'd already kept her from doing for forty minutes. In the second place, she'd never had a manager chastise her for personal calls. He was treating her like she was a newly hired sales associate instead of a salaried assistant. She had a brief, satisfying vision of bludgeoning him with the stapler.

"I'll try not to let it happen again," she managed to get out before she reached for her purse. "I'm going to lunch."

When she walked through the breakroom, Brian and Dawn were staring at her with their mouths hanging open. They'd obviously overheard Rodney scolding her. She gave them a weak smile and kept walking. The last thing she needed was a staff mutiny during Christmas season.

By the time she made it to the food court, she barely had time to get inside a stall in the restroom before tears streamed down her flaming cheeks. She *hated* him, and worse, she hated that he could make her cry. She never cried at work; she couldn't stand women who reacted emotionally to every frustration or admonishment. She finally blew her nose, splashed water on her face, and did her best to repair her makeup. Even though she'd lost her appetite, she forced herself to eat a sandwich before she went back to work, determined to keep her distance from Rodney.

Unfortunately, he was still stressing out about the impending visit from Corporate. Even though Shrinkage Guy was only coming to discuss their shoplifting problem, Rodney was convinced he was some kind of spy, so he was determined that everything in the store would be perfect. Which, as long as they had customers, was impossible. Unattended kids made messes in Children's. Shoppers reshelved books incorrectly or took books from displays and end caps, leaving gaps in the merchandise. There was never enough staff to keep everything in order and also help the customers.

Keelie resigned herself to a long day.

When she got home that night, Keelie barely had time to speak to Hamlet before she dragged herself into the shower and tried to scrub away the excruciating hours she'd spent with Rodney. She smiled when she remembered her mother's way of making unpleasant things better and began singing about washing that man right out of her hair.

She felt human again by the time Ivy arrived with the food. They ate with a rerun of *The West Wing* on low volume in the background, and Keelie told Ivy about her day.

"You know, I expect to have rough days," Ivy finally said. "After all, I work with a bunch of men who pick on my politics all day. But you'd think that anyone working in a bookstore would be kind of laid back. Even fun."

"Most are," Keelie said. "I just got a bad apple with Rodney."

"More like the worm," Ivy said. "Don't worry. Some bird will come along and snap him up one day."

"If I don't feed him to the fish first," Keelie said.

Keelie threw away their takeout containers. They slouched on the sofa after Ivy got Hamlet from his cage to let him crawl in and out of an empty toilet paper roll on her lap.

"This feels good," Ivy said. "To just hang out."

"It's been a while," Keelie said, trying to sound casual. She felt like Ivy was taking a big step by coming over, and she didn't want to scare her away.

"I was thinking about what Holly said last night," Ivy said. "I guess I was kind of a bitch to her. I realized later how selfish I was being. I know I'm going to be lonesome for Daddy, so I don't want Mom to be away, too. But Holly's right. It would be fun and different for Mom to be in Hawaii at Christmas. And something else occurred to me."

"What?"

"If Mom's not here, maybe Holly could take the boys to Scotland to spend the holidays with Dave. I know they all have passports. I'm sure they can afford the trip. Finnergy might even pay for their trip as a bonus for Dave."

Finnergy Oil & Gas was the company where Ivy worked as a tech editor and Dave worked as a project manager. Dave was one of Bill Finn's most valued employees, and the company probably did want to keep Holly's husband happy.

"She and the boys would have a blast in Scotland," Keelie said. "But do you think she'll leave you if your mother's gone, too?"

"You'll be here. So will Evan. It's not like I'll be totally without family."

Keelie smiled, always happy to be considered family, and said, "What about your grandmother?"

"I thought maybe instead of Granny coming here, you, Evan, and I could drive up to Coventry on Christmas Eve when you get off, then drive back Christmas night. It's far enough north that we might even get a white Christmas. Wouldn't that be fun?"

Keelie nodded thoughtfully and said, "I've never had a white Christmas. Of course, with my luck, we'll get snowed in, and Rodney will drop dead because I'm not back at work the day after Christmas."

"That would be better than a Christmas bonus!" Ivy said.

"Are you sure you want to do all that driving in two days?" Keelie asked.

"We'll take turns at the wheel."

"I meant do you want to be on the road that much."

"You and Evan are the ones who have to work on your feet every day during the holidays. If y'all don't mind the trip, I won't. I don't particularly want to be in Houston."

Keelie remembered the year before, when they'd all been at the Johnson house together to see Ivy open her engagement ring from Mark. There were probably a lot of memories Ivy didn't want to relive this year. "Sure. If Evan's up for it, I am," Keelie said.

"I'll e-mail Dave and tell him to make the Scotland suggestion to Holly. Before he does, I'll try to talk her into going to Coventry. So when Dave calls, she'll think I've already got my heart set on taking y'all to Granny's and she'll be more willing to leave me."

"You're so sneaky," Keelie said. A peculiar expression flickered across Ivy's face, and Keelie said, "What? Did I say something wrong?"

"No." Ivy patted Hamlet one last time before putting him back in his cage. Keelie had the feeling that Ivy was avoiding looking at her and seemed to be on the verge of leaving.

"Ivy? Is there something you want to talk about?"

Ivy finally met her eyes, then she flopped back down on the sofa and said, "I'll be so glad when this year is over."

"It hasn't been much fun for you, has it?" Keelie asked softly. She wasn't sure if she should bring up Mark's name.

Ivy was quiet for a few minutes, then she said, "You know Mark works for Finnergy, too."

"Is he still in the New Orleans office?" Keelie asked.

Ivy nodded and said, "If I tell you what happened, you can't tell Holly."

"It seems like you'd want Holly to know," Keelie said. "You're not just sisters, you're twins. You always share everything."

Ivy's laugh sounded a little bitter, then she said, "I'll get to that later. It's because I know Holly would be totally on my side that I haven't told her. She'd be furious and tell Dave, and Dave could get Mark fired."

"What happened? What did Mark do?" Keelie asked. "I won't tell Holly."

"Or Evan," Ivy said.

"I promise."

"You remember that I met Mark when he had to work on a project in our office a couple of years ago."

"Right. He's a project manager, like Dave."

"He's a project manager, but he's nothing like Dave," Ivy said cryptically. She paused for a minute, then went on. "There was an instant connection between us. You've been around him. You know how funny and smart he is. We clicked. What you don't know, and probably Dave doesn't know, is that when I met Mark, he'd recently broken an engagement."

"Uh-huh," Keelie prompted when Ivy stopped talking.

"He met her at a frat party in college; they'd been dating for over seven years. Mark wasn't sure he was ready to settle down, but she basically told him that either they started talking marriage, or she would walk. She wanted proof that their relationship was going somewhere. According to Mark, he wasn't madly in love with her, but he was comfortable. Once she got an engagement ring on her finger, she was happy for a while. Mark lived and worked in New Orleans, and she had a job in Mobile. Then she started pressuring him to find a job there. He realized that he'd rather keep his job than his fiancée, so he broke things off."

"Then he met you."

"Right. We stayed in touch through phone calls and e-mail. The more I got to know him, the more perfect he seemed. We had so much in common. We started flying between New Orleans and Houston nearly every weekend, and now and then, he'd suggest that I look for a job in New Orleans or see if Finnergy would transfer me or let me work remotely from there. The only thing holding me back was that he never talked about marriage. Or even living together. Sometimes I wondered if he was repeating himself, having the same uncommitted relationship with me that he'd had with Susan. That was his ex's name."

When Ivy stopped talking again, Keelie got the wine bottle from the kitchen counter, refilled their glasses, and said, "Then he proposed to you last Christmas."

Ivy took a deep breath and said, "I was totally surprised and thrilled. But he'd once been engaged to

Susan, too, so I wasn't about to push for a wedding date or get caught up in plans until I was sure we were both ready. Then Daddy died."

As tears began streaming down Ivy's cheeks, Keelie got a box of Kleenex, set it on the sofa between them, and said, "You don't have to talk until you can."

"You're such a good friend," Ivy gasped. "You don't know how hard it's been not telling you this." After a few minutes, she blew her nose. "I needed Mark so much, and he was there for me. It meant everything to be able to lean on him. To cry on his shoulder. To feel supported the way Dave supported Holly and Carla supported Scotty."

"I don't get it. What changed?"

"Nothing changed," Ivy said with a shaky laugh. "I just didn't realize how much hadn't changed. A couple of months after Daddy died, I was having a bad week, so I called in sick one morning. My manager suggested that I take a few days off. I tried to call Mark at his office, but he wasn't in, so I left a message that I wanted to come to New Orleans. I packed, and instead of catching a flight, I decided to drive. Sometimes when I feel really bad, it helps to get in the car and go somewhere. Turn the music up loud, be away from the rest of the world, cry if I feel like it."

Keelie knew exactly what Ivy meant. Although she lived alone except for Hamlet, there were times she wished she could escape and indulge a desire for self-pity. "It's not as easy to do that on the bus," she said.

"You can always borrow my car if you need to," Ivy said. "I got to Mark's apartment around three in the afternoon. His car wasn't in its space, so I used my key and let myself in. I assumed he was still at work."

Keelie's stomach lurched, and she said, "Susan was there, wasn't she?"

"She was *so* there," Ivy said. "It was one of the eeriest experiences I've ever had. We introduced ourselves, then I asked what she was doing there. She asked what *I* was doing there. I held up my left hand as my answer. She looked at my ring then held up *her* left hand. We were wearing identical two-carat, emerald cut diamonds. Identical!"

When Ivy paused, Keelie took a big gulp of wine and counted to three to stop herself from saying anything terrible about Mark. Experience had taught her that bashing someone's ex could be counterproductive.

"I didn't know what to say, so I wandered away from her," Ivy said. "I walked into Mark's bedroom, and it was like stepping into an episode of *The Twilight Zone.* Where my picture usually sat, there was one of her in the same frame, or one just like it. Her lingerie was in the drawer where mine usually was. Her shorts and T-shirts were in my other drawer. She had clothes hanging in the part of the closet where mine usually hung, and shoes on the rack where I'd left a few pairs so I didn't have to pack them every time I went there. It was that way in his whole apartment. There were different DVDs on top of the TV. My favorite coffee cup wasn't in the kitchen. The shampoo in the bathroom was different."

"That's horrible," Keelie said.

"I know! It was Pantene, and I'm an Aveda girl." Ivy laughed when Keelie did, then she blew her nose again. "Mark was playing golf with some vendors, so Susan and I had a lot of time to compare notes before he got home. He'd told her about me, but not that we were involved. And obviously not that we were engaged. He told her that I was this crazy woman who worked in the

Houston office and was obsessed with him. I guess he was covering his butt in case she ever intercepted a call from me. She'd begged him to let her tell me to back off. He told her that I'd threatened to kill myself if I couldn't have him. He said he was afraid if she made contact with me, it would push me over the edge."

"What an asshole!" Keelie exploded.

"All my life, I've had to share. I don't mind being a twin, but think about it: Not only is my birthday on Christmas, but it's also Holly's birthday. We had to struggle to have separate lives and interests. People were always lumping us together. But damn, there are some things no one should have to share."

"Did you stay there until he got home?"

"Of course. That's when it got even more bizarre. Susan had been this totally sane, rational person while we were talking. But when he showed up, she went nuts. She was screaming and slapping him and crying. Not that I blamed her, but it stole my thunder. I wanted to be the wronged woman and lose my shit. But she had seniority. I gave the ring back, asked him to mail my stuff to me, and left."

"Have you talked to him since?" Keelie asked.

"No. He left messages until I sent him a note to let him know that if he contacted me again, I'd go to Bill Finn and tell him the whole story. In his messages, Mark tried to convince me that Susan's the one who's crazy. That she wouldn't let go of him, and she'd lied to me to break us up."

"How do you know that's not true?"

"Come on, Keelie." Ivy shook her head. "You always believe the best of people."

Keelie wondered what was wrong with that, but said, "I don't believe the best of Rodney."

"Who could? Think about it. Why would Susan have a key to his apartment? How would she have known exactly which stuff was mine so she could switch it for hers? How could she have guessed that I was coming there on that day? How would she have known to buy a diamond identical to mine? He was trying to pull the same con on me that he pulled on her, making me think she was nuts, when the truth is, he's a pathological liar and a cheat."

"You *should* have told Dave or Bill," Keelie said. "You should have gotten Mark in trouble."

"I was tempted. But the idea of having everyone at work know how stupid I'd been was humiliating. Even worse, I couldn't stop thinking about Daddy's funeral. How Mark stood there letting everyone in my family think what a great fiancé he was. The thought of Mom and Holly finding out the truth turns my stomach."

"I wonder if Susan stayed with him?"

"Who cares? If anyone at the office knows about her, I've never heard about it. I swear, I'm *never* falling in love again. It's not worth it." She looked at the TV. "I feel like I've been talking forever. Why the hell is *The West Wing* still on?"

"It's Bravo," Keelie said. *"The West Wing* is always on."

"I call that *Law and Order* Syndrome," Ivy said. "That's the show that's always on."

"Or some version of *Star Trek,"* Keelie said. "I can't believe all this happened to you and I knew nothing. How do you feel about Mark now? Is that a stupid question?"

"I don't know. I never want to see him again. It's not the kind of breakup you had with Jason, where you can stay friends. Do you still talk to him?"

"Yeah, but he's got a girlfriend in Baltimore, and now that I've heard your story, I think maybe I shouldn't keep in touch with him. I wouldn't want her to feel like he hasn't moved on. 'Cause he totally has."

"Do you think we'll be old maids?"

"Nobody says that anymore," Keelie said. "We're . . . progressive. Self-sufficient and independent. We don't need a man to complete us. We're not Bridget Jones."

"Right actress, wrong movie," Ivy said.

"I didn't see the movie. I read the book, and I'm still not Bridget Jones. I don't have a weight problem, I don't smoke, and I'm not desperate for a man."

Ivy nodded solemnly and said, "So how many times a day do you check out a total stranger and try to imagine what your kids will look like?"

"No more than two or three," Keelie said. "Actually, I never get past the bedroom part. And dealing with kids at the store has killed my desire to have any."

"Understandable. Plus you don't have to send a hamster to college."

"Or give him the car keys. If I had a car."

"I'll bypass you and put a Hamlet-sized car under the Christmas tree," Ivy said. "You know, Keelie, that's our problem. Bridget Jones."

"Bridget Jones is our problem?"

"Okay, not Bridget. Books. We've read too many novels about some perfect man who sweeps a woman off her feet to live happily ever after. But men in novels fall into one of four 'R' categories, and in real life, they're all fatal."

"Um," Keelie said. "Tell me more about this theory. Who are these 'R' people?"

"There's the Rake. Like Rhett Butler. And frankly, my dear, he dumped her as soon as she told him she loved him. Then there's the Rulebreaker. Like Rochester in

Jane Eyre. That may be the category Mark falls in, since he practically had two wives."

"Rochester got better."

"After the nutty wife jumped to her death, and he ended up burned and nearly blind. Fun! Then there's the Romantic. Romeo. The kind of guy who inspires a suicide pact."

"Maybe we should just avoid men whose names begin with 'R'," Keelie suggested. "What's number four?"

"The Remnant."

"What the hell's that? A vampire?"

"The Remnant starts out with one personality, changes, and wins the girl. Like Darcy in *Pride and Prejudice.*"

"How can you find fault with Darcy?" Keelie asked. "He was wonderful by the end of the book."

"No, he was wonderful *during* the book. Everything that made him irresistible was whipped out of him by the end. Leaving only the Remnant. I stand by my theory. No matter which 'R' you get, your love story is doomed. I'd rather be a spinster. A spinster who gets good sex now and then."

In spite of the light note that ended their evening, when Keelie went to bed later, she couldn't get comfortable and ended up twisted in the sheets. She kept thinking about Ivy's story, analyzing every minute she'd spent around Mark and trying to remember if she'd had any inkling that he was a lying bastard who was leading a double life. It was like something on one of those afternoon talk shows, and she was the dumb friend who'd say, "No, he seemed like the *nicest* guy."

Even though he'd turned out to be a snake, Ivy's

theory about men was just her bitterness talking. They weren't all bad. Were they?

Keelie reassured herself that it didn't matter anyway. She wasn't looking for a man to make her happy. If someone came along, that was fine, but she was satisfied with her life the way it was. At least that's what she kept telling herself—and anyone else who acted like she should panic because, two years away from thirty, she was still single. Like her grandmother—

"Oh, crap," she muttered, punching the pillow. She'd forgotten to return Gram's phone call.

She looked at the clock. It was an hour later in Georgia, but her sister was a notorious insomniac, so she picked up the phone.

"This better be good," Misty said. "Matt and the kids are spending the night at his parents' house so they can chop down a Christmas tree tomorrow. I just took a long bath, and I'm sitting here drinking a glass of Merlot with my boyfriend."

"It's TiVo," Keelie said. "You can pause your boyfriend. Your obsession with Jon Stewart is unhealthy, anyway."

"This from the person who spent her teenage years kissing photographs of gay pop stars."

"I didn't know they were gay when I was a teenager. Do you have any idea why Gram's trying to get in touch with me? I don't want to call her back until I know what you and Mom have done to her."

"She probably just wants to know how big a check you want for Christmas."

They both laughed at the absurdity of that, and Keelie said, "Right. I could use some new clothes."

"I hope you like shopping at Goodwill."

"It's where I got your Christmas present," Keelie said.

Chapter 3

Keelie's hope of sleeping late on her day off was shattered when the phone rang at eight. She peered at the clock as she fumbled for the receiver, certain that it was Rodney. Either he or Charlotte would want to trade shifts. As tempted as she was to let Call Notes save her, Keelie's conscience got the best of her.

"I've been trying to reach you for days," Gram said. "If you're not going to return my calls, maybe I should call you at Buy Our Books."

Keelie bit her tongue before she could correct the store's name. The last thing she needed was Gram calling her at work. Rodney would probably implode. She perked up and said succinctly, "Buy *The* Book. I was going to call you later. After I woke up. On my day off."

"I've been up for hours," Gram said. "Cooked breakfast, cleaned the kitchen, paid bills, and read the paper. Although I don't know why. The news is always the same. Murder, inflation, and carjacking. Or Martha Stewart. A woman makes a little money, and the world goes berserk."

Gram loved Martha Stewart almost as much as she

loved money. The two combined was nearly more happiness than she could stand. It had always mystified Keelie that her grandmother could admire Martha without appreciating that her own daughter had followed a similar path to success.

"I'm sure Martha will land on her feet," Keelie said. "Even if she makes her shoes from license plates."

"Very funny," Gram said dryly. "I'm coming to Houston."

Since the phone was already precariously balanced between her ear and her shoulder as she tried to get her sweatpants down to use the bathroom, Keelie watched helplessly as it fell and skidded across the bathroom floor. "Hold on, Gram!" she yelled. "I dropped the phone!"

Of course her grandmother had hung up by the time she flushed and retrieved the phone. Gram would never waste money listening to Keelie pee. Keelie started a pot of coffee and hit speed dial.

"Coming to Houston," Gram repeated in lieu of a greeting. "This Friday. I realize you don't have a car, so I'll take a shuttle from the airport."

Keelie's brain circuits overloaded. Her grandmother never went anywhere. Certainly no place that required airfare. Or a shuttle.

"Are you staying with me?" she asked weakly, mouthing an apology to the innocently snoozing Hamlet. "For how long?"

"I'm staying at the Westin Galleria. I thought it would be more convenient for you. I'll be there one night."

"How come Mom didn't tell me?" Keelie asked. She couldn't believe her mother hadn't warned her.

"Polly doesn't know I'm coming. And you're not going to tell her. This is between you and me."

"What's wrong? Are you sick? Are you coming to the medical center?"

"We have doctors in Columbus, dear. And the South's best hospitals are in Atlanta. Why would I come to Houston to be sick?"

"Why are you coming?"

"Your hospitality overwhelms me. I'll see you Friday night."

"Wait! That's all you're going to tell me?"

"If I wanted to discuss this on the phone, I could save myself the cost of a trip, couldn't I? Remember: It's our little secret."

Keelie couldn't believe it when Gram hung up. She mimed banging the receiver on the counter before tossing it on the sofa.

"That's all she said? I wonder why she's being so mysterious?" Holly asked. She'd picked up Keelie to do laundry at her house and help wrap the boys' Christmas presents while they were at school.

"She makes me crazy," Keelie said, reaching for the tape. "Why couldn't I have a cool grandmother like yours?"

"If by cool you mean salty, count your blessings," Holly said. "Granny has no filters, which drives Mom crazy, as you know."

"Our grandmothers got the wrong families. Gram would be happy with a daughter who was as sweet-natured as your mother, and she'd consider you the next best thing to Martha Stewart. Whereas your grandmother would think my mother has moxie and would never nag me about finding a husband."

"Right. She'd insist that you live in sin, so when you got tired of one man, you could trade him in for a better model." Holly paused at the CD player and asked, "Anything you want to hear while we're wrapping?"

"I don't care, as long as it's not Christmas music," Keelie said.

"You're still being Scrooge? It's less than two weeks until the big event."

"I've shipped my family's presents to Georgia, but that's all I've done."

"You could put lights and little ornaments on a tiny tree next to Hamlet's cage. That would be just silly enough to get you in the mood."

"Maybe Hamlet's Jewish," Keelie said.

"Fine. Buy him a dreidel. We got some little antlers this year to put on Fernando."

"Where is he?" Keelie asked, looking around warily. Like all cats, Fernando unnerved her by staring at her for long periods of time, making her think he knew all her secrets and wasn't impressed by them.

"Probably draped over the dryer. He loves laundry days."

While they wrapped presents, Keelie casually said, "I saw Ivy last night."

"Really? Did y'all go out?"

"No. Just hung out at my place."

"Was she in a better mood?"

"She was fine. Except she shared a gloomy theory about men."

Holly listened without comment as Keelie explained Ivy's categories of "R" men, then she said, "I think that's just post-breakup talk. What about responsible men? Reliable men? Or Mr. Right? Those are all 'R' men, too." She grinned and waved her arms to indicate the pile of unfolded clothes she'd taken out of the dryer to free it for Keelie, her sons' toys that were piled in front of the fireplace, and the mess of wrapping paper and boxes in front of them. "Who'd give up a chance at all this?"

"You make a good point," Keelie said, rolling her eyes.

"It's not so bad. Maybe Dave's waist is a little thicker and his hair's a little thinner. He's more likely to bring home a bag of mulch than a dozen roses on our anniversary. My boys have two volumes: loud and super loud. But I like my life, even if I rarely have time to do more than brush my teeth and hair and hit the mommy trail. That reminds me. When's your next day off?"

"Next week. Tuesday."

"I'll get Melissa to sit with the boys. Let's book time at Evan's salon. Get massages. Pedicures. Haircuts. My treat. Consider it an early Christmas gift."

"You really are determined to inflict comfort and joy on me, aren't you?"

"Somebody has to. Did that shrinking guy show up and move the art books yet? I still have shoplifting to do."

"Shrinkage," Keelie corrected her with a laugh. "No. I'm hoping he's there today so it'll all be over when I go back. I don't think I can stand watching Rodney follow him around with his nose up his ass."

"If you could have your dream job, what would it be?" Holly asked.

"I don't know. Why? Do you know someone who's hiring for the position of dream job?"

"No. I never wanted a career. I wanted to get married and have babies. Ivy was the dreamer. She was going to move to New York and become a hotshot editor at Doubleday or some other big publisher. She planned to discover the next great American novelist."

"I wanted to *be* the next great American novelist,"

Keelie said. "My writing teachers shot that idea to hell. They said I should focus on nonfiction. Sure enough, I help shelve it five days a week."

"And Ivy edits technical reports."

"Maybe she'll discover the next great American engineer."

By the time Holly and her sons took Keelie home that night, she was happily exhausted. As she put away her clean clothes, she thought about Holly's life. She did seem content as a stay-at-home mom, and although Keelie's job had given her an aversion to most children, she thought Holly's sons were great. Jon was eight and Ryan was six. They'd whipped Keelie's tail at video games and kept her laughing with their running commentary on random topics throughout the evening— mostly about how gross girls were.

The Sadlers presented a cozy picture of domesticity, but it didn't make Keelie envious. Maybe her problem was that she'd never envisioned a dream life, so she wasn't compelled to make it a reality.

"Is there something wrong with living in the moment?" she asked Hamlet. "You do, and you seem pretty happy. Except for the crazy lady who hounds you with questions every night."

Predictably, Hamlet said nothing.

Keelie was scheduled for the closing shift the next day, and as soon as she stepped inside Buy The Book, the tension in the air made her sure what her dream job was *not*. Kenny was the supervisor on duty and he stopped her on her way to the office.

"Brace yourself."

"The guy from Corporate? He's here? He wrote up our store? He fired Rodney? What?"

"Don't shoot the messenger. Charlotte quit. Without notice."

"Oh, crap," Keelie muttered. "We're an assistant short?"

"Yep. No more days off for you, I guess, until she's replaced. And you know Rodney hates all the supervisors, so he won't promote any of us."

"Great," Keelie moaned, not bothering to toe the company line and defend her manager, because Kenny was right. Rodney was definitely going to hire an outsider whose only loyalty would be to him. "So is the guy from Corporate here?"

"Uh-huh. Total Type A personality. He probably wanted to be in the Secret Service when he grew up, but he never got beyond store detective. Takes himself way too seriously. It's not too late to save yourself. Go to the nearest mall phone, call Rodney, and tell him you're quitting, too."

"How would I pay my rent?"

"Open a meth lab?"

"Tempting, but my landlords might not like it." Keelie squared her shoulders and said, "I'm going in."

"Good luck."

She expected Rodney to look like he'd been visited by the Grim Reaper, but instead he looked . . . happy. Almost jovial. His eyes were bright, and red spots of color stained his cheeks, like he'd run into an Avon lady with a grudge.

"Here she is now," he said, spotting Keelie as she walked through the stockroom toward the office.

The man sitting in the guest chair stood and turned around. As his steel-gray eyes bored into her, she felt guilty. She was ready to confess to things she hadn't done just so he'd stop staring at her.

"Keelie Cannon," she said, moving her purse to her left hand so she could shake his hand. She saw his eyes flicker over the purse and blushed. *Yes, it's a Kate Spade,* her mind screamed. *I didn't steal it. It was a gift from my mother!*

"Ted Hughes," he said. His grip was firm, almost crushing, and she tried not to wince.

"Like the poet," she said. When his face stayed blank, she chattered, "He was married to Sylvia Plath. He was the Poet Laureate of England—"

"I know who Ted Hughes is," he said, his voice a little frigid. "Believe it or not, you aren't the first person to make the connection."

Just shove my head in the oven and bake at 350 until done, she thought and turned to Rodney to say, "I hear Charlotte resigned."

"Without notice," Rodney said in a tone that made it sound like a joyful proclamation. "Interesting that she would do it while our shrinkage issue is under investigation."

"You've got to be joking," Keelie blurted. "Charlotte would never—she plays the organ at her church!"

"Bibles are the most shoplifted items in bookstores," Ted said sagely.

Keelie looked from Rodney to Ted and couldn't stop herself from saying, "Yes, it's true. Charlotte, a fifty-five-year-old woman who barely clears five feet, is running a Bible ring. Late at night, buyers drive up to her house. They pay in cash, get the goods, and skulk off to churches all over Houston to read and worship in their secret Cult of Hot Bibles."

"As you can see, Keelie keeps us all in stitches with

her humor," Rodney said, looking completely una-
mused. "I've repeatedly told her and Charlotte that their
low-key approach on the sales floor is wrong. You have
to let customers know they're being watched so they
won't steal."

"I should be on the floor now," Keelie said. "I've noticed that our *Shoplifting for Dummies* books are going
awfully fast. Nice to meet you, Ted."

Kenny was working in Fiction when she walked out
of the stockroom. She just rolled her eyes at him and
went to the cash wrap area.

"Oh, man, did you see the guy from Corporate?"
Dawn asked. "He's hot."

"Not my type," Keelie said. "How are you on change?
Do you need to make a cash drop?"

"I'm good," Dawn said. "Hot men are not your type?"

"I guess not," Keelie said. She shrugged and walked
away, realizing that she hadn't registered anything
beyond Ted's eyes. As she tried to remember other details about him, the only things she could come up with
were that he'd been wearing a suit and his tie looked expensive. She should have scrutinized it the way he'd
checked out her purse.

She managed to keep herself busy on the floor until
Rodney left for the day. She noticed that Ted went with
him. No doubt they were going out to dinner, where
they'd discuss the possibility that Keelie was part of
Charlotte's Bible ring. Once she was sure they weren't
coming back, she went to the office and called Evan at
home, bringing him up to date.

"Maybe they'll make you take a lie detector test,"
Evan said. "I always wanted to do that. I'm all about
high crimes and misdemeanors."

"Bright lights and rubber hoses," she said. "Shrinkage Guy is totally film noir."

"They could think you're stealing cookbooks and ask for a stool sample to see what you've been eating."

"I'll sneak in some of Hamlet's droppings to confuse them," she said.

"You dirty rat," Evan said in an abysmal James Cagney imitation.

"Okay, I'm looking at the schedule for next week. Now that we're down to two managers, he's readjusted our hours. I'm no longer off on Tuesday, but I don't come in until four. Do you think you can schedule Holly and me early at the salon? Even if I can't do any of the other stuff, I have to get my hair cut."

"Yeah, I'll set up everything tomorrow," Evan said.

Keelie pinched the bridge of her nose, trying to ward off a headache, and said, "I have another favor to ask. My grandmother will be in town tomorrow. I open in the morning, and she wants to see me when I get off work; she's staying at the Westin Galleria. I don't know what this is about or if she wants to go to dinner. I might need to be rescued."

"I'll pick you up," Evan said. "Just call my cell in case I go somewhere."

"Are you sure? If you have a date—"

"I haven't had a date this century," Evan said. "What does Shrinkage Man look like? Is he gay?"

"I barely remember him, and I don't know," she said. "But it's nice of you to offer up yourself to distract him from me and my Kate Spade purse."

"Anything for a friend," Evan said.

"I think this was his only day here," Keelie said. "I'm sure there are other stores that he must protect from the Charlottes of this world."

"Poor Charlotte," Evan said. "I wonder why she quit?"

"I don't," Keelie said. "I wonder why I stay."

Keelie got up early so she could clean Hamlet's cage before she went to work. She let him stay in his hamster ball until she got out of the shower. Her phone rang just as she was putting him back in his cage and reminding him that she'd be home late that night.

"Remnant," Ivy said when Keelie picked up the phone.

"I beg your pardon?"

"I just finished getting an update from Evan. I believe you've met a future Remnant."

"You two waste no time. I assume you're talking about Ted the Shrinkage Guy? What makes him a Remnant?"

"You bristled upon meeting him. You feel intense dislike. In no time at all, you'll start noticing his strong jaw. The way his mouth twitches when you say something stupid. You'll sniff the air for a trace of his aftershave."

"You need therapy," Keelie said. "I'm sure he's on his way back to New York by now."

"Uh-huh. Just wait. I'll bet he suddenly acquires a sickly old aunt in the Houston suburbs. He'll feel that it's his duty to stick around so she won't have to spend her last Christmas on this earth alone. He's not going anywhere until you're smitten with him."

"I have a bus to catch. Goodbye," Keelie said.

"Call me on your lunch break. I have to know the Remnant's excuse for staying in Houston."

Keelie sighed at the heaviness of the air when she stepped out of her apartment. Maybe the reason she couldn't get into the Christmas spirit was because it so seldom got cold in Houston. As she went down the stairs, Mrs. Atwell came outside and waved at her. Her artfully tinted blond hair was enormous, as always. Evan often expressed his gratitude that Texas women continued to faithfully believe that big hair took them closer to God. Keelie and Ivy suggested names for his dream salon like Colossal Coiffure, Mammoth Mane, or Titanic Tress.

"On your way to work?" Mrs. Atwell called.

"Yes, ma'am," Keelie said.

"I'm going that way. I'll be glad to drop you at the Galleria."

"You don't have to do that."

"It's no trouble," Mrs. Atwell said. "It beats riding the bus, doesn't it?"

As she fastened her seat belt, Keelie said, "Thanks for the ride. I hate waiting for the bus when it's so muggy out."

"It sure doesn't feel like December," Mrs. Atwell agreed. "Do you have Christmas plans? Are you going home?"

"I don't have enough time off," Keelie said. "I'm going to Coventry for one night with some friends though."

"Isn't that near Dallas?"

"Somewhere northwest of it. Near the Brazos River, maybe?" Keelie shrugged. "My friend Ivy's grandmother lives there. I've never been. I think the town is really small."

"It should be colder there," Mrs. Atwell said. "Will we need to check on Hamlet while you're away?"

"I'll take him with me," Keelie said, squelching an image of Hamlet nesting in Mrs. Atwell's hair. "Thanks for offering, though."

It was wonderful to get to the Galleria so quickly and

be dropped at the entrance closest to Buy The Book. Keelie unlocked the door, relishing the quiet, then frowned when she realized that the lights in the back of the store were on. She was sure she'd turned them off the night before.

"Good morning," Rodney said, emerging from Supernatural and Metaphysics.

"Jesus, you scared me," Keelie gasped. "What are you doing here? You scheduled me to open today."

"As long as Ted Hughes is here, I feel like I should be in the store," Rodney said.

Keelie wanted to kill Ivy when she felt herself blushing as she asked, "He's still in Houston?"

"I believe he'll be here for a few more days," Rodney said. "He has to interview the entire staff, including you. You really shouldn't have been so flippant when you met him. Employee theft is not a joking matter."

"My schedule today is not a joking matter either," Keelie said. "I can't close tonight. I have plans."

"I still intend to close," Rodney said, following her through the store.

She was dismayed to see that Ted was already in the office. She wasn't going to get her usual quiet morning, especially with him hogging the desk to talk on the phone.

"Can he do that somewhere else?" she hissed at Rodney.

"You won't need the office this morning," Rodney said. "I already did the report from yesterday and finished the deposit. I've even done the duty sheet."

"So I see," she said, feeling disgruntled. He was stepping all over her managerial toes without a hint of remorse. She frowned at the duty sheet. "Uh, Rodney?"

"Yes?"

"Why is my name on here?"

"Really, Keelie, you're not above helping maintain the store. I only assigned you to straighten Children's."

Ted had hung up the phone and was listening, so she merely said, "Is this a new policy?"

"What?" Rodney asked.

"To include managers on the duty sheet. Should I start writing down your name, too, when I *normally* do it as part of opening the store?"

"Haaaa," Rodney brayed. "You're not the manager, Keelie. *I'm* the manager. No, you don't need to assign me a duty. Now, since I've taken care of everything back here, maybe you can start on Children's?"

"Sure thing," Keelie said. She'd never hated him more than at that moment. She gave both men a sweet smile and headed for Children's. She was going to have to call Charlotte. Maybe she'd defected to Barnes & Noble or Borders and could get Keelie a job, too.

She was still in Children's when Dawn and Tamala descended on her.

"You know I can't vacuum, Keelie," Tamala said, rubbing her excessively pregnant stomach. "It hurts my back. Don't make me call the Texas Employment Commission on you."

"I don't think they'll help you," Keelie said. "Go right to the EEOC. Seriously, I'm sorry. I didn't do the duty sheet."

"It's okay," Dawn said. "I'm supposed to do restrooms. I'll trade with you, Tamala. How come Rodney's here? And how come your name's on the duty sheet, Keelie?"

Keelie shrugged and reshelved *The Chronicles of Narnia*.

"You want me to get Z-Man to come in and intimidate Rodney for you?" Tamala asked.

Keelie grinned in spite of herself and said, "Your husband is a high school science teacher, Tam."

"You know that. I know that. But Rodney's just gonna see a big black man and think he's a gangsta."

Keelie felt her face get hot as she spied Ted at the end of the aisle. She wondered if he'd overheard.

"Restrooms," Tamala sang and walked away.

"I'll get the vacuum cleaner," Dawn said and made her own quick exit.

"Could I speak to you, Keelie?" Ted asked. She followed him, assuming they were going to the office, but instead, Ted walked to the Art section. "Before I came, I looked at the store's floor plan. As I recall, this section is supposed to be Bargain Books."

"It used to be," Keelie said.

"Why did Joyce change the sections?"

"Actually, it was changed after Joyce left," Keelie said, wondering if he was testing her to see if she would say bad things about Rodney. He must have overheard Tamala and wondered if Keelie was creating dissension among the staff.

"It's a bad idea to put high-dollar items right by the door," Ted said. When Keelie didn't answer, he went on. "After all, the sensors don't really do anything. People could just walk out of here with a two-hundred-dollar coffee-table book."

His words were uncomfortably familiar, and Keelie felt her face get hot again. But he couldn't possibly know that he was repeating exactly what she'd said to Evan and Holly a few nights before.

"If you think changes need to be made, you should tell Rodney," she said.

"Um-hmm. Since you're only an *assistant* manager."

That jolted her, and she kept her voice casual when

she asked, "I guess since you just came from New York yesterday, you haven't had time to see any of Houston yet. Is this your first visit here?"

"Actually, I've been in town for several days. My brother just married a local girl, so it started as a personal trip. But now I'm here on business. As I was saying, since the store's surveillance cameras are connected to *nothing*—"

"Are you two having a nice chat?" Rodney boomed.

It was the first time Keelie had ever been happy to see him, and she said, "Ted was just making a suggestion about Art. I need to get the registers ready for opening. Excuse me."

"What the hell were the chances?" Keelie asked Ivy on the phone later. "Why would he have been in Bennigan's, of all places, when I shot off my mouth to Holly and Evan about Rodney and the store? Stop laughing!"

"I don't know why you're surprised," Ivy said. "I told you that Ted Hughes is your Remnant. It's going to be one contentious encounter after another until he admits that you're wonderful, fires Rodney, and gives you his heart and the manager's job at Buy The Book."

"Would you stop that? I don't want his heart. I don't even like him!"

"Of course you don't. But you will," Ivy said. "However, just when you come to love the eavesdropping, overbearing, annoying man that he is, he'll turn into a pussycat. And you know you don't like cats."

"I'm hanging up on you," Keelie said.

Ivy just laughed again and hung up first, so Keelie left the bank of phones and walked through the Galleria. She wondered if Gram was already at the Westin as she passed it on her way to Nordstrom. She still had over half an hour to find a gift that would soften the old lady up. Although Keelie wasn't sure if her grandmother needed softening up, since she had no idea why Gram was in Houston.

She charged more than she should have for a beautiful watch, then stopped for a minute to listen to the man who played the grand piano on Nordstrom's street level. She wished she could curl up on one of the sofas in Women's Shoes and listen all day—until she realized that he was playing "Winter Wonderland."

"I *hate* Christmas," she muttered for the millionth time since Thanksgiving.

"Oh, honey, don't we all," she heard a man say. She turned to see Santa Claus standing behind her. "How many brats have tossed their Christmas cookies on *you* today?"

"None so far," she said.

He pulled a giant candy cane from his black bag, handed it to her, and said, "Don't eat this. They taste like crap. But it might be useful if you need to beat a mother over the head."

"Thanks; you're my kind of Santa," Keelie said and turned to walk back to Buy The Book.

Chapter 4

Growing up, whenever Keelie and Misty spent an afternoon at their grandmother's house, Gram would include them in her cocktail hour ritual. Sometimes they would have apple juice on the rocks, garnished with a cherry and served in crystal tumblers. Other times, they had grape juice in wine glasses. And on special occasions, Gram gave them Fresca in champagne flutes.

"Thanks to you, my daughters will one day be in a church basement drinking bad coffee and sharing lost weekend stories with strangers," Polly had once said.

"Nonsense," Gram answered. "Many times I sat next to my own grandmother on the front porch with a Brewton jar full of cocoa and sugar, and I have never dipped snuff as an adult. Besides, we don't have alcoholics in our family."

So it was no surprise to Keelie that Gram thrust a whiskey sour on her just a few seconds after they shared a stiff hug of greeting. She noticed that her grandmother didn't bother with the hotel mini-bar, but poured the drink from her own full-sized bottles of liquor and mixes.

What did shock her was that Gram was in a hotel room with an adjoining parlor. Although Keelie didn't know the rates at the Westin Galleria, they had to be beyond Gram's usual preference: cheap and cheaper.

"You came here right from work?" Gram asked, giving Keelie the once-over.

"We dress casually. Especially when we work long hours," Keelie said defensively. She quickly scanned the room for potential conversations that didn't include her appearance and said, "This room probably has a great view of all the buildings and the holiday lights along Post Oak. You should open your curtains."

"Draperies," Gram corrected her with a small sigh. "I saw enough of Houston on the drive from the airport. We had to get off whatever highway we were on because of an accident. Then, as we were going through a residential neighborhood, I saw the most bizarre thing. A girl running down the road with a goat on a leash."

"She's probably showing the goat at the rodeo in March," Keelie said. "Kids can win big scholarships that way. You still haven't told me why you're here."

"I can't believe they let you work in sneakers," Gram said. "Maybe that's why you don't get promoted."

"They're black leather," Keelie said. "We're on our feet all day, Gram. Plus I have to climb ladders and move stock." Gram had made her more exhausted in five minutes than Rodney could during an entire shift. She was afraid her mother's Three Count Rule wasn't going to help. She might have to count to a hundred. "May I use your bathroom?"

"Of course," Gram said, pointing the way.

Keelie was relieved to see that her assumption had been correct; there was a phone on the vanity. As she flushed and ran water, she dialed Evan's number. When the call went to voice mail, she hissed, "Save me! She's like those things in *Harry Potter* that suck all the joy out of everything." She gave him Gram's room number, hung up, and examined herself in the mirror, trying to see herself as her grandmother saw her. Her makeup was okay. She'd sprayed her bangs back so they wouldn't be in her eyes. She was wearing a navy blazer over a black jersey shirt and black pants. Her outfit was no different from the rest of the staff's. Corporate encouraged them to wear black, navy, or if they were daring, the occasional khaki. Of course, Rodney always wore a tie and was even dressing in suits while Ted Hughes was in town.

Maybe that's why you don't get promoted.

She took a deep breath, counted, and returned to her grandmother. After she sat down, Gram grimly said, "I didn't come to Houston alone. I'm with Major Byrnes."

It took Keelie a minute to remember that Major Buford "Boots" Byrnes was Gram's neighbor, a rather distinguished man of imposing height and a crown of white hair. He'd retired from Fort Benning when Keelie was in junior high, but he and his wife, Shirley, had owned the house next to Gram's even longer than that.

"Is Shirley here, too?" Keelie asked.

Gram frowned and said, "Shirley died four years ago. I know you couldn't come home for the funeral, but it seems like you might remember something as significant as a death."

"Oops," Keelie said. "Good thing I didn't say that in front of the major, isn't it? Wait! Are you and Major Byrnes—"

"We're eloping." Gram's tone made it sound more like a trip to the dentist, and Keelie just blinked at her. "We'll only be in Houston tonight, then we're leaving from Galveston on a cruise ship. We'll be married in Cozumel."

Keelie leaned over, patted Gram's hand, and said, "Did Major Byrnes knock you up?"

Her grandmother cracked her first smile and said, "Sometimes you're just like your mother."

"Why didn't Mom tell me?" Keelie asked. "I think it's very romantic."

"She doesn't know," Gram said. "And you're not telling her. I tried to put together a Christmas celebration, but Polly and her husband are going to Connecticut to visit his family, and your sister is giving a big party on Christmas Eve. If they're too busy for me, I see no reason to tell them my plans."

"Well, I wish I'd known," Keelie said, removing Gram's present from her bag and holding it out. "I'd have gotten a gift for both of you instead of this."

Gram's eyes lit up at the silver Nordstrom box, but she frowned a little when she looked at the watch. "Can you afford this?"

Can't you just say "thank you," Keelie wondered silently. "Of course. Do you like it?"

"It's lovely," Gram said. "But I think you spent too much. One of these days, your generous impulses will get you in trouble, Keelie." She put the lid back on the box without removing the watch. "Misty is the same way: always doing things without thinking of the consequences. Do you know what she did?" When Keelie made a noncommittal noise, Gram said, "She had her bellybutton pierced. Have you ever heard anything so silly? A grown woman with two small children."

"But she has a really cute tummy," Keelie said in defense of her sister.

When Gram just stared at her, Keelie felt herself blushing, and Gram said, "Don't tell me you did it, too?"

"The last time I was home," Keelie admitted. "We all thought it would be fun, and it was."

"All?" Gram repeated. "I hope that doesn't include your mother."

Keelie counted, took a swallow of her whiskey sour, and said, "Where's the major? I want to congratulate him."

"He took a walk through the Galleria so I could tell you our news," Gram said. "He'll be back soon."

Not soon enough, Keelie thought as the silence stretched between them.

"I didn't realize that Mom and Huck planned to spend Christmas in Connecticut," Keelie finally said.

Before Gram could answer, they both turned toward the door as it opened and Major Byrnes came in. He looked older than Keelie remembered, but he still had a full head of white hair. Keelie jumped up. She wasn't sure if she was supposed to hug him, but he took her hand and smiled when she welcomed him into the family. Then he made a beeline for the bar as she asked about wedding details.

"Booked one of Carnival's golf cruises," the major said. "Playing in Progresso, Cozumel, at Playa's course in the Mayan jungle, and in Belize. Challenging courses, all of them. Can't think of a better way to spend a vacation. Do you play golf, Keelie?"

"I never have," Keelie said.

"Shame," the major said, patting his flat stomach. "Good exercise for your grandmother and me."

Keelie didn't remember golf being one of Gram's pastimes, but she kept her mouth shut while the major told her in excruciating detail who had designed each of the courses where they'd be playing on their cruise. She thought he sounded almost British with his tendency to clip words out of his sentences, although maybe that was the result of barking orders in the Army for so many years.

"Iguanas come right out of the jungle onto the fairway," the major said. "Damnedest thing."

"Do you still have that gopher, Keelie?" Gram asked.

"He's a hamster," Keelie said. "Yes, I still have Hamlet."

"I imagine that's a practical pet," Gram said. "Since the maternal instinct seems to have bypassed you, and it's probably a lot less trouble than a dog."

Maybe I need to start counting in square roots, Keelie decided as she made it to twenty before the major spoke.

"Gophers," he said. "Hell on greens." He rattled his ice cubes, then went back to the bar to refresh his drink and Gram's after Keelie said she didn't want another one. She wished Evan would show up before the major got completely wasted or she was driven mad. Probably in a golf cart.

"You're not actually getting married on a golf course, are you?" she asked Gram.

"Of course not," Gram said. "It's a garden wedding. It's all been arranged by a travel agent who coordinated the wedding, the cruise, and the golf. We're having the ceremony videotaped. You can see it the next time you come home. When will that be?"

"Probably April," Keelie said.

"Not the first week," Major Byrnes said. "Masters in Augusta."

"I always heard it was impossible to get tickets to the Masters," Keelie said.

"Cost a fortune, but you can get them," the major assured her.

"Would you prefer to have dinner here, Keelie, or shall we go to one of the Galleria restaurants?"

"I didn't know we were having dinner," Keelie said. "A friend is supposed to meet me here to give me a ride home."

Gram got her tight-lipped expression and said, "When will she be here?"

"He," Keelie corrected. "My friend Evan. I'm not really sure. If the two of you want to go ahead—"

"We can wait," Gram said.

"Good courses in Houston," Major Byrnes said. "Champions. Carlton Woods. Seventeenth hole at The Woodlands is famous. The 'devil's bathtub.'" When Keelie didn't comment, he added, "Water hazard."

"Why don't I just order dinner for four? Hand me that menu, Boots, and let's see what Keelie and Evan might like."

"I really don't—"

"Best meal I ever had was at Westwood in Canada," the major said.

"Excuse me," Keelie said, heading again for the bathroom.

"If you have a bladder infection," Gram said, "you shouldn't be drinking alcohol."

"Cranberry juice," Major Byrnes said. "Fix you right up."

Keelie shut the door behind her and furiously punched numbers on the phone. When Evan answered, she whispered, "Where the hell are you? When will you be here?"

"Is now soon enough?" Evan asked, and she heard rapping on the door of the hotel room.

"Thank you," she breathed and hung up. By the time

she flushed and left the bathroom, they'd already introduced themselves, and Evan was sitting with his legs crossed, a drink in his hand, and an interested expression as the major extolled the merits of Mexico's golf courses—except for those pesky iguanas—while Gram silently scrutinized him.

"What's your handicap?" Evan asked when he could get a word in.

"Do you play?" Major Byrnes asked, regarding Evan with interest.

"I've played miniature golf," Evan said.

The major looked crestfallen, and Gram said, "What do you do, Evan?"

"I'm a hairdresser," Evan said.

Gram stared at him for a moment, and Keelie silently prayed she wasn't about to say anything derogatory, but Gram chose a more familiar conversational gambit when she glanced at Keelie and said, "Why on earth haven't you done something with Keelie's hair?"

"Oh, I have," Evan said. "I made her grow her bangs out so I could give her a new style. Our appointment is still on for Tuesday, right?"

"Yes," Keelie said, grateful that he'd absolved her of blame for her bangs. She'd have been more grateful if he'd said they were cutting her hair that night and had to leave immediately.

"Even though I don't play," Evan said, looking at the major, "I'm an avid golf fan. Who was that Irishman that helped win the Europeans the Ryder Cup in—when was that?"

"Oak Hill in 1995," Major Byrnes said. "Phillip Walton."

"Right," Evan said. "And how about Tiger Woods's dramatic comeback at Pebble Beach?"

Keelie tried not to gape at Evan. She'd had no idea he knew so much about golf. When she said as much to him two hours later as they trudged through the parking garage, Evan just laughed.

"Are you kidding? I don't know a bogey from a baseball. But do you realize how many golf widows look fabulous thanks to me? A hairdresser who listens knows a little about everything."

"I'm dazzled," Keelie said. "Thanks to you, Major Byrnes talked golf all through dinner. Although Gram managed to cover all the bases before you got there, insulting my family, my job, my clothes, and my hamster."

"Bases? Ah, baseball," Evan said, imitating the major. "Great sport. Plenty of fresh air. Ruined when brats run out on the field, though. Like iguanas. Need discipline."

"I wouldn't know," Keelie said. "Gram said I have Hamlet instead of maternal instincts."

"Pay no attention to the bitter old woman behind the faux pearls," Evan said. The rest of his words were lost in the roar of his motorcycle, and Keelie climbed on behind him.

"Why does Gram always make me feel like I'm doomed to be alone forever?" she asked Evan later as they sipped decaf in her apartment. *"She's* getting married, and I can't even get a date."

"Yeah, but she's marrying a golf-crazed bore who shares a name with a character from *MASH* and can't speak in complete sentences," Evan said.

"The major's okay," Keelie said. "I wonder if I should tell my mother?"

"I'm sure she'll be relieved to know the major's okay."

Keelie stuck out her tongue at him and said, "That they're getting married. Gram told me not to tell anyone."

"Who would you rather have mad at you? The one

who'll leave you money one day, or the one who's fending off iguanas with someone called 'Boots'?"

"Good point. I'll call Mom tomorrow. How was your day? Before you got stuck with the golfer and the gorgon."

Evan propped his feet on the wooden chest that served as Keelie's coffee table, closed his eyes, and said, "Brutal. Three highlights, two cuts, and someone who wanted to be red-streaked and crimped for a Christmas party. Cleo was on a rampage about something. Every time she came near me, I turned on my dryer so I didn't have to listen to her. PMS is not pretty."

"I think you need a uterus to have PMS. This time last year she was in the hospital having hers removed."

"Oh, yeah. But since she's lived without a beating heart for years, I'm sure Cleo can manage periods without plumbing. In better news, Mama Johnson is going to Hawaii for Christmas, and Holly and spawn are going to Scotland. The rest of us, as managed by Ivy, are set for Coventry. I am all about getting away. Even if it's only for a day."

"I wish it could be longer," Keelie agreed. She waited a beat and said, "You're sure you wouldn't rather go home for Christmas?"

Evan opened his eyes and said, "To Edna, Texas? I'm not invited unless I recant my sinful lifestyle." He snorted. "Like there's been much sin lately."

"Do you ever hear from your Jason?" Keelie asked.

"About as often as you hear from yours," Evan said. "He's still in Russia. He's living with someone named Levka. I think they're just roommates. There's also a woman living with them. Maybe Levka belongs to her. Or maybe Jason does. Jason was always a little confused."

"Russia seems like a strange place to figure things out," Keelie said.

"I think of it as cold and bleak," Evan agreed. "Like my last few months with Jason before he moved there."

"It's the name Jason," Keelie said. "It's evil, I tell you."

She was rewarded by a flash of Evan's smile lines, then he said, "I'm out of here. I'm sure we're both facing hellish days tomorrow." Keelie walked him to the door and thanked him again for saving her from Gram. He kissed the top of her head, lightly brushed her bangs back, and said, "You'll feel like a new woman after Tuesday. I promise."

The fortunes of Cleo Popper—which Evan swore was his boss's real name—had paralleled the circumstances of its Montrose location. When Cleo had opened the hair salon in the eighties, unimaginatively calling it "Cleo's," it had been a small, depressing shop with only one shampoo station and three chairs. Cleo had doggedly stayed in business even when her clients, mostly gay men, began moving away or dying. In the mid-nineties, Cleo's took an upward turn. Properties that had been gentrified by their previous owners were snatched up by an influx of new residents. They were mostly young and upwardly mobile straight people like Ivy, who loved the arty appeal and village-like quality of this small area nestled between downtown Houston and affluent River Oaks.

Cleo's new clients wanted more than a good haircut. They wanted *services,* and once she was making money again, Cleo expanded into the space next to her original shop, and finally into the empty space above. She added manicurists, massage therapists, and aestheticians to her staff. The fading gold "Cleo's" was scraped off the window and replaced by the green neon "Cleo's Urban Oasis," which ended with a glowing palm tree, across the building's brick storefront.

Based on photographs that Keelie had seen throughout the shop, Cleo herself hadn't changed over the years. Everything about her was big. She was nearly six feet tall, with a huge head of bright red hair that rivaled any drag queen's wig. Although everyone else in the shop was required to wear green smocks, Cleo was always draped in colorful blouses and stirrup pants. She was all stomach over spindly legs, and her arms were also thin and in constant motion. Evan said she looked like an Easter egg with limbs, and Keelie had to agree, especially since Cleo's face was always decorated with a generous slathering of makeup.

Loud, brash, and outspoken, Cleo intimidated Keelie, who usually arranged her appointments during Cleo's absences. But because of her new schedule and Holly's need to get their appointments out of the way before she left for Scotland, Keelie was forced to skitter past Cleo on her way upstairs for her massage. Fortunately, Cleo was complaining loudly about the new Aveda salon around the corner to anyone who would listen, and she barely glanced at Keelie. Holly headed for Evan's chair so she could get her hair cut before she was waxed and plucked to perfection for her reunion with Dave.

Although Keelie's massage hadn't begun on a high note—Denise told her she was wound tighter than a golfer's watch in church, an analogy that made Keelie wince—her body felt like warm wax by the time she sank into Evan's chair. When he turned her away from the mirror before he began snipping at her hair, Keelie had a feeling he was cutting more than her bangs.

Holly was relaxing in the chair next to her since the stylist, Patsy, didn't have a customer. They were talking about Holly's trip to Scotland.

"I don't know," Patsy said in her deep Texas drawl, "I don't think I could understand a word they say over there."

"They do speak English," piped up Peggy, the hairdresser on Evan's other side.

Keelie slid her eyes Peggy's way to see how she was dressed. The green smock couldn't hide her many-colored layers of diaphanous clothes that ended in a pair of combat boots. As usual, she had a stick of incense burning, and she was wearing a necklace with several crystal pendants.

"I thought they spoke Scotch," Patsy said.

Peggy sighed and said, "Scotch is a drink. You mean Scottish, but it's still English. I'll bet they couldn't understand a word *you* say."

"I speak as God intended," Patsy said, sounding huffy. "American."

"See what I put up with?" Evan asked. "Every day, sandwiched between Peggy Pagan and Pentecostal Patsy."

"I'm not Pentecostal," Patsy said. "I'm Methodist."

"Y'all stop bickering," Keelie begged. "I've been hearing enough of that in my phone messages."

Everyone brightened, anticipating good gossip, and Evan said, "Do tell. Is this about your boyfriend, the Remnant?"

"His name is Ted, and he's not my boyfriend," Keelie said. "If Ivy was here, I'd kick her. I might kick you, Holly. You're a good Ivy substitute."

"Who's been leaving you messages?" Holly asked after she shifted her legs away from Keelie.

"My mother and sister." She let Evan bring them up to date on Gram's pending nuptials, since he could make it sound funnier than she could. Then she told them about the messages from her mother and sister.

What do you mean, they're getting married? Polly had bellowed in response to the first message Keelie left on Wonderful Wife's voice mail. *Call me with details.*

Predictably, her mother had gone into efficiency mode, making sure that Gram and the major would have flowers and champagne from the family waiting in their room on the cruise ship.

How come she told you instead of us? Misty complained in her first message. *You've always been her favorite. I call her all week. Take her shopping and put up with her moods and insults. Matt's constantly going over there to fix something because she thinks her house is falling down around her. Yet she tells* you *about her wedding?*

Don't get mad at your sister, their mother followed up Keelie's terse reply to Misty. *She's just stressed out about the holidays. She did invite your grandmother for Christmas, but of course, Gram makes it seem like we're all neglecting her.*

Mom and Huck aren't even leaving for Connecticut until the day after Christmas, Misty said in another message. *You're* never *here at Christmas, but Gram's not mad at* you.

At least her mother and Misty were sticking up for each other. Keelie had no idea how she'd become the bad guy, and she reminded them that they should be happy. The major would give Gram something else to focus on. And when Gram moved into his house, he could pay someone to fix things and Matt would be freed from his servitude.

The whole ordeal had strained Keelie's nerves, which were already overtaxed by spending so many hours at Buy The Book with Rodney. Ivy had been right. Ted Hughes was still in Houston and was always lurking around the store, catching Keelie in her worst moments. But his mouth never twitched with amusement, and she still didn't sniff the air for a whiff of his aftershave.

"Evan, can you please grab the phone?" she heard Cleo yell.

"Oh, sure, why not," Evan grumbled. "My client's not as important as whatever you're stuffing into your face back there."

"My grandmother got remarried," Peggy said. "To a guy seventeen years younger than her. He ended up cleaning out her bank account and disappearing into the night."

"People just don't respect the sanctity of marriage anymore," Patsy said sadly. "Everybody lives in sin. If they do get married, they end up divorced."

"Uh, how many times have *you* been divorced?" Peggy asked.

"Those divorces weren't my fault," Patsy said. "George is living off the state in Huntsville because of that little thing with the cars—"

"*Little* thing," Peggy said. "He stole a tractor trailer carrying six Ford F-150s."

"At least he went with American-made. And Bubba's ex-gay thing didn't take."

"Where's Bubba now?" Holly asked.

"In Galveston with a man named Pedro and two Chihuahuas."

"Bubba didn't go with American-made," Peggy said.

When Evan came back, Keelie blocked out the squabbling between Patsy and Peggy and thought about work. She had to admit that Ted hadn't been entirely awful. In fact, he seemed to bother Rodney a lot more than he bothered her. Ted had insisted that Rodney turn over some of the departed Charlotte's managerial duties to the supervisors until another assistant was hired. And he'd wreaked havoc on Rodney's budget with his plan for an after-hours shift to move the Art and Bargain sections back to their original locations. He'd promised that the store would provide pizza and drinks to anyone who agreed to work overtime. But just because Ted seemed almost human didn't mean she was falling for him, so she wasn't about to tell her friends about those developments.

"Are you still with us?" Evan asked, nudging her shoulder.

Keelie's eyes fluttered open. "I'm going to be worthless at Buy The Book later. Which is fine. I don't think even Rodney can ruin—"

She broke off and everyone else froze when they heard a bloodcurdling scream from the back of the shop. Before she realized what she was doing, Keelie jumped up and ran in that direction, aware that several people were on her heels.

She rounded the corner to see Cleo's eyes bulging out of her head as she gasped and pointed toward the bathroom. A rapid series of images went through Keelie's mind when she pushed past Cleo. First she braced herself to see a hairdresser lying murdered on the tiled floor of the bathroom. Then she remembered telling Hamlet that she was going to meet a handsome homicide detective who'd fall in love with her. And finally, she realized that Cleo's black stirrup pants and purple thong were around her knees, which was not a picture Keelie wanted to carry with her.

The bathroom was empty, and Keelie looked back at Cleo's beet-red face. "The toilet!" Cleo shrieked.

Keelie walked cautiously through the bathroom and looked with apprehension into the toilet. She heard Evan roar with laughter behind her as he saw what she saw.

A rat, a young one judging by its size, was bobbing in the water, his dainty feet unable to get traction on the porcelain. He looked wet and pitiful, and he made Keelie think of Hamlet.

"Does anyone have a pair of tongs?" Keelie asked.

"For what?" Evan asked.

"So I can get him out of there."

"You must be kidding. It's a *rat,* Keelie."

"I've got tongs," Denise said from the doorway. "I use them to take my massage stones out of hot water."

"May I have them, please?" Keelie asked.

Evan rolled his eyes at her, then he spotted Cleo in the doorway. Thankfully, she'd pulled up her pants. "Aw, Cleo, how precious," Evan said, glancing down at the rat. "I didn't even know you were pregnant."

Keelie swallowed her giggle as Cleo's face turned the same hue as her thong. Evan could end up being the murdered hairdresser on the tiled floor of the bathroom.

Cleo's eyes glittered, and she said, "That's it. Pack up your stuff and get out of here."

Since Cleo had fired Evan at least twice a month for years, no one paid any attention to her. She moved aside as Denise returned with the tongs. Keelie gingerly approached the rat, who was looking at her with terror.

"I won't hurt you," she promised. She kept thinking of Hamlet, instead of rats, so that her grip on the tongs was firm when she closed them around his body just behind his front legs. Everyone gave her a wide berth as she held him away from her while he pawed the air. Evan led her out the back door of the shop, and they watched the rat tear off the second his feet touched the ground.

"I can't believe you did that," Evan said, shaking his head. "For a half-drowned rat. It could have been rabid. It could have bitten you."

"He was just scared," Keelie said.

"Who wouldn't be scared to see Cleo's bare ass coming at them?"

Keelie walked inside and held the tongs toward Denise, who backed away from her and said, "No, thanks. You can throw those away."

"He's not that different from . . . a Chihuahua," Keelie said.

"He was in the *toilet,*" Denise reminded her.

"There is that," Keelie conceded. She dropped the tongs in a trash can and followed Evan back to his station.

"I meant what I said," Cleo insisted as soon as she saw him. "I want you out of here now."

"Don't be ridiculous," Evan said. "I have to finish Keelie's hair."

"Not here you don't," Cleo said.

"You know what? It will serve you right to lose me. Don't call me back this time. I quit!"

"Evan," Holly warned.

"Do you know how many years I've put up with her crap? I'm done."

"You're past done," Cleo said, pointing toward the front of the shop. "Get your ass out of here."

"That's just what the rat said," Evan said and breezed past her.

Keelie looked at her reflection and said, "I hate to seem selfish, but under these sweats, I'm coated in more oil than a french fry. I have on no makeup, and my hair's half cut. I can't go to work like this."

"I'll finish your hair," Cleo said, picking up Evan's scissors.

"You just fired one of my best friends!"

"He quit," Cleo said calmly. "Get in the chair."

"Sounds like something they'd say to George up at Huntsville," Peggy said, and Patsy smacked her arm.

Letting someone who was angry and embarrassed cut her hair didn't seem like a good option to Keelie. She looked at Holly, who was hurriedly writing a check. When Holly met her eyes, both of them started giggling. Keelie grabbed her purse, and they walked out of Cleo's together.

Evan was smoking a cigarette next to his motorcycle. "Where did you get that?" Holly asked, taking it away from him and stamping it out.

"I always have an emergency pack stashed on my bike," Evan said. He looked at Keelie's damp, half-clipped hair and said, "You look like Cyndi Lauper, circa 1985. I guess I should have taken my stuff before I walked out."

"It's not like you aren't going back," Keelie said.

"I'm not," Evan insisted. "As Peggy says, when it's time to make a change, if you don't do it, the universe will do it for you. Holly, if you'll take Keelie home, I'll meet y'all there in less than an hour. With scissors. No tongs."

Chapter 5

Because of her schedule, Keelie wasn't able to go with the others on their two separate trips to the airport to send Mrs. Johnson to Hawaii and Holly and the boys to Scotland. Holly made Evan drive them in her Expedition and told him to keep the keys for their trip to Coventry.

"Like I can afford the gas for this monster," Evan complained when he and Ivy called Keelie from the road.

"Are you sure we should still go?" Keelie asked. "Don't you have to look for a new job?"

"I've got enough funds to last me a couple of unemployed months," Evan said. "Besides, we'll only be there overnight."

"Let me talk to Ivy." When Ivy took the phone, Keelie said, "The whole Coventry idea was mostly to make Holly go to Scotland. Now that she's actually in the air, we don't have to go. It seems like a lot of trouble for one night."

"Actually, for me, it's going to be more than a night," Ivy said. "That's why Holly offered her car."

"What do you mean?"

"I planned to use the rest of my vacation time between the Christmas and New Year's holidays so I wouldn't lose it. But I just found out our office is closed that entire week. So my vacation has already started."

"And you want to go to Coventry early," Keelie surmised.

"If I don't, who knows if Granny will even have a tree? I want to give you and Evan a real country Christmas, but you know Granny isn't exactly a domestic goddess."

"Like you are?" Keelie heard Evan say with a snort.

"At least I know how to decorate a tree," Ivy said. "So I'm driving up tonight, and Evan will drive y'all up on Christmas Eve. I'll give Evan money for gas."

"No, you won't," Evan said.

"Can you two argue about this later? I have a bus to catch."

"There's nothing to argue about," Ivy said.

"Are you taking Fernando with you?" Keelie asked nervously. She didn't want to be trapped in a strange house with Holly's inscrutable cat.

"No. The boys' sitter, Melissa, is looking after Fernando. Tell Hamlet he's safe."

After they hung up, Keelie turned off the coffeemaker, gave Hamlet a mini carrot, reminded him that she'd be home late because of the after-hours shift, then locked the door behind her.

Mrs. Atwell was kneeling next to one of the flowerbeds. Her hair didn't seem quite as large as usual, and she wasn't wearing makeup. She looked wonderful. She waved Keelie over and held out some flowers wrapped in brown paper.

"Don't look at me," she begged. "I just rolled out of

bed and didn't even comb my hair. I thought you could take these to your boss. I remember how much she likes cut flowers."

"Thanks," Keelie said. She didn't feel like telling Mrs. Atwell that Joyce was no longer her boss. She could put the flowers in the bookstore office and that would be almost like giving them to Rodney.

She clambered on board her bus, found a seat, and stared out the window. She was weary from her long hours at Buy The Book and a little homesick. More than anything in the world, she wished she could wake up on Christmas morning in her old room at her mother's house and open presents with her family. But even if she could go to Georgia, Misty did Christmas morning at her house now, because of the kids, and her mother and Huck were going to Connecticut.

You're just feeling sorry for yourself, Keelie scolded internally. *You have great friends who'll make Christmas fun. Even tonight will be fun, except for Rodney and Ted.*

The bus lurched to a stop because of a train, and Keelie looked at her watch. She was going to be late, giving Rodney another reason to bitch at her. At least Dawn had offered her a ride home that night. She was tired of the bus, tired of the bookstore, and tired of her life.

"What'd you say?" someone across the aisle asked.

Keelie glanced over to see an elderly man with grizzled hair and beard. "Did I say something?" she asked.

"You said you're tired of your life," he said. "You having one of those Jimmy Stewart days?"

She smiled and said, "Who are you? An angel? Or Santa Claus?"

He guffawed and said, "That's me. Metro Santa."

A woman in front of them turned and said, "If he tries to make you sit on his lap, hit him with your purse." Then she looked at Keelie's purse and said, "Maybe not. I'll hit him. You don't want to mess up that Kate Spade."

"Snob," Metro Santa said.

"Pervert."

"You two stop," Keelie begged.

"It's okay," the woman said. "He's my uncle."

"Uncle-in-law," he said. "How come you're tired of your life?"

"I'm not really," Keelie said. "I just wish I could have a real vacation instead of one day off."

"Be careful what you wish for," the niece said and turned around to face forward as the crossing gates lifted and the bus began moving again.

Keelie closed her eyes for a moment, then opened them, knowing that if this were a movie, her riding companions would have vanished. But they were both still there, and the man grinned at her as if he'd read her mind.

"If I could make wishes come true, she wouldn't be taking me to the doctor or deviling me every day of my life," he said.

"Yeah, your cholesterol would have killed you by now, and *I'd* be on a real vacation," his niece said, but Keelie could see that she was smiling.

When they reached her stop at the Galleria, Keelie left the flowers on the seat as she got up to leave the bus.

"Hey, Jimmy Stewart, you forgot—"

"No, I didn't," Keelie said and kept walking. "Merry Christmas."

She felt better by the time she walked into the bookstore, which was filled with customers. She barely said hello to Rodney when she dropped her bag in the office before putting on her name badge and hurrying to the cash wrap area.

"Take a break," she said to Tamala. "I'll run your register."

"I'm not on break for another hour," Tamala said. "Rodney will—"

"I don't care what Rodney says," Keelie interrupted. She took ten dollars out of her blazer pocket and said, "Don't go to the breakroom and you won't even have to see him. Take this, get yourself something to drink, and sit down before you go into labor."

As Tamala grabbed the ten and walked out the door, Keelie motioned to the next customer in line. Then she saw Ted watching her from Business and sighed inwardly. No doubt she'd be in trouble for making an employee take an unscheduled break.

"No good deed goes unpunished," she muttered, her mood plummeting to where it had been before she met Metro Santa.

"I'm sorry?" her customer said.

"I said, have you ever read *Crime and Punishment?*" She looked down at the book he'd placed on the counter: *Anatomy of Greed: The Unshredded Truth from an Enron Insider.*

When she looked up, she saw the desperate shopper look in the man's eyes as he asked, "Who wrote it? Do you think my wife would like it?"

"No," she said. "Buy your wife something from Victoria's Secret. Anything, as long as it comes in their gift wrap. She'll think you're romantic."

"Thanks," he said.

Ted walked by and said, "Nothing like suggestive selling. Although I think the idea is to suggest something we actually sell."

Since she seemed to have no control over blurting out her thoughts, Keelie bit her lip as she smiled at the next customer.

"Alvin!" the man said.

"Pardon?"

"I've had that stupid chipmunk song in my head all day, but I couldn't remember the chipmunk's name. Until I saw your teeth sticking out. It was Alvin. Now who were the other two?"

"You think I look like a chipmunk?" Keelie asked. "Just for that, I'm not telling you."

"Aw, come on. I'll add a couple of gift cards to my pile of books."

"Gift cards first, answers later," Keelie said. After she ran his credit card and bagged his books, she said, "Theodore and Simon."

"Wow, you really know your chipmunks. Do you want to go out sometime?"

"I think you're just swept away by the moment," Keelie said.

"I'll be back after Christmas," the man vowed, picked up his bag, and moved on.

Dawn looked over at her. "Did that guy just ask you out?"

"Sort of."

"Must be a full moon."

When they finally closed the store, Keelie was what Gram called "bone tired," but as she watched Ted come through the door with a stack of pizza boxes, her spirits lifted. Even with a lot of hard work in front of them, the staff was always fun during after-hours shifts. She worked with bright, funny people—except for Rodney—and they rarely got a chance to socialize while they worked.

"Keelie," Rodney blared, as if she'd been evading him for hours, "why don't you set up the pizza and drinks in the breakroom? Then you can do today's report so I can get right to work on the floor tomorrow morning. When you finish the report, you can load the carts in the stockroom. I'll supervise moving the sections."

She really wished she was one of those Texans who carried a gun. She'd never actually shot a gun, but it would be fun to practice on Rodney.

"I was kind of looking forward to spending time with—" She broke off as she heard their employees approaching. She could tell by the way they were whispering and giggling that something was up, and for a fleeting moment, she hoped that Rodney's obnoxious instructions were part of some holiday surprise for her.

"Look what we did," Kenny said, leading the pack as they emerged from the bookshelves. He was holding out a white sweatshirt, and Keelie laughed when she saw that it matched the shirts everyone else was wearing. Someone had altered a photo of Hamlet, putting a Santa hat on him, and transferred it to the sweatshirts. Then they'd sewn little red and green bells into a kind of collar for him. Keelie got a lump in her throat as everyone jingled around her.

"I love this," she said. "Thank you!"

"We couldn't ignore our Buy The Book mascot at Christmas," Kenny said as Rodney rolled his eyes and walked away.

Keelie couldn't stop smiling while she was doing the daily report. Her pizza might be cold. She might be stuck in the back while everyone else was on the floor, and Rodney was worse than Scrooge. But Christmas wasn't really so bad.

She glanced up as Ted and Rodney came into the

stockroom, then looked back at the computer monitor and hit PRINT. The printer spit out one page, then stopped. She looked over and saw a blinking light. Of course. Rodney never refilled the printer tray. With a sigh, she reached into a bottom drawer and found an empty paper package.

"I hate him," she mumbled. "Hey, Rodney," she called, "could you bring me a ream of paper?" When Rodney gave her an annoyed look, she refused to let it rattle her. "Never mind. I'll get it."

She walked to the shelves in the stockroom where they kept office supplies, but all she saw were rolls of cash register tape.

"Look up," Rodney said.

Don't help me or anything, she thought, dragging the ladder to the shelves. She climbed up, grabbed a pack of paper, and was going back down the ladder when her foot slipped. She felt it twist as she went down. Her ankle took all her weight, then she fell into a bin of mass market paperbacks.

"Are you okay?" Ted asked, hovering over her.

"I'm not sure," Keelie said. "I think romance cover model Mike Dale might be wedged up my butt. And not in a kinky, fun way."

"I can't believe it's not Fabio," Ted said.

Keelie started laughing, but as she tried to stand up, she lost her balance and fell against Ted's chest. "Ouch! I must have twisted my ankle."

"I wish you'd done it while the food court was open," Rodney said. "You probably need to put ice on it. I don't know where we can get ice."

Ted helped Keelie hobble to a chair, then he turned to Rodney and said, "She doesn't need ice. She needs an X ray."

"I'm sure I'll be fine in a minute," Keelie said.

"She didn't fall far," Rodney said.

Ted looked at Rodney with disbelief and said, "Call mall security. Tell them we need a wheelchair. Then write down directions to the closest emergency room. I'm taking Keelie for an X ray. You can stay here and fill out an incident report."

"I've never had a workers' comp case," Rodney said, looking at Keelie like she'd deliberately blemished his perfect record.

"Really, I'll be fine," Keelie insisted.

"Really, loss prevention is my job," Ted said. "I'm taking you for an X ray."

Keelie was dreaming she was at Starbucks in a body cast when the phone rang and woke her. She grimaced as she turned over and her right leg landed on her left leg.

"Oof," she said into the phone.

"Good morning," her mother said brightly. "Is there something you want to tell me?"

Keelie stared down at her splint and said, "No. I don't think so."

After a beat, her mother said, "Are you sure there's nothing you want to tell me?"

"Do you have a camera in here?" Keelie asked.

"No. You have a sister who called you first thing this morning. A man answered the phone, so she hung up."

That explained the coffee aroma that had found its way into Keelie's dream. Ted must have brewed it before he left. At least she assumed he was gone. The apartment felt empty.

"Misty always was a snitch. It's not what you think.

I didn't hear the phone ring earlier. Must have been the drugs."

"This gets better and better. Drugs and a man who answers your phone before breakfast."

"Last night I sort of fell off a ladder at work. Ted, a guy from our corporate office, was there and took me to the emergency room. We didn't get home until after four, and he insisted on staying on my sofa in case I needed anything. Since they gave me a shot and some Vicodin, I slept like the dead."

"Are you okay? You must not be okay if they gave you drugs."

"I just have a splint on my ankle," Keelie said, hoping to minimize the damage.

"You need to come home."

"I can't," Keelie said. "I don't want to deal with crutches and holiday travel."

"Crutches? You broke something, didn't you? Huck! Come here! We can't go to Connecticut."

"Mom, I'm not coming home. I'll be fine. I just have to stay off my feet and keep my leg elevated for a while."

"How long is 'a while'?"

"I'm supposed to see an orthopedic doctor after Christmas. He'll put on a cast if the swelling has gone down."

"A cast! I knew you broke something. Your leg?"

"My ankle. It's not exactly broken. More like a little cracked. And I strained some ligaments. The good news is that I won't need surgery or pins and screws."

"Oh, then what am I worried about?" her mother said, then shrieked, "*Good* news? I'm not going to let you spend Christmas alone in bed! It's awful to be alone at Christmas."

"I'm still going to Coventry," Keelie said, not sure if that was true. She hadn't talked to Ivy or Evan yet. "The doctor said as long as I keep my leg elevated on the trip, I can lie around there as easily as here."

"How long will you be out of work?"

"They don't know. It depends on how quickly I heal and whether they can put a walking cast on my leg. At least three weeks."

"Do you need money?"

"Ted said our workers' comp covers all the medical stuff and will pay part of my salary while I'm out."

"Stay out as long as you can. If you need money, call me. Not only could you use the break—if you'll pardon the term—and the recovery time, but maybe Rodney will finally realize how good he has it with an assistant like you."

"Wow, I seem to remember a lot of bitching about your employees and workers' comp," Keelie said.

"They weren't my daughter. Stick it to the man," her mother said.

"They'd rather deal with workers' comp than have me sue them," Keelie said. "Since Ted's the head of Corporate Loss Prevention, I imagine he's staying one step ahead of me."

"That'll make it easier for you to kick him in the ass with your cast. Are you sure you're okay? With only a few calls, I can cancel Connecticut and be in Houston tonight."

"Maybe after I get my cast, I'll come home," Keelie promised.

After they hung up, she used her crutches to get to the bathroom. They'd put her in scrubs in the emergency room. She giggled as she remembered the woman who'd taken her information. Ted kept butting in, until the woman finally made him leave the room.

"Is he your boyfriend? Did he cause the injury?"

"No! I work with him. Sort of. He was there when it happened, and he brought me in."

"I have to ask these questions. In case you're battered. Are you sure you're not battered? It doesn't always show. You could be battered."

"I work in retail; only customers are allowed to batter me."

"Buy The Book, huh?" the woman asked, looking at the intake form. "Hey, do y'all have that book that was on Oprah last week? Wait. Maybe it was Letterman. It had a blue cover. I get lousy TV reception, though. It could have been green."

"Yes," Keelie told her.

As she leaned on a crutch and sipped the coffee Ted had made, Hamlet emerged from his bedding and twitched at her.

"I know. A man finally spends the night, and I don't get any action. I can't help it. He was nice to me, but he still doesn't make my teeth sweat."

She called Evan, who was less distraught than her mother but promised to be in her apartment within the hour. She took a bag of peas from the freezer and was about to go back to bed when she heard the key click in her door.

"You're awake," Ted said, walking in with a grocery bag. "Shouldn't you be lying down?"

She held up the frozen peas as an answer, and he set down the groceries, followed her into her bedroom, and hovered over her as she lay down. Then he arranged the pillows under her leg, wrapped the peas in a towel, and gingerly set the bag on the splint.

"Does it hurt? Do you need another pill?"

"That Vicodin makes me feel stoned," Keelie said and hastily added, "Not that I've ever been stoned."

"Or shoplifted," Ted said solemnly. "And you help old ladies cross the street, you recycle, and you file your taxes on time."

"Don't become likeable, okay?" Keelie asked.

"Too late," he said. "You had nothing in your refrigerator. I got juice, eggs, bread, and bacon. I'm cooking you breakfast."

"That goes way beyond the call of duty," Keelie said. "Oh, man, I have to talk to Rodney."

"Already taken care of," Ted said.

"Is he furious? Overwhelmed?"

"We're flying in an assistant from Dallas and another one from Nashville."

Keelie stared at her bulky leg and said, "I can't believe I did this during Christmas season. He's never going to let me forget this."

"We'll see," Ted said, rolling up his sleeves as he headed back to the kitchen.

Evan got there just after Ted set up a tray next to her bed, and the two men eyed each other warily as they introduced themselves.

"You're the shoplifting guy, right?"

"And you're the hairdresser," Ted said. "I remember you from Bennigan's. Great job on Keelie's hair."

Since the bathroom mirror had conveyed a sad story, Keelie didn't know if she was blushing about her bed hair or because Ted had just admitted that he'd overheard her conversation at Bennigan's.

"It looks fine when she actually brushes it," Evan said. "Which she barely has time to do, thanks to Buy The Book."

"Hey, these are good," Keelie said after taking a bite of eggs. "You can cook!"

"You've just got the munchies because of your Vicodin buzz," Ted said.

"They gave you Vicodin?" Evan asked. "If you don't use it all—"

"I'll flush it down the toilet," Keelie said firmly.

Evan glanced at Ted and said, "Oh, yeah. I'm all about preventing drug abuse. You don't want to end up with Vicodin flashbacks."

Ted laughed and said, "Who knew Vicodin is the gift that keeps on giving?"

"That's chlamydia," Evan said. "Chlamydia's like a bad Christmas gift."

"I've heard that," Ted said. "Like the song says, have yourself a merry little chlamydias."

"Or a holly jolly chlamydias," Evan said.

Since they were obviously about to embark on a game of one-upmanship, Keelie quickly said, "I'm eating. Let's take the chlamydia out of Christmas."

There was nothing gratifying about having a couple of men competing to amuse her when one was running a mental tally of how much she was costing the company and the other was her gay best friend. Where was the romance? Wasn't it supposed to be Jake the Armored Truck Guy who caught her as she fell off the ladder, then rushed her to the emergency room? Or couldn't her doctor have been sexy instead of puffy-faced, sporting a bad comb-over, and afflicted with a wedding ring?

"The story of my life will never be on Oprah or Letterman," she muttered and reached for another slice of bacon.

"I'd have cooked for you," Evan said. "You should have called me last night. You know I'm not working."

"Me, either," Keelie said. "Did Ivy already leave for Coventry?"

"Ivy?" Ted asked. "The brunette from Bennigan's?"

"One of them," Keelie said, wondering how many times he could work Bennigan's into the conversation. "Her hair's auburn, not brown."

"Yeah, she's gone," Evan said. "If we'd known about your gimpy ankle, she could have waited so we could all ride up together."

Ted looked a little sad as he stood up, headed for the kitchen, and said, "I'll just clean up my mess and get out of here."

"No, wait!" Keelie said, thinking what a gem Ted had been in the emergency room. Not to mention that he'd cooked breakfast. "Aren't you eating?"

"I grabbed a bagel on my way to the grocery store," Ted said.

"I'll take over from here," Evan said. "I'm sure you need to get to work and bust Bible thieves."

Keelie quickly said, "Thanks for staying with me in the emergency room last night. And bringing me home." She frowned at Evan. "He practically had to carry me up the stairs and put me to bed."

"It was nothing," Ted said. "I'm sure you'll be back at work in no time."

"Crack that whip," Evan said.

"I wonder if they got the sections moved last night," Keelie said. "I guess you're finished in Houston and ready to fly back to New York."

"No. I'm off until the second week of January. My brother's my only family, so I'm hanging out here. He gets back from his honeymoon on New Year's Eve."

"It's awful to be alone at Christmas," Keelie unthinkingly repeated her mother's words. When she realized how heartless she sounded, she said, "You should come with us to Coventry."

Evan's eyes bugged out at her, and Keelie tried not to wince when she heard Gram's voice in her head: *One of these days, your generous impulses will get you in trouble.*

"I couldn't impose," Ted said, but Keelie could have sworn that his gray eyes lit up.

When she noticed how both men were staring at her, it occurred to her that they might have the wrong idea and think she was interested in Ted, which was the last thing she wanted.

"It's the least I can do after making everyone in St. Luke's Minor Emergency Center suspect you of breaking my ankle," Keelie said weakly.

"I thought that woman was going to have me arrested," Ted agreed, then added doubtfully, "Are you sure it's okay?"

"It'll just be friends hanging out," Keelie said. "You won't be crashing a big family gathering."

"Don't you think you should call Ivy?" Evan asked.

"Trust me, Ivy will be delighted," Keelie said, dreading the comments she was going to have to endure from Ivy about Ted the Remnant.

Chapter 6

Evan put the seats down in the back of Holly's Expedition, and Keelie slept through most of the trip to Coventry, tucked under a blanket with her leg propped on Ted's suitcase. She wasn't sure what gestures Ted and Evan were making toward becoming friendlier, but occasionally their conversation got loud enough to wake her. It was like junior high, when every boy had to be noisier than every other boy. She would shift or clear her throat, and their voices would drop. It might have been the effects of the Vicodin, but she could have sworn they were still competing over gross Christmas songs and that she heard one say, "I'll be home for chlamydias" and the other reply, "It's beginning to look a lot like chlamydias." Either she was dreaming, or they'd permanently regressed to age fourteen.

As groggy as she was, she didn't register much when they got to Granny's house until Ivy helped her get in bed. "All those books," Keelie said, looking around her. "It's like being at work."

"This is the library," Ivy said. "When my mother was a teenager, she had mono one summer and they put the daybed in here so it would be easier to take care of her. Somehow it never got turned back into just a library. Holly and I used to love to sleep here on visits." She tucked the covers around Keelie. "Are you warm enough? I can light a fire. Granny has central heat, but the fire makes it cozier."

"I'm fine," Keelie said.

"Good," Ivy said, scooting next to her on the bed. "Evan was sketchy on the phone, so you can tell me how your Remnant ended up here."

"Please stop calling him that," Keelie begged. She told Ivy about her fall off the ladder, the emergency room, and how nice Ted had been. "He's really not as bad as I thought, and I felt sorry for him when I found out he was going to be alone at Christmas. But he's not my Remnant; there's no chemistry between us."

"Okay, Madame Curie," Ivy said.

"I know I should have asked you before I invited him—"

"It doesn't bother me at all," Ivy assured her. "If he was nice to you, that's good enough for me. *I* feel sorry for him if he thinks he's going to get a Norman Rockwell Christmas. Granny's idea of cooking Christmas dinner is throwing Stouffer's Turkey Tetrazzini in the microwave and buying a can of cranberry sauce. The gelled kind with can lines around it, not the real thing."

"I don't like the real thing," Keelie said.

"Me, either." Ivy stood up. "I'll try to keep the Rem— Ted fed and entertained somehow. We're kind of off the beaten path here."

"Is it snowing?" Keelie asked hopefully.

"Not a flake. But it's still a week until Christmas, so you never know." Ivy looked at Hamlet's travel case. "I think there's an old aquarium in the attic. I'll find it and clean it so the kid can have more space."

"He doesn't care," Keelie said. "But if you could locate a carrot—"

"I haven't been shopping yet, but I'll find something he can eat," Ivy promised. She brushed Keelie's hair off her face and said, "Sleep. You're hours from the evil Rodney, and we've got days to talk."

Waking up in a room full of books that she didn't have to sell reminded Keelie of how much she loved to read. She gazed at the shelves for a while, trying to pick out familiar titles from among books that looked decades old. She spotted Nancy Drew and Hardy Boys collections and smiled, thinking of all the children who'd probably enjoyed them over the years. But there were also lots of paperbacks, so the library must have been kept fairly current even after it became a guest room.

She studied other details of the room. Elaborately carved molding, stained instead of painted, set off the pressed tin ceiling. The walls were painted a deep blue, and a faded Oriental rug covered hardwood floors. The stone fireplace was surrounded by a carved mahogany mantel. A built-in secretary and the bookshelves were also mahogany, and reading chairs that looked old and comfortable were positioned throughout the room next to tables and reading lamps. The lower parts of the windows were covered with wooden shutters, and the upper windows were stained glass. She couldn't appreciate the windows' details because the sun wasn't fully up, and the library was on the west side of the house.

The early hour and the quietness probably meant she

was the first one awake. She decided to do a little exploring with the help of her crutches. She paused outside the library to admire the stained glass transom over the front door, then stared appreciatively at the wooden staircase, wondering if the house was two or three floors and where everyone else was sleeping.

Two parlors and the dining room were painted in deep greens and blues and also had elaborate molding, tons of windows, some with stained glass, and more Oriental rugs protecting the buffed hardwood floors. It was awkward maneuvering with the crutches, but unlike many old houses, including her own grandmother's, Granny's was free of clutter and sparsely furnished.

The kitchen was big, with blue walls, another tin ceiling, white cabinets with dishes gleaming behind glass doors, and a black and white tiled floor. Everything was spotless, which wasn't surprising since Granny apparently never cooked. Most of the small appliances were tucked inside an old pie safe; even the microwave was concealed in an antique cabinet. Keelie rummaged around until she found everything she needed to make a pot of coffee.

She fell in love with the yellow bathroom's beadboard wainscoting, thick molding, and hexagonal tile floor. The room's sunny quality was enhanced by a stained glass window full of greens and yellows, and by a number of hanging ferns. A glass-walled shower with a marble bench had been added next to a claw foot tub. The shower would make it easier for Keelie to keep her leg dry. She went back to the kitchen and found a trash bag to wrap around her splint. After taking her toiletries and a change of clothes to the bathroom, she took a long, fragrant shower, which not only made her feel better, but allowed her to do something with the disaster that was her hair.

She was still the only one up, and she found a travel cup with a lid for her coffee and took it and a small piece of apple to the library without dropping anything. Hamlet emerged from his pile of bedding long enough to take the apple. She grabbed the first book she saw that she hadn't read before, a mystery by Janet Evanovich, and sank to the daybed, feeling stupidly weak from so much exertion. She took a Vicodin, propped her leg on pillows, rested for a while, and finally opened the book.

She read a few pages then said, "Hey, listen to this. Stephanie has a hamster, too, named Rex." Hamlet didn't seem to care, but she read all the Rex parts out loud to him anyway. At some point, she dozed off, waking up when Granny came in.

"You washed your hair?" Granny asked. "I'll light the fire so you won't get chilled."

Keelie watched her, thinking that no one looked less grandmotherly than Ivy and Holly's granny. She was a big-boned woman with iron gray hair that she kept short in a cut that was more practical than stylish. She was wearing a pair of jeans and a man's denim shirt, the bottom two buttons undone to allow room for her ample hips. She clumped through the room in a pair of leather cowboy boots that were as weathered as her face.

When she was satisfied that the fire was going, she turned back to Keelie and said, "Tell me about this fellow you brought with you. He's taken over the kitchen and even has Ivy doing something with the blender. I've never used that blender for anything but margaritas. It's likely to go into shock."

Keelie explained who Ted was. When she saw the

knowing look in Granny's eyes, she said, "I barely know him. I don't know what provoked me to invite him here."

"Doesn't curl your toes, huh?"

"Nope. But he's been awfully nice about my ankle. I don't think Evan likes him."

Granny snorted and said, "Evan is used to being the only man in you girls' lives. It's high time he found a man of his own. You reckon Ted is gay?"

"I don't think so. I don't know. But even if he were, I don't think he curls Evan's toes, either."

"Some relationships start that way."

After a pause, Keelie said, "I just realized I don't know anything about your husband. Is there a Mr. Granny somewhere?"

"Yep. I can't believe the girls never told you about him."

"You could tell me."

"I'm not sure it's a before-breakfast story," Granny said with a grin. "I think it was fate, because Fred was a second son. Do you know the story of Coventry? The town, I mean."

"No."

"Thomas Albright was the second son of a British earl. He quarreled with his family over his inheritance, which was apparently slim pickings. When he asked how he was supposed to live a gentleman's life with such a stingy family, his father told him he could damn well go to Coventry."

"That's a city in England, right?" Keelie asked.

"Yes. There was a prison there, so being sent to Coventry meant you were cast out of society. Albright decided to make his fortune in the New World, and he got here just in time to fight on the losing side of the War Between the States. When the war ended, like

many Confederates, he headed west. He made money—
probably underhandedly, like most of the robber barons
of his time—and he stopped moving when he made it to
the Brazos River, founding our little town and naming
it Coventry as his last shot at his family.

"My great-grandfather, Ellison Rourke, also a second
son, was a friend of Albright's. He staked claim to thou-
sands of acres of land and my family became cattle
ranchers. By the time my father inherited, he was more
interested in oil than cattle, so he sold off a lot of our
land piecemeal, keeping the drilling rights. All my
brothers went into the oil business, too, and some of
them got rich. They live in Dallas, San Antonio, and
Houston. They didn't have much interest in this house,
so Fred and I got it by default, though my family didn't
think much of Fred."

While she talked, Granny opened the shutters, allowing more light into the room, added a log to the
fire, and gently plumped up the pillows under Keelie's
foot, somehow making it more comfortable. Keelie decided Granny was more grandmotherly than anyone
suspected.

"Fred and I met after the Second World War. He'd
been too young to join the Army in time to see combat,
and he couldn't seem to settle on a vocation. Not much
ambition, but that was all right by me. I had enough
money to take care of us. Fred did keep up what was left
of the family land, repairing fences and barns and such.
But after our kids were grown and out of the house,
Fred decided it was time to see a bit of the world again.
He joined a motorcycle club and travels all over the
States. Hell's Antique, I call him. He buzzes back into
Coventry now and then until we remember that we get

on each other's nerves, then he's off again. I was never crazy about a conventional life, so Fred suits me."

Keelie grinned and said, "You are *so* much cooler than my grandmother."

"My children think I'm an old fool, but I do better with my grandkids," Granny admitted. "Since Ivy's gotten herself in a state about this Christmas thing, I called Isaac—he runs our hardware store—and asked him to get us a tree. We've got decorations in the attic. I haven't done all that since the kids grew up. As you know, I usually go down to Houston and agitate my daughter at Christmas. I can't imagine why she decided to go to Hawaii," Granny finished with a gleam in her eye.

"I appreciate your letting us all come here," Keelie said. "Your house is beautiful."

"You're welcome, even if I'm not much of a hostess," Granny said. "Who knows, maybe Fred will ride in and make things more festive." She slapped her knees and stood up with a glance at Keelie's crutches. "You get around all right on those things?"

"They helped me snoop all over the downstairs this morning," Keelie confessed.

"Let's head to the kitchen and see if Ivy killed the blender or Evan killed Ted. I do love a good time."

By Keelie's second afternoon in Coventry, she was dreaming about mobsters and hot men thanks to Janet Evanovich's books, two of which she'd finished between Vicodin naps. She wasn't sure what everyone else was doing, except that Granny apparently spent most of her time on her computer.

When Keelie hobbled into the kitchen, Ivy and Ted

weren't around, but Evan was getting directions to the hardware store so he could pick up the Christmas tree.

"I want to go," Keelie begged.

"You're supposed to stay off your ankle," Evan reminded her.

"I'm not putting any weight on it. If I have to lie in that bed another minute, I'll go out of my mind. Even Hamlet is sick of me. He stays buried in his new aquarium. I think he hates Rex, the hamster in the books I'm reading. Maybe there's a hamster wheel at the hardware store."

"Probably," Granny said. "Isaac's got a little bit of everything there."

"All right. Dress warmly. And hurry. I don't want to drive back in the dark."

"If you get lost, anyone can give you directions to the Rourke house," Granny said.

"This road is weird; I understand why you didn't like driving it in the dark," Keelie said later, looking out at the landscape. There wasn't much to see but pastures, most of which were empty except for an occasional cluster of cattle and a horse or two. If there were houses, they were either tucked behind random patches of tall trees or down little graveled side roads that curved away from the one Evan was driving, which she finally learned from a sign was Old River Road.

"According to Ted, who's suddenly an expert on the area," Evan said dryly, "the original roads were designed to parallel the river and to impact the cattle ranches as little as possible. As land was divided and sold and new roads were put in, they started making the roads go north-south, east-west, whatever. Granny says the locals like it this way because it confuses the tourists."

"Tourists? Why would tourists come to the middle of nowhere?"

"I hear drugs are the latest micropolis craze."

"The what?"

"Micropolis. Ask Ted. He says it's a town with more than ten thousand and less than fifty thousand people."

"This is Texas. High school football is the only micropolis craze," Keelie said.

When Evan took a right onto Oak Road, Keelie said, "Easy to see where this road got its name. I'll bet it's beautiful in the summer when the trees have leaves. Maybe the tourists come to look at the trees?" Then without warning, they were suddenly in town, and Keelie gasped and said, "Oh, it's so charming! Look at all the old buildings and Victorian houses like Granny's. And everything's so clean."

"There's even a town square," Evan said. "Which is where I turn for the hardware store."

"Every place has Christmas lights," Keelie said.

"You hate Christmas, remember?"

"It's like one of those little ceramic villages Holly decorates with," Keelie said, as if she hadn't heard him. "Who knew there was anything so quaint in Texas?"

"You need to get out more," Evan said. "There are lots of towns like this. They all have old buildings, a town square, and bored teenagers who get the hell out as soon as they can."

"Not that it's all about you," Keelie said.

"Edna never looked this good," Evan vowed.

When he started to turn into a spot in front of Phillips Hardware, Keelie said, "Could you park at the drugstore instead? I want to get some Tylenol. I'm tired of being stoned or knocked out on Vicodin all the time."

"You're on the cutting edge of the micropolis trend,"

Evan said. After he parked, he helped her inside Rook Drugs, where they both stopped and stared around them.

"A real soda fountain," Keelie whispered. "We've gone back in time. It's like Pleasantville."

"Actually, I think we've found the North Pole," Evan said and nodded toward the man behind the counter, who was bald and had the requisite white beard and twinkling blue eyes of Santa Claus.

"What can I get you folks?"

"Coffee," Evan said.

"Hot chocolate," Keelie said.

Evan looked around and spotted some empty plastic milk crates at the end of the counter. "Do you mind if I put a couple of these under her foot?"

"Help yourself," the man said. After he put steaming mugs in front of them, he went to the other side of the drugstore and began stocking shelves.

"Maybe he really is Santa Claus," Evan said. "According to Ted the Expert, Coventry's main industry other than agriculture is a toy factory."

"Why are you so hard on Ted?" Keelie asked and took a sip of her hot chocolate, which was exactly the right temperature. Santa apparently had many talents.

"I don't like the way he acts toward you," Evan said.

"What? He was nice about my ankle, but he barely knows I'm alive."

"Exactly," Evan said. "He should act more like a boyfriend. He hardly checks on you. Instead, he spends all his time pestering Granny with questions and conspiring with Ivy about something. Christmas dinner, I think."

"But I don't want him to be my boyfriend," Keelie said.

"If you weren't interested, you wouldn't have invited him to spend Christmas with you."

"I didn't want him to go through Christmas with nothing but Rodney to divert him," Keelie said. "Ugh. I don't want to think about work." She looked around and said, "I can't remember ever being the only customer in any store in Houston."

"You should shop in the middle of the night like I do," Evan said. "I'm going to the hardware store to get the Christmas tree. You stay off your feet."

"Don't forget to look for a hamster wheel," Keelie reminded him. "Solid. No rungs."

After Evan left, Keelie swiveled around so she could see the square. A couple of kids were bundled up and playing near the fountain, and Keelie peered at it, wondering if her eyes were deceiving her. She looked around for Santa and said, "Excuse me?"

"Need a refill?" he asked, stepping behind the counter.

"I was wondering about the fountain," Keelie said. "Is that statue a naked woman on horseback?"

"Of course," he said. He held out his hand and said, "I'm Nelson Rook. You must be Ivy Johnson's friend."

"How did you know—"

"Broken ankle," Nelson said. "I read about you in Storey Time."

Keelie was at a loss and said, "I'm sorry; I don't know what you're talking about."

"Elenore Storey's online journal," he said. "You didn't know she has a Web log? It's called Storey Time, and she mentioned her visitors from Houston."

"Granny wrote about me?" Keelie asked. "For anybody on the Internet to read?"

"There's not much to read, since all you've done is sleep," Nelson said.

"Good grief," Keelie said, wondering if Ivy knew about Granny's blog. "Back to the naked woman on the horse . . ."

"It's Lady Godiva," Nelson said, as if it should be obvious.

"Why is there a statue of Lady Godiva in the fountain?" Keelie asked.

Nelson put another cup of hot chocolate in front of her and said, "Are you ready for a little history lesson?"

"Granny told me about a man named Albright who founded Coventry," Keelie said.

"There's a lot more to our town's story than that," Nelson said. He pulled up a stool on his side of the counter and sat down. "Lady Godiva was one of the more famous residents of Coventry, England. She lived in the eleventh century, and her horseback ride through the village was a challenge to her husband to lower the townspeople's taxes."

"Was she really naked?" Keelie asked.

"Probably not," Nelson admitted, "but it makes a better story if she was. Coventry thrived over the centuries. Then it was badly bombed in two German air raids during World War II. In fact, Coventry and Dresden, Germany, formed a partnership after the war to promote reconstruction and peace.

"Some of our Coventry's citizens sent money and supplies to the original Coventry to help with relief efforts during and after the war. Our mayor issued a proclamation declaring us sister cities, and that's when we renamed our two main streets Godiva and Dresden, to recognize that we're all part of one world."

"I love that," Keelie said.

"A few years after the war ended, England's Coventry erected a statue of Lady Godiva. Plenty of people from our town have visited the statue and learned more about the city that gave us our name. In the 1960s, we began holding a Godiva Festival every summer. An anonymous British benefactor commissioned a smaller-scale reproduction of England's Godiva statue and donated it to our town. Theirs is on a pedestal; ours was designed to be part of a fountain. That's the one you see today."

"I like your story," Keelie said, looking at the statue with new appreciation.

"You should come back in the summer and enjoy our festival. Lots of folk art, crafts, entertainment, food, and of course, the crowning of our own Daughter of Godiva."

"Does she have to ride across the town square naked?" Keelie asked.

Nelson grinned and said, "No. Back in the seventies, a lot of the girls wouldn't cut their hair for years because of the festival. Now they wear wigs. But they've always been dressed. We have a whole pageant, with knights, jousting, and a Medieval Ball."

"I'd love to see it," Keelie said.

"By then, you won't be on crutches, and you could really enjoy it," Nelson said.

"Sold!" Keelie said. "I should pay for our drinks before Evan comes back. And I need some Tylenol. I'm weaning myself off Vicodin. I'm telling you this in case Granny mentions my substance abuse on her blog."

Nelson grinned, rang up the Tylenol, and said, "Drinks are on me this time. Thanks for letting me bend your ear. Could you take these limes to Elenore? She'll need them for *Sex* night."

Nelson turned to answer the phone just as Evan came

through the door. He seemed eager to help Keelie outside to the car, so she didn't get a chance to ask Nelson
if he'd actually said "sex night."

"It's huge!" she said as she saw the tree splayed
across the top of Holly's car.

"Yeah, I'm all about the size. I hope Isaac did a good
job of tying it down. You should have met him. What a
character. I got a hamster wheel for Hamlet. Solid. No
rungs."

"Thanks. Santa's name is Nelson Rook. He was a
fountain of information."

Evan listened with interest as Keelie told him Coventry's history, then he said, "What better role model
could there be for Texas girls than a woman with as
much hair as Lady Godiva?"

"I totally want to come back for their festival in the
summer," Keelie said.

"It sounds like a smaller version of the Renaissance
Festival," Evan said. "Isaac didn't tell me about the
town's history, but he did tell me about the toy factory,
and now I get the whole Godiva connection. A couple
of A&M college boys who grew up in Coventry devel-
oped a video game called Godiva. I guess they made a
lot of money, and they came back here and bought an
empty manufacturing plant to make educational toys.
The wife of one of the guys is creating a doll that's sort
of like Barbie, but she's not a fashion doll. The doll is
named Godiva, and the early versions are supposed to
encourage girls to break through the glass ceiling. So
far, there are plans for CEO Godiva, Doctor Godiva,
and President Godiva."

"Wow, who knew there were such forward thinkers in
small-town Texas?" Keelie asked. "Speaking of com-

puters, did you know Granny has a blog and she's been talking about us on it?"

"She's a pistol," Evan said, showing his smile lines. "I think I just passed Old River Road." He made a U-turn, took a right on the winding road that led back to Granny's house, and said, "Isaac said something weird as I was leaving. I'm not sure I heard him right. I swear he said he hoped we have fun on sex night."

"You're kidding," Keelie said. "Nelson gave me a bag of limes to take to Granny for sex night. I didn't get a chance to ask him what he was talking about, because that's when you came to get me."

"Big cities have nothing on our little Texas micropolis," Evan said. "What the hell is sex night?"

Keelie's only answer was a shriek as Evan took a curve too fast and had to swerve to avoid a man on horseback. The car spun around, and she got a good view of the horse rearing and unseating his rider. By the time Evan jammed the car into park, she was outside the Expedition, standing on one foot and watching the man get up. He swore as he grabbed the horse's reins and brushed himself off.

"Are you all right?" she called.

"Why the hell were you driving so fast?" he snapped.

"We weren't expecting to see a horse—"

"You're in the country," he said. "I could have been a deer, a cow, a skunk—were you driving with that *thing* on your foot?"

"She wasn't driving; I was," Evan said. "Are you hurt? Do you need help?"

The man turned away and ran his hands over the horse's legs. He finally looked back at them. He didn't appear any more composed, but his voice had dropped an octave when he said, "The horse seems fine, no thanks to your *excellent* driving skills." He put one foot in the stirrup, swung his leg over the saddle, and rode away from them without another word.

"What a jerk," Keelie said.

"I did nearly run him down," Evan said, leaning weakly against the car. "My adrenaline is pumping, so his must be off the chart."

"Whatever. It's not like you were going that fast. It was a blind curve. He shouldn't have been in the middle of the road."

Evan checked the tree and seemed satisfied that it was still tied securely to the roof. Then he held Keelie's arm while she hopped back to the car and got inside. He slid into the driver's seat, started the car, and turned it in the right direction.

"It could have been a lot worse," she said after a few minutes of silence from Evan. "The car's okay. The horse is okay. Even the tree's okay."

"I wish he'd given me a chance to apologize to him. I feel like such an idiot."

She endured more of Evan's silent brooding, then said, "Why did I think the country would be laid back? Blogging grannies, naked statues, mysterious sex nights, and furious cowboys."

"Don't forget drug-peddling Santa Clauses," Evan said, but she could tell his mind was elsewhere.

Chapter 7

"I don't like theme trees," Ivy was saying as Keelie limped into the parlor. Ivy and Ted were sitting among piles of boxes, with ornaments spread around them. Granny was nowhere to be found, so Keelie had put the limes from Nelson Rook in the refrigerator before she gave Hamlet his new hamster wheel. He hadn't seemed very interested, but Keelie was sure he'd take it for a test run most of the night while she was trying to sleep.

"Did you misplace Evan?" Ted asked in a hopeful tone.

"He's untying the tree from the car's roof."

"I left the tree stand on the front porch. Should I go help him?"

"It might be better if you let him do it himself," Keelie said. "He's in a mood."

"He's been in a mood ever since y'all got here," Ivy said. "What's up with that?"

"I don't know," Keelie said vaguely. "Maybe he's worried about finding a job."

"Yeah, he's all about work," Ted said, mimicking one of Evan's favorite phrases. Ted cleared a place for

Keelie on a tapestry loveseat and set her crutches within reach before he turned back to Ivy. "Did your family have theme trees?"

"My mother is a Christmas fiend," Ivy said. "She always has three trees. The one in the living room is her theme tree. Daddy called it the 'company tree', because that's the one everyone sees. One year it was all silver garland and red balls. Other Christmases, it was just wooden Santas, or all angels, or little Mardi Gras masks and purple, green, and gold beads and balls. The tree is always pretty, but I like the one in the den better. It has a mish-mash of ornaments that she's collected over the years. The third tree is on the landing upstairs. She decorates it with all the crap that Holly, Scotty, and I made when we were kids. And now stuff that Holly's sons, Jon and Ryan, make. It isn't very pretty, but it has character."

"And lots of memories," Ted said with understanding.

"My grandmother does theme trees," Keelie said. "They're boring."

Ted nodded and said, "My grandmother had one of those silver trees with that spotlight thing that turned and made the tree red, green, and blue."

"Those are popular again," Ivy said.

"Bad taste never goes out of style," Ted said.

"Kitsch," Ivy corrected him.

"My mother always does a tree like the one in your mother's den, Ivy. Loaded with whatever ornaments will fit on it. What kind of trees did your mother do, Ted?"

"My brother and I were raised by my grandmother. So it was just the silver tree and tons of presents. I guess one of the few advantages of having your parents die when you're a little kid is that you get really spoiled at Christmas."

"Sorry," Keelie said meekly.

"It was a long time ago; don't sweat it," Ted said. He stood up when they heard a thump on the front porch.

"Go help Evan," Ivy said, waving her hand with resignation. "I'll make Tiny Tim over there help me untangle these lights."

When they heard the front door close behind him, Keelie said, "Why do I always say the wrong thing to him?"

"I don't think it bothered him," Ivy reassured her. She tossed a strand of lights to Keelie. "I'm glad you invited him. He's amazing in the kitchen. Today we went grocery shopping. He's planning a real Christmas dinner. Turkey with all the trimmings. Much better than anything Granny and I could have done. Did you enjoy your trip to downtown Coventry?"

"I did," Keelie said. "I met Nelson Rook at Rook Drugs. He told me lots of stuff about Coventry's history and the Godiva Festival."

"Good old Nelson," Ivy said. "He's looked the same since I was a little kid. I used to think he was Santa Claus."

"Evan still thinks he is," Keelie said. "I know one reason Evan's in a bad mood. Because of you, he believes that I'm interested in Ted. He thinks Ted should be paying more attention to me. I want you two to stop this."

"I think Ted's a real catch. Are you absolutely, positively sure that you aren't interested?"

"Yes," Keelie said, hoping that was the end of it. "Another reason Evan's cranky is something that happened on the way home."

As she explained how they'd nearly run down the enraged man on horseback, she noticed that Ivy sat up straighter and got a gleam in her eye.

"I don't know how you do it," Ivy said almost before Keelie had finished.

"Do what?"

"First, the Remnant. Now the Rulebreaker."

"What are you talking about?"

"It's just like when Jane Eyre met Rochester. Except he was the one who hurt his ankle when his horse slipped on ice. But still—"

"Right," Keelie said. "There was Jane, nearly mowing Rochester down with her SUV, then offering her little shoulder to help him walk lamely to his horse. After that, she carted her best friend off to the loony bin."

"Poor Darcy. You've dumped him for Rochester. What does Rochester look like?"

"Even if I wanted to indulge your demented fixation, I don't remember. I was just quaking in my splint because he was yelling. But don't start one of your fantasies about how we met angry and are destined to fall in love, because he was yelling at Evan, not me."

"Details," Ivy said dismissively. "Your suitors span two centuries. Where will it end?"

"With me strangling you with these lights," Keelie said.

"Oh, goodness," Granny said as she walked into the parlor and looked around. "What a mess." She had to step aside when Evan and Ted tromped through the door carrying the tree.

"Where do you want it?" Ted asked.

Keelie focused on untangling the lights, keeping her face down so no one could see her grin as Granny and Ivy made the men move the tree four times before it ended up in the first place they'd tried.

"I'm done," Evan pronounced. "This tree is sticky. I need a shower and some food."

"It's too bad we can't call out for pizza," Ivy said.

"We don't need pizza," Granny said. "I picked up chicken while I was out, and once the girls get here, we'll have tons of food."

"The girls?" Ivy asked with a slight frown.

"It's *Sex* night," Granny said. She looked surprised when all four of them stared at her with a mixture of curiosity and apprehension. "Dorothy, Lois, and Arliss come over once a week for *Sex* night."

"I'm afraid to ask," Ivy said weakly.

"I'm not," Evan said. "Isaac at the hardware store talked about sex night. The guy at the drugstore talked about sex night. What are you, Dorothy, and the rest of the Golden Girls up to? Is it some kind of sex toys party? Because I've been to those, and while I'm all about the toys, I—"

"Aaaaa," Ivy said, covering her ears. "She's my grandmother!"

"It's just my friends and me spending an evening with Carrie and her friends," Granny said.

"I get it!" Keelie yelped, and they all looked at her. "The Golden Girls watch *Sex and the City.*"

"Arliss has the first two seasons on DVD," Granny said. "We limit ourselves to one episode a week. We're trying to make them last. That Carrie Bradshaw inspires me. I may not have a newspaper column or my picture on the side of a bus—"

"But you have a blog," Evan said.

"You heard about that?"

"Mr. Rook knew my name, that I have a broken ankle, and I sleep all the time," Keelie said.

"Oh, Lord," Ivy said, looking at the ceiling.

"I don't say anything bad," Granny defended herself.

"Usually I share whatever we talk about on *Sex* night. *Some* people think old ladies have good sense."

"I'd like to read your blog," Ted said.

"We'll see," Granny said. "You're welcome to join us for *Sex*." She laughed as Ivy shuddered. "We drink margaritas. You might even be able to talk my friends into helping you decorate that monster of a tree. After the show, of course. Nothing comes before *Sex*."

"You really love finding ways to use that word in a sentence, don't you?" Ivy asked.

"I'm definitely up for *Sex*," Evan said. "But first, a shower."

"My caller ID says 'Fred Storey,'" Misty said. "Who's Fred Storey? Is that the guy who answers your phone in the morning?"

"Ivy's grandfather," Keelie said. "Remember? I'm in Coventry."

"Oh, yeah. How's your ankle?"

"Still broken. Misty, do you think there's something wrong with me?"

"How much time have you got?"

"I'm serious. I just spent an evening with some of the most amazing women. Ivy's grandmother is seventy-three. She's happily married to a man who's zooming around the country on a motorcycle. Granny keeps a blog. I don't even have a computer, much less an e-mail account, and she's writing stuff about her life that everybody in town reads and talks about. Once a week, she gets together with three of her friends. These are not little old ladies who knit."

"I think little old ladies who knit are a myth. Gram doesn't knit. I don't know anybody who knits. Wait, I take that back. Matt works with a guy whose son knits. Knitting: It's not just for little old ladies anymore."

"Let's drop the knitting," Keelie said. "Granny's best friend is Arliss. Arliss is in her late fifties. She went to U.T. and got a degree in political science. Then she got married, had a son, and became a homemaker. A few years ago, her husband died. She said people started treating her like her life was over. So she ran for mayor and won. She's running an entire city!"

"Coventry's not exactly—"

"They're friends with Dorothy."

"They're lesbians?"

"Not friends *of* Dorothy. Friends *with* Dorothy. Dorothy is sixty. She's the high school principal. When other Texas schools started freaking out about standardized tests and changed their curriculum to teach to the tests, Dorothy went the other way. She got the school board to approve more art classes, music programs, and reading clubs. She's also a proponent of sex education. Coventry High has low drop-out rates, almost no teen pregnancies, and some of the highest test scores in the state."

"These kids all sound above average," Misty said. "Are you sure you're not in Lake Wobegone? Aren't there any normal, and by normal, I mean dysfunctional, people there? You're scaring me."

"Their other friend is Lois. Lois is a stay-at-home mom. She's only thirty-five and she has four kids. Her husband is a Coventry policeman who shuttles her with the other two women to Granny's one night a week so they can have a few margaritas and not worry about driving. Lois helps organize the town festival every summer, because you know, with four kids, she has nothing else to do."

"I don't know why these women intimidate you," Misty said. "You grew up with Polly and Gram as your role models."

"Mom I get, but Gram?"

"Gram serves a purpose. She gave her daughter and her granddaughters someone to react against. We didn't want to be crabby old women who marry for money and spend our time polishing silver and worrying that someone else might have more than us."

"These women's accomplishments don't intimidate me. I'm just . . . Today, Evan nearly ran down a man on a horse. We started talking about it while we were trimming the Christmas tree with Granny's friends. Arliss asked what the man looked like, and I couldn't remember. I could tell her the horse was black and the man was pissed off. Evan, on the other hand, said that the man was taller than six feet and had brown hair and brown eyes. He then described the guy's haircut—well, Evan is a hairdresser, so maybe that's not a big deal—and said he probably hadn't shaved in a couple of days. Then he told her what he was wearing, right down to the height of the heel on his boots. And all I could do was drool and say, 'Black horse,' like I was three years old. Stop giggling, or I'm hanging up on you."

"I can't help it. So you couldn't describe a stranger. What's the big deal?"

"Then there's Ted Hughes, the guy who answered my phone when you called. The women at work all think he's hot. Ivy says he's a real catch. When he's not in front of me, I can barely remember what he looks like. However, if you asked, I could describe in detail all of Granny's friends tonight, including their hair, their makeup, and what they were wearing. What is wrong with me?"

"Maybe *you're* the lesbian," Misty said. "With a thing for older women."

"I may as well be a nun," Keelie said. "I'm twenty-eight years old and my libido doesn't even register a handsome man."

"What about the armored truck guy?"

"Don't mess with my theory, Misty. I'm telling you, I'm not normal."

Misty sighed and said, "Shut up and let me talk you down. Do you know how many women Mom and I meet through Wonderful Wife who are obsessed with finding a man? They can have great jobs, apartments, and friends, but do they appreciate themselves? No. They feel like they're nothing because they haven't found a soul mate with a penis. They answer personal ads, meet men online, and hook up with the biggest losers because they *must have a man*. It's pathetic. Maybe the reason you don't obsess over every handsome face that comes along is because you aren't desperate. Could it be that you're relatively happy with your life? That even if your job has its miseries, you enjoy it? That you're content with good friends? That your hamster, an interesting book, and your own company are enough to keep you from putting on too much mascara and a sleazy outfit and troll for men who don't offer half of what you deserve?"

After a few seconds of silence, Keelie said, "When did you get so smart?"

"I've always been this smart. I admit that I'm probably not the best judge of what it feels like to hear your biological clock ticking while you're trying to sleep solo. Sometimes I'm ready to kill for an hour alone in my own house. To go to the bathroom without a kid or a dog poking their head in the door. But like you, when

I am alone, I'm in good company. Well, as long as I've got Jon Stewart and *The Daily Show*. Mom raised us right, Keelie. That's your curse. If you never get married and have kids, you'll be fine with it."

"Marriage? Kids? I just want someone to make my teeth sweat," Keelie said.

"Be careful what you wish for."

"You're the second person to say that to me in the last week," Keelie mused. "The first person said it after I wished for more than a day off at Christmas. And now I'm laid up with a broken ankle and forced to live on a reduced salary."

"Since you're my sister, I'll give you a Wonderful Wife discount for this consultation," Misty promised.

Keelie had put Janet Evanovich's mysteries aside and was deeply involved in *Jane Eyre* when Granny brought firewood into the library.

"I was afraid I'd wake you if I came in earlier," Granny said. "Did you have fun last night?"

"I had a great time," Keelie said. "I wasn't taking Vicodin, and my ankle didn't even hurt."

"Laughter's the best drug I know," Granny said. "Mind if I visit a while?"

"I'd love it," Keelie said.

Granny pulled a rocking chair near the daybed and said, "This is my favorite chair in the house. Fred bought this Windsor rocker when I was pregnant with my first baby. It's got a good creak. Babies sleep better when they hear a good creak. All my grandkids were rocked in this chair, too, and now my two great-grandkids. I guess when Scotty and Carla come back from Hawaii, their baby will be rocked in it, too."

"I'll bet almost everything in this house has a story," Keelie said.

"That's what makes a home," Granny said. "See how the end of this arm looks a little worse for wear? It's a baby magnet. As soon as they can pull up, their little mouths go right to it. They like it better than a teething ring."

Keelie laughed and said, "I'm sure my little baby, Hamlet, would like to get his teeth into it, too."

Ivy stuck her head in the door and said, "Oh, good. You're awake. Am I interrupting something?"

"No," Granny said. "The more the merrier."

Ivy had to move *Jane Eyre* as she sat on the bed, but other than a raised eyebrow, she made no comment.

"I was telling Granny how much fun I had last night," Keelie said. "I slept like a rock."

"My phone has been buzzing all morning," Granny said. "You sure made an impression on Dorothy. She asked me if you've ever considered teaching. I think she'd hire you in a minute."

"Teaching?" Keelie asked. "Not really. I didn't go that route, although I knew a lot of English majors who got teaching certificates."

"I think they're so desperate for good teachers these days that they hire you and let you get certified while you're working," Ivy said. "Maybe you should think about it."

"Why? What has Ted said? Am I going to lose my job?"

Ivy bit her lip then said, "If I tell you something, you can't act like you know."

"Bad idea," Granny said. "When somebody confides in you—"

"Well, he didn't say I *couldn't* repeat it," Ivy said.

"Ted told me that Rodney is a jerk. I get the impression he already thought so, but the night you hurt yourself, I guess Rodney didn't react the way Ted believed he should."

"If Ted hadn't been there, I probably could have ended up suing because Rodney didn't take my injury seriously," Keelie said. "Ted's just protecting the store. That's his job."

"Ted actually said you're a better manager than Rodney. So I don't think your job's in jeopardy. But you haven't seemed happy there for a while. Maybe Dorothy has the right idea."

Keelie considered it for a minute, then said, "I think a teacher needs to have passion for the job. I lack that passion. I'm flattered by Dorothy's suggestion. And I admit that this break from Buy The Book is making me think about my future. I can't stand working for Rodney, and I can't be promoted at my store. Maybe I should either move, so I can get my own store, or I should try a different profession." She sighed. "I wish I enjoyed my job the way you do, Ivy."

"What makes you think I enjoy my job?"

"You never complain about work the way Evan and I do. Plus you put in all those extra hours."

"I enjoy being an editor. But everyone I work with thinks he's a great writer and, thanks to spell check, a great editor, so to them, I'm just an unnecessary person who delays their reports."

"Does Dave think that?" Granny asked.

"Dave is at too high a level to deal with such pettiness," Ivy said. "And the last thing I'd do at work is give the impression that I whine to him. I can handle it, but sometimes the political crap gets the best of me."

"Office politics?" Keelie asked.

"My politics. Not that I spend my days at work talking about what I believe, although if someone baits me with some ignorant or hateful remark, I'll call them on it. That seems to happen more on Mondays, when Evan and I have lunch. There are people at work who know he's gay, and for some reason, seeing us together is all the encouragement they need to tell me their religious beliefs. I don't want to be subjected to that any time, but especially not at work. There's this one guy who can never resist an opportunity to say something stupid about gay people. Then he turns around and invites me to his church. I guess he wants to save me from myself. Oddly, he's the same guy who gets the receptionist to lie to his wife whenever he has lunch at Hooters."

"I'm sure he only goes there for the wings," Keelie said.

"Right. Everybody goes to Hooters for the wings. The funny thing is, I don't care who goes to Hooters. It's his hypocrisy that bothers me. And I can't stand a liar. I don't even know what religion he is, but he's the last person who'd ever get me into a church. Or into Hooters, for that matter."

Granny grinned and said, "I've got a story, if you want to hear it."

"Is it about Hooters?" Keelie asked.

"No. A few years ago, a preacher from one of those cold states—maybe Nebraska—got crazy about our Lady Godiva statue. He said it was wicked and a bad example for our children. He wrote letters to the *Coventry Chronicle* about it. We didn't pay much attention to him. I reckon he travels around and sticks his nose in other towns' business all the time, and he decided to bring a group to demonstrate against the statue and our yearly Godiva Festival."

"Like that's the most pressing problem in the world," Ivy said, rolling her eyes.

"I don't know if you noticed the little church on the square, Keelie, but it's nearly as old as the town."

"The one with all the stained glass? It's lovely," Keelie said.

"Remember, Coventry's founder was an Englishman, so that church was Episcopalian to start with. Even though our town was also settled by Lutherans, Catholics, and Presbyterians, the Episcopal church had the most members, so they eventually moved to a larger building, which is the one they still use today: Christ Church. The old church stayed empty for many years, then Quakers used it for a while. Finally, it became First Coventry Church, which as far as I know, isn't connected to any denomination."

"Is Gary Black still the minister there?" Ivy asked. When Granny nodded, she said, "I always thought he was the meekest little man. Scared of his own shadow. I could never imagine him preaching hellfire and brimstone."

"He was the minister when this traveling preacher took issue with our statue. Apparently, some of his parishioners jumped into the fray and demanded that Pastor Black make a statement. Which he promised to do if the festival was actually picketed by the Nebraskans. Or they could have been from Iowa. No, I think it was definitely Nebraska."

"Did they show up?" Keelie asked.

"Yes. On a Sunday. It was a good year for the festival. All the bed-and-breakfasts were full, and so were the hotels on the highway that goes southeast to Fort Worth. You probably haven't seen that part of town, Keelie. Our suburbs," Granny said with a grin. "We call that part of town New Coventry. It's where the people who commute to Fort Worth and Dallas live. And where you'll find chain stores, Wal-Mart, and fast food restaurants."

"So what happened?" Ivy asked impatiently.

"The square was full of people, and First Coventry was having its regular Sunday morning service, when the traveling preacher and about a dozen followers showed up with a megaphone and stood outside the church, predicting the town's eternal doom if we didn't change our ways. Inside, the parishioners got restless, and the police chief interrupted their service to ask Pastor Black what he should do. The group didn't have a permit to protest, and they could have been hauled to jail, or at least to the city limits." Granny looked at their spellbound faces, grinned, and said, "I think I need to put another log on the fire."

"Make one move, old woman, and I'll sit on you," Ivy said.

"Pastor Black stepped outside the church, followed by his parishioners, and everyone held their breath. Nobody knew what his opinion was on the matter. Was he going to tell all the tourists they were sinners for gathering around Lady Godiva? That would have aggravated the businesses who depend on tourist money. Not to mention being a buzz kill."

"Gram would *never* say 'buzz kill'," Keelie complained.

"Pastor Black started off real quiet," Granny said, her eyes a little distant. "He didn't have a Bible in his hand, but he quoted scripture about how Jesus never turned away anyone who came to him. He welcomed the sinners and the believers. The rich and the poor. The sick and the healthy. The old and the young.

"When he turned and looked at Lady Godiva, there wasn't a sound in the crowd. He told us how he often wrote his sermons while staring out the window at her.

To him, the statue represented compassion for the downtrodden. Even if the story of Lady Godiva wasn't entirely true, it could be seen as a parable in which someone risked comfort to show love toward her fellow man. Pastor Black didn't see the statue's nudity as shameful. He saw the woman on horseback as a creature naked before God and man with nothing to offer but her good heart.

"He said it was our duty to show hospitality to the strangers among us, and to remember that God's love isn't always revealed to us in comfortable ways. He invited the Nebraskans to break bread with the good people of Coventry and all our other visitors."

"What did they do?" Ivy asked.

"They got in their bus and drove away," Granny said. "Never heard another peep out of them. But First Coventry's members were mighty popular that day. And that, Miss Ivy, shows why Gary Black will go to *heaven,* not Hooters, to get his wings."

"Okay, I like Gary Black," Ivy said, "and I love the Godiva statue, but I still don't like being preached to at my job."

"Then you know what I say. Do something about it," Granny said and put the Windsor rocker back in its place.

Chapter 8

"I don't care what the forecast says, it's not going to snow," Ted said when he came in the back door, letting in a gust of cold air.

"Are you also a meteorologist?" Evan asked.

Evan and Keelie were rolling rum balls from a mixture that Ted had concocted earlier. It seemed to Keelie that Evan's mood had improved over the previous couple of days. Even his question sounded more like he was teasing Ted than criticizing him.

"No, but I'm a New Yorker, and I know my snow."

"Did you grow up in Manhattan?" Keelie asked.

"Albany," Ted said. He washed his hands and sat at the table with them, tearing off a sheet of wax paper and spreading it in front of him so he could help with the rum balls.

"I really want it to snow," Keelie said. "I might even decide to like Christmas if it snows."

"It looks like it's snowing in this kitchen," Ivy said as she walked in. "Your hair is full of powdered sugar, Keelie." She opened the refrigerator door, stared blankly inside for a while, then closed the door and sat at the table. "What are y'all doing?"

"Making rum balls," Evan said.

Ivy picked up one and ate it, made a noise of approval, and picked up another one.

Granny walked into the kitchen, gingerly carrying a vase filled with juniper foliage and red roses, and said, "Keelie, I'm afraid you won't be getting your white Christmas." After she surveyed the rows of rum balls on the table, she set her vase on the counter and said, "I picked up this stuff at the florist, but damned if I can make it look good."

"Let Ted do it," Evan said.

"Sorry," Ted said. "My talents don't include floral design. Nice vase."

"It's Waterford," Granny said. "Arliss gave it to me several years ago. It's more her taste than mine. You should see her house. She's got Waterford vases, bowls, lamps, glasses of every variety, decanters—if it's Waterford, she bought it back in the days when she was bored. I used to wonder how a little boy could ever be himself in that house. But as far as I know, Grayson never broke anything. He was always outside."

"Grayson's her son?" Keelie asked.

"Yep. You met him."

"I did?"

With a smirk, Granny said, "You remember how Arliss was asking all those questions after hearing that Evan nearly collided with a horse? I'd bet it was Grayson riding the horse. He's a few years older than the twins."

"I sort of remember him," Ivy said. "Didn't he go away to school?"

"The Marine Academy in Harlingen. He went to

college in California, then he and a friend started a horse ranch in Wyoming. After his father died, he moved back here. He bought land from me and built himself a snug little log cabin on it. We don't see much of him. He's always traveling because of his horses. You must have scared the hell out of him, Evan, when you tried to kill his horse. He probably saw his bank balance flash before his eyes."

"I didn't try to kill it," Evan said.

"I remember!" Ivy said loudly, making them all jump. "Mom talked about it. Didn't Mr. Murray cut Grayson out of his will?"

"Donald Murray was a hard man," Granny said. "He was always on Grayson about something. Grayson was as stubborn as his father, and Arliss had to run interference between them. That's probably why she's a good mayor. She knows how to deal with conflict. The silly thing about Donald trying to disinherit Grayson was that most of the money is Arliss's. Arliss," she added, looking at Keelie, "is a descendant of Thomas Albright. While the family fortune isn't what it was in the early 1900s, I reckon Grayson isn't hurting for money. In spite of his father. I also think he does pretty well with those horses he raises."

"Finished," Evan pronounced and stood up to wash his hands. "I'm going out for a while. Does anyone need anything?"

"Can I—"

"No," Evan cut Keelie off. "You're keeping that ankle elevated and on ice."

Keelie glared at him as he left the room, then she said, "I wonder what he's up to?"

"What do you think? It's the day before Christmas Eve. He's a man," Ivy said.

"Maybe I should go with him," Ted said.

Ivy laughed and said, "See? They're all alike. And I'm no better. I have to do a little last-minute shopping myself." She walked to the vase and said, "You can go with me, Ted. I'll try to do something with Granny's flowers while you get ready."

Ted walked out of the kitchen with Granny on his heels, and Keelie hissed, "I need to shop, too! I'm covered for you and Evan, but I thought I had more time to shop for Granny, and I have nothing for Ted."

"The last thing you should be doing is maneuvering on crutches around crazed shoppers," Ivy said. "Ted was complaining about not having enough warm clothes with him. There's an Old Navy out on the highway. I think there may even be a Gap. I'll pick something out for you to give him. Any idea what you want to get Granny?"

"Yes, but I'm not sure if you can find it. A set of margarita glasses and a pitcher. Not Waterford! Something more cool, like Granny."

"Great idea. If Ted's looking for something to get her, maybe we can find one of those salt rimmers for the glasses. She'll be the queen of *Sex* night." Ivy wrinkled her nose. "That's not something I ever thought I'd be saying about my grandmother."

Keelie woke up from her afternoon nap to an empty house. She wrapped her leg in its trash bag and took a shower to get rid of her coating of powdered sugar and because she felt out of sorts. Her ankle was aching a little, and she couldn't stop feeling guilty about Buy The Book. Today was retail's last full shopping day, so tonight and Christmas Eve would be a madhouse. Even though Ted had assured her that the two substitute assistant managers would be adequate to help Rodney run the store, she felt like she'd let everyone down.

She wasn't in the mood to read, so she picked up the phone. First she called home, and they put her on the speaker phone.

"You sound down, baby," Huck said. "You know it's still not too late to come home. I'd drive all night and get you myself if you don't want to fly."

"No, I'm fine here in Coventry. In fact, I've kind of fallen in love with this town. It's so pretty and . . . I don't know. Fun. In a quirky way."

"Tell us about it," her mother urged.

They seemed genuinely interested in the town's history, laughed about Granny and *Sex* night, and listened quietly as she described how charming the town itself was.

"It sounds like the perfect Christmas town," Polly finally said.

"It's weird. I think of myself as a city girl," Keelie said. "But there's something about this place that just feels good. I'm probably romanticizing it. I haven't been to the newer part of town, which sounds pretty generic. I'm just seeing the quaint part. And meeting the nicest people. I'm sure Coventry has its problems."

"There's good and bad everywhere," Polly said. "I miss you so much, but I feel better knowing that you're recuperating with friends. With a sexy grandmother to look after you."

"Have y'all been in touch with Gram?"

"She called to let me know they got the flowers and champagne. And she's Mrs. Byrnes now. Can you imagine her on a golf course? I don't know what she's thinking."

"I picture them doddering around like that old couple in *Caddyshack*," Huck said, and Keelie laughed, knowing that Gram and Major Byrnes were not the doddering type.

She felt better after they hung up, so she called the Atwells and wished them a merry Christmas. Mrs. Atwell was worried about how Keelie would handle the stairs to her apartment when she came home, and Keelie assured her that she'd probably get one of those walking casts and would be fine.

She finally took a deep breath, followed her mother's Three Count Rule, and called the store, happy when Dawn, not Rodney or one of the unknown assistants, answered the phone.

"I'm looking for a book," Keelie said in her dumbest voice.

"We're all out of books," Dawn said. "You rat. How's your ankle?"

"It hurts. How are things there? Awful?"

"Busy, but not too bad. The two assistants they brought in are so cool. One of them used to work with Joyce. I can tell they don't like Rodney either. He's sort of whipped. I guess Ted Hughes didn't give a glowing report about Rodney to Corporate. Ted's gone, by the way. We haven't seen him since the night you fell off the ladder."

"How's Tamala? Is Rodney making sure she's taking it easy?"

"One of the new assistants set her up full time at the information desk," Dawn said. "Rodney was against it, of course, but he lost. So Tamala just looks up titles for people, or answers calls and gets the rest of us to find books and put them on hold. She loves it. And customers are really nice to her. I think they're afraid she'll go into labor if they abuse her. They keep looking around like they expect to see three wise men and a few camels. How's Hamlet?"

"I don't think he's as happy as Tamala," Keelie said. "He doesn't seem perky."

"Rub his furry little head for me," Dawn said. "Oh! Speaking of furry heads, Jake, our armored truck guy, came in while he was off duty."

"Uh-huh," Keelie said, her heart beating a little faster.

"He brought us boxes and boxes of Krispy Kreme donuts, and he showed us the engagement ring he's giving his girlfriend for Christmas. I should go. Rodney has passed me twice now."

"Tell everyone hello," Keelie said. "I miss all of you."

"Sure you do. Next year, I'm breaking my ankle. We'll make it a holiday tradition."

"I don't recommend it," Keelie said. She hung up the phone and sadly said, "Bye, Jake. It's official. I am doomed to a life of sweat-free teeth. I hate Christmas."

As a treat for Keelie, who'd obediently spent most of the day in bed, everyone decided to go into Coventry to eat dinner at Lady's Ryde Restaurant, which overlooked the square. The fountain was turned on, and Keelie stared out at the Godiva statue, which was illuminated with red and green lights.

"Looks just like my grandmother's Christmas tree," Ted commented.

Keelie glanced across the table at Ivy, who was also staring toward the statue. She seemed to be lost in thought, and Keelie decided that getting out of Houston and away from work had been good for Ivy. She and

Holly were equally pretty, but when Ivy was relaxed and happy, she was a knockout.

As if sensing Keelie's scrutiny, Ivy's eyes shifted to her, and she said, "I keep feeling like something's about to happen."

"Snow!" Keelie said.

"Santa Claus," Evan said.

"Your birthday," Ted said.

"If Evan doesn't mind driving us, we can take a spin around town after dinner," Granny said. "It takes less than ten minutes to see Old Coventry, and the lights twinkling in all the stores are pretty at night."

"I'm all about the lights," Evan said.

Keelie focused on Evan, who seemed awfully mellow, then she was distracted by the arrival of their food. But it struck her again later, as they drove around town, that he was being more agreeable than he had during their entire trip.

She appreciated the sights, as few as they were. Granny directed them by city hall, various bed-and-breakfasts, a nursery school, the Early Bird Café, and several office buildings where Coventry's law, insurance, and medical offices were located. As they turned back onto Oak Road, Keelie noticed a couple of buildings hugging one corner. With their green siding and exterior stairs, they stood out from the brick-front stores and Victorian homes, and she saw a sign between them. "Rourke Apartments?" she asked.

"My family owns those," Granny said. "They're filled now, mostly with young married couples who can't afford a house and want to live in town. Most of the houses you see in town have been in the same families for generations. It's rare that anyone sells, so newcomers live in New Coventry neighborhoods. That's where the schools are, too."

"Funny we didn't run into you shopping today," Ted commented to Evan. "I think Ivy and I hit every store out there."

"I must have been just ahead of you," Evan said.

They rode in silence down the twisting Old River Road until Granny pointed out one of the graveled drives and said, "That's the way to Grayson Murray's cabin. He must have been somewhere near here where you tried to run him down."

Evan merely grunted, and they were all quiet again, probably as full as Keelie was from dinner. She'd almost nodded off by the time they turned toward Granny's house, but she was suddenly wide awake when she saw lights bobbing and weaving along the driveway. As they got closer, she realized a group of motorcyclists were taking spins around Granny's house.

"Figures he'd show up now," Granny said.

As Evan pulled up, Ivy jumped out of the car and Keelie heard her yell, "Grandpa!"

Granny got out of the car, but Evan and Ted seemed to hold back, as Keelie did, until after the family reunion.

"I don't know why I thought Mr. Storey rode around with a bunch of old men," Keelie commented. "These people are all ages, and I'm definitely seeing women."

"Grandpa's got to be nearly seventy-five," Evan said. "There can't be many senior motorcycle gangs."

"I pictured him as bigger. Burly. He's just a little guy," Keelie said, watching as Ivy danced with excitement around her grandfather. Both she and Granny were taller than he was, and his leather jacket and worn jeans made him look like a kid playing dress-up—except that most kids didn't have wisps of gray hair.

"He's seventy-three," Ted said. "Ivy told me he's just a passenger. He doesn't have his own bike. He rides behind a woman named Molly. I hope they don't think we're rude. Maybe we should get out and meet them before they leave."

"No way," Keelie said. "I'm not exposing myself to biker scorn for breaking my ankle by falling off a ladder."

A woman detached herself from the other riders and walked toward the car. The harsh glow of floodlights and headlights made her face look weathered. She wasn't wearing a helmet, and her hair was pinned up. Keelie got the impression that it was long and might have softened her features if it were down.

Ted and Evan got out and introduced themselves, and she shook their hands, saying, "I'm Molly Reed. Which one of you is the hairdresser?"

"I am," Evan said. "Do you need a haircut?"

She smiled and said, "Yep. But mostly I want to talk to you about something. If you'll be around tomorrow, do you mind if I come back out? Around noon, maybe?"

"That's fine," Evan said, looking mystified.

"I'll explain everything then. I'm beat right now."

She gave Keelie a friendly wave and walked back to her motorcycle. That seemed to be everyone's signal to leave, and Keelie watched as the riders and their passengers roared down Granny's driveway.

"I wonder why she wants to talk to you?" she asked, getting out of the car and leaning on her crutches.

"No idea," Evan said. "I have a strange feeling Granny's blog is at the bottom of it."

"I *have* to see that thing," Ted commented.

* * *

Ted had gone upstairs, but the rest of them were sitting in the parlor staring at the Christmas tree in a stupor when Ivy's grandfather joined them after a soak in the tub. Granny introduced everybody.

"Don't call me Mr. Storey," he chastened Keelie. "It's Fred. I've been having a look around. When did we start keeping rats captive in the library?"

"That's my hamster," Keelie said. "Hamlet."

"A pet rodent," Fred said thoughtfully. "To think of all the rats we used to shoot by the woodpile."

"That was a thousand years ago. Maybe you should raise hamsters as a hobby instead of riding all over the country like Evel Knievel," Granny said.

"Didn't one of our boys have a hamster?"

"Freddy Jr. It was a gerbil."

"I'm taking part of your advice. I've seen all I want to see on the road. I'm back to stay. I've already found a new occupation."

"What daredevil notion have you got in your head this time? Skydiving?" Granny asked.

"Snake handler?" Ivy suggested.

"Helicopter pilot," Evan said.

"Granny's husband," Keelie said and dodged as Granny threw a pillow at her head.

"Aren't you a bunch of comedians," Fred said. "I'm taking a job with Grayson Murray. Maybe I'll be one of those horse whisperers."

"Maybe you'll be shoveling shit out of stalls," Granny said. As she stood up, she asked, "Are you hungry? We ate out tonight, but I'm sure there's something in the kitchen. Bacon and eggs?"

"I wouldn't sleep a wink if I ate this late," Fred said.

He gave Ivy a hug. "I just wanted to say goodnight to the young folks. These old bones need to turn in."

Evan was openly yawning, and it wasn't long before Keelie and Ivy were alone in the parlor. "Where's everybody sleeping?" Keelie asked. "I haven't braved the stairs yet."

"Granny and Grandpa are in their room. Evan's in one of the two guest rooms. I don't like the other guest room, because it has a small bed, so I'm in the bedroom my mother shared with her sisters, which now doubles as Granny's computer room."

"So you're the one with the most likely access to Granny's blog," Keelie said.

"No. She has a laptop, and she moved it to her bedroom. She's cunning."

"Where's Ted sleeping?"

"He claimed the little room on the third floor. It's really part of the attic, but when my aunts and uncles were growing up, my grandparents enclosed a section so Freddy Jr. could have his own room. Probably because of his pets. The gerbil was just one of them. He also had a tame squirrel named Crazy. Several turtles. And at least two snakes. Thus the aquarium that Hamlet's using now."

They were quiet a while, then Keelie said, "Your prediction at dinner was right. Something did happen. Your grandfather came home."

"I guess," Ivy said. She looked like she was about to say something else, then she glanced toward the front windows with a puzzled expression.

"Is that headlights?" Keelie asked.

"Seems to be. I can't imagine who'd drive out here this late. I know none of the rest of the family is coming for Christmas."

They heard the sound of a car door slamming, and Ivy hurried across the room to prevent their visitor from knocking and disturbing everyone else. Keelie heard her open the front door, then there was silence.

"Ivy?" she called.

Ivy walked back into the room and said, "I *knew* something was going to happen."

Keelie's eyes widened when she looked past Ivy and saw Mark Page. He was as good looking as she remembered, with prematurely graying brown hair and dark eyes. His closely shaved beard was new, but other than that, he looked much as he had the last time she'd seen him: at Mr. Johnson's funeral. The memory of how miserably he'd betrayed Ivy made Keelie squirm inside. She wished she was the kind of person who made scenes, because she wanted nothing more than to scream at him. She also wished Evan hadn't gone to bed, or that Holly was there. She had a feeling that even without knowing the details of her twin's breakup, Holly would kick Mark out of their grandparents' house.

"Hi, Keelie," he said.

"Hello," Keelie said in a frosty tone. She paused in the act of reaching for her crutches when she saw Ivy give a little shake of her head.

"How did you find me?" Ivy asked, turning back to Mark without inviting him to sit down.

"It wasn't hard to find out where you're spending Christmas," Mark said. "Everybody at Finnergy knew. But I only came here once with you. I had a hell of a time on Old River Road. I don't know how many times I got lost."

"Why would you bother?" Ivy asked. "I made it clear months ago that I don't want to see you."

"I left you several phone messages," Mark said. "Keelie, would you mind if I talk to Ivy alone?"

"I mind," Ivy snapped. "There's nothing you can say that I want to hear."

Keelie sat uncomfortably frozen in place. She desperately wanted to leave the room but felt like she'd be abandoning Ivy if she did.

"I haven't seen Susan for months," Mark said. "I broke it off for good."

"Lucky Susan," Ivy said. "And you think I've just been waiting for this news so we can pick up where we left off?"

"Couldn't we at least have a friendly conversation?" Mark asked.

"Why?"

"Is there someone else?"

Ivy made a noise of frustration and said, "The only someone else was me. We've had nothing to talk about from the time I was made aware of that. No thanks to you. I want you to leave."

"Ivy, it's the middle of the night—"

"I'm sure there are motel rooms in New Coventry," Ivy said. "You can get a good night's sleep before you go back to New Orleans." She made another noise. "This is all so silly. Please just go."

"I'm not leaving until—"

"What's going on?"

Keelie jumped and looked toward the door. Ted was leaning against the doorframe. She had no idea how long he'd been standing there.

"Oh for fuck's sake," Ivy said, which drew all eyes back to her. It was uncharacteristic of Ivy to swear. "I'll put you in the extra guest room. One night, just so everyone can get to bed. I hope you realize how rude it is for you to show up uninvited."

"If you'd returned my calls—"

"Get your suitcase," Ivy said between clenched teeth. "I'm tired, and I'm not talking about this tonight."

Ted moved aside as Mark walked out of the room, then he said, "You don't have to let him stay. Unless that's what you want."

"I just want to go to bed," Ivy said wearily.

Ted and Keelie watched silently when Mark came back inside and Ivy said a curt goodnight to them before leading him upstairs.

"I can't believe she's letting him stay," Ted finally said. "I got the idea it was a bad breakup."

"Oh," Keelie said with sudden understanding as she looked at Ted's face. "God, I'm dense. Does Ivy know how you feel?"

"No, and I'd rather you didn't tell her," Ted said. He walked inside the room and sat next to Keelie. "Confession time. You remember that night at Bennigan's?"

"Will you ever let me forget it?"

"It was Holly who caught my eye," Ted said. "I thought she was pretty, and I started eavesdropping. You know everything you said about the store that night was accurate. I'm sorry if it made you uncomfortable to realize I overheard you. Normally I wouldn't have told you. I understood you were just blowing off steam. But I had to find an opening, because you were joined by a drop-dead gorgeous version of Holly."

Keelie frowned at him and said, "I don't think either of them would like your description."

"I know, but come on. Ivy's beautiful. And the hell of it was, Holly was the one who was sweet and funny that night. Ivy was in a bad mood. It didn't matter. I knew I had to meet her. I figured once I got to know you, I could tell you the truth, you'd introduce us, and we'd see what happened."

"You weren't exactly friendly to me," Keelie said.

"Likewise," Ted said. "You have a little chip on your shoulder at work." When she opened her mouth, he held up his hand to stop her. "I know it's Rodney, okay? And he was always in my face whenever I tried to talk to you."

"That's true," Keelie said, thinking back to the times they'd all been in the store.

"The whole thing felt awkward. I thought maybe Ivy would visit you at Buy The Book and I could introduce myself to her. But that never happened. Then you broke your ankle—"

"And I played right into your hands by inviting you to Coventry," Keelie said. She tried to be mad at him, but she started smiling. "You know what? It doesn't matter. You and Ivy obviously get along. You've practically been inseparable since we got here. And it explains why she was so eager to throw me at the Rulebreaker."

"The what?" Ted asked.

"Never mind. Nobody deserves to be romanced more than Ivy. I hope it works out for you."

"I thought I was making progress," Ted said. "Then *he* showed up."

"I know what Granny would tell you," Keelie said with another smile. "Do something about it."

Chapter 9

Keelie had a few dicey moments on the stairs as she went to the second floor of the Storey house, but she was a woman on a mission. Unfortunately, once she successfully reached her destination, she realized that she had no idea which bedrooms were Evan's and Ivy's. She leaned on her crutches and stared at closed doors, doing the eenie-meanie rhyme in her head. She didn't want to wake Ivy's grandparents, nor did she feel like dealing with Mark.

She was still trapped by indecision when a door opened and Evan walked into the hall, looking tousled, sleepy, and confused to see her.

"Hey," she said. "I need your help." He just peered at her, and she said, "Can you drive me to a vet? I think something's wrong with Hamlet."

He made a one-minute gesture with his hand and went into the bathroom. When he came out, he looked a little less rumpled and she could smell toothpaste.

"I'll get dressed," he said. "Wait for me before you go downstairs. If you fall and I take you to the vet, they might shoot you."

Once they were in the car, Keelie said, "I've noticed that Hamlet seemed a little off the last couple of days. I was keyed up when I went to bed last night, and it took a while for me to realize what I was missing. He didn't run on his wheel at all. But he ate some of the carrot I gave him, so I put it out of my head. This morning, he hadn't burrowed under his bedding. He was lying in his food bowl, and he didn't react when I was petting him."

"I haven't had coffee," Evan reminded her. "My brain is still stuck at why you were keyed up. Where are we going?"

"I looked up a vet in the phone book. It's on Oak Road, a few miles outside of town. The other side of town from us," she added.

"Should be easy enough to find," Evan said. "And you were keyed up because . . ."

"You'll never believe who showed up last night. Mark Page."

That woke him up, and he darted a disbelieving look her way and said, "What?"

"Uh-huh, and Ivy was not happy to see him. He said he's been trying to get in touch with her and they need to talk."

"I hope she sent him packing," Evan said.

"She let him stay." She hastily added, "In a guest room."

Evan thought it over and finally said, "Since I don't know why they broke up, I guess I'll reserve judgment. I never trusted him, though."

"You didn't? You never told me that."

"Too smooth," Evan said. "I like knowing a person's flaws. When someone seems a little too perfect, it makes me wonder what they're hiding."

Keelie barely looked around as they drove through

Coventry. She kept checking Hamlet in his travel case and reproaching herself for not doing something sooner.

"He'll be okay," Evan assured her. "As soon as I get the two of you inside the vet's office, I'll make a coffee run for both of us."

"You don't have to bring me coffee," Keelie said. "Just get yourself—oh, you have that meeting today. With that woman. Molly."

"Not until noon," Evan reminded her. "We'll have Hamlet safe at home long before then."

She reached over, squeezed his arm, and said, "You're kind of comforting in an emergency."

"I'm no Ted Hughes," Evan said and flashed his smile lines.

She felt edgy when they'd driven a few miles past town and still saw no sign of a veterinary clinic. In Montrose, there was practically a vet on every corner. "Maybe I should have looked for a vet in New Coventry—"

"There's the sign," Evan said, pointing. "Michael Boone, DVM." He let out a low whistle. "Wow. Look at that."

Keelie caught her breath as Evan turned into the driveway. The two-story house was large, but it wasn't a mansion. What made it spectacular was that the entire exterior was covered with rocks. Not flat or cut stones, but an assortment of river rocks in every hue of brown that she could imagine. A porch that curved from the front to the side of the house was red concrete, its ceilings supported by square columns covered in the same rock as the rest of the house.

"I love rock houses," Keelie said. "I always wanted to live in one."

"With the sun hitting it, it looks like honey," Evan said.

To the right of the house was a second, smaller rock

building with a sign that said "Boone Animal Clinic." Evan parked the Expedition there, then he took Hamlet's case while Keelie slowly climbed the stone steps. Keelie wondered if the interior would make her feel like she was inside a castle, but the plaster walls were painted a light shade of blue, and everything was stainless steel and modern.

"Hi," a girl behind the desk said. "Do you have an appointment?"

"No," Keelie said. "I'm from out of town, and my hamster's sick."

"The heat's on, but this part of the building takes longer to warm up," the girl said. "Could you fill out this form? I'll put him in an examining room, where he'll be warmer."

After she took Hamlet and went through a door behind her desk, Evan asked, "How old do you think she is?"

"I don't know," Keelie whispered. "About twelve? Did you notice her eyes?"

"Yeah. She's a little fox," Evan said. "She'll break hearts when she gets older."

Keelie focused on filling out the form, then she said, "You don't have to stay. Go somewhere and get your coffee. I'll be fine."

"Are you sure? I don't want you to feel abandoned."

"Go," she said. "You'll probably be back before I see the vet."

When the girl returned, she smiled at Keelie, told her it would be just a few minutes, then sat down at the desk again. Keelie had to smile at her professional manner, because she could see just enough of the computer monitor to know the girl was playing solitaire.

Evan was right, though. She was beautiful. Her light

green eyes were ringed by thick, black eyelashes, and her dark eyebrows were naturally arched. Her ivory skin was flawless. She was in the transitional stage between baby fat and a teenage figure.

A 'tween, Keelie reminded herself. Thin, all legs, almost coltish in appearance, especially with her chestnut hair.

The girl looked up, caught Keelie staring at her, and said, "He's with a sick cat." She noticed Keelie's shudder and said, "You don't like cats? I guess you wouldn't. A cat probably wouldn't be too nice to your hamster."

"Probably not," Keelie agreed.

Keelie heard a buzzing noise, and the girl said, "If you go through that blue door, your hamster's in there. Dr. Boone will be right with you."

"Thanks," Keelie said.

She stood beside the examining table and opened the top of Hamlet's case, reached inside, and patted his head. "You'll be fine," she promised.

When another door opposite her opened, she glanced up, expecting to see someone who looked like an old country doctor. Instead, she was confronted with a pair of green eyes that matched those of the girl at the receptionist desk, and a smile that made her heart stand still. He had longish brown hair parted in the middle that he'd tucked behind his ears. The structure of his face was amazing: sharp jaw line, perfect chin, high cheekbones. With that face and his slender height, he could have been a model pretending to be a veterinarian for a magazine ad.

"Hi," he said, holding out his hand. "I'm Michael Boone."

"Keelie Cannon," she said weakly, her fingers tingling where they'd touched his.

"And who've we got here?"

"Hamlet," she said, realizing that she'd once again turned into a three-year-old incapable of providing more than a one-word answer to anything.

It's the lab coat, she told herself. *He reminds you of your father when you were little. An authority figure. It's intimidating. He's intimidating. He's beautiful . . .*

"Let's hope your noble son is not mad," he said.

Oh, my God, he knows Shakespeare . . .

"Biter?" he asked.

"Not usually," she said, trying not to stare at his mouth with thoughts of biting it.

"Dwarf hamsters can be a little testier than some of the others."

He washed his hands. She felt dizzy as she watched him scoop Hamlet out of his case. His hands were beautiful, the fingers long and sensitive, and she abruptly sat down as he gently examined Hamlet, who seemed too listless to bite or try to get away.

"Broken ankle?"

"He has a broken ankle?"

"You," Dr. Boone said.

"Oh. Yes." *Hi, my name is Keelie, and I'm a moron.*

He listened through his stethoscope with a frown, then he returned Hamlet to his case just as delicately as he'd removed him.

No wedding ring. Which meant nothing. She'd read enough James Herriot books to know where vets' hands had to go, and a ring or a watch would be out of the question.

"Age?"

"Twenty-eight."

He looked up and said, "I meant the one without the broken ankle."

Oh, my God, someone please shut me up. "Between one and two."

He asked her several more questions about Hamlet's diet, exercise habits, and any previous problems, which she managed to answer without making more of a fool of herself.

"He's got a little respiratory thing going on." He flashed his impossibly white teeth at her again. "That's some of my technical jargon. Can you think of anything that's changed in his daily life?"

Yes, his mother has lost her mind. "We live in Houston. He has a cage there, and a water bottle. Here, he's staying in an aquarium and drinking from a little bowl."

"And he's off his food."

"He is this morning."

"Bedding?"

Yes, please. "I usually use shredded toilet paper." *Wait. That sounded wrong. Keep going. He knows you meant for the hamster.* "But I only had one roll, and we left Houston in a hurry, so my friend grabbed a bag of bedding from the pet store."

"Wood chips? Labeled safe for hamsters?"

"Yes."

"I think I've identified the problem. It's not your fault. It happens to a lot of hamster owners. If the bedding has any cedar or pine, it can be deadly because it irritates their respiratory tracts. Don't buy that fluffy bedding either. They can get the fibers wrapped around their legs and end up losing a foot. I've got hay I can give you. It's free of toxins, mites, and allergens because I use it for sick animals."

"Do you think he'll be okay?"

"I'm going to give him a small dose of antibiotics. Not much, because it's hard on their digestive systems.

Keep an eye on him, and keep him warm and his cage clean. How long will you be in town?"

"I'm not sure. Probably until after the new year."

"Here's my card. You can call that number any time, day or night, and I'll meet you here immediately."

"Thank you. That's really nice of you."

"I just live next door," he said with a grin. "I can be in the clinic in less than a minute."

"You live in that beautiful house?"

He nodded and said, "I'll be right back. Don't go anywhere."

Ever, she thought.

When he returned, she watched anxiously as he gave Hamlet a shot. Then he set a bag of straw next to the travel case. "His coat looks healthy, and he's a good weight. Those are promising signs. Do you trim his nails?"

"No. He's got a little sandpaper box in his cage. And a solid wheel. Lots of toys. At home I have a Habitrail and a hamster ball. He also gets a milk bone for his teeth."

"You're a good hamster mom."

"Do you have a lot of hamster patients?"

"None," he said. "Mine is a large animal practice. Primarily equine and bovine."

"You seem to know a lot about hamsters."

"I learned a few things from a hamster named Rex."

She narrowed her eyes and said, "You got your hamster expertise from Janet Evanovich's mysteries?"

"Don't tell," he begged. "I used to wonder about some of the things bounty hunter Stephanie Plum feeds her hamster, so I researched hamsters on the Internet."

"Shocking," Keelie said with mock disapproval. "I love those books."

"Me, too," he said. "I keep wondering who Stephanie will end up with."

"Me, too!" Keelie said. "And by the way, I never feed Hamlet sweets. Do you really think he'll be okay?"

"I haven't lost a hamster yet."

"Hmmm," she said, her heart racing because unless she'd totally forgotten the signs, Dr. Boone was flirting with her, which had to mean that he was single. "So how long has your sister worked for you? Aren't there laws against child labor?"

"My sister?" When she inclined her head in the direction of the waiting room, he said, "Oh, Jennifer. My office manager is soaking up sun in the Bahamas this week. Jennifer is out of school and bored with nothing to do next door, so she likes to sit at the front desk. She's my daughter."

In spite of the way her heart sank, Keelie kept a fixed smile as she said, "Your daughter? You don't look old enough to have a—how old is she?"

"Thirteen. I'm thirty-four." He grinned. "And you're twenty-eight." She nodded. "You didn't drive yourself, did you? With that ankle?"

"No. A friend brought me. He went to get coffee. Is Jennifer your only child?"

"Yes." He stuck his head out the door and said, "There's no one out here. Jennifer? When Mrs.—" He broke off and looked back at her.

"Miss," she said.

"When Miss Cannon's friend gets back, let us know." He pulled up a stool and sat across from her, saying, "Tell me about your ankle. I won't bill you, I promise. Judging by your splint, it must be a recent injury?"

She told him about the ladder, and he went to a business card file and pulled out a card. "Dr. Jenkins has an orthopedic practice. If you'll be around another week or so, you should let him take a look. He could put your cast on."

"Thanks," she said. She knew she needed to get out of there, because the news that he had a daughter living with him—which would surely indicate that he had a wife—wasn't making him any less appealing. But her version of Tourette's Syndrome seemed to have returned when she said, "Tell me about your house. It took my breath away."

"I guess I take it for granted," he said. "It's got a colorful and somewhat unsavory history."

"I love unsavory histories." *Do you keep cyanide in your office,* she wondered.

"My great-great-grandfather, Jeremiah Boone, was from Alabama. I'm sorry to say that he owned slaves. When the war was over, and his fields and house were in ruins, I'm sorrier to say that he managed to hold on to some of his slaves with promises of giving them their own land if they'd continue to work for him. But not in Alabama. He hauled his poor wife, children, and former slaves to Texas, where an uncle had left him some land."

"This land we're on now?"

"Yes. His wife, Martha, was not happy about being uprooted, and the only thing that would placate her was his promise to build her a big house. But she didn't want just any house. She wanted a house built with rocks. Not from Texas. She hated everything about Texas. Instead, he was to get them from Alabama. So after making that long journey here, the former slaves were ordered to go back to Alabama and return with wagons full of Alabama rock."

"And they did it?"

"They didn't want to leave their families, but they felt

they had no choice. Here's where the story gets fun. Everybody in Coventry knew everyone else's business, of course, and Jeremiah had quickly made a few enemies. One of them was our town's founder."

"Thomas Albright," Keelie said.

"Excellent. I see you've been learning some local history."

"I'm staying with Elenore Storey. She told me about Albright."

"I know Elenore well," Dr. Boone said. "Albright intercepted Jeremiah's men. He contacted a friend with the railroad and some of his former comrades in the Confederate Army, and arranged to have Alabama rocks transported to Houston by rail. Then he sent the men and their wagons there to pick them up."

Keelie stared up at him, memorizing every detail of his face and voice while he talked. It was agonizing to keep her expression impassive when her heart felt like it might explode out of her chest.

"Meanwhile, Albright placed a small wager with the unsuspecting Jeremiah. If the men returned with the rocks within a certain amount of time, Jeremiah was to treat them as free men and let them settle wherever they wanted and work for whomever they chose. Since Jeremiah felt reasonably sure that it would be months before they returned, he agreed."

"And of course, Albright won. Because of the railroad," Keelie said.

"Albright wasn't entirely altruistic. Convinced that it would take some time for the cotton industry to recover, he'd acquired several sheep farms. He wanted to open a wool textile mill, and he needed workers."

"Including the former slaves," Keelie surmised.

"He was a fairer man than my great-great-grandfather, though. Albright deeded them the land around his mill to build their houses. Men and women worked there. When they wanted to start a school so their children could learn to read and write, Albright flatly turned them down."

"Just when I was starting to like him," Keelie said.

"Hold on. It gets brighter. Albright bitterly resented the class system of England, since it hadn't done right by him, and even though he'd fought with the Rebels, he despised slavery. As time passed, he studied what was happening in the postwar South. Ultimately, and without much resistance from the white townspeople, many of whom depended on him for their livelihood, he built one school for everyone. It's been gone a long time—there's a nursery school where it used to be—but Coventry's schools were fully integrated long before the twentieth century, and included the children of Albright's black, Mexican, Native American, and white employees."

"That's an amazing story," Keelie said. "What happened to your great-great-grandfather?"

"He died of pneumonia not long after Martha's house was finished. Which was probably best for everyone all around. She hightailed it back to Alabama with her two youngest children. My great-grandfather became a doctor and built this clinic with the leftover Alabama rocks. His entire practice was in what's now the reception area. My grandfather and father were dentists and converted it to their dental office, adding a couple of rooms at the back. Then I took it over for my vet practice when my father and mother retired and moved to Galveston. I left the exterior as it was, redid the interior front, and had the back of the building completely renovated and expanded. Would you like a tour?"

"I'm not all that mobile," she said, pointing at her crutches.

"I have a solution."

He left the room and came back with a gurney that made her smile. It was identical to a hospital gurney, but about half the size.

"Cute," she said. "But how do you fit a horse on it?"

"I do occasionally treat a smaller animal," he said.

"Your daughter told me you were with a cat earlier." She ignored his outstretched hand and stood up on her own, but realized she'd need his help to hop up on the gurney. She felt a little dizzy again when he put his hands on her ribs and hoisted her up, and blushed when she heard herself say, "You're strong."

"I'm used to pushing cows around," he said. Then he gave her an apologetic look and said, "I didn't mean—"

"No, that's okay," she said. "Everybody gains weight during the holidays, especially when incapacitated. Kick me when I'm down."

"You're just a calf," he said. He put her crutches next to her and pushed her out the door and down the hall, pointing out another examining room, a pharmacy, a lab, the surgical and radiology areas, and his office.

Everything was sterile, and she said, "It doesn't smell of animals."

"Just wait," he said. He went through another door into a room full of cages and said, "Small animal vets usually have separate kennels for their cats and dogs, but I treat so few that it's not an issue for me."

"There's the cat," she said, spotting it lying in a cage. "I don't much like cats. What's wrong with him?"

"Her," he said. "Broken leg. Some internal injuries, but she'll be okay. She's a stray, but she has a beautiful disposition, so I suspect she's a drop."

"A drop?"

"People often drive their animals into the country and drop them," he said. "Some mornings, I walk over to find a box of puppies or kittens at the clinic door. I try not to turn them over to Coventry's shelter, because they're strained as it is. One of my techs is passionate about placing strays and drops, and she's never failed to find good homes yet. Usually by offering free vet services, bless her heart. We always spay or neuter them before we place them. Cats aren't hard to place, because they kill rodents in people's barns and gardens."

"See? That's why I don't like them." As he pushed her down a long corridor, she said, "You'd never know all this was back here. It's not visible from the road."

"That's the magic of a good architect and a good landscaper," he said.

"I meant to ask you: Is there still a feud between the Albrights and the Boones?"

"Grayson Murray, who's the last of the Albrights, is one of my best friends. I take care of his horses. The old wool mill closed down in the 1940s, but if you've seen Independent Seven Toys, it's the same building. The four little houses around it comprise a historical landmark and serve as the town's museum, where you can see some of the old equipment from the mill and desks from the first school. Those houses are what remain of the original homes built by Jeremiah's freed slaves. The name 'Independent Seven' comes from those men. One of their descendents, Terry Bowen, is another friend of mine. He's part owner of Independent Seven Toys."

"I love a happy ending," Keelie said, but she felt hollow inside. In the space of a few minutes, she'd become helplessly infatuated with a man who could never share a happily ever after with her. Why did he have to be handsome, a good hamster doctor, kind to stray animals, and married? Fate wasn't playing fair.

"Wow," she said when he opened another set of doors. "This is huge."

"Really? I feel like there's never enough space." He pointed out long rows of stalls and said, "That's the lameness workout area, the mare and foal stalls, and behind them are the isolation stalls. Down that way is the feed room."

Two boys who looked like teenagers, dressed in jeans and T-shirts and wearing Wellingtons, were hosing down some of the stalls. While she watched them, a brindle greyhound padded up, and Dr. Boone reached down and scratched his ears.

"Who's this?" she asked.

"This is the one who made me break my own rule," he said. "I never let Jennifer get too close to the strays, or I'd end up with a house full of dogs. But Rip is special. I don't think he was a runaway. I think someone dropped him, and he probably lived on his own for quite a while, because he was nothing but bones when he followed Jen home from the woods one day. He had everything imaginable wrong with him. His ears were full of ticks. He had kennel cough. And he had a skin condition. Plus you can see all those nicks and scars on him, which gave me pause. Greyhounds aren't normally aggressive, but if he was, it would be unethical to adopt him out. It would also make him a bad animal to have around here."

"Apparently that wasn't the case," Keelie said.

"Not long after he came out of isolation from the kennel cough, he proved his worth with one of Grayson's mares, who is one hundred percent bitch. My guys," he nodded toward the two boys, "hate working with her. She'll bite. She'll kick. She's impossible for anyone except Grayson to handle. She danced with somebody's barbwire fence, and her wounds got infected. When Grayson brought her in and led her to a stall, Rip padded along and invited himself in with her. She nosed him and decided he was okay. From then on, as long as Rip was with her, she was—well, not perfect, but at least manageable."

"I hope you pay Rip well," Keelie said.

Dr. Boone reached down, grabbed Rip's nose, and gently swung his head. "He's curious, good-natured, and well-behaved. He's insanely devoted to Jennifer. I don't know where he's been—you know every one of those scars has a story—but he's never given me a single minute's regret about getting him healthy again and making him part of the family." He turned around and looked Keelie in the eye. "I guess some things are just destined to be."

"I'm sorry it took me so long to get back," Evan said later as he drove Keelie away from the clinic. She forced herself not to look back at the rock buildings in their bucolic setting.

I found my 'R' man, she mentally told Ivy. *Regrettably married.*

"No problem," she said, staring dully from the window. She was surprised when Evan took a right off of Oak Road and parked the SUV at the intersection of Dresden and Old School Roads, keeping the engine running. "Why are we stopping?"

"Do you believe in destiny?" Evan asked. When Keelie burst into tears, he looked alarmed and reached for her hand. "I'm sorry. Is it Hamlet? You said he was going to be okay. Are you still worried about him?"

"It's not Hamlet," she said. "I'm tired. I feel guilty about work. Not just because I'm not there. There's a part of me that doesn't want to go back. But I know I will. And my ankle hurts. Mostly, I don't like my life or myself very much at this moment. I'll snap out of it."

"You're always too hard on yourself," Evan said.

"Why did you ask about destiny?"

"It'll keep," Evan said. "Let's get you and Hamlet back home."

Chapter 10

Evan couldn't be dissuaded from his belief that Keelie was the overly emotional mother of a hamster and that he was at least partly to blame for Hamlet's illness, so Keelie made the most of it. While Evan cleaned out the aquarium and replaced the old bedding with straw, she found a discarded Christmas wrapping paper tube. By the time Evan cut it in lengths that would suit Hamlet perfectly, he was tired of playing hamster uncle and reminded Keelie that he had to cut Molly's hair at noon and still hadn't taken a shower. Since no one else was at the Storey house, Keelie got what she'd wanted all along: solitude.

She propped up her leg, put her arms behind her head, and examined the reality that she was actually the overly emotional admirer of a married veterinarian. Rather than try to convince herself that she'd exaggerated his charms, she took inventory of them.

First, there was the superficial. He had the body type that she found most appealing: tall, slender, not quite the reed that Evan was, but certainly not muscular like the men Ivy preferred. Although Keelie could see the appeal of a brawny body—like Jake the Armored Truck Guy—usually that wasn't what caught her eye. She thought that Ted might have a better chance with Ivy than he realized, because physically, he actually had a lot in common with Mark.

For a moment, Keelie was diverted by curiosity about where Ivy and Mark were and how their unexpected reunion was going, but her thoughts quickly returned to Dr. Boone. He was a man who seemed physically strong—he'd certainly had no problem lifting her—without being rugged. It was the kind of contradiction that appealed to her.

Beyond that, she loved the way his face was built. She'd always been a sucker for good bone structure. It was the first thing she'd noticed about Jason, and she'd never gotten tired of looking at him, even when the sizzle had left their relationship. Jason and Dr. Boone might not be the kind of men that most of the women and some of the men she knew drooled over, but they were Keelie's preference.

She wished that she could stop there and convince herself that she was experiencing a shallow case of lust for a man she found handsome. She could even chalk up to desire the tingling sensation she'd felt when he'd shaken her hand and lifted her onto the gurney. While it was reassuring to know that the fear she'd expressed to her sister—that a handsome man didn't register on her libido—wasn't accurate, she couldn't stop feeling like there was more to it than merely the sexual jolt he gave her.

She'd fallen for his daughter, his dog, his house, and his conversation. She had the idea that he'd also sensed the attraction between them. She'd even been sure that he was deliberately charming her. It was doubtful that he provided a tour of his clinic and a glimpse at his family history to everybody who brought a sick animal to him. He'd made the choice to prolong their time together and tell her all the things that he had.

There was only one glaring omission from his conversation: his wife.

Keelie could think of two explanations for that. Either he was divorced, or he was a philanderer like Mark Page. It would be simple to find out whether he was divorced by asking Granny or Ivy, but she'd have to do it carefully. She didn't intend to give Granny material to use on her blog for the entire town to read. And she'd been able to tolerate Ivy joking about Ted and calling Grayson Murray her Rulebreaker because those men meant nothing to her.

But she didn't want to be teased about Dr. Boone, whether or not he was married. Her attraction to him made her feel vulnerable, and if he was married, she'd rather no one ever knew about her crush. Even worse, she was worried that finding out he had a wife wouldn't make the crush go away. If she was brutally honest about her dating history, she knew why it had been so long since there was a man in her life. She didn't get crushes. She didn't have casual sex. She didn't fault anyone who did; it just wasn't in her nature. When she fell, she fell hard, and that was why she'd stayed with Jason longer than she should have. She was even slower to break up than she was to get involved.

She knew herself well enough to understand that if Dr. Boone was like Mark—unfaithful, dishonest, and deceitful—she'd never let anything develop between them. It would be a betrayal of herself, and she wouldn't let someone's wife suffer because of her. Even the idea made her squirm. She thought about how devastated Ivy had been by Mark's double life. She thought of Holly and Misty: their faith in Dave and Matt, their desire to build something solid for their children. The commitment, energy, and trust—Keelie could never be part of damaging a family. Especially since she'd actually seen his daughter. Jennifer Boone had been utterly adorable playing the part of his receptionist, and if the impact she'd made on Keelie was just as sudden as her father's, it was even more consequential. Gram might be right in saying that Keelie had no maternal instincts, but Keelie would never even indirectly hurt a child.

After thinking all that through, she felt lighter and surer of herself. She'd been caught off guard by the sensation of something she didn't even believe in—love at first sight—but she hadn't lost her mind or her principles.

"And anyway," she told Hamlet, who was hiding in one of his new tubes, "I always swore I'd never get involved with anyone in the medical profession. Having a father who was a doctor was the reason I don't remember him very well. Dr. Boone may be a vet, but animals are like people. Their emergencies are no respecters of birthdays, weekends, vacations, or a good night's sleep."

"It cracks me up when you talk to Hamlet," Ivy said as she practically waltzed into the library.

Keelie's apprehension that Ivy might have overheard Dr. Boone's name was immediately replaced by dread. Ivy was radiant, and Keelie darted a nervous look at her left hand. She felt relieved to see that Ivy wasn't wearing her engagement ring. Then she realized that a man who was smart enough to juggle two women for as long as Mark had wouldn't give back a ring that was a duplicate of Susan's.

"You look happy," Keelie said cautiously.

"You can't imagine just how happy I am," Ivy said. "I haven't felt this good since last Christmas. It's amazing."

"Because of Mark?" Keelie asked, hoping it wasn't.

"Absolutely. Now that everything's okay, I can admit how awful the months since April have been. I don't want to feel that kind of loneliness ever again. I knew I was coming out of it when I told you the truth about what happened. It was so hard to be honest about Mark and me."

"Uh-huh," Keelie said. "But—"

"I told you the truth because I felt like I no longer had any feelings for Mark. But it's easy to deny your feelings when you don't see someone, and you bury yourself in your work."

"And now that you've seen him . . ."

"I told you. I'm happy." Ivy smiled at Keelie. "Thank goodness he came, even though at first I was annoyed because I thought it was rude of him. But when we talked, he said everything I needed to hear. He told me what a fool he'd been. He told me that he'd changed. He apologized for everything he put me through. He's sorry about the lies. He's sorry for that awful meeting I had with Susan. He hasn't seen her for months, and it's really over. I'm the only woman for him. He's never felt for any other woman the way he feels about me. He's been even more miserable than I have, because he had to face the truth that he'd hurt the one person he loves most in the world. I've probably thought a million times about what Mark should say to me, and I don't think he missed even one of them. It was wonderful. Can you believe it?"

"No," Keelie said, suppressing what she really wanted to say. She didn't understand how *Ivy* could believe it. Or how she could forget her hurt over Mark's farce at Mr.

Johnson's funeral. Keelie suddenly felt like she didn't understand her friend at all, and her disappointment was acute.

Ivy sighed and said, "I'm not the kind of person who enjoys being mean to other people, Keelie, but I'm only human. So I confess. The pleasure I took in asking Mark to leave and never get in touch with me again was almost diabolical. Do you think I'm a terrible person?"

Keelie burst out laughing and said, "You are the most evil person I've ever known, because you totally planned how you were going to tell me this. You knew you were giving me the wrong impression."

"I didn't think you'd fall for it. Don't you know me at all? He is one smooth operator, that Mark Page, but there wasn't a single fiber of my being that wanted to believe what he was saying. Or even cared. I'm happy because now I know for sure that—"

"He's dead to you!" Keelie said dramatically.

"Deader than the battery in my car, which I had towed in because you and Evan disappeared this morning. Where were you?"

"Hamlet's sick, so Evan took us to a vet," Keelie said.

"Is he okay? What's wrong with him?"

"He has a respiratory infection caused by his bedding. He got a shot and new bedding. I think he'll be fine. Tell me more about you and Mark."

"When I got up, he was the only person here. I'm sure Granny whisked Grandpa out of the house so Mark and I could be alone. I don't know where Ted is. I guess it's for the best, because everyone was spared Mark's act of contrition. I don't doubt for a second that an act was exactly what it was, and I don't really believe Susan's out of his life. Or if she is, it was probably her choice, not his. Even if he did break things off and he's a changed man, he can take his transformation into his next relationship, because I'm not interested. And I can be sure that I'm never going to endure another meeting with him, because I've made a decision. This is for your ears only."

"What?" Keelie asked.

"Granny was right. If I'm unhappy at work, I should do something about it. It's a sweet situation for me because the salary is great, the benefits are good, and I've got job security as long as Dave is there. They'd never get rid of me and risk making Dave mad. But the job isn't the right fit for me, and some of the people I work with are even more unendurable than I told Granny. It's time for me to take a risk and find a place where I love my job and feel like the work I do is valued."

"You're going to quit?"

"Not immediately. I'm not that brave. I want to see what else is out there and whether or not anyone will hire me."

"Oh, please. You're smart. You're professional. You have a great wardrobe. And people are not exactly repelled by your looks. You'll be turning down offers."

"We'll see," Ivy said. "I'm glad my car just needed a new battery. I don't want to be held hostage by Finnergy because I take on a car payment."

"Do you think . . ."

"What?" Ivy asked when Keelie trailed off.

"Do you think you'll have to move? Because that would suck."

Ivy looked a little sad and said, "If I were offered a position that I really wanted, yeah. I'd be willing to relocate. You're right, though. It would suck leaving you, Evan, Holly, and Mom."

"None of us would hold you back," Keelie said. "We can always meet for Christmas in Coventry."

"Listen to you, already anticipating the worst. Who knows what the future holds?"

Keelie rode into Coventry with Evan, Ted, and Ivy when they went to pick up Ivy's car at Bailey's Texaco. Her new knowledge of Ted's interest in Ivy made her speculate about what he thought of Ivy's near-giddy behavior. At the very least, Ted had to realize that Mark was history, but he asked no questions. Since Keelie and Ted were in the back seat of the Expedition, she could see the affection play across his face while Ivy talked.

"Did you cut Molly's hair today?" Ivy asked Evan.

"I did."

"She's the town scandal, you know."

"How so?"

"Molly was always as reliable as the day is long. She owns Molly's Salon—did she tell you that she's also a hairdresser?"

"Yes."

"You could set your clock by Molly. Six days a week—even on Mondays!—she opened her salon at nine in the morning. On Sundays, she was always in the third pew on the right at Christ Church, and she drove two of Coventry's oldest widows to church, too. Whenever anyone died, she was the first to bring a dish of food to the grieving family. On Sunday afternoons, she always visited her mother at the nursing home, and if anyone was in the hospital, Molly would go by in the evening for a nice chat. As you would imagine of the town's hairdresser, she knows everything about everybody, but she never repeats anything that shouldn't be told."

"And this is scandalous? She sounds like a saint," Keelie said. "I'm starting to dislike her."

"Rumor had it that Molly never married because the man she loved abandoned her for another woman." Ivy turned around and grinned at Keelie when she said, "She was the town spinster."

"This sounds like a Faulkner story," Ted said.

"She always did for others and never thought of herself. Then her mother died, and everything changed."

"She turned the salon into a bordello?" Ted asked.

"That might have been acceptable," Ivy said. "At least she'd have been taking care of the other half of the town's population. No, she did something much worse. A couple of years ago, at the Godiva Festival, Molly met a man."

"That's always where a story goes to hell," Evan said.

"In Molly's case, it's where a story hits the road. Perry Watson roared into town with his biker friends on the last afternoon of the festival, probably because that's when they select the Daughter of Godiva who'll be crowned at the Medieval Ball. They came to ogle the pretty girls. But it wasn't any of Coventry's fair maidens who caught Perry's eye. It was one of the judges: Molly Reed. The next thing you know, it was Sunday morning and no one picked up the widows for church. Everyone thought Molly might be sick. When she didn't answer her phone, a group of Episcopalians went to her apartment—she lives over the salon—and that's when they saw the sign in Molly's window that said, *CLOSED UNTIL FURTHER NOTICE.* Foul play was suspected, and our police chief was summoned. He let himself into Molly's apartment, but there was no sign that anything was wrong. Except that Molly had vanished."

"It isn't a Faulkner story," Evan said. "It's a country song."

"The entire town was in an uproar, especially since all

the Old Coventry women had to go to New Coventry to get their hair done by strangers. And the strangers charged them more than Molly ever had."

"So how did they find out what happened to her?" Keelie asked.

"Granny told them. She is so bad, that grandmother of mine. She knew all the time where Molly was. Molly loves my grandparents like they're her own. That day at the festival, Grandpa said that he wished he could know what it was like to see the country on a motorcycle, and Granny and Molly wanted to indulge him. When Perry started flirting with Molly, she asked if they would take on a couple of passengers, and for some insane reason, the bikers agreed. I'm sure they thought that Grandpa and Molly would ask to come home after a few hours, but they underestimated Grandpa's stubbornness. It wouldn't have mattered if he was miserable, he'd have stuck with it. But he wasn't miserable. He was having the time of his life. So Molly took training to operate a motorcycle, got her license, bought her own bike, and she and Grandpa have been on and off the road ever since."

"What about Perry?" Ted asked.

"According to Grandpa, Perry proposes to Molly about once a week, and she turns him down."

"What do you think she'll do now that Fred's hanging up his leathers?" Keelie asked.

"No idea. I hope she marries Perry if she loves him. But Molly's sense of duty is so ingrained that I fear that without the necessity of taking care of Grandpa on the road, she'll be back in that shop six days a week and in the third pew on the right on Sundays."

"Maybe Perry should settle down in Coventry," Ted said.

Ivy turned around, looked at him, and said, "What would *you* do?"

"If I loved a woman, I'd follow her to the ends of the earth," Ted said.

"Ted!" Evan said, and Keelie could see him eyeing Ted in the rearview mirror. "I had no idea you were such a feminist."

"Why should a woman always be the one who changes her life?" Ted asked. "It's a new age."

"I'm not sure the new age has reached Coventry," Ivy said.

When Evan got to Godiva Street, he turned the opposite way that he'd taken to go to Phillips Hardware and Rook Drugs, and Keelie's heart skipped a beat when she saw a sign that said "INDEPENDENCE PARK" and the building that bore the name "INDEPENDENT SEVEN TOYS." It was like a secret connection to Dr. Boone.

Somehow she wasn't surprised when they turned into Bailey's Texaco and she saw the veterinarian getting into his truck. She could see that he had a passenger. She stifled a sigh when she realized that the person riding with him wasn't small enough to be Jennifer, but she couldn't see if it was a man or a woman.

Of course it's a woman, she scolded herself. *It's Mrs. Michael Boone. And you need to put Ivy's and Ted's notions of giving up everything for love right out of your head.*

"Which of you is riding back with me?" Ivy asked.

"Let Ted," Evan said. "I'll chauffeur Keelie so she can stretch out on the back seat with her leg up."

"I'll only be a second," Ivy said as she reached for her door handle. "I'm sure Mr. Bailey is eager to get home since it's Christmas Eve."

"Have I ever mentioned that I hate Christmas?" Keelie asked.

* * *

Keelie spent a restless night trying not to think about Dr. Boone. She refused to take a Vicodin and slept fitfully, but she got her first Christmas present at four in the morning when Hamlet emerged from one of his tubes and took a run on his wheel.

"Aw," she said, sitting up to stare at him in the dim light from the lamp she'd left on across the room. "That's better than Santa coming down the chimney."

She chose to see it as a good omen, and she shared it with the others at a pancake breakfast cooked by Ted and served with gusto by Ivy.

"I was sure Hamlet would be fine when you said you took him to Michael Boone," Granny said. "He knows what he's doing."

"We met his daughter," Keelie said. "Evan called her a fox."

"The reason *I* knew your little fellow would be okay," Fred said, "was because I got a visit from the Rat of Christmas Past last night."

"Don't listen to him," Granny said. "All day yesterday—"

"Don't spoil my surprise, Elenore," Fred warned her.

"How long has Dr. Boone been divorced?" Keelie asked in an indifferent tone.

"He's not divorced," Granny said and made a grab for the syrup when Evan put it down.

"I thought I heard the Rat of Christmas Past last night, too," Evan said. "In the attic."

"I remind you that I'm not only the provider of those pancakes you're shoving into your mouth, but I also control your Christmas dinner," Ted said, waving a spatula at Evan.

"Don't taunt the chef," Ivy said. "Anyway, the Rat of Christmas Past has gone back to New Orleans. When do we open presents?"

"Presents!" Keelie said, relieved that in the chaos, no one had noticed her less-than-subtle way of finding out that she was right: Dr. Boone was married. "I just remembered it's your birthday, Ivy."

"Everybody always forgets," Ivy said. "Usually Holly is with me and we sing happy birthday to each other to make everyone feel guilty."

"I didn't forget," Ted said. He stepped onto the porch and came back with a three-tiered birthday cake. "It's one of today's desserts, but this is why the rat was noisily going up and down the stairs all night."

Ivy jumped up, threw her arms around him, and said, "Thank you! I'm getting my digital camera and Granny can e-mail a photo to Holly. We talked last night, which was very early morning for her. The boys got them up before dawn, of course, to check out their loot. She'll call again today to talk to everybody else."

"I'm sure your mother will call, too," Granny said.

"I think next year, if Scotty and Carla are still in Hawaii, we should go there," Fred said. "I always wanted see a real luau."

Keelie picked up her crutches and went to the kitchen window. "No snow," she said sadly. "Next year, maybe I'll go to my stepfather's family's house in Connecticut. I've always dreamed of going over the fields in a horse-drawn sleigh."

"Be careful," Evan warned. "You almost sound like someone with Christmas spirit."

"It's a fantasy," Keelie said. "In reality, next year, I'll have my one day off from Buy The Book. And no Christmas spirit."

"But you do have Christmas presents," Ivy said. "When do we get to open presents?"

"I'm all about the presents," Evan agreed as he stood up. "I'll do the dishes later."

"I can clean up the kitchen," Granny said.

"Nope. Today, you and Grandpa get to sit around and relax. We're doing everything. We even have jobs for Keelie," Ivy said.

"I think my ankle is hurting then," Keelie said.

"Nice try," Ivy said. "You've been running all over Coventry for days when you're supposed to be in bed. It's too late to pretend you're lame now. I hope you're getting all this down, Ted."

Ted picked up Ivy's camera, took a picture of Keelie standing by the sink, and said, "All I needed was photographic evidence."

"I'm ruined," Keelie said.

Later, she was sitting on the floor with piles of paper, ribbon, and bows around her when Fred went outside. He came back carrying something that looked like an oversized wooden drawer and set it in front of Keelie.

"Freddy Jr. made this for his science project one year," he said. "He taught his rat to go through it for cheese."

"It was a gerbil," Granny said. "Fred found the maze, cleaned it up, and replaced the top with new screen. Hamlet can run through it for exercise, and we bought treats and toys at the pet store for him to find in it."

"You guys are so great," Keelie said. "He'll love it."

"It's even got little tunnels," Evan said. "We may never see him again."

"I know those critters can get out through a pinhole," Fred said, "but Freddy Jr. did a good job on the design. As long as you latch the lid, it should be secure."

"I've never had problems with him trying to escape," Keelie said. "It's perfect. Thank you so much."

As the others continued opening presents, Keelie pulled things from the stocking Granny had given her, almost as excited by Hamlet's new toys as if they were hers. She'd felt that way in the past when she'd watched Holly's boys open presents, too, and she knew Ivy must miss spending this day with her nephews, but when she looked up, Ivy looked perfectly content. Keelie glanced at Ted, who smiled as he watched Ivy open another gift. She wondered how long it would be before Ivy became aware of Ted's feelings.

"I think," Evan said softly beside her, "you may have lost the Remnant."

"And I'm okay with that," Keelie said. "Do you like him better now?"

"You know what I like about him?" Evan asked.

"His flaws?"

"You got it. What you see is what you get. And if his worst flaws are that he's inquisitive and smart, who am I to think he's not good enough for our girl?"

"You're all about the romance," Keelie said. She started to put the stocking aside, then realized there was something flat in the bottom of it. She pulled out an envelope and gave it a puzzled look, because she could swear that her name was in her sister's handwriting. She looked up and realized that all eyes were on her. "What's this?"

"Open it," Ivy said.

When Keelie opened the note, Evan said, "Read it out loud."

"Dear Keelie," she read, "you said you didn't have an e-mail account, so Mom and I got you one. We love you, Misty, Mom, Huck, and Matt." She looked up with bewilderment and said, "I don't get it."

"Your sister overnighted that note with very specific instructions from your mother," Ivy said. "Ted and I had a lot of fun shopping with somebody else's money." She pulled another box from under the tree, and Ted passed it to Evan, who handed it to Keelie.

The box was heavy, and she set it on the floor to open it, her eyes getting huge when she realized that it was a laptop. "Oh, my God. They bought me a computer?"

"Yes!" Ivy said. "And an AOL account that your mother's paying for. Ted and I set everything up on it yesterday."

"I don't believe it," Keelie said, opening the box and pulling out the laptop. "I haven't had a computer since Jason moved to Baltimore."

"It's like riding a bicycle," Evan said. "It'll come back to you."

"It was definitely easier to put together and hide than a bike," Ted said.

"Right," Ivy said. "We didn't have to stay up all night looking for missing ratchets."

"I'm in shock," Keelie said. "I need to call them right now."

"Why don't you just send them an e-mail?" Granny asked. "I've got high speed Internet access."

"All the way out here?" Evan asked.

"When your best friend is the mayor—not to mention that I used to babysit the man who now runs the cable company—you can get things done," Granny said. "I'll show you how to set up everything, Keelie."

"Yeah, and show her how to find your blog," Ted said.

* * *

Keelie sat on her bed late that night, her splinted leg stretched out and her other leg serving as a desk for her laptop. She was slowly getting used to the touchpad instead of a mouse. She looked down at Hamlet, who'd stopped exploring his new maze for a bout of chewing.

"You racked up," she said. "That Rex never had it as good as you, with a maze, all those chew toys, and your very own car from your Aunt Ivy. You are one spoiled hamster."

Hamlet darted into a tunnel for some peace and quiet, and Keelie turned her attention back to her computer. She lightly ran her fingers over it, loving the way it looked and felt, and took stock of the day. Phone calls with her mother and Misty. Phone calls from Holly and Mrs. Johnson. An incredible meal cooked by Ted that had them lingering at the table for hours, telling stories of other Christmases and their various family traditions. She knew Ivy had to be missing her father on this first Christmas without him, but the only time she'd gotten a little emotional was when she blew out the candles on her birthday cake. Evan had been right there to put an arm around her and say something funny to break the tension.

Keelie hadn't thought of the store even once, nor was she going to brood over what tomorrow would be like when people started exchanging books and using their gift cards. Buy The Book would be fine without her.

She tried to imagine Christmas day at the Boone house, remembering some of her favorite presents when she was Jennifer's age. Her mother had always managed to know just when she and Misty stopped wanting toys and were finally happy to get clothes and more grown-up presents.

Jewelry, she thought. *Perfume. And we were at the right age when CDs and videotapes got popular. But*

Mom always managed to find us something fun. Some
little toy that we would pretend we were too old for and
secretly loved. I hope Jennifer's mother is like that, be-
cause Dr. Boone, like Huck, may not get it.

And yet she'd loved her stepfather's gifts, too, even
when they were unusual, because they came from him.
She couldn't remember ever having a bad Christmas,
even when Gram was in one of her moods. She'd only
started hating the holiday when she was swallowed up
by the world of retail.

She looked again at the computer and understood
why it was the perfect gift, even if her mother couldn't
have known. It wasn't the e-mail account, which was
going to make keeping in touch with her family easier.
It wasn't having access to the Internet or the hours of di-
version that could provide.

Instead, it was exactly what she needed to work her
way through her futile preoccupation with Michael
Boone. It would give her an outlet from the stress of her
job. If she had to move away from Houston to get her
own store, or if Ivy moved away for a better job, there
was one way the computer would provide stability and
keep her engrossed.

She took a deep breath, counted to three, looked at
the blank screen, conjured up a mental image of Rip the
greyhound, and began typing.

Every one of his scars had a story . . .

Chapter 11

Had it not been for the fight it provoked between her and her sister, Keelie would never have remembered one of the Sunday afternoon movies they saw as kids. *The Perils of Pauline* starred Pat Boone, and Misty thought it was hilarious. Keelie found it silly and implausible that Pauline and George could repeatedly miss each other by mere seconds as Pauline went from one catastrophe to the next, the hapless victim of various nefarious characters.

Minus the nefarious characters and the perils, Keelie's experiences with Dr. Boone made her change her mind and decide that the movie had gotten it right. Or rather, her lack of experiences with Dr. Boone. When she was away from the Storey house with Ivy and Ted one afternoon, Dr. Boone came by to check on Hamlet. Annoyed that she'd missed him, and determined to show her gratitude for his care of her hamster, Keelie stole a plate of Ted's homemade cookies and coaxed a ride to the veterinary clinic out of Fred Storey. They found the office locked. A sign on the door explained that Dr. Boone was taking care of an emergency on someone's farm. Keelie could only hope no wild animals would steal the cookies from the back steps of the house where she left them.

Dr. Boone came by the Storey house again when Keelie was at Dr. Jenkins' office getting her ankle X rayed. He left a note next to Hamlet's cage thanking her for the cookies. When she called to thank him for thanking her, a taped message informed her that the Boones were spending the New Year in Galveston. They would undoubtedly be returning on the same interstate that Evan and Keelie would take to get back to Houston. It was maddening.

Keelie hid her frustration from her friends and assured herself that fate was playing a game of keep-away as a reminder that it was folly to fall for a married man. That stupid Pauline had no idea how good she had it, being kept from a potential lover by pygmies, Russians, and crazy millionaires instead of one small-town wife.

After Keelie returned to Houston and got her walking cast, her doctor said he couldn't release her for work until he saw her again the second week of January. Other than calling Rodney to let him know, she was able to shove Buy The Book from her thoughts. But the only way she could stop thinking about Dr. Boone was indulging herself in a different obsession.

She filled her days with the story she was writing about a twelve-year-old girl named Destiny. To get inside Destiny's head, Keelie at first tried to remember herself at twelve. Then she found that it was easier to recall things about Misty. Misty had been twelve when Huck came into their lives. But Destiny's life was nothing like the Cannon sisters' lives had been. Destiny lived in a trailer in rural Alabama. She didn't have a loving family, but a neglectful, even somewhat abusive one.

Destiny wasn't Keelie, or Misty, or Dr. Boone's daughter Jennifer. She shared qualities with all of them, but mostly she was a lonely girl who escaped the dreariness of her life by walking through the woods to the small town nearest her. She made friends with shopkeepers and the waitress at the town diner. She sometimes did odd jobs at the beauty shop or the drugstore to pick up a little money.

Keelie put a lot of detail into Destiny's town. She didn't use Columbus; Keelie felt no particular attachment to the city where she'd grown up. She hadn't appreciated that a place could have a unique personality until she went to the University of Georgia. Athens had the energy and contradictions of most college towns, and she'd loved living there.

When she and Jason moved to Houston, they'd found an apartment close to where he worked. Keelie had disliked living in a complex where every apartment was the same, and the landscaping made it look like every other complex in the city. They heard about Montrose and decided to check out its bar scene. The first time they'd driven down its main street, Westheimer, Keelie had excitedly pointed out the jumble of shops. The faded and decaying features of some of the buildings made it look like a Southern town to her. The sidewalk procession of young mothers, gay men, goth girls, and boys in dreadlocks reminded her of Athens.

When Jason moved away, she'd lived with girlfriends in an apartment close to the Galleria because it was all she could afford. Moving behind the Atwells' house had finally brought her to the edge of Montrose and its bohemian charm. Although Destiny's fictitious hometown in Alabama couldn't provide exactly the same kind of environment, Keelie infused it with the spirit of Athens and Montrose. She also borrowed from Coventry, where she'd learned that a small town's residents could be full of delightful surprises. She drew from Coventry's colorful history to create one for Dresden, whose name was her nod to the city that had become a partner to England's Coventry after World War II.

There was no veterinarian in the story she wrote, but Michael Boone's influence was on every page because of Destiny's best friend. This was the point which always thwarted Keelie. No matter how she wrote the dog or changed his name, he always turned into Rip the greyhound. She finally gave up trying to fictionalize him. Since she was only writing for her own pleasure, there was no reason why she had to disguise Rip. The relationship between Rip and Destiny had the affection of Keelie's with Hamlet, but Rip, like Destiny, had been forced to cope with a harsh youth, as indicated by his scars. When Destiny found Rip in the woods, it was the beginning of a new and richer life for both of them.

The story was with Keelie when she went to bed at night. She dreamed about it, and the first thing she wanted to do every morning was power up her laptop and keep writing. There were days when the only reason she took a shower or tidied her apartment was the certainty that Mrs. Atwell, Evan, or Ivy would check on her and bring her groceries. She didn't want them to know what she was doing. There were even times when she was so caught up in writing that she didn't stop to clean Hamlet's cage, letting him spend the day in his maze. It didn't matter to Hamlet, because he only slept all day anyway. But it was indicative of a shift in her priorities.

She understood why she was keeping the story a secret. It was hard to shut out the negative voices of her grandmother and some of her old writing teachers. She would tell herself that she wasn't trying to write the perfect novel. In fact, sometimes it felt like Destiny's story was writing itself and she was only a typist. Other times, she'd worry over some detail in her head while she was trying to sleep and realize that she was putting far more energy into it than she wanted to admit. She revised, restructured, and polished almost constantly, and she knew that if Evan, and especially Ivy, a fellow literary scholar, said anything disparaging about her attempt to write, it would crush her. The story of Destiny and Rip was being written from a deep part of her soul, and it felt fragile. She wanted to protect it.

She was caught off guard one afternoon when Evan showed up without calling first and began what seemed like an interrogation. "What are you up to, Keelie?"

"Huh? I'm stuck in my apartment in a cast."

"Something's different. Your mind always seems like it's somewhere else. Do you realize that since we came back from Coventry, you never call Ivy or me? We have to call you. You haven't asked either of us to take you anywhere. You haven't tried to see Holly since she came home from Scotland. Something's going on, and I'm afraid I know what it is."

"What?" she asked, trying not to look guiltily at her laptop.

"You're the only person I know who's getting zero exercise and still losing weight. Have you looked at yourself in the mirror?"

"Do I need another haircut?"

"Your hair is fine. Are you eating anything?"

"I have more food stockpiled than a Mormon," Keelie said. "Nobody comes through that door without bringing something to eat. And I do get exercise. I go up and down the stairs every day in this stupid cast to walk around Mrs. Atwell's gardens."

Evan shook his head and said, "It's the Vicodin, isn't it? You're hooked."

She laughed and said, "No! I don't even know if I still have Vicodin. I didn't refill my prescription because I'm not in pain."

"Are you sure? I know you're not telling me something. Do you have a secret boyfriend?"

"You and Hamlet are the only men in my life," Keelie swore. "I suppose I could be wasting away because of missing Rodney."

"Don't try to joke your way out of it. You'd tell me if something was wrong, wouldn't you? You can always tell me anything. I won't judge you."

"I promise you, there's nothing to tell. I'm fine."

His eyes bored into her, and he said, "Is it the Internet? Ivy told me that the Atwells gave you access to their wireless. Are you spending your time in chat rooms? On message boards? Having cyber sex?"

"No. Although I did find Granny's blog. It's fun to keep up with the people in Coventry. It's not at all the racy exposé that Ted suspected it was. It's homey and sweet. I miss Coventry."

"It was a good Christmas," Evan said. "I'll have to take your word for it that everything's okay. I need to go out of town for a few days, but Ivy and Holly are just a phone call away. If you need anything—"

"I'll call them," she assured him. "Are you going to Edna?" When he made a noncommittal noise, she said, "So that's how it is. You can keep secrets, but I'm not supposed to have any."

"I'll tell you everything when I get back."

After Evan left, she went to the laptop, but her guilty

feeling remained. Instead of opening Destiny's story, she sent e-mails to her mother, Misty, and Granny. Then she succumbed to an urge she'd been suppressing, opened a search engine, and typed "Michael Boone."

There were a zillion entries that weren't her Michael Boone—or someone's Michael Boone—and only two that were. One was a listing for his practice. The other was about a paper he'd presented at a conference at Texas A&M on equine nutrition. Fortunately, the paper wasn't available online, or she'd have had to face just how unnatural her obsession was by reading something just because he'd written it.

She daydreamed for a while about being in a classroom with Dr. Boone as her professor. She'd never had a crush on any of her teachers, most of whom had been preoccupied with publishing papers on obscure aspects of long-dead writers. But if Dr. Boone had been one of her teachers, and Jason hadn't been in the picture, and Dr. Boone hadn't been married . . .

"Stop," she said.

She then typed in "Mrs. Michael Boone" and got nothing. She stared at the screen for a while and finally tried "Boone," "Coventry," and "married" together, getting two hits: the listing for Michael's practice and a link to Storey Time.

"Granny," she said, "maybe you came through for me."

She found the blog entry, which was from the year before, and began reading.

It's a known fact that Coventry produces the prettiest girls in Texas. We've taken two Miss Texas titles and seen our beauties walk down the runway at the Miss America pageant. They always grace the class beauty pages of their college yearbooks, and one of our girls has even had movie roles in Hollywood. However, I freely admit that the crowning of our Daughters of Godiva is not my favorite part of our festival. This year's high point was the runaway terrier at the dog show, who turned our entire square into a scene worthy of a Disney comedy. The last time I remember having that much fun at the festival was the year Lisa Fleming (who later married every horse owner's favorite vet, Dr. Michael Boone) was crowned the Daughter of Godiva. If you recall, that was the year when two amorous skunks decided to join the Medieval Ball and ended up with the entire mead hall to themselves.

"Oh," Keelie moaned. "His wife is named Lisa, and she was pretty enough to be crowned a Daughter of Godiva. Suddenly I'm in a Daphne du Maurier novel. I feel like the second Mrs. de Winter. Ivy didn't cover this with her 'R' men. Evan was right. I'm a mess."

She went to the bathroom to study herself in the mirror. Maybe it was the power of suggestion, but her face did seem thinner. She didn't think she'd lost weight, but because she hadn't worn anything for days other than sweats or baggy flannel pajama bottoms with oversized T-shirts, she had no way of knowing. She kept her skinny jeans deep in the back of her closet, and since she couldn't get them over the cast, she couldn't use them as a means of measurement. She plundered her wardrobe until she found a skirt that she hadn't worn since she was with Jason. It had been tight even then— her sexy skirt that she wore when they went out.

She slipped out of the pajama bottoms and pulled the skirt up, shocked when the zipper was not only easy to close, but the waist was actually loose.

"Maybe what I should be writing is a new diet book,"

she said, staring at her reflection. *"Break Your Ankle and Write Your Way to Weight Loss."*

She tossed the skirt on her bed, wrapped her cast in its trash bag, and got in the shower, resolutely scrubbing away thoughts about what would happen next in Destiny's story. Even if she couldn't go back to work, there was no reason why she had to shut herself away from the world.

After she dried her hair, she stared out the window. It would be easy to stay home and write. Houston's version of winter had finally arrived. The weather was cold and wet, certainly not anything someone in a cast wanted to be out in. But she was determined to break out of her routine, so she finally packed up the laptop and called a cab to take her to one of Montrose's coffee shops.

It suited her mood to be alone in a crowd, in a place that smelled of coffee, feeling warm and dry while rain streamed down the windows. She thought about the trailer that her character Destiny lived in and how the rain must sound against the roof. It wasn't long before her fingers were flying over the keys of her laptop as they tried to keep up with her brain.

When she finally looked up, it was dark outside and the faces of the shop's clientele had changed. She watched lights from passing cars make diamonds of raindrops on the window.

"Is anyone using this chair?"

Keelie looked up at the man who'd asked the question and shook her head. He pulled the chair to the next table and set down a backpack and an umbrella. She pretended not to stare while he took off his thigh-length raincoat and walked to the counter to order.

He wasn't the kind of man who'd get a second look

from most people, but Keelie thought he had nice eyes. And his butt wasn't bad, either. She was tired of men in baggy jeans and appreciated the way his hugged his body.

She continued to watch while he got his coffee and walked to another counter to doctor it. But as he reached for a carafe of cream, one of the coffee shop employees snatched it away from him. He reached for another, and she tonelessly said, "I have to fill these. I have to fill them all."

"I just need a little cream for my coffee," he said.

"I have to fill them all," she repeated. She picked up his coffee and handed it to him so she could wipe down the counter. He tried to wait her out, but she clearly had a routine that didn't involve giving him access to the cream. He finally walked back to his table, sat down, and glared across the shop at the woman.

Keelie smiled and said, "You can have some of my cream. I made them give me the individual ones." She pointed to her cast. "Because I'm handicapped."

He thanked her and took the cream, stirred it into his coffee, and said, "Does that also work for parking in blue spaces?"

"I don't have a car, but I suppose I could slap a handicapped sticker on my cast and park my ass in one if I wanted to."

"That could turn into a funny story. A homeless guy gets one of those blue handicapped placards that people hang on their review mirrors and puts it on his Kroger's shopping cart. So he can sleep in parking places closest to public restrooms."

"Let me guess," Keelie said. "You're in the writing program at Rice."

"University of Houston," he said.

"Impressive," Keelie said and meant it. "It's not easy to get in that program."

"You?" he asked, pointing to her laptop.

"I'm not a student. I got my degree in English—oh, a few years ago."

"You're not going to flirt with me until you know how old I am, are you?" he asked. "You're afraid you're too old for me."

"If you're in the MFA program, you must be older than twenty-two," she said.

"Twenty-five. See? We're the same age."

She laughed and said, "Smooth. I'm twenty-eight. I'm Keelie Cannon."

"You're kidding."

"Why? Did someone forget to tell me that I'm famous?"

"My name is Stephen Cannon. We may be cousins."

"I suppose we should stick to watching Crazy Coffee Woman then. We wouldn't want our children to be mutants."

"How many children were we going to have?" he asked.

"Two."

"I'd ask you out, but I don't have a car either," he said.

"It seems we're just two former English majors that pass in the night."

"It could have been so beautiful," he said.

"I can't believe you're quoting Tiffany lyrics to me."

"I was quoting Mandy Moore's version."

"See? The age difference is already affecting us. I'll always be Tiffany and eighties pop; you'll always be Mandy and nineties pop."

"We could start over in this century," he suggested.

There was a lull in their banter as a group of people

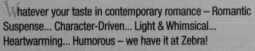

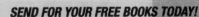

To start your membership, simply complete and return the Free Book Certificate. You'll receive your Introductory Shipment of FREE Zebra Contemporary Romances, you only pay $1.99 for shipping and handling. Then, each month you will receive the 4 newest Zebra Contemporary Romances. Each shipment will be yours to examine FREE for 10 days. If you decide to keep the books, you'll pay the preferred subscriber price (a savings of up to 30% off the cover price), plus shipping and handling. If you want us to stop sending books, just say the word... it's that simple.

If the FREE Book Certificate is missing, call 1-800-770-1963 to place your order.

FREE BOOK CERTIFICATE

Yes! Please send me FREE Zebra Contemporary romance novels. I only pay $1.99 for shipping and handling. I understand that each month thereafter I will be able to preview 4 brand-new Contemporary Romances FREE for 10 days. Then, if I should decide to keep them, I will pay the money-saving preferred subscriber's price (that's a savings of up to 30% off the retail price), plus shipping and handling. I understand I am under no obligation to purchase any books, as explained on this card.

NAME _____

ADDRESS _____ APT. _____

CITY _____ STATE _____ ZIP _____

TELEPHONE (_____) _____

E-MAIL _____

SIGNATURE _____

(If under 18, parent or guardian must sign)

Offer limited to one per household and not to current subscribers. Terms, offer and prices subject to change. Orders subject to acceptance by Zebra Contemporary Book Club. Offer Valid in the U.S. only.

Thank You!

CN026A

||..|..|||.....|||..|.|..|.|..|..|..||..|.|..||.|..||..|

Zebra Contemporary Romance Book Club
Zebra Home Subscription Service, Inc.
P.O. Box 5214
Clifton NJ 07015-5214

PLACE
STAMP
HERE

at the table next to his pushed back their chairs, shared long and loud goodbyes, and finally left the coffee shop. Just as Stephen was about to say something, Crazy Coffee Woman came over and began pushing the chairs under the empty table. He waited for her to stop making noise so he wouldn't have to yell to be heard. After four chairs were tucked under that table, she began moving the extra ones to his table. Then she stopped and stared at him.

"I have to move that chair," she said.

"My chair? The one I'm sitting in?" he asked. When she nodded, he said, "Move it where?"

"It goes with her table," Crazy Coffee Woman said, pointing at Keelie.

"All the chairs are alike. Why don't you take one of those and put it at her table?"

"I have to move that chair," she said stolidly.

He stood up and waited while she arranged the chairs to her satisfaction. When she picked up his coffee and began wiping his table, he said, "I'm not finished with that, and I'm still sitting here."

"You're standing up. I have to clean this table."

He knew when he was beaten and said, "If you'll give me my coffee, I'll sit at her table."

Crazy Coffee Woman eyed Keelie with a look that said she knew they were conspiring against her, but she reluctantly gave him his coffee. Just as she finished wiping his table, a couple sat at the other vacant one, and she moved toward them and said, "I have to clean that table."

"This is the most difficult pickup I've ever attempted," Stephen said.

"Can you really pick up somebody when you don't have a car?" she asked.

"See? It's like the gods are determined to keep us apart."

"Probably because we're cousins," Keelie said.

"They're all against us," Stephen said. "Can I have your number anyway? Maybe we could meet in a more sane environment for a meal sometime."

"Do you like hamsters?" Keelie asked.

"I'm a vegetarian."

"Do you eat tuna salad?"

"Anything that once had a face is meat," he said.

"Too bad. I have lots of tuna salad at my place."

"I eat popcorn," he said. "We could watch a movie."

"You're probably into suspense."

"I like chick flicks," he said.

"How sexist. You assume because I'm a woman that I like chick flicks."

"You assumed I like suspense because I'm a man. Our first fight," Stephen said. "What kinds of movies do you like?"

"Chick flicks."

"Oh, boy. You're related to Crazy Coffee Woman, aren't you?"

"I don't think so. Then again, until a few minutes ago, I didn't know I was related to you."

"Julia Roberts or Meg Ryan?" he asked.

"Sandra Bullock."

"It was a trick question. I was trying to see if you'd say Sandra Bullock," he said.

"It was a trick answer. I was trying to see if you knew I meant Kate Hudson."

"There's one thing we can agree on," Stephen said. *"Glitter* is the worst movie ever made."

"It was that cat!" Keelie said. "The cat was the best actor in the movie, and I don't like cats!"

"I have a cat."

"It's over," Keelie said.

"Too bad. But I want you to know, I will always love you."

She narrowed her eyes and said, "When you look at me and say that, are you thinking of Dolly Parton or Whitney Houston?"

"Burt Reynolds," he said.

She nearly spit out her coffee when she laughed, then she said, "That almost makes me want to try again."

"Maybe after time passes, we can salvage a friendship out of our broken dreams."

Keelie's face hurt from smiling when she unpacked her laptop at home later. She'd forgotten how fun it could be to flirt. She'd given Stephen her number, but she didn't think he'd call. Even if he did, she knew they'd never go beyond friendship. Stephen didn't make her teeth sweat. But he did make her feel like she could pull herself out of her Dr. Boone-induced funk.

"I definitely think I'm over it," she told Hamlet. "Next thing I do is go back to work. Then I stop saying no any time someone asks me out. Eventually, I'll click with someone. If I don't break out of this pattern, I could end up spending all my time wearing pajamas in this apartment and talking to you." She glanced at the flannel bottoms she was holding, then frowned at Hamlet. "Don't say a word, you little rat."

The next morning, Keelie called Holly and opened with, "I've been a terrible friend."

"You have?" Holly asked. "What have you done?"

"It's what I haven't done. I haven't seen you even once since you got back from Scotland. I haven't seen pictures from your trip. I haven't thanked you for your gift, which you shouldn't have bought, by the way. You gave me that wonderful spa day at Cleo's, and—"

"Wonderful? Evan got fired, you had to save a rat from drowning, and you looked like you had mange when we ran out the door with Cleo brandishing scissors at you."

"It was a fun day," Keelie said.

"I can't promise you another one like it, but I can visit you. Why don't I bring you lunch today?"

"You can come over, but please don't bring lunch. I have a ton of food here."

"Are you sure?"

"Positive."

"I'll see you around noon then."

"Bring pictures," Keelie ordered.

Later, looking across the table at Holly after they'd caught up on everything—or at least everything that Keelie was willing to share, Keelie said, "You look different."

"Everyone always says that when they've spent a lot of time with Ivy then see me again for the first time."

"I've never had any trouble telling you apart," Keelie said. "Something's different."

Holly shrugged, picked at her sandwich, and said, "I still can't believe you broke your leg after I left for Scotland."

"I don't think there was a connection." She watched Holly tear the crust off her sandwich and break it into little pieces. Tuna salad was one of Holly's favorites, but maybe something was wrong with it. Keelie took a bite of her own sandwich, but it seemed fine. She narrowed her eyes. "You're pregnant."

"What? Oh, my God, how can you tell? You shouldn't be able to tell!"

"I knew it," Keelie said then repeated more enthusiastically, "You're pregnant! That's great. I'm so happy for you."

"Are you sure?" Holly asked.

"Of course. Why wouldn't I be? This time, you'll have a girl and name her Keelie."

Holly smiled and said, "I can't promise that. No one knows I'm pregnant except my doctor, Dave, Ivy, and Scotty. You won't tell my mother will you? Or anyone else?"

"Of course not. Did you get pregnant in Scotland?"

"No, I was pregnant when I went to Scotland. Apparently, Dave is in the zero to six percent of men whose vasectomies don't work. But even unplanned, we're happy about it."

"Why are you keeping it quiet?"

Holly sighed and said, "Here's the deal about being pregnant. The first time it happens, everyone is thrilled. It's the only thing they talk about, and the baby comes, and it's the most wonderful baby ever. The second time, everybody says how good it is to provide a sibling for number one. But they don't marvel over every detail with you. After all, you already proved you could do it. But the third time, people look at you as if they're thinking, *Don't you know how to stop that?* Like you're just being a showoff now, and inflicting too many offspring on a tired planet."

"That's insane," Keelie said.

"It's a syndrome," Holly said. "There's probably even a name for it. This Isn't China Syndrome or something."

"Well, I'm thrilled," Keelie said. "Besides, you can use up my quota, because I don't plan to have children. Is Ivy excited?"

"Uh-huh. Oh, I wanted to talk to you about Ivy. She told me everything about Mark. She was right not to tell me sooner. I would have nagged Dave to get Mark fired or something, and it wouldn't be right to interfere with a person's job, even if he is a cheating, lying sack of shit who deserves it."

"Tell me how you really feel," Keelie said.

"In all honesty, I don't feel like wasting much energy on Mark. But I admire my sister a lot. She could have been vindictive. She could have gotten involved with someone on the rebound. Or shrieked about him all the time—she was certainly entitled—but instead, she rose above it. And considering the grief she was going through about Daddy, that took a lot of strength."

"Are you mad at me for not telling you?"

"No. Maybe if you'd known all along, I'd have wanted to know, too. So I could be supportive of her. I think you were a good friend by not repeating what she told you. Plus it makes me sure you won't tell anyone I'm pregnant."

"You'd better hope they don't try to serve you a tuna salad sandwich, or the jig will be up. Does this mean Finnergy will send Dave home?"

"You have to ask all the hard questions, don't you?" Holly asked. She took a deep breath. "Dave needs to manage this project for at least another year. There's really no way to dodge it. But I'm not going through a pregnancy and childbirth without him. The boys and I are moving to Scotland. That's the part you *really* can't tell anyone yet."

"Your mother is going to freak out," Keelie surmised.

"Yes. Scotty's asking his company to transfer him back to Houston. If that works out, it'll give Mom something else to focus on."

Holly told her everything Mrs. Johnson had said about Scotty and Carla's baby and her trip to Hawaii, then she talked about the difficulties of moving a household and finding a school for her sons in a foreign country.

Keelie couldn't stop feeling a little sorry for herself. Holly was going away. If Ivy moved to a different city for a new job, Keelie would be left behind by two of her dearest friends. She reminded herself that she'd still have Evan. Anyone would be lucky with a friend like Evan. And he didn't have to be her only friend. If she kept her promise to herself and got out of the rut she was in, she could meet lots of new and interesting people. One of them might even turn into a boyfriend.

Even Stephen, she thought, and smiled at the rhyme, although she hadn't changed her mind about not dating him.

"I told Dave about Ivy's 'R' men theory," Holly said. "He says he's Retro Man. Because he's the breadwinner to a stay-at-home mom and two—nearly three—kids. Do you think I should get a job?"

"Why do you always do this to yourself? Raising kids *is* a job," Keelie reminded her. "My sister was talking to me about this just the other night. When my mom started her company, her clients were women struggling to prove they could do it all—be good employees and good wives and mothers. Now she has a different kind of client—the woman that some people scorn because she wants to stay home with her kids."

"What does your mother's company do for them?" Holly asked.

"She helps them create their own jobs. Work from home. Telecommute. Find clients who contract their skills and services without expecting them to be full-time employees in an office everyday. Wonderful Wife still does things for busy working women, but it also helps stay-at-home moms find a means to make income from home offices. Isn't it crazy that just a few decades ago, a woman was terrible if she went to work, and now she's terrible if she wants to stay home? It's supposed to be about choice. If your staying home works for the Sadler family, who cares what anyone else thinks?"

"You're always so positive," Holly said.

"You wouldn't think so if you'd been stuck with me and my bum ankle at Christmas. Ivy nearly drove me crazy with all that 'R' stuff. First it was Ted, then it was a man in Coventry that I saw a grand total of one time. She's like a pit bull when she clamps on to an idea."

"Who was the man?" Holly asked.

"Arliss Murray's son."

Holly got an odd look on her face and said, "Grayson?"

"Yes." Keelie told her about Evan's near-collision with Grayson and his horse, and Ivy's subsequent insistence that Grayson was Keelie's Rulebreaker. Then she hastily concluded, "But your Expedition was fine. Not a scratch on it."

"I'm not worried about the car," Holly said. "Actually, I was thinking of letting you and Evan share the Expedition while I'm living in Scotland. Dave's car was leased by Finnergy, so they just turned it over to another of the project managers. But we own the Expedition, and I don't want to deal with selling it. Or worry about getting another car when we come back from Scotland and I'm taking care of an infant."

"That's generous of you," Keelie said.

"The car will be better off if someone's driving it and maintaining it," Holly assured her. "If y'all don't want to use it, I was going to leave it at Granny's. They're used to driving pickups. Mom doesn't like driving anything big. Even if Scotty gets transferred home, Carla drives a minivan, and Scotty likes sporty little cars. The Expedition's not sexy enough for Ivy. She's a car snob.

Dave and I would still pay for the insurance. Do you think Evan will do it?"

"Considering how often it rains in Houston, he'd probably jump at the chance to drive a car to work instead of riding his motorcycle. When he gets another job, that is. If he doesn't want to keep the Expedition at his place, I can keep it here. Mrs. Atwell has always told me that if I had a car, I could use the third space in their garage."

"That's one thing off my list," Holly said with relief. "I got sidetracked. I was going to tell you that there's no way Grayson Murray would be romantically interested in you."

"Thanks!" Keelie said. "Not that I wanted him to be, but damn."

Holly laughed and said, "Grayson is gay. I guess Ivy doesn't know that."

Keelie let out a sigh of satisfaction and said, "I only hope that she brings his name up again. I can't wait to spoil the fun she tries to have at my expense."

That night, Keelie settled in front of the TV with a bowl of popcorn, but when the Lifetime movie she tried to watch was about three tormented women who met in a Lamaze class and turned their lives around, her mind wandered to Holly's news. She wondered if it bothered Ivy that Holly was married and kept having babies. Ivy had never seemed to measure her life against her twin's. It was funny how they could be so alike and yet so different.

Then again, she and Misty were the same way. In their case, it was Misty who had the husband and the babies, although she also had a busy career. Keelie examined that, wondering if she was jealous of her overachieving little sister. She didn't think so. Her mother and Misty would welcome her into the business if she wanted to open her own division of Wonderful Wife. She could even do it in Houston. The prospect had never appealed to her. She didn't want to run a business and put up with all the challenges the two of them thrived on.

And as she'd told Holly, she didn't feel compelled to have children. She liked kids okay, especially when they got to be older. But the idea of having a baby didn't make her go all gooey inside. She didn't look at parents in the Galleria with their babies and envy them. If a child came into her life . . .

"Oh, I see where this is going," Keelie muttered and muted the television. "Snap out of it. Jennifer Boone already has a mother."

She reached for her laptop and her literary child.

Chapter 12

It was Ivy's car, not Holly's, that Evan borrowed on the day Keelie saw her doctor again. The cast was removed, a smaller one was put in its place, and Keelie got her release to return to work.

"It's a bittersweet thing," she said, waving the form at Evan once they were back in the car. "I'm free. Yet not free. I get to be Rodney's underpaid minion again."

"On the bright side, I have a feeling no one will ever make you climb another ladder," Evan said.

"Unfortunately, Rodney won't even let me climb a figurative ladder. Do you have anywhere to be?"

"My entire day is yours. Until we pick up Ivy from work."

"Inside, I'm screaming and counting to a hundred, but I guess I should go to Buy The Book and tell Rodney to put me back on the schedule."

"You could just call him," Evan said.

"But then the first time I walk through the door again, I'll be working. Baby steps."

"You know I'm all about shopping at the Galleria," Evan said agreeably.

It was slower to walk with the cast and the special shoe the doctor had given her than when she used her crutches, but she wasn't sorry to leave them in the car. Evan left her at the door of Buy The Book, mumbling something about Aveda, so she walked in alone.

When she was sixteen, Huck had treated the family to a weekend in Atlanta. Keelie and Misty had gone to a movie in a mall theater, and when they came out, Keelie was disoriented. She'd forgotten they weren't in their usual mall at home. When she saw different stores across from the theater, it took her a few seconds to remember where she was.

She experienced that feeling again as she looked around the bookstore. She knew her confusion wasn't just because she'd been away for nearly a month. Everything looked different. Art and Bargain were back where they were supposed to be. But the displays were different. The books on the new arrivals table were unfamiliar, and she didn't recognize a single face in the cash wrap area. She felt like she'd stepped into a Buy The Book in a different city.

"Could I help you find something?"

Keelie looked at a waifish girl who was nothing but teeth and said, "Is Rodney here?"

"Rodney?"

"The manager?"

"You mean Jarvis?"

"Jarvis?"

"The manager?"

"What?"

"Our manager is Jarvis Kennedy," the girl said.

"Is he here?"

"Sure. I'll page him."

Keelie stood rooted to the spot, desperately hoping

that a familiar face would pass by, until a man emerged from Business, looked at her ankle, and said, "I'll bet you're Keelie! You're a legend around here. I'm Jarvis Kennedy. How's your ankle? Are you ready to come back to work?"

The barrage of questions overwhelmed Keelie, but not as much as Jarvis did. He was tall. Very, very tall. She almost felt off balance as she stared up at him while he shook her hand.

"I don't—what happened to Rodney? Where is everybody?"

"Wow, you didn't hear?"

"Hear what?"

"Maybe we should go back to the office," he said. As she slowly followed in his wake, he called out to another employee that she didn't recognize, "Salli, this is Keelie!"

What he lacked in information he certainly provided in enthusiasm, as did Salli, who rushed over and said, "You're Keelie? It's so good to meet you."

Salli adjusted her pace to Keelie's as they followed Jarvis to the office. He pulled in an extra chair from the breakroom so Keelie and Salli could both sit down, then he closed the office door and took the chair behind the desk.

"I'll let Salli tell you about Rodney, since she was more directly involved," Jarvis said.

"You know Tamala, right?" Salli asked.

"Of course," Keelie said.

"Rodney and I had a little conflict about her. See, I decided to put her permanently at the information desk during the Christmas rush."

"Oh," Keelie said. "You're one of the temporary assistants."

"Not anymore," Salli said. "I transferred here from Nashville. Anyway, I'm sorry if you like Rodney, but he was on a big power trip. I don't know if he really cared about Tamala's assignment, but he definitely cared that it was my idea. He just couldn't let it go. Especially when business slowed down. He wanted her back on regular duties. But the woman is seven months pregnant. I didn't think she should pull eight-hour shifts on her feet. The first thing he said that hit me the wrong way was that Tamala shouldn't ask for special treatment. I thought I'd let that slide, and I told him it wasn't Tamala's idea. She hadn't asked for anything. It was my decision."

"Rodney likes to make the decisions," Keelie said.

"Definitely. But then he crossed a line. He told me, and I quote, 'Tamala isn't that delicate. After all, she comes from people who squatted in the fields to have babies then went back to work.' Can you believe that?"

"Holy shit," Keelie said. She tried not to look at Jarvis for his reaction, but she couldn't stop herself, and when their eyes met, she felt her face get hot.

He grinned at her and said, "It's okay. We don't have to pretend like I'm not black."

"What was he thinking?" Keelie moaned. "He never said anything like that in front of me. Rodney had equal contempt for all of us."

"That's not the philosophy of Buy The Book," Salli said, then went on like she was reading from the employee handbook. "A manager shouldn't make disparaging remarks about anyone for any reason. I called the district manager, Jimmy, who talked to Rodney, and the end result was Rodney's termination."

"It wasn't just the one incident," Jarvis said. "I don't know details, but apparently Jimmy's gotten several

employee complaints about Rodney. There was another
assistant manager here—"

"Charlotte?" Keelie asked.

"Yes. You didn't hear this from me, but she wrote a
detailed letter to Corporate about Rodney when she
quit. She said he made remarks about her age. I think
Rodney was on his way out anyway. The Tamala remark
just moved things along a little faster."

"I can't believe him," Keelie said. "What an idiot."

"I don't know how you worked with him," Salli
commiserated. "I'm eager to be part of the manage-
ment team with you. Do you know when they'll let you
come back?"

"I got my release from the doctor today," Keelie said.

"Outstanding," Jarvis said. "I'll put you on next
week's schedule. Everything we've talked about today
is confidential, of course. Tamala has no idea any of this
happened."

"Of course," Keelie said. "It looks like there's been
some turnover other than just Rodney."

"I'll bring you up to speed on everything when you
come back," Jarvis assured her. "Like Salli, I'm looking
forward to it."

"Me, too," Keelie said, although she wasn't sure she was.

"What do you think that means?" Evan asked later as
they ate dinner at Barnaby's with Ivy. She'd told them
everything, sure that even though the tables at the tiny
restaurant were close together, there were no Ted-like
lurkers to overhear her talking about Buy The Book.
The other patrons were much too involved with their
own tables' dramas to care about hers.

"I'm not sure. I feel really disconnected from the

store. Like everything changed while I was gone. Don't get me wrong. Jarvis and Salli seem nice. I should be thrilled that Rodney's gone. Instead, I just feel weird."

"Maybe you were comfortable with the devil you know?" Ivy suggested.

"Maybe."

"That's the way I used to feel about Cleo," Evan said. "Every time she had one of her fits and fired me, I'd think I should take her up on it. Then I'd wonder if it would really be better anywhere else. I've never worked in a salon that wasn't run by someone with behavior ranging from diva to dictator. At least I knew what to expect from Cleo, and I loved the other stylists and my clients. Most of them. A few of them. God, why did I stay there so long?"

"The devil you know," Ivy repeated.

"But I have worked with other managers," Keelie said. "Rodney hadn't been in the store that long, and Joyce was a great manager. If she was back at our store, I'd be jumping for joy. Or at least hopping on one foot."

"Are you sure?" Evan asked.

"What do you mean?"

"Maybe it isn't just the store that's changed. Maybe you've changed."

She thought that over while he and Ivy compared notes on which guys in Barnaby's were hot. Finally she said, "Do *you* think I've changed?"

"I think we all have. It was Coventry. It's like the town cast a spell on us, and we can't break free. It's probably that damn Lady Godiva statue. Maybe it's enchanted."

"I think she's still under the spell of the Rulebreaker," Ivy said.

Evan scowled and snapped, "Stop doing that. You know she doesn't like it." When both women looked at him with surprise, he said, "She only saw the man once. It's not like they had some big fling while we were there."

"You're the one who's changed," Ivy said. "You don't even look the same."

Keelie looked at Evan. Ivy was right; there was something subtly different about him. A jaded quality that he'd worn like a mask from the time his Jason left for Russia was gone. He seemed relaxed. Happy. Yet there was something anxious about him, too. It occurred to her that his focus was on anything but her or Ivy, as if he didn't want to meet their eyes.

Unlike Holly, however, Evan couldn't be pregnant, so Keelie asked, "Are you addicted to Vicodin?"

"What?" he asked, finally looking at her.

"You're the one with a secret, aren't you?"

"No, she is," he said, pointing at Ivy.

"What secret?" Ivy asked. "What are you talking about?"

"You stole Keelie's Remnant away from her."

"He wasn't my—"

"I did no such thing," Ivy said. "Stop calling Ted that." Her eyes widened, and she said, "Oh. I get it."

"Get what?" Keelie asked. She felt like they'd suddenly started speaking Japanese.

"Are you going to pretend like nothing's going on? Admit it. You're in a romance with Ted Hughes," Evan said.

"He's back in New York," Ivy said.

"That's not an answer."

"So what if she is?" Keelie asked. "They're both free and over the age of twenty-one. And he was never my Remnant."

"And Grayson Murray was never *your* Rulebreaker," Ivy said.

Keelie frowned at the way she said it, then she remembered the little detail about Grayson she'd gotten from Holly. She looked at Evan and said, "You sneak! You were seeing Grayson on the sly in Coventry, weren't you?"

Evan sniffed and said, "I think it's time to ask for the check and fight over who owes what."

"I don't think so," Keelie said. "I want dessert. After all, the weight is just falling off of me because of my Vicodin addiction."

"Oh, be quiet," Evan said.

"You're not weaseling out of this," Ivy said. "We want full disclosure now."

"You might get more than you bargained for," Evan said.

"Why? Did you? Tell us all about Grayson's attributes."

"What is it with you straight women? All you think about is sex," Evan huffed. "It wasn't like that."

"Then why don't you tell us how it was?" Keelie asked.

Their waiter stopped to get Keelie's dessert order, giving Evan time to compose his thoughts. Finally he said, "That day when we nearly ran down Grayson in the car, it hit me like a ton of . . . a ton of . . . horses."

"That's awful," Ivy said and laughed at him.

"I never claimed to be poetic."

"Remember what he said in the car the night you told us the story about Molly?" Keelie asked. "When you meet a man, the story always goes to hell."

"At least the metaphors do. A ton of horses," Ivy said and snickered again.

"Do you want to hear this or not?" Evan asked.

"Do the rest of us have to hear it, too?" a man at the next table asked.

"Be quiet," his companion said. "I love romance. Go on, Evan."

"Do I know you?" Evan asked.

"You used to cut my boyfriend's hair," the man said.

He told Evan his boyfriend's name, which started a conversation between them. Keelie ate her cheesecake in silence and shared a few eyerolls with Ivy, who was equally impatient to hear about Evan and Grayson.

"I'm paying the check," Ivy said firmly when Evan turned his attention back to them. "Then we're going to Keelie's to get the rest of this story."

"I can't help it if I'm not like Keelie," Evan said later as his opening.

"What does that mean?" Keelie asked.

"You don't mind being single. When your Jason left, you were fine. I do better in a relationship. Or at least I was happier being unhappy with my Jason than I was being unhappy without him."

"Could we all take a vow?" Ivy asked. "Could none of us date another Jason? I know you can't shake a stick without hitting a Jason these days, but share the wealth. Let the other men and women of the world have their chance with Jasons."

"Fine by me," Evan said. "Okay, so I saw Grayson that day on the road, and it was like—"

"Horses hit you. Yeah, we got that part," Ivy said.

"And I thought I was crazy. There's no such thing as love at first sight. Is there?"

"You'd be surprised," Keelie said. "No, it's probably not love. But I think it is possible to have your entire world rocked the first time you meet someone. Maybe it's some kind of genetic memory."

"Oh, that old argument," Evan said. "Nature or nurture. Genes or environment."

"You're getting off topic," Ivy said.

"I was totally shaken up," Evan said.

"You almost ran Holly's Expedition up a horse's ass," Keelie said. "Of course you were shaken up."

"I barely noticed the horse. It was Grayson who took my breath away."

Ivy slowly smiled and said, "Of course he did. As I told Keelie, it was like Jane Eyre and Rochester. Only *you* were Jane Eyre, not Keelie."

"Whatever," Evan said. "This is my story, not some Jane Austen movie."

"Charlotte Brontë, but do go on."

"I had to find out who he was. But I couldn't exactly ask around. In the first place, for all I knew, he was married and had a half-dozen kids. And even if he wasn't, I was a gay man in a small town. All I needed was an angry mob coming to Granny's with pitchforks. *Give us your homosexual!"*

"You could have asked Granny about him. She has no problem with your being gay," Ivy said.

"Except Keelie had just informed me that Granny was putting all our business on her blog. Angry mob. Pitchforks."

"So what happened?" Keelie asked.

"I did find him again," Evan said. "I noticed that Arliss asked a lot of questions on *Sex* night, and the next morning, Granny confirmed that Grayson was Arliss's son. I found his cabin. I'm very resourceful when I need to be. And he seemed to appreciate my . . ."

"Resourcefulness."

"Yes. It was quite clear that he admired my resourcefulness and that no wife or kids stood in my way. We talked a few times—"

"You never went shopping at all," Keelie complained. "Every time you disappeared, you were sneaking off for a rendezvous with Grayson. And pretending I couldn't go because of my stupid ankle. You abandoned me for a roll in the hay. Actual hay!"

"Like I said, y'all always think it's about sex. We talked. A lot. Not that whole tortured story of our young lives routine. Just stuff. Horses and hair and Lady Godiva. I'm sure it sounds stupid—"

"It sounds sweet," Keelie said. "And romantic."

"And itchy. Because of the hay. Then what happened?" Ivy asked.

"I hated leaving Coventry," Evan said. "But you don't just uproot your life because you meet a lovely man and sense that you could have something special with him. It could have just been one of those things that happens because it's convenient, then it's over. I was born in a small town—"

"And unlike John Mellencamp, you didn't plan to be buried there," Ivy said.

"I remember what it was like. I spent my time and energy on men that I had nothing in common or a future with, because there weren't enough of us to be picky. For all I knew, Grayson was taking advantage of an opportunity and nothing more. Let's face it. He's like Coventry aristocracy. His ancestor founded the town. His mother is the mayor. He comes from money. He went to college. He owns a horse ranch. I'm not even from the good part of Edna. I make my living cutting hair. I don't know Jane Austen from Charlotte Brontë, and I've never been on a horse in my life."

Keelie slapped Evan's arm and said, "Listen to me.

You are smart. Funny. Handsome. And you have one of the biggest hearts of anyone I've ever met. You have a way of putting other people at ease. You never meet a stranger. You're the best friend in the world. You're generous. And your Jason was stupid to let you go. Do *not* put yourself down to me."

"Don't be nice to me. You're making me feel worse."

"Why?"

"Because there's more to the story," Ivy said. They both turned to look at her, and she said, "Trust me, I know where this is going."

"You, too, huh?" Evan asked, and she nodded.

"Can someone fill me in?" Keelie asked.

"It kind of goes back to Ivy's story about Molly," Evan said.

"You fell in love with her, too?" Keelie asked. "Was it like being hit by a ton of motorcycles?"

"Shut up," he said. "Molly did proposition me. About her salon. Granny had told Grandpa to come home because Ivy was visiting, but she'd also told him about you and me. Grandpa saw me as the solution to Molly's problem."

"Oh," Keelie said, and her heart sank. "I get it. If you take over the salon, Molly will be free to stay on the road with what's-his-name."

"Perry," Evan said. "The morning I took you and Hamlet to the vet, I went back into town to get coffee, remember?"

"Yes."

"I ran into Molly at the Early Bird Café. That's why it took me so long to pick you up. Even though she was planning to see me at Granny's at noon to get her hair cut, we walked down the street to take a look at her salon."

"On our way home, you pulled over at that corner,

didn't you?" Keelie asked. "Where the beauty shop is. And you asked me if I believed in destiny."

"And you started bawling because Hamlet was sick. I knew it wasn't a good time to tell you about Molly's offer."

"Did you tell Molly you'd do it?" Ivy asked.

"I promised to think about it. It seemed like a good opportunity. You know I always wanted my own shop, and this one has a built-in clientele that Molly says would love to come back to the salon instead of going to New Coventry. Molly would move out of the apartment over the salon, and I could have it. The cost of living there is lower than here, and I'd be able to save money and eventually buy out Molly. But . . . this is Houston. You know? I love it here. I love Montrose. I have a life here. What would I have in Coventry except work?"

"What about Grayson?" Keelie asked.

"Yeah, what about him? I didn't want to move there hoping for something that would never be. I didn't want him to think I had expectations."

"But you do, don't you?" Ivy asked.

"Yeah," Evan admitted. "I went back. To Coventry."

"Is that where you went when you told me that you were going out of town?" Keelie asked.

"Yes. I took my bike. I didn't tell anyone I was coming. Molly or Granny. I went to Grayson's. I took a chance and told him how I felt. I had nothing to lose, right? Except maybe my dignity."

"What did he say?"

Evan smiled and said, "He's the kind of man who needs to process things. He knew I was exhausted from the trip. It was freaking cold going there on my motorcycle. He invited me to spend the night. Not in his bed. He's only got one bedroom, but he has this little upstairs loft. The bed is next to the chimney, and he keeps a fire burning, so it was cozy. Sometime in the middle of the night he came upstairs, and it was even cozier."

"Aw," Keelie said. "I *love* this story."

"The next morning, we had breakfast, then we went into Coventry. We sat in the shop with Molly, and Grayson asked her if she could do anything she wanted with it, how would she change it. She told him how it could be improved. I talked about what I'd want in a shop. Grayson is really smart about business, so we spent the next couple of days developing a plan for me. He even introduced me to a loan officer at Coventry Central Bank and vouched for me. I applied for a small business loan, and if I get it, I can turn Molly's shop into something a little closer to my dream salon."

"You're doing it?" Keelie asked. "You're moving?"

"Uh-huh." He gave her a look like he expected her to start beating on him. "Don't think I'm jumping into anything with Grayson. I'll be living over the shop. But still . . ."

"It definitely sounds like he's as interested as you are," Ivy said. "He wouldn't help you change your whole life if he didn't think there was something worth exploring."

"Yeah, I definitely think he's all about exploring," Evan said and showed his smile lines. "Your turn, Ivy."

"No, this is your moment. Let's talk more about Grayson."

"Shit," Keelie said. She couldn't believe it. First Holly was going to Scotland. Now Evan was going to Coventry. And Ivy would probably end up going to New York. "Just spill it, Ivy. I can take it."

"I don't have definite plans," Ivy assured her. "I'll

admit that I had a lot of fun in Coventry with Ted. I couldn't help but notice that he was lavishing attention on me. But I honestly wasn't looking for a relationship. In fact, after Mark and I broke up, I swore I'd never let a man get that close to me again."

"I remember," Keelie said.

"Nothing happened," Ivy said. "Okay, there were a couple of moments under some mistletoe. But nothing beyond that. Mostly, we talked. Then he came back to Houston and stayed with me. I met his brother. He met my mother and Holly. And . . . I really like him. A lot."

"You don't have to convince us," Evan said. "He's the first man who's ever gotten you to wear an apron."

"I know!" Ivy agreed and laughed. "How did that happen?"

"I think it's because he's willing to be in the kitchen with you," Keelie said.

"You may be right," Ivy mused. "He's so different from some of those chauvinists I work with. There are a lot of good signs. Like the way he gets along with Evan—at least after they stopped bristling around each other. I love a straight man who's not all hung up about his masculinity around gay men. You know the type I mean. They have to be all macho so no one thinks they might be gay, too."

"I hate that," Keelie said.

"And Ted's up for anything. He can shop. He can carry on a conversation that's not about sports or Pamela Anderson. He can cook."

"And he knew he was named after a poet," Keelie said.

"Yes! He reads. I sound terrible, don't I? I'm as narrow minded as those men I work with. I act like all straight men are pigs. But you two weren't much better.

I don't know why you were so negative about him. Especially you, Evan."

"Because you and Ted were obviously flirting with each other while Keelie was languishing in her sickbed—"

"Oh, brother," Keelie said.

"They were! In all the ways she just mentioned. Playing Julia Child and Wolfgang Puck in the kitchen. Taking long walks. Going shopping together. Telling each other stories about Christmases past. Comparing books they liked."

"Acting like two crazy kids in love," Keelie said.

"I wouldn't go that far," Ivy said.

"How far would you go?" Keelie asked. "All the way to New York?"

"You know I want another job," Ivy said. Keelie nodded. "I'm sending out résumés. Because of Buy The Book, Ted has a few contacts in the publishing world. No one spectacular, but they can get my name and résumé to people who might find an editorial position for me."

"Holly told me that was your dream job," Keelie said. She smiled. "I think you're both doing the right thing. It's not as if you're changing your whole lives because of a man. It's like when you have the guts to pursue a dream—your own salon, Evan, or a job in publishing, Ivy—everything falls into place. You meet people who can help make your dreams a reality. Maybe even be part of your new, exciting lives. Do y'all think I'm such a bad friend that I'd wish you anything but happiness?"

"But I don't want to leave you," Evan said.

"Me, either," Ivy agreed.

"I'm not excited about that part either," Keelie

said. "How can I be so happy and miserable at the same time?"

She asked her mother the same question when she called her later. Polly sighed and said, "Trust me. I understand. It's your version of the empty nest. I think three of the hardest days of my life were when you and Misty went away to college, then when you moved to Houston."

"At least Misty came back," Keelie said. "Now you probably see her so much that you're sick of her."

"Never," Polly said. "When your father died, I did a lot of soul searching about what I wanted for my daughters. I felt like it was the three of us against the world."

"Or at least against Gram," Keelie said.

"Your grandmother actually gave me good advice," Polly said. "She told me that I was your mother, not your friend. She and I fought so much when I was growing up. I had all the usual feelings. She was mean. She was unfair. She was hopelessly out of touch. But she knew that if she ever stopped acting like a mother and tried to be my pal, I'd have run right over her. You and Misty were a lot easier to raise than I was."

"You were a good mom," Keelie said.

"I tried. But during your teenage years, there were moments when I wanted to tear out my hair. Especially with Misty. She was a handful. You were harder on yourself than I ever would have been. I used to worry that I gave Misty too much attention and not enough to you."

"You must have done something right. We both turned out okay. Didn't we?"

"Well, I think so. But I'm a little biased." Polly

sighed. "Even though we're all friends now, I'm still your mother. Which means I can't stop myself from giving you advice."

"Okay," Keelie said.

"Stop comparing yourself to other people. You don't have to be like me and Misty and make your mark on the business world. You don't have to be a mother like Holly. You don't have to be as ambitious as Ivy. You're on your own path and your own timetable. Everything that you do is going to take you where you're meant to go. Try to enjoy yourself along the way and trust that it'll all turn out the way it's supposed to."

"What would you tell me to do if I were one of your clients?" Keelie asked.

"I'd tell you to set realistic goals for yourself," Polly said. "And by realistic, I don't mean practical. I mean figure out what feeds your passion, then decide what steps you need to take to get it. But, and I can't emphasize this enough, don't be so driven that all you think about is the end result. Not only does that cheat you out of truly living every day, it can set you up to feel like a failure if it doesn't come fast enough or if it's different from how you envisioned it. You have to be adaptable and leave some things to—"

"Destiny," Keelie said.

"I was going to say chance. Chance is random. Destiny sounds like everything's been determined already. I guess either way, some things are out of our control. But think how boring it would be if everything went according to our plans."

"And miserable," Keelie said. "Like if Evan didn't take a risk by quitting his job, he wouldn't be opening his own salon. And if Ivy never let herself love anyone else because Mark hurt her, or if she let her paycheck keep her in a job where she feels like she doesn't fit. Or if Holly stayed safely at home and pregnant instead of embracing the experience of an entirely new country."

"See? You don't need me to tell you anything. You already know it."

Okay, Keelie thought later as she scrolled through the first two hundred pages of Destiny's story. *At least have the guts to take* one *risk.*

She wrote Ivy an e-mail and attached the story to it. Then she rested her hands on the keyboard and looked at Hamlet, who was chewing on a wood block with joyful concentration.

"Should I?" she asked. For once, Hamlet stopped what he was doing and stared at her. She smiled. "Here's your literature lesson for the night. I named you for a character whose tragic flaw was his inability to take action." She looked back at the screen and hit SEND. "Destiny," she told him, "is out of my hands. At least for now."

Chapter 13

Keelie's first day back at work made her feel like a bride. The kind of bride who experienced the unpleasant realization, as she walked down the aisle, that she'd rather be anywhere else, but it was too late to turn back without causing an uproar. She thought that if she kept smiling and pretending everything was fine, it would become fine. Or it was possible that she'd wake up in two decades and realize that she'd thrown away the best years of her life.

She tried to shake off her gloom as the day began early with a mandatory staff meeting, where Jarvis made a big show of welcoming her back. She was relieved to see familiar faces among the new ones. But Kenny was gone; he'd been made an assistant manager in the Phoenix store. Brian had decided to go back to school, would only work an occasional shift on the weekends, and couldn't be at the store meeting. Tamala had opted to go out early on maternity leave. Keelie had the feeling she wouldn't be back.

Keelie's name and Salli's weren't on the duty sheet, so at least that ridiculous practice of Rodney's had been eliminated. Everyone new seemed as easygoing and pleasant as Jarvis and Salli, so she wasn't sure why she continued to feel unsettled as she slipped back into her Buy The Book routine.

Unlike Rodney, Jarvis was sensitive to her moods, and one afternoon when business was slow, he asked her if she wanted to go home early.

"Are you sure?" she asked.

"Salli's willing to close," Jarvis said. "I'd rather you ease back into things than get injured again."

She jumped at the chance to leave, and she was just getting out of her work clothes at home when her phone rang.

"Hi, Cousin Keelie," a man's voice said when she answered.

"I hope you're not about to hit me up for money, Stephen. We may be fake-related, but I'm broke."

"Yesterday was my birthday," he said.

"I can't believe I forgot after all the years we've known each other," she joked. "Happy belated birthday."

"My mother—hmmm, how can I describe my mother? You know how some people think all blondes are dumb?"

"I'm an ash blonde," Keelie said. "I've heard the jokes."

"My mother is the inspiration for those jokes. She sent me a bunch of DVDs. I don't have a DVD player. But I do have popcorn. So I thought if you had a DVD player—"

"As it happens, I do. My mother is also a blonde; she gave me a DVD player, but I don't have any DVDs."

"We're like an O. Henry story. But at least you can rent DVDs."

"Why would I? I can watch yours."

"Is now a good time?"

"Come on over," she said.

She fluffed up her hair a little but changed into her usual slouchy clothes. She wasn't worried about making a good impression on Stephen. As she stuffed a stack of mail into a drawer in a halfhearted attempt to straighten up her apartment, she glanced outside. Mrs. Atwell, hair higher than usual, was talking to Stephen and walking him through her gardens. As Keelie watched, Stephen bent down and looked around the bottom of some plants, then he stood up and they talked some more.

Keelie shrugged and washed the few dishes that were in her sink. At least Mrs. Atwell was giving her time to make the apartment decent.

After Stephen knocked and she let him in, she asked him what he and her landlady had been talking about.

"I was admiring her flowerbeds," he said. "She's worried because something seems to be eating some of her plants, so I was checking them out."

"Are you a gardener?" Keelie asked.

"My parents own a nursery," he said. "I worked there in the summers when I was a teenager."

"Did you identify her bug issue?"

"Yep. And more. She just hired me to redesign some of her beds this spring. You're good luck for me, because I can use the extra money."

"You can buy your own DVD player," Keelie said as she took the DVDs he removed from his backpack.

Stephen looked around and said, "Wow, you live here alone?"

"Yes."

"Sweet. I hate my apartment. The whole place has, like, two windows, and I have a roommate whose girlfriend never leaves. They bicker all the time. I can never study or write at home."

"Roommates," Keelie said sympathetically. "I liked my college roommates. Then I lived with my boyfriend, which was sort of like living alone in that he left everything about the apartment up to me. He just wrote checks. When we broke up and I tried roommates again, I'd gotten too used to having things my way." Stephen put a bag of popcorn in the microwave while she looked at the DVDs. "Your mother has eclectic taste."

"I think it's a John thing," Stephen said. "Waters. Hughes. Huston. Schlesinger. She loves her Johns."

"You make her sound like a hooker," Keelie said. "Should I be worried that she sent you *Serial Mom?*"

"Nah, she's harmless," he said.

It was a relaxing night, and she enjoyed Stephen's company and the chance to binge on popcorn and pizza, but it confirmed again for Keelie that nothing was going to happen between them. No chemistry; no sweating teeth. She felt like she was with another of her gay friends. That wasn't a bad thing, when she thought about it, since her current friends were leaving Houston at an alarming rate.

Jarvis had arranged Keelie's schedule so she could have three days off in a row and go with her friends to Coventry. They were moving Evan's belongings and getting him settled into his new apartment over the salon. Keelie rode with Hamlet, Ivy, and Holly in Holly's car. Holly's sons had been left with their grandmother for the long weekend. Evan followed the Expedition in a rented van with Holly's cat, Fernando, in a cat carrier on the seat next to him. Fernando was going to be living with Granny for the next year.

Keelie thought it was pathetic that everything Evan owned could be packed into a van only because it was also true of herself. She felt like she, at twenty-eight, and Evan, at thirty-five, should at some point have become more like Holly. Holly's days were a constant logistical challenge as she arranged for professionals to pack and move the Sadlers' belongings. Finnergy was leasing their house as a temporary home for the family of one of the company's executives, so Holly had to divide her household between those things that would be shipped to Scotland and everything else, which would be placed in storage.

It vexed Keelie that Ivy, who was also single and childless, owned all of her furniture, unlike Evan and Keelie, whose furnished apartments reflected the tastes of their landlords. Keelie had been luckier in that regard than Evan, because even the Atwells' castoffs were worthy of a River Oaks home. Still, it was depressing that six years after graduation, she continued to have the unfettered life of a college student.

"Where has all my money gone?" she wondered aloud to Holly and Ivy after expressing her discontent to them. "Shouldn't I have something tangible to prove I'm a grown-up?"

"Books," Ivy said. "Clothes. Music. Eating out. Bars. All the great things that people unencumbered by families and mortgage payments can buy and do."

"I'm glad Evan's stuff can fit into a van," Holly said, "since we're the ones who'll be hauling it up the stairs to his new place."

"Don't pay any attention to me," Keelie said. "I'm

just bitter because everyone's going places, and I'm staying behind."

"I'm not moving," Ivy said.

Yet, Keelie thought, but she didn't say it out loud. The other thing she didn't say was what was really bothering her. Ivy must have received her e-mail with Destiny's story. Even if she hadn't had time to read it, it seemed like she could have told Keelie that she'd gotten it and was going to read it. Keelie was afraid that Ivy's silence meant that she'd read it and was trying to decide the most gentle way to tell Keelie how bad it was.

I should have never given it to her, Keelie thought. *I put her in an impossible position. What was I thinking?*

She squirmed whenever she pictured Ivy reading her work. Now Ivy would know she was a lousy writer, and it would change something between them. Keelie would never be able to forget that her writing hadn't met Ivy's standards, and Ivy would probably feel sorry for Keelie for her feeble attempt.

"What's wrong with you?" Ivy asked. "Does your ankle hurt? Do you need to stop for a Coke so you can take a pill?"

"My ankle's fine," Keelie said.

Holly turned down the radio and said, "You probably feel like everybody's abandoning you. But I'll be back. Evan's not really far away. And who knows? Ivy could find the perfect job in Houston."

"I know," Keelie said. She wanted to change the subject. "Did I tell y'all about Crazy Coffee Woman?"

She embellished the story a little, making it better so they would laugh and stop feeling sorry for her. She was doing enough of that on her own.

"Montrose is full of quirky characters," Ivy said. "It's part of the charm."

While Keelie tried to decide if there was a hidden message in that—maybe Ivy was trying to tell her to write what she knew instead of making up a story about a twelve-year-old in Alabama—Ivy began telling them about a time when she and another woman at Finnergy had decided to help the homeless.

"We didn't do it through an agency," Ivy said. "Jenna had gone to a performance of *The Nutcracker* at the Wortham Center, and she noticed a group of people living under a nearby overpass. We were having a cold winter that year, so she asked if I'd help coordinate collecting coats and blankets from our coworkers. We did, and one Saturday we got up early and drove there. They'd divided themselves up with appliance-sized cardboard boxes, but they had a communal Christmas tree. When we opened the back of Jenna's Jeep, one man came out to meet us. The rest of them watched. After he found out why we were there, he motioned to them, and they descended on the Jeep."

"It's so sad," Holly said.

"I know. One woman wasn't wearing shoes, but at least she got a big blanket. Actually, what I liked was that they didn't act all humble and pathetic. They snatched that stuff out of the Jeep and went back to their cubbyholes to get warm, and I was glad. I didn't want them to treat me like a do-gooder or act like I might think I was better than them. As far as I'm concerned, most of us are only a paycheck or two from living under a bridge ourselves. I just wanted them to be warm. One of the men pulled out a sweater. It was one of those sweaters like you see people in the Midwest wearing. You know, with an Alpine theme? Snowflakes or elk or whatever on it?"

"I know the kind you mean," Keelie said.

"So he pulled it out and said, 'What is *this*? Who'd want this?' And threw it down and took a blanket instead. Someone else took the sweater. When we left, Jenna started crying, then she calmed down, and we couldn't stop laughing. Just because you're homeless doesn't mean you have no taste. That man gave me one of the best Christmas stories ever."

"I guess the moral of your story is that I should stop pissing and moaning and be grateful for what I have," Keelie said. "There's no place to plug in my laptop under a bridge."

"There must be," Ivy said, "because their Christmas tree had lights on it."

"No more Christmas stories," Keelie ordered. "I don't have to think about Christmas again until—"

"July," Holly said, "when they start selling Christmas stuff in the stores."

"Pretty soon it'll be Christmas season in retail year round," Ivy agreed.

"That's when I'm getting a different job," Keelie said. "I don't think I can listen to that freaking drummer boy song all year. Just play your damn drum and shut up, kid."

"That one doesn't get to me as badly as 'The Twelve Days of Christmas,'" Holly said. "All that leaping and milking makes me edgy."

"The question of the ages," Ivy said, "is when poor Alvin will get his hula hoop."

"Poor Alvin almost got me a date once," Keelie said. "With a man who thought I looked like a chipmunk!"

She told them the story of the customer who couldn't remember the chipmunks' names.

She and Ivy began trying to top each other with bad date stories, which kept the mood light until they were in Coventry. It was dark. The stores were closed and the streets were empty, but it all looked comfortably famil- iar. Keelie got a lump in her throat; it felt like coming home. She would never understand the hold Granny's little town had over her heart, but the one advantage of Evan living there was that she'd always have a reason to visit.

They left Fernando yowling in the van while they went upstairs to check out Evan's apartment for the first time. It wasn't anything fantastic, just a basic one- bedroom, one-bath. But Evan said there were hard- woods under the worn carpet, and he had lots of plans for improving it.

"That's one good thing about having no furniture yet," Holly said. "You won't have to keep moving stuff around as you do the work."

"Is it awful?" Evan asked, noticing Keelie's frown.

"It's wonderful," Keelie said, and her eyes filled with tears. "You're going to get that loan, improve things, make lots of money, and own it all yourself one day. It will be home, not just some place you're passing through. You'll put down roots, judge the Lady Godiva pageant, marry Grayson Murray, and live happily ever after."

"I like the way you tell a story," Evan said.

Keelie avoided Ivy's eyes and said she wanted to check out the bathroom as she walked away from them.

* * *

Since she was more mobile on this visit, Keelie and Hamlet were put in Granny's guest room with the single bed. Evan was in the same room as last time, and Holly and Ivy were bunking together in their mother's old bedroom. Keelie took the bathroom first, while everyone else visited with Granny and Fred, then she settled into bed, reading another Janet Evanovich mystery that she'd scored from Granny's library. Hamlet's wheel provided a familiar sound as he took up residence again in the aquarium next to her bed.

Just as she decided she should turn off the light and get some sleep, there was a light tap on the door. Ivy stuck her head in and said, "Are you still up? Do you feel like talking?"

"Sure," Keelie said.

She tried to keep her expression blank when she realized that Ivy was carrying a thick stack of paper. Apparently, she'd printed Keelie's story. She set it next to Hamlet's aquarium, then sat cross-legged at the foot of the bed.

"Do you want me to tell you what I think as your friend or as the future editor at a publishing house?" Ivy asked.

"Both," Keelie said.

"As your friend, I love it."

"Really?" Keelie asked. She hoped that Ivy couldn't tell how hard and fast her heart was beating.

"Really. And as an editor," Ivy paused as if searching for the right words, "I love it."

"You do?" Keelie asked. "You're not just saying that?"

"Have you ever known me to sugarcoat anything?" Ivy asked. "I have nothing in common with Destiny. Her life is as far from mine as a life can be. But when

I was reading, I felt like I was inside her skin. Every word rang true. The reason it took me so long to get back to you was because I devoured the story, then I realized that I'd only been reading it for enjoyment, and you'd want me to read it more critically. So I read it again. Twice. I love it."

Keelie leaned forward and grabbed her, so grateful and relieved that she didn't know if she wanted to laugh or cry. "Thank you."

"Don't thank me. I did finally find some suggestions I could make about it. And some wordsmithing; what editor can resist that? I'm in love with Destiny and Rip. And Merle at the diner—she's so earthy and real. You have to keep writing. I need to know what happens next. Are you crying?"

"I can't help it. I was so afraid that you'd hate it."

"Hate it? Keelie, it's amazing. You have totally nailed this child's voice. I can't say that I'm an expert on young adult fiction, but I do know a compelling story when I read one. You have to finish this. You have to submit it. I'll help you any way I can. We'll get agents' names. I'll talk to a couple of published writers I know. We won't stop until we find someone who believes in Destiny as much as I do." She laughed. "That sounds funny, doesn't it?"

"It sounds wonderful," Keelie said. "You just turned my whole mood around."

"I don't know why you'd ever doubt yourself," Ivy said. "You, Keelie Cannon, are a writer. You have a gift. This book will be published. I know it. I hope you're not sleepy, because I have about a million questions and comments for you."

"I don't have a tired bone in my body," Keelie said.

* * *

It took them only a couple of hours to move Evan's meager possessions into his apartment the following morning, then the four of them cleaned up and walked down the street to the Early Bird Café for lunch.

After they ordered, Ivy looked at Keelie and said, "Can I tell them?"

"Tell us what?" Evan asked. "I hope you haven't found a Reprobate or whatever the hell you call these men you keep trying to force on Keelie."

"My batting average is not so good. I'm not finding any more men for Keelie."

"Oh, come on," Keelie said. "You never found me the Rake and the Romantic. I still have some single friends who can walk off with them."

"No, I've retired," Ivy said. "I have a new project."

Keelie sat back, letting Ivy say whatever she wanted to about Destiny's story. After days of feeling like she would regret letting Ivy read it, she was ready to relish some praise along with her BLT and fries.

Unfortunately, she didn't have long to do so. She heard Gram's voice in her head saying, *Pride goeth before a fall,* when she saw Dr. Boone walk into the café with a woman who was laughing at something he said. Keelie pretended to listen to Ivy as she covertly watched the couple. She was glad he sat down with his back to her. She didn't want an introduction to his wife, and she was sure her friends would immediately sense her awkwardness if it happened. She assured herself again that Dr. Boone was only a passing infatuation that no one needed to know about.

She was consumed by jealousy as she casually let her eyes return to his wife, who looked nothing like Keelie had envisioned. Because she'd known Lisa Boone was once crowned a Daughter of Godiva, she'd expected her to look like a younger version of Mrs. Atwell, or maybe a Miss America contestant: blond, big hair, Chicklet teeth, consistently fake smile.

But Lisa was pretty mostly because her face was so animated as the two of them talked. Her dark, straight hair was pulled back in a ponytail, and she had dark eyes and skin. Apparently, Jennifer had inherited most of her father's features, because Keelie would never have guessed this woman was her mother.

Dr. Boone's laugh squeezed her heart and made her turn her attention back to her friends. She had to stop tormenting herself about him; it wasn't healthy.

"I want to read it," Evan was saying.

"Me, too," Holly said.

"Not yet," Keelie said. "Ivy gave me some good ideas last night that make me want to change a few things before I start writing again. I promise that when I have a final draft, I'll let you read it. If you're sure you really want to."

"Of course," Holly said. "I'd have wanted to even if Ivy wasn't so positive about it, because you wrote it."

"Am I in it?" Evan asked.

"You would ask that," Keelie said. "Not unless you have the personality of a twelve-year-old girl."

"I do love Kelly Clarkson," Evan said.

"That proves nothing," Ivy said. "My mother thinks Kelly Clarkson is the shit."

"I'm sure she said it just that way, too," Evan said with an eyeroll.

"Weren't we talking about me? My story is all fiction," Keelie assured Evan.

"I'm so proud of you," Holly said. "Do you still have time to write now that you're back at Buy The Book?"

"I haven't been working on it, but I brought my

laptop this weekend in case I get inspired," Keelie said. "We're done talking about me now. It makes me feel weird."

"You do look a little flustered," Holly said.

"It's hot in here. If y'all don't mind, I want to go outside. I've never seen the Lady Godiva fountain close up. Why don't you meet me there when you finish eating?" When they nodded, she slipped out of their booth and said, "See you in a few minutes."

As she passed Dr. Boone's table, she managed to shrug into her coat in such a way that her face was hidden from him. Once she was outside the café, she breathed a sigh of relief. The cold air felt good on her hot face, and she walked slowly around the corner and toward the town square.

The fountain wasn't running—it was probably too cold—but Keelie sat on its edge and stared up at the bronze statue. Lady Godiva was naked except for her long hair, which fell over her left breast in a way that allowed her some modesty below the waist. She was sitting in a side saddle position, although the horse had a folded cloth instead of a saddle, and she held the reins in one hand. Lady Godiva's lowered head made her look sweetly humble and contrasted nicely with the horse's obvious pride in the rider he carried.

It occurred to Keelie that if the statue were in Washington, D.C., some idiot would probably miss the entire point and demand that its subject be covered up. But there was nothing salacious about the statue, and Keelie loved it and loved that Coventry was proud of it.

"Hi, there," a voice said, and Keelie turned around.

The man who'd spoken was bundled up against the cold, which probably made him look bigger, but he towered over her and helped block the biting wind that was whipping her hair around.

"Hi," she said shyly. "I was just admiring your town's statue. At least—you're not a tourist, are you?"

"This time of year, we don't get many tourists," he said. "I'm Isaac Phillips. And this is my grandbaby, Rochelle."

Keelie spotted the little girl peeping out from behind his legs. She was nothing but coat, shiny brown eyes, and big puffs of black hair that her knitted hat couldn't quite subdue.

"Hi, Rochelle, I'm Keelie." She looked back at Isaac and said, "You own the hardware store, right? You met my friend Evan before Christmas when he picked up a tree for Elenore Storey."

"I remember," Isaac said with a nod. "You're the one with the broken ankle and the hamster. How's that ankle doing?"

"Much better, thank you," she said, extending her leg so he could see the cast and shoe.

"Do your toes get cold?" Rochelle asked, then ducked her head.

"Yes. That's why I have this ugly old sock over them," Keelie said, and Rochelle nodded gravely, as if she'd been wondering about Keelie's bad taste in footwear.

"Rochelle has to visit the fountain every day, even if it's not on," Isaac said. "The story goes that if you toss a shiny new quarter in the water, your wish will come true."

"What do you wish for?" Keelie asked.

"Can't tell," Rochelle said.

"I wonder if I have a quarter," Keelie said. Before she

could dig in her purse, Rochelle held out her hand and said, "You can have my wish."

"Oh, no, I can't take your quarter," Keelie said. But Rochelle pressed the coin into her hand. "Let's throw it in together. Maybe then we'll both get our wish."

Rochelle flashed her dimples, nodded, and kept her hand in Keelie's as Keelie tossed the quarter into the water.

"A few years ago, that wish would have only cost you a shiny nickel," Isaac said. "Then it became a shiny dime."

Keelie laughed and said, "Who knew inflation affected wishes?"

Rochelle looked up at the statue and said, "It's not true about the horse's leg."

"What about it?" Keelie asked, but Rochelle had evidently imparted all she intended to because she retreated behind her grandfather again.

"Some people say that if a horse has one foot off the ground, its rider died from battle wounds," Isaac explained.

"How did Lady Godiva die?"

"Old age. Doc Boone says the horse statue story is one of those urban legends."

"He knows everything about horses," Rochelle volunteered from behind Isaac's legs.

"He knows a lot about hamsters, too," Keelie said. "You'll have to meet my hamster sometime. If you want to."

She saw the hair puffs nodding furiously. Isaac shook his head and whispered, "Shy."

"I've always been a little that way myself," Keelie said.

"Okay, baby girl, let's get you back inside where it's

warm." He looked at Keelie. "Good to meet you. Don't stay out in this wind too long, or you'll be laid up at the Storey house again."

"I won't," Keelie promised. She watched them walk toward the hardware store, then looked back up at Lady Godiva. "Ha. You thought I'd make some stupid wish about Dr. Boone, didn't you? Nope. I just want you to help Destiny."

Chapter 14

Sunday was the momentous day that Evan decided to pull the different factions of his life together. Grayson Murray had invited them all to his house for lunch and a ride afterward.

"I don't know," Keelie said, looking down at her leg with doubt.

"Listen, if I have to ride one of those monsters, you do, too," Evan said.

"Nothing to it," Holly said. "Ivy and I started riding when we were practically babies."

"Grayson wouldn't put an injured amateur on one of his best horses. You'll get a gentle ride," Granny promised.

"We'll see," Keelie said. She'd ridden years ago, but she'd rather have all her limbs in good working order before she attempted it again.

"Take your laptop," Ivy suggested. "That way, if you decide not to ride, you can write by the fire."

"She's determined to make you finish that book," Evan said, then looked at Ivy. "Are you practicing for your future career, or what?"

"I just want to know what happens," Ivy said. "Her story's that good, and I'm in limbo here."

"I could take the laptop," Keelie said. "If you don't think Grayson will mind."

"If he's acting like Evan has been all morning, there's only one thing on his mind, and that's seeing the new man in his life," Holly said. "The rest of us will be lucky if they even notice we're there."

"Dress warm," Granny said. "We're finally getting that cold snap we should have gotten in December."

"It'd better not snow after I go back to Houston," Keelie said. "Not after thwarting me at Christmas."

They were in high spirits as Evan drove them in Holly's Expedition down the winding gravel road that led to Grayson's house.

"It really is a log cabin," Keelie said when they pulled up.

"I told you it was."

When they went inside and Evan made the introductions, Keelie observed that this version of Grayson was much more pleasant than the one she'd seen on the road that day. He still had the stubble, which made him look a little rugged and sexy, and he gave her a warm smile and said, "My mother tells me I was rude to you the first time we met."

"Apparently, near-death experiences rattle you," Keelie said.

"I never came anywhere near hitting that horse," Evan protested.

While Holly and Ivy helped Grayson put lunch on the table, Evan gave Keelie a tour of the cabin. It was snug, cozy, and made Keelie wish that Evan wasn't going to live over the salon. When she whispered that to him, he asked why.

"Because I can totally picture you here," she said.

"You and Grayson stretching your legs out in front of the fire after a long day. Like an L.L. Bean ad. All you'll need to complete the scene is a golden retriever."

"I blame the Vicodin," Evan said sadly. "Before that, you didn't have Ivy's romance psychosis."

"Moonlight rides on horseback," Keelie went on dreamily, as if she hadn't heard him. "Me sleeping in the loft upstairs next to the warm chimney."

"Who invited you on this honeymoon?" he asked rudely. "You can stay with Granny."

"You're so mean to me."

Grayson told them about his horse operation during lunch. Keelie was barely aware of what he said because she was mesmerized by his voice. He really was an alluring man; he might even be good enough for Evan. Especially if he continued to look at Evan like he wanted to devour him whenever Evan added anything to the conversation. She felt a pang of envy that she instantly suppressed. Evan deserved all the happiness he could get. They made a striking couple, both of them tall and lean. Evan's blond hair and light eyes were a great contrast to Grayson's dark hair and eyes. If some couples ended up looking like bookends, Evan and Grayson were more like salt and pepper shakers.

After they finished eating, Keelie helped Evan clean up. Then they all sat lazily in front of the fire, until Grayson finally said, "Up. We'll fall asleep if we stay around here much longer."

"Would it bother you if I don't ride?" Keelie asked. "My ankle."

"Not at all," Grayson said. "There's not much to do here, though."

"I brought my laptop," she said. "I can entertain myself."

"She looks at porn," Evan said.

"Shut up!" Keelie said.

"I can show you where I keep my collection," Grayson offered with a smile.

"No, thank you," Keelie said. "A person's porn is a private thing. I mean, I've heard."

Grayson cleared his desk for her laptop, and Keelie sighed with contentment when they were all gone and the only noise in the cabin was the crackle of the fire. She looked around at the sturdy furniture, the rustic paneling, the bleached wood floors, and the stone fireplace. Everything about the cabin was masculine, and its good vibe made her like Grayson even more.

She knew some people thought Evan was either all light heart or all drama, but she understood him. He really was a small-town boy who could be satisfied living a quiet life with a good man. No matter what he said about renovating the apartment over the salon, this was where he was going to end up, and she was sure he'd be happy here.

It was funny how that near-accident on the road had led him to a man he could share his life with. If she hadn't broken her ankle, they wouldn't have even been in Coventry. Ivy probably wouldn't have met Ted . . . Evan wouldn't have met Grayson . . . And if Hamlet hadn't gotten sick and needed to go to a vet . . .

She pushed her thoughts aside and opened Destiny's story. As she went back through it, adding things that she and Ivy had talked about, altering other things, and thinking about what she intended to write next, she lost track of time. She finally realized that the words were starting to blur on the screen and glanced at the clock. She'd been working for nearly two hours, and she was yawning nonstop.

"Fresh air," she said.

She layered herself in a sweater, scarf, coat, hat, and gloves before carefully going down the front steps of the cabin. After walking a few minutes, the cold began to penetrate her clothes, so she headed for a barn.

It was much warmer inside. She took off her hat and scarf and walked along the stalls, murmuring soft hellos in response to the nickering of horses as she passed them. She knew from Grayson's conversation at lunch that these were his work horses, not the Arabians that were the heart of his ranch.

She stopped to rub the muzzle of a black mare who extended her head for Keelie's hand.

"Maybe you're not one of the money girls, but you're awfully pretty," Keelie said.

"Keelie?"

She whipped around and found herself staring at Dr. Boone. *Not fair,* she thought, as her heart pounded. "Hi," she said. "How are you?"

"Great. How are you? How's your ankle?"

"Getting better every day."

"I didn't realize you were still in town," he said.

"Oh, no, I went back to Houston after New Year's. Elenore's granddaughters and I are just helping Evan move here this weekend."

"Your friend who's taking over Molly's," Dr. Boone said.

It was crazy how everyone in town always knew more about her than she knew about them, but for some reason, she liked it.

"Elenore should have let us know," he said. "The women of Coventry would probably throw a big party in your honor."

"Yes, I'm losing my hairdresser to them," she said.

"You can't appreciate how tragic that is, because I have really difficult hair."

He reached over and brushed a strand of it back from her face, saying, "It looks fine to me."

"How's Rip?" she asked quickly.

"Great. Actually, you'd probably be a little mad at him these days. He's got it in for a rat that's taken up residence in my foal stalls. How's Hamlet? I assume he had a complete recovery."

"Hamlet's fine," she said. She was about to ask how Jennifer was, then decided it would make him think she equated his daughter with their animals. Instead, she said, "I have a confession to make."

One eyebrow arched and he said, "Yes?"

Her knees felt weak. If he kept looking at her that way . . . Why was he looking at her that way? Maybe she could forget between one moment and the next that he had a wife, but he shouldn't find it that easy.

"I started writing a story, and I stole Rip from you. I didn't even change his name or breed."

"Rip would be honored," Dr. Boone said. "I didn't know you were a writer."

"I didn't either," she said. "But my friend Ivy assures me that I am."

"I'd like to read it sometime. I gave you my card, didn't I? You could e-mail me. Your story, I mean."

"Hmmm," she said. She was finding it hard not to be distracted by his mouth. How had she managed to forget how much it made her want to kiss him?

"Or you could tell me about it," he said, perhaps thinking that her noncommittal answer was a no.

Just say no and get away from him, she thought, and said, "Really? You want to hear about it?"

As his answer, he walked away to get a stool for her

to sit on. He looked even better than when he'd been dressed in scrubs. He was wearing cowboy boots, jeans, and a henley shirt with a dark green wool shirt over it that set off his eyes. She had to stop staring at his eyes; they were deadly.

After he sat across from her, he said, "So tell me this story about Rip."

She loved the way he listened to her, his face still, his eyes never leaving hers. It was like he really heard her, and she found herself telling him more than she'd intended about Destiny and Rip. Sometimes he smiled a little at the things she said.

Don't think of the smile . . . don't look at the eyes . . .

She stood up too quickly and got a head rush, which made her sway a little. He stood, too, and reached out to steady her.

"I . . . um . . ." Her vision swam, because his face seemed awfully close, and then he did it. He kissed her. Her body leaned into his as her mind emptied of everything except the warmth of his lips. The slightly minty taste of his tongue. The way his face scratched against hers. The smell and feel of him. She'd known she hadn't been the only one who felt the attraction. He wanted her, too, enough to dispense with wasting time and . . . *his wife.*

She pulled away and said, "We shouldn't—I don't—" His eyes looked a little too sure of the effect he was having on her, and she was suddenly furious at him. She was not interested in being anyone's other woman, and she wasn't someone who would just fool around in a barn and pretend that his marriage didn't matter. "I have a boyfriend," she heard herself saying before she could stop the words.

"Oh?" he asked. He backed away a step.

"Stephen," she said. "He's in Houston. He's a writer, too."

"He's a lucky man." The emotion had left his face, which was now merely pleasant, like a stranger's, as if he hadn't just kissed her and turned her world inside out. "I guess I should get back to work."

"Yes," she said. "Me, too."

"Will you e-mail Rip's story?" he asked in a tone that made it sound like the entire fate of his happiness rested on it.

"I'll think about it," she said, determined that the kiss that shouldn't have happened would be the last private part of her life she shared with him.

She refused to cry as she walked back to the cabin. She'd been an idiot for allowing herself to think about him. Dream about him. Think about his kisses, which were even better than in her imagination. She wished she'd never met him.

Maybe that wasn't entirely true. He'd taken good care of Hamlet, and his daughter and his dog had inspired Destiny's story. She couldn't regret that. Instead, she wished she'd never seen him again. That his disloyalty to the woman who'd looked at him with such affection at the Early Bird Café hadn't spoiled her illusion about the man he was.

That was the worst part of it. Even if she'd known nothing could happen between them, he'd become a kind of emotional companion to her. She liked thinking about his family history, his beautiful rock house. She liked imagining him helping Jennifer with her homework, or going on long walks with Rip. She liked remembering how strong and sensitive his fingers were when he was taking care of a sick animal.

But that wasn't the real man. The real man was one

who'd kiss another woman even though he was married. The real man was one for whom she'd come up with a lame excuse about a boyfriend that didn't exist.

Why had she lied about Stephen instead of making him tell the truth about his wife?

What the hell is wrong with me, she wondered. *When am I going to start living for myself instead of letting other people tell me who I am? Like Gram. Or being so dependent on my friends that I go into a tailspin when their lives don't include me? Or letting a loser like Rodney make me feel lousy about a job that I love?*

Except . . . she didn't really love it anymore. The only times she felt really happy these days were when she was with her friends or when she was writing. Maybe the reason she lived in some fantasy world about Dr. Boone was because her real life had stopped being a life she liked.

She looked over the cold, flat landscape and remembered something Evan had said once. If she didn't change her life, the universe would do it for her.

"Destiny is in *my* hands," she said with determination.

"I don't understand," Jarvis said, looking across the desk at Keelie.

"I know," she said. "I'm sorry."

"Is it money? Is it something I did? Can we talk it out?"

"It's not you," she said. "I think I want to move back to Georgia. My family's there, and I'm homesick."

"Where are they?" he asked. "Maybe you could try to transfer or—"

"There's no Buy The Book in Columbus," Keelie

said. "I'll work out a notice, but then I'm leaving the company."

"There's nothing I can say to change your mind?" When she shook her head, Jarvis sighed and said, "All right. I'll let Jimmy know."

"Please don't tell anyone in the store yet," she said. "I don't want a big deal made out of it."

"I'll keep it quiet," he promised.

She realized that her entire body was shaking when she walked back on the floor. She began straightening shelves so she'd look busy if any of the employees passed by her. She didn't want them to see the tears that threatened to spill over.

She hadn't told anyone except Jarvis her decision to leave Buy The Book. She didn't have a rational explanation for her friends or her family. She just knew that after spending time in Coventry, being in Houston made her feel like she was moving underwater. Weightless but sluggish. Trapped in some murky, unfamiliar world.

She'd just gotten her composure back when she was paged to the phone. She answered in a cheery voice that was the opposite of her real mood.

"Keelie, it's Jimmy. What's going on?"

"Jarvis already called you?" she asked.

"Of course. He's very upset. He feels like you haven't given him a chance."

"I'm not leaving because of Jarvis," she said. "Jarvis is great. So is Salli. The store hasn't been running this well since Joyce left."

"So why are you leaving? Jarvis said you're moving?"

"I'm thinking about it."

"Is this because I didn't promote you to manager?" Jimmy asked. "I have to follow protocol, Keelie, but if you're willing to relocate, I'm sure there'll be a store manager position opening up in the near future."

"It's not that," Keelie said. "Really, Jimmy, I'm not mad at you or anyone here. I think it's just time for a change. For me, I mean. Maybe it has been for a long time, but I felt like I was needed here. Which is silly. The store will be fine without me."

"I have to talk to Corporate," Jimmy said. "You're still under workers' comp for your injury, and you'll need rehab—"

"I'm not going to sue the company," Keelie said. "You're not worried about that, are you?"

"I want to make sure the situation is resolved to everyone's satisfaction," Jimmy said.

"Okay. Just let me know what I need to do," Keelie said. She hadn't thought about the cost of rehab. There was no way she could afford a lot of medical bills. She hadn't looked for another job or considered the benefits she was giving up. She'd resigned impulsively, without worrying about the consequences. Sometimes she wondered if she was really her mother's daughter.

When she got home that night, she sat in the dark and cried. She felt like she couldn't call Ivy or Holly, who would ask a lot of questions that had no answers. She was afraid to call her mother, who would think she'd lost her mind and was behaving irresponsibly. And if she talked to Evan, she'd probably spill the whole story about Dr. Boone. Evan was too perceptive any time she tried to keep secrets from him.

She took a shower and played with Hamlet when he woke up. Then she fed him, gave him a new dog biscuit for his teeth, and stared unseeingly at the television. Finally she picked up the phone and called Stephen.

"You know how sometimes you do something that seems really stupid because you just have to?" she asked.

"It's a Cannon family trait," he said.

"Can you come over? I need someone to talk to."

"Sure. Are you hungry? Or are you on a hunger strike?"

"I was going to make a grilled cheese sandwich and tomato soup," she said.

"Do you have enough to feed an impoverished graduate student?"

"Definitely."

"I'm on my way."

She had the food ready by the time he got there, and he ruffled her hair before sitting at the table. "Talk to me."

"For starters, did you know you're my boyfriend?"

"It happens in even the best families," he said.

She told him everything about Michael Boone, from their first meeting to their last. Stephen didn't react in horror. He barely reacted at all, just hearing her out.

"How do you know he's not divorced?" he asked when she was finally quiet.

"I asked someone. He's not divorced. And I saw them together. They didn't act like a couple in trouble. They had that comfortable look."

Stephen frowned and said, "Does that add up for you? That a man who'd cheat on his wife would look all cozy with her?"

"Yes. I have a friend who was in a similar situation. The man wasn't married, but he was seeing my friend and another woman at the same time, and neither knew about the other. In fact, he was engaged to both of them. He even gave them identical rings."

"God, men suck," Stephen said.

"I know. Anyway, I never would have guessed my friend's ex was doing that. They seemed like the perfect couple. Maybe that's part of a cheater's act. It's how they get away with so much, because they never let their guard down."

Stephen frowned as he silently stared at her. Then he shook his head, picked up their dishes, and took them to the sink. Finally he turned around and said, "I don't know this guy at all. But there's something about you . . . Don't take this the wrong way, okay?"

"What?" she asked.

"You're the kind of woman a man feels like he can introduce to his family," Stephen said and looked embarrassed. "What I mean is, you're not somebody I'd just try to nail. You're nice. You have this sweetness about you."

"Everybody's buddy," Keelie said. "I'm not offended. I've been through the 'you're a great friend' routine with guys when I wanted to be seen as someone sexier. I just can't pull off sexy."

"I didn't say you're not sexy," he said. "It's just hard for me to believe that a man would think you'd get involved in some sleazy affair. Okay, some men do suck. But you don't seem like the type who's easily fooled."

"I didn't know about my friend's ex," she reminded him.

"That's different. You didn't have anything on the line. You weren't interested in him; she was."

"I don't know," Keelie said. "I've been told that I only see the best in people. Maybe I'm a poor judge of character."

Stephen shook his head like he didn't believe her, but

he only said, "What was the stupid thing you did because you had to? Kissing the cheating horse doctor?"

"No. Today, I gave my notice at work. I have no other job lined up. I don't have any idea what to do next. It was impulsive. Stupid, like I said. Plus I don't know if workers' comp will still cover my medical bills."

"Dude. That was a little rash," Stephen said. "Can you change your mind?"

"I don't want to change my mind. I want to change my life. Drastically. And I know a way you can help me."

"I don't want to pretend to be your boyfriend in front of the horse doctor," Stephen said.

Keelie rolled her eyes and said, "This isn't ninth grade. I'm talking about my apartment. You don't like where you're living. You're going to be helping Mrs. Atwell around here this spring. If I leave, you should move in here." When he started to say something, she held up her hand. "Don't be like me and make a rash decision. You like the apartment, and the rent is reasonable. Everything's included except my phone. There's a bus stop at the corner. At least I assume you use Metro and not your bike to get to campus."

"Yeah."

"I'd feel better about going if I could find the Atwells a good tenant. It's not like they need the rent money, but I feel an obligation to them. They've been good to me."

"How much is the rent?" he asked.

When she told him, he said, "That's about what I pay even with a roommate. Are you sure you want to do this? You've got a sweet setup here."

"I'm pretty sure," she said.

"You're making me nervous. You're quitting your job

and giving up your apartment without a definite plan. It makes me wonder if . . . you know . . ."

"No," she said, bewildered. "What?"

"If you're planning to put rocks in your pockets and wade into Buffalo Bayou."

"In the first place, I would never get in water that dirty looking. In the second place, such acts of desperation are limited to tortured, brilliant writers. I haven't suffered for my art. However, if the day comes that I decide to end it all, I'll leave you my DVD player."

"In that case, do what you have to." He grinned. "You seem a little tortured. And I have no proof that you're not a brilliant writer. You know one of the best ways to judge your own writing? Let someone read it out loud to you. I've been told I have an excellent reading voice."

"It would be easier to sleep with you than let you read my story," Keelie said.

"Is that some kind of weird compliment? It doesn't sound like a compliment."

"I don't have to compliment you," she said. "We're family."

Chapter 15

Keelie had promised to spend her day off working on Destiny's story. After cleaning Hamlet's cage, she sat down at the laptop with her second cup of coffee and stared blankly at the screen. She'd finished all the revisions that she and Ivy had talked about, but she wasn't sure what to write next.

"See?" she asked Hamlet, who'd gone back to sleep under his bedding. "If Destiny were older and I was writing a romance, it would be time for the love interest to show up. I wonder if he'd be the Rake, Remnant, Rulebreaker, or Romantic? I wonder why I got a hamster who sleeps all day and never answers me?"

She tapped her fingers on the keyboard, then realized she needed to cut her nails, which she always kept short. They were too long.

Finding her fingernail clippers took half an hour; cutting her nails took two minutes. She still didn't know what to write next, but while looking for the clippers, she'd noticed her bathroom could benefit from a good cleaning.

That used up another half hour, and she figured while

she had all the cleaning stuff out, she might as well do her kitchen, including the refrigerator, a job she always hated. In fact, there were several jobs she hated, so she balanced her checkbook, wrote a check for her Nordstrom bill, dusted, and vacuumed. Then she decided to find space on her bookshelves for the pile of books she'd bought and never had time to read.

She was reading the back cover of one of the books and trying to figure out why she'd bought it when someone knocked on her door.

"Saved!" she said. "From a bad book and the reproachful hum of an untouched computer."

She opened the door expecting to see Mrs. Atwell and squealed with surprise when she was enveloped in her mother's arms. Misty, standing behind Polly with a smirk on her face, said, "I hope we didn't get you out of bed."

"I've been up forever," Keelie said. "What are you two doing here? Why didn't you call me and—"

"Warn you?" Polly asked, standing back to look at her daughter. "Your clothes are hanging off of you. Are you eating?"

"Aren't you supposed to be on crutches?" Misty asked.

"We went to the Galleria from the rental car place and found out you were off today. But we passed this great restaurant called EatZi's that had takeout food—"

"Which is getting heavy," Misty said, nodding at the bag she held. "Are you going to let us in?"

"Stop!" Keelie said, covering her ears. "Yes, come in. I'm thrilled to see you!"

They came inside. Misty put down the bag and hugged Keelie, then she joined their mother for a quick inspection of the apartment. When they came back,

Keelie was unloading more food than they could possibly eat. It was one of her mother's few inefficiencies that she always bought too much.

"Everything's so clean," Misty said. "Did someone at the bookstore call you and tell you we were on our way?"

"Hush," Polly said. "She was always neater than you are. Should you be on your feet, Keelie?"

"The cast isn't much more than a formality now," Keelie assured her mother. "I can't believe you're both here."

"Don't worry. We'll get a room somewhere—"

"No, you won't," Keelie said. "You two can share the bed, and I'll sleep on the sofa. It'll be like a slumber party."

While they ate, they gave her all the news from home. Gram had put her house up for sale and was in the process of moving into the major's house. Matt and Huck were on a camping trip with the kids. And Wonderful Wife was doing its usual booming business.

"I can't believe you're off today," Misty said. "We were going to shop all day at the Galleria, then go out to dinner and drive you home tonight."

"We can still shop," Keelie said. She saw her mother's doubtful look and said, "I'm completely mobile. Slower than usual, but I'm not in pain."

"I do need to take you shopping," Polly said. "How much weight have you lost? You need new clothes."

"Only ten pounds," Keelie said. "I'm just in my baggy clothes."

"Get changed and let's go," Misty ordered. "I've got two new credit cards with zero balances, and I'm ready to do some damage."

"Y'all can bring in your stuff from the car while I get ready," Keelie said. "I mean it. You're staying with me."

Keelie slept like a rock that night after hours of shopping and talking. While she got ready for work the next morning, Misty stayed in bed, covers over her head, and her mother made breakfast.

"I don't really have time to eat," Keelie said, although she gratefully sipped the coffee Polly handed her.

"You have plenty of time," Polly said. "It only takes a few minutes to drive to the Galleria."

"Yeah, but the bus—"

"I'm taking you," Polly said. "Now eat. You can't afford to lose any more weight."

"Do I look bad?" Keelie asked as she obediently sat down and picked up her fork.

"I think you look wonderful," Polly said. "I love the way your hair is cut. I wonder if I could get Evan to do something with mine?"

"You could if you wanted to drive several hours to his new salon," Keelie said.

"That's right. I forgot that he moved. Misty and I have directions to all the places we want to explore today while you're at work. But do you think we'll get a chance to meet Holly and Ivy? I've heard so much about the Johnsons that I feel like I know them."

"I'll call them and see," Keelie promised. "What great Houston sites are you planning to visit?"

"Highland Village," Misty called from the bedroom. "Did you see all those stores?"

Polly rolled her eyes at Keelie and said, "I want to see more of the houses in River Oaks, and also West U and the Heights. Of course, Major Byrnes suggested we visit the golf courses."

Keelie giggled and said, "I'll make a list of some of my favorite places, and you can look them up online to get directions." She pointed at the laptop and added, "Since you made that possible. It's always connected, because I have access through the Atwells' wireless service."

"I wish you didn't have to work today," Polly said.

"We'll talk about that later," Misty yelled cryptically.

When Keelie raised her eyebrows at her mother, Polly just shrugged and said, "More toast?"

"If you keep pushing food, I won't be able to wear any of those clothes you bought me yesterday."

When she went into work, she felt more upbeat than usual. She loved wearing new clothes, but mostly she loved knowing that she had only a few more days at Buy The Book. Even though she still had no idea what she was going to do, having the powerhouses from Wonderful Wife in Houston fortified her. If anyone could help her organize her life, it was those two.

By the time they picked her up that evening, Keelie wondered if Jarvis was rethinking letting her work out a notice. She'd been on and off the phone most of the day coordinating dinner with her family and Ivy's. Mrs. Johnson had insisted that they come to her house.

Within ten minutes of their arrival, it was as if they'd all known one another forever. Misty scurried off to the den to play video games with Holly's sons, while Polly tossed a salad and chatted with Mrs. Johnson in the kitchen and told the others to stay out of their way.

"Your mother and sister are like a whirlwind," Ivy said. "I'm dizzy."

"You should have grown up with them," Keelie said.

"I think there were about three years after Misty started talking that I never got a word in edgewise."

"You're definitely the quiet one," Holly agreed. "In our family, that was Scotty. He left me totally unprepared to deal with my noisy boys."

True to her reputation, Misty chattered all the way through dinner. Holly's sons had apparently decided she was okay for a girl, and they were sillier than usual. After they ate, Holly banished them back to the den while the rest of them had coffee and dessert. Keelie loved having all her favorite women together, but she was sad that her favorite man wasn't with them. She'd always wanted her family to meet Evan.

One day, she reminded herself, sitting quietly as the rest of them talked. Holly told them about her move to Scotland. Mrs. Johnson showed off pictures of her new grandbaby and talked about her excitement that Scotty and Carla were moving back from Hawaii. When there was a lull in the conversation, Keelie intercepted a look between her mother and sister, as if they were telepathically coming to some decision. Before either of them could speak, Ivy broke the silence.

"I guess now is as good a time as any to share my news," she said, giving Holly a nervous glance. When Holly nodded supportively, Ivy said, "I found a job."

"With a publishing house in New York?" Keelie asked, bracing herself for the news that Ivy was leaving, too.

"Not exactly," Ivy said. When she saw Keelie's hopeful expression, she went on. "It is in New York. At an agency. I'll be negotiating foreign rights for several literary estates."

"Congratulations," Keelie said with a puzzled look. "So you'll be selling the work of dead writers?"

"That about sums it up. Ted passed my résumé to someone he knows, who forwarded it to someone else. They liked my background in detailed technical and legal writing. So you see," she said, looking at Keelie, "if you lay the groundwork, eventually it can pay off if you meet someone who's in a position to help you."

Keelie got the message. If she kept working on her novel, Ivy might be able to get her manuscript read. "When do you start working there?"

"If all goes as planned, within a couple of weeks."

"Yikes! You'll be leaving the same time Holly does. I don't know whether to kiss Ted or kick him."

"Ted," Misty said, sounding bemused. Then her face cleared. "Isn't that the guy who spent the night with you, Keelie?"

Mrs. Johnson's cup clattered against its saucer, and Ivy and Keelie giggled.

"It's not how it sounds," Keelie said. "He stayed at my apartment the night I broke my ankle. On the *sofa*."

"I thought you broke your ankle on a ladder," Misty said.

"Stop playing dumb. Don't pay any attention to her," Keelie said soothingly to Mrs. Johnson. "She's just kidding around."

"I know," Mrs. Johnson said. "I've met Ted. He seems like a fine young man."

"Oh," Polly said. "Is Ted your boyfriend, Ivy?"

"He appears to think so," Ivy said.

"Never tell them you approve of their boyfriends," Polly warned. "That's the kiss of death."

"Don't I know it," Mrs. Johnson said. "You should have seen some of the men Ivy brought home when she was in college." She looked at her daughter and smiled grimly, saying, "Remember Jason?"

"You had a Jason, too?" Keelie asked.

"Everyone's had a Jason," Ivy said. "I'd like to forget mine, please."

"I never had a Jason," Misty said.

"Me, either," Holly said.

"I want to know about your Jason," Keelie demanded.

"No!" Ivy said.

Holly laughed and said, "They had one date. They went to dinner, and she got a blinding headache from the drinks he ordered, so he took her home. She went into the bathroom to take aspirin, and when she came out, he was waiting for her under the sheets—"

"Without a stitch of clothes!" Mrs. Johnson and Holly said simultaneously, obviously mimicking Ivy.

"Ugh," Ivy said. "He had hair on his shoulders. I thought I'd never get rid of him. He wasn't even embarrassed at how horrified I was."

"I can't believe you never told me that story," Keelie said. "No wonder you don't like Jasons."

"I took enough crap about it from my roommates," Ivy said. "It's one of those things I want to forget."

Polly nodded and said, "The worst date I ever had was about a year after my first husband—the girls' father—died. I wasn't ready to date, but my mother set it up."

"Uh-oh," Misty said, then added, "Gram doesn't really get Mom."

"He was a podiatrist. We went out to dinner, and he spent the whole meal describing foot diseases to me. I haven't been able to eat shrimp scampi since."

Everybody laughed except Keelie, who said, "Thanks for that. Now you've ruined it for me."

"I'm glad I married Matt and skipped that whole

single girl thing," Misty said, and Holly nodded. "What was your worst date, Keelie?"

Keelie looked at Ivy and Holly, and all of them said, "Trent Carpenter."

"He took me to the rodeo," Keelie added.

"That doesn't sound like something you'd enjoy," Polly said. "Keelie's very softhearted about animals."

"Except my poor Fernando," Holly said. "He's a cat."

"No, she was never much of a cat person," Polly agreed.

"The Houston rodeo has tons of great performers," Keelie said. "We were supposed to see Destiny's Child. But Trent wanted to watch bull riding, which was the last event before the concert. Except he was a big wienie, and the first time he saw a bull toss a cowboy, Trent tossed his cookies. On me."

"Ew," Misty said.

"I didn't get to see Beyoncé," Keelie said sadly. "I don't know why it is that wherever I go, people are always throwing up. Maybe I'm the reason people bring their children to Buy The Book to vomit. I'm cursed."

She caught yet another look between her mother and Misty, but before she could say anything, Misty said, "May I help you with the dishes, Mrs. Johnson?"

"Oh, no, you're my guest—"

"We'll all help," Keelie said, getting to her feet. "Grandmothers get to relax."

"How do you really feel about Ivy's news?" Polly asked later as the three of them sprawled over Keelie's bed.

"I wasn't exactly surprised. I told you she was looking for a new job and that she might have to go somewhere else. I'm happy for her. Because of the job and Ted. I don't want her to move. That part I hate. Especially since Evan moved and Holly will be away, too. My life is going to change. A lot. But Ivy's had a rough time, and Ted's a good person. I'm glad she'll know someone in New York, and if things work out between them . . . Who am I to whine about true love?"

"Just think. She'd never have met him except for you," Misty said. "Isn't it weird how things turn out?"

"Isn't it weird that for more than twenty-four hours, you two have been exchanging meaningful glances, and I don't know why?" Keelie asked.

Her mother took a deep breath—Keelie was sure she was counting—and said, "I've been a little worried about you."

"I told you. My ankle's healing. I'll make new friends. Besides, Holly will be back in a year, and Evan's not that far away."

"It isn't that," Polly said and sat up. "You haven't seemed happy for a long time. All your friends are moving forward, doing exciting new things, and you appear to be stuck somewhere you don't want to be. I thought now that you have a new manager, you'd be happier at Buy The Book. But you've barely mentioned the store since we got here. I remember when you used to talk about everything that was going on there. Good and bad."

"Actually, I have a little confession to make," Keelie said in a small voice. "The reason I haven't been talking about the store is because I gave them my notice."

Misty sat up, looking like she might explode with excitement, but Polly gave her a warning glance and said, "What are your plans?"

"I don't know," Keelie admitted. "I know it sounds crazy to quit a job when I have nothing else lined up. I was thinking maybe I'd go back to Columbus and try to figure things out. If you and Huck wouldn't mind me staying with you for a while."

"Of course not," Polly said, but she looked thoughtful.

"You could always stay at Gram's until her house sells," Misty said.

"I don't think so," Keelie said. "If I had to live next door to Gram, my next residence would probably have bars on the windows and a Nurse Ratched."

"A what?" Misty asked.

"A character in a movie," Polly said. "Before your time. You know I don't mind if you come home, Keelie. In fact, I'd love it. But I'd rather hear about what *you* want."

"Please don't give me the Wonderful Wife treatment," Keelie begged. "I don't want to be your client."

"How would you like to be our employee?" Misty asked, and Polly gave her a sharp look.

"Is that what the big secret is? Y'all want me to open a Wonderful Wife franchise? That's really generous, but I'm not like you two. I don't want to run a business. In fact, I think I'd suck at it."

"Frankly, so do I," Polly said. She smiled at Keelie's expression. "I'm only agreeing with you. It's not because I don't think you're capable. I just know it doesn't appeal to you, and it's so demanding and crazy that you have to love it to do it. Misty and I love it."

Keelie went over to Hamlet's cage and pulled him out, hoping he'd be a good distraction. She wasn't sure how much she wanted to tell them or where the conversation was going. Everyone was quiet for a moment as they watched Hamlet run back and forth between Keelie's hands.

Polly's voice was gentle when she said, "It always strikes me that people are afraid to express what they really want. When you ask them if they could do anything, what would it be, they'll give you some grand answer. Like everything they'd do if they won the lottery or were suddenly rich. Or how they'd like to find a cure for cancer or AIDS. Big dreams are important, but most of our lives play out on a smaller scale. Even so, we're not small people, and the things we want matter. What would make you love to get up in the morning?"

"I've started a novel," Keelie said after a long pause. "That makes me happy. I don't mind working, but I'd rather have a job that wasn't so many hours or wouldn't take so much energy that I'm too tired to write." She looked around and laughed. "I'm sure it doesn't seem like my life could get much simpler than this. I don't have a mortgage or a car. I'm not in a relationship. Not that I'd mind having a man in my life, but I haven't met the right one."

"Too bad you and Ted didn't hit it off," Misty said. "That seems to have helped Ivy get out of her rut."

"I think what Ivy's doing is exciting, but a city like New York would eat me alive. I'm more envious of Evan. Visiting Coventry made me realize that urban life has worn me down. I used to love all the things I could do here. Having so many choices. But I get tired of the traffic and the sheer number of people. I get tired of hearing news stories about crime. I'd like to be somewhere prettier, with changing seasons. Maybe I wouldn't like it forever, but there was something about Coventry. I could see myself living in a little place close to Evan. Taking walks in the country where Ivy's grandmother lives. Knowing my neighbors. Having the people who own the stores in town know me by name."

She looked up from Hamlet and met Misty's eyes. Misty grinned at her, and Keelie couldn't stop herself from smiling back. Misty still looked so much like the little girl who'd plagued Keelie's childhood and teenage years.

"You sound like you're apologizing," Misty said. "What's stopping you from moving to Coventry?"

"I have to make a living. One of Granny's friends suggested that I teach, but I don't want to. Talk about putting in long hours. I doubt there are many choices in Coventry other than retail jobs in the newer section of town. Retail's what I'm trying to get away from. But I have to work. Even if I get a book published one day, I don't think many authors make a lot of money."

"You never know," Polly said. "It's time for me to make my pitch about putting you on the Wonderful Wife payroll." She held up a hand when Keelie started to protest. "I'm not talking about a franchise. Or paying you to do nothing. Misty and I came here to make you a proposition, even before we knew you'd quit your job. It's not charity. It's part of the reason we got you the laptop. We need your skills."

"What skills?"

"Your writing skills. Your organizational skills, because you have the gene whether or not you admit it. It's a Wonderful Wife is in eight cities now, and every office has its own way of doing things. We have an outdated operations manual and mission statement. We need someone who can take boxes of material and develop a more realistic and workable set of operating procedures. One book of standards that apply to everybody, then individual procedures for each office."

"The best part for you," Misty said, "is that you can work out of a home office anywhere. As long as you have access to the Internet, a phone, and a fax machine, it doesn't matter where you are. You can set your own hours."

"Although I'd want you to give us at least thirty-five hours a week," Polly said. "So you can be eligible for benefits." She tapped Keelie's cast. "I'm sure you've seen some of your bills and realize that you need health insurance."

"Oh, yeah," Keelie said.

"Like Misty said, you can figure out a schedule that works for you. One that allows you the energy and time to write."

"I want to read your novel," Misty said. "What's it about?"

Keelie felt like they'd lifted a huge weight off of her. Not just because of the job offer, but because they listened with interest as she talked about Destiny's story. It felt good to be taken seriously and to feel like they believed in her.

"I think it sounds wonderful," Polly finally said. "I can't wait to read it. So what do you think? About the job?"

"It sounds great, if you think I can do it."

"Of course you can do it. If you want to travel to any of the offices, meet the staffs, interview them, we'll arrange all that. Or you can do it by phone and e-mail." Her mother smiled and added, "The best part for Misty is that we'll get to do more shopping while we're in Houston. You need a desktop computer in addition to the laptop. A cell phone. The fax machine. A printer. Desk. Work table. Filing cabinets. It can be daunting to set up a home-based office, but we've done it for so many clients that we're experts now."

"How long do you think this project will take?" Keelie asked.

"Realistically, about a year."

"And then what?"

"That depends on you. We pay an agency to develop our publicity materials, handle our mailings. You could do that as easily as they could. Or if it doesn't interest you, I know plenty of business people who contract out their documentation. They could hire you—through us, naturally, so you'd still be on our payroll with benefits. But remember: Dream big. Maybe your novel *will* be a bestseller, and you won't need us anymore."

"I'll always need you," Keelie said, hugging her mother. "It never occurred to me that I could fit myself into the family business."

"The sad thing is, it didn't occur to me, either," Polly said. "One night I was complaining to Huck about how daunting this task was and how hard it would be to find someone I trusted to do it. I said I wished I had another Misty. She's too good at what she does for me to load her down with this project. The next night, you and I talked on the phone, and I told Huck how miserable you seemed. He pointed out that there was only one Misty, but I also had a Keelie." She shook her head. "So much for women helping women."

"You and Misty *are* helping me," Keelie said. "Huck's the power behind the throne."

"Don't tell Gram that," Misty said. "Half the time she belittles what we do, and the rest of the time, she takes credit for Mom's success."

"Well, I'm no Martha Stewart, but I do all right," Polly said.

"Evan always tells me to keep you happy because you'll make me rich some day," Keelie said.

"I don't know about rich, but I can help you keep my grand-rodent well-fed," Polly said as Hamlet crossed the bed toward Misty's outstretched hand.

Chapter 16

Keelie submerged herself in the bathtub and leaned back until her chin was just above the water's surface. The bathroom's only illumination came from the glow of twenty tealight candles in the cylindrical iron holder that Holly had given her for Christmas. Although Keelie generally preferred to take showers, being able to bury both legs in water in the oval spa tub was an indulgence she hadn't been able to resist. She pulled her feet out of the water and stared at her legs side by side. Even in the dim light, her skin still looked icky where the cast had been, and one leg was smaller than the other. But being able to dispense with a cast, splint, or orthopedic boot was as good an omen as any for her new life, as was the comfort she felt in her new bathroom.

She watched the light flickering on the tile walls, peered over the edge of the tub at the stained concrete floor, then turned her head to look at the windows by the tub. She had the blinds down, but she'd already figured out that in the summer, when the oaks were full of leaves, they'd provide privacy and make her feel like she was taking a bath in a tree house. She couldn't wait.

She closed her eyes. The past few days hadn't left her much time for reflection, but she shouldn't have been surprised. Once her mother had a goal, nothing slowed down until everything was done. But Keelie had never imagined how many changes would be set in motion once she told her mother that she'd quit her job.

Polly negotiated with Buy The Book's corporate office to ensure that the remainder of Keelie's medical care, including the rehab she'd need, would be paid for. Keelie knew that had gone easier than it could have because Ted, as the head of Loss Prevention, was the one who made the final recommendation on her case. It seemed ironic that the man who'd suspiciously eyed her Kate Spade purse when she met him would turn out to be her biggest ally. Her mother's more practical and jaded view was that Buy The Book was afraid of a lawsuit, but Ted knew Keelie wouldn't sue the company. Even if Ted was partially motivated by his blossoming relationship with Ivy, it worked in Keelie's favor and took away some of her financial anxiety.

Her mother had stayed behind when Misty returned to Columbus. Although Polly intended to set up Keelie's home office in her apartment behind the Atwell house, once Ivy found out that Keelie wanted to move to Coventry, everything began falling into place with dizzying speed. A couple living at Rourke Apartments had just moved into a home they'd bought in New Coventry, and Granny offered Keelie their apartment. It was two bedrooms and unfurnished, but Ivy wanted to sell most of her furniture before she moved to New York. She let Keelie and Evan have first pick of anything they wanted. Keelie bought all of Ivy's bedroom furniture, and Evan took her living room furniture and a kitchen table.

Her mother hired movers to pack everything, and on the day Keelie moved out, still pinching herself to believe it was all happening, Stephen moved in. Mrs. Atwell wasn't charging him rent until his lease was up at his old apartment. She said he could work it off with his landscaping, but Keelie knew better. In the long run, the Atwells would probably pay Stephen for whatever work he did. It was gratifying to know that she'd helped the three of them find one another.

The hardest part of leaving had been saying good-bye to everyone from Buy The Book. They'd gotten together for an after-work dinner to wish her luck. Tamala, who looked like she might give birth any minute, had even come with her husband to say good-bye. Everyone laughed over old times, compared horror stories, and promised to stay in touch. Maybe they would for a while, but the slow slipping away of her college friends had prepared Keelie for the inevitable day that Buy The Book would be just an entry on her résumé. However, she would have some tangible reminders of those friendships, thanks to the gift certificates they'd given her to stores in New Coventry, where she could buy things for her new home. But her bookstore friends would move on, until the day came when there'd be no one left at the store who remembered her or their little mascot Hamlet. It made her sad, but she had too many good things happening in her life to dwell on it.

She pulled her feet out of the water and smiled at her legs again. Her doctor had been pleased with how her ankle had healed. She'd been secretly worried that all the pillows, beanbags, ice, careful showers, and sporadic rest had been negated by the way she'd never stayed as inactive as she'd been ordered to. Fortunately, she must be a fast healer. She made a vow to follow orders once she started rehab. And walking between her apartment and Evan's, and all around her new hometown, should also help her leg get back to normal.

Her new hometown . . . She again looked around the bathroom with a sigh of satisfaction. Like the rest of her apartment, everything was clean and packed away. After her mother finished setting up Keelie's office in the second bedroom, she went back to Georgia. Now Keelie just had to wait for the boxes of Wonderful Wife materials to begin arriving so she could start her new job. In the meantime, she had Destiny's story to keep her busy. And she and Evan would be making one more trip to Houston to see Holly and Ivy off on their new lives; then they'd come home to Coventry.

After she finished her bath, Keelie put on socks and a warm robe and wandered through her new apartment. She ran her hands over the oak bedroom furniture, trying to get used to the fact that it was hers and not Ivy's. Since she'd moved up from a double bed to a queen size, her mother had bought all new bedding. Keelie's only request had been that her mother make it homey, maybe with a quilt instead of a comforter. Her mother had gone wild at January white sales, buying her four sets of Ralph Lauren sheets, and a beautiful Nautica quilt set with shams and a bed skirt. Keelie loved the blues, grays, and pinks of the quilt. It all managed to look inviting without being overly feminine.

She blocked out an image of Michael Boone lying on the quilt, stopped to say hello to Hamlet, then continued her tour. The bathroom was the only room that had been updated in the 1950s-era apartment, but Keelie didn't mind. The kitchen cabinets were aluminum covered by several layers of paint, the most recent being white. Evan thought she should strip them down to the

aluminum and get new stainless steel appliances to re-
place the old white stove and refrigerator, but Keelie
liked the dated look of the kitchen. She'd decided to use
her gift certificates to buy reproduction retro appliances like a toaster, blender, and coffeemaker. She'd
also held off getting a table because she wanted to find
a chrome and Formica dinette set.

Her mother had already bought her new cookware
after Keelie vowed that cooking would be part of her
new life. She would have to adjust to not having every
kind of takeout available, but she could always get food
from Lady's Ryde Restaurant or the Early Bird Café.
She wouldn't starve even if it took her a while to get
more proficient in the kitchen.

She grinned at the package she'd received that day
from Gram. The enclosed note said,

If you can read, you can cook.

Accompanying the note was *The Martha Stewart
Cookbook: Collected Recipes for Every Day* and *The
Martha Stewart Living Cookbook.* If Keelie could figure
out what pistachio gelato was or could manage a clam-
bake for a crowd, she might win Gram's approval yet.

The kitchen and dining and living areas were all one
big room, and Granny had loaned Keelie furniture until
she could afford to buy her own, including an eggplant
leather sofa, the Windsor rocker from the Storey library,
and a coffee table.

A couple of inexpensive rugs provided warmth and
color against the pine floors, and Keelie looked around
the room, trying to decide what style of lamps she
wanted. Then she reminded herself that she could look

at pictures online, so she walked into her new office, her favorite room in the new apartment.

One entire wall contained oak bookcases. The boxes of books were the only thing they'd left for her to unpack, because everyone had a unique system for arranging a personal library. Even though there was more space for books than she'd ever had before, Keelie glanced at the still-taped boxes and knew it wouldn't be long before the shelves were full. The same would be true of the drawers in the oak filing cabinets. Right now, she was only using one for her personal papers, but all those empty drawers would make organizing her Wonderful Wife project much easier.

An oak credenza held a fax machine and a printer. Her new computer was concealed inside a special compartment of the desk, with only the flat-screen monitor in sight. And her laptop was also up and running. Her mother had contracted a consultant through one of New Coventry's computer stores to set up Keelie's wireless network, so both computers shared files and accessed the printer. If anything went wrong with her system, she had his card—the first one in the special binder her mother had given her for business cards.

"I finally feel like a grown-up," Keelie said, looking around with pleasure. In time, she'd choose artwork for the walls, but even without all the finishing touches, her new apartment felt like home.

She sat down at her desk, the drawers of which were fully loaded with all the supplies she could possibly need, and began doing online searches of lamps. Before she knew it, over an hour had passed, and she had to get ready because her friends would be over soon. Ivy was in town, and she, Evan, and Grayson were taking Keelie to dinner.

By the time they arrived, Keelie was dressed, made up, and still trying to torment her hair into submission. Evan rolled his eyes, dragged her to the bathroom, and in less than five minutes had done something wondrous that she couldn't have achieved in two hours.

"I don't get it," she said. "You're using my brushes and combs and my hair products, so why can't I manage this?"

"Do not question the ways of the hair god," Evan said. "Merely worship me."

"My hair followed you to Coventry," Keelie said. "But you can forget the worship part. Remember, I've seen you at your worst."

"I have no worst," Evan insisted, giving her hair one last spritz and declaring her done.

They joined the others, and Keelie sat on the sofa to put on her socks and boots. But almost as soon as she stood, she sat back down and said, "The boots are a mistake. I guess my ankle's swollen." When Grayson knelt in front of her to remove the boots, she grinned and said, "Speaking of worship, this is the way a man should be. On his knees."

"Don't I know it," Evan said, opening her refrigerator and shaking his head. "I wish your mother had stocked me up before she left town. This is definitely a mom refrigerator."

"It's the same way inside the cabinets," Keelie said as she tied her shoelaces. "She couldn't believe how little I had in my old apartment."

"Who needed groceries when we had Niko Niko's? Barnaby's? Crostini?" Evan asked.

"Baba Yega," Keelie said dreamily. "Jalapeños. Café Adobe. Carrabba's."

"Churrascos. Vincent's. Ruggles Grill," Ivy said.

"Did you people do anything in Houston other than eat?" Grayson asked. "Evan always talks about the restaurants there like they're shrines on a pilgrimage."

"My collection of menus takes up a drawer in my desk," Ivy said. "The only thing I ever cooked was an occasional frozen pizza or baked potato."

"Why would you cook a baked potato when you could get one loaded from Jason's Deli?" Evan asked.

"Or potato pancakes from Katz's Deli," Keelie said.

"Or a potato knish from Kenny and Ziggy's Deli," Evan said.

"I'm starving," Ivy said. "Where are we going?"

Grayson told them about a restaurant outside of town called Broadgate Tavern, which he said was fashioned after a British pub.

"We have a place like that in Montrose," Evan said. "The Black Lab."

"The food's not the best," Grayson warned. "Broadgate's appeal is its atmosphere."

Evan was right; the tavern reminded Keelie of the Black Lab. The wooden tables and chairs were scarred and rustic. The ceiling had exposed beams, and portraits of several British monarchs hung on the walls. The entire back wall of the dining room was glass, and beyond it, Keelie could see a bar with pool tables, dart boards, and a couple of game tables where people appeared to be playing chess or checkers. There weren't many people dining, but the games room looked full and lively.

She chose a chair facing the glass wall so she could people watch, then found that she had more fun watching Evan and Grayson. Anyone who walked in or out spoke to Grayson, and he invariably introduced them to his dinner guests. It amused Keelie to see how Evan stayed on his best behavior.

"You're a little like one of these kings hanging on the wall," she told Grayson. "Coventry royalty."

"You don't know how exhausting it can be when your mother is queen," Grayson said. "Charles and I chat about it all the time."

"So is Evan your blushing Diana or your secret Camilla?" Ivy asked.

"Neither," Evan said. "I'm the prince consort, and I expect a little more respect from you two now."

"Seriously," Keelie said, "do people in Coventry know you're gay, Grayson?"

"I never hid it," Grayson said. "That was one of the reasons I was banished from the kingdom until after my father died."

His tone was light, but Keelie suspected there was a lot of pain underlying those words, and she let the subject die. It was enough for her to know that, Ivy's joke notwithstanding, Evan wasn't going to be Grayson's dirty little secret. It wasn't a role that would suit him, and she knew that having to live again the way he had when he was growing up in Edna would kill Evan's soul.

While the others talked, she thought about a conversation she'd had with her mother before she went back to Georgia. Polly had warned her that she might suffer culture shock as she adjusted to small-town life.

"I know," Keelie said. "You probably think I'm being typically Keelie and not seeing things the way they really are. I'll try to remember that the world is not always a shiny, happy place."

"But Keelie, for you, it is," Polly answered. "You expect the best from people, and that's why you so often get it.

But as charming as Coventry is, there will be people who think your business—and Evan's—is their business. I wouldn't dream of suggesting that either of you change who you are. Just try not to let it get you down when you run up against people who don't accept you."

Keelie felt a surge of protectiveness as she looked at Evan, but she knew he'd be okay. Judging by the way the women of Coventry were flocking to his salon, he was winning them over one hairdo at a time. As they came to know him, she was sure they'd adore all the things about him that she did. His wit, his cheerfulness, and his discretion . . .

On that thought, her eyes drifted past him to the games room, and she saw Michael Boone playing darts with two other men. One of them was black, the other was white, and they seemed to be about his age. After carefully checking to make sure no one at her table was paying any attention to her, she shifted her focus back to the group in the games room.

Dr. Boone looked wonderful. He was dressed much the way he'd been on the day she saw him in Grayson's barn—in jeans and layered shirts. His friends were dressed similarly, and as they talked and laughed over their game, she searched the bar for Lisa. She didn't see her, or any women who might be attached to the men. Apparently it was boys' night out.

She dropped her eyes, annoyed by the way her entire body was tingling. She didn't understand why this thing wouldn't die. Why just the sight of him could set her pulse racing. She hadn't moved to Coventry so she could be closer to him. In fact, that possibility had almost kept her away until she'd defiantly convinced herself that she was giving him too much power. Yet here she was, all of her senses on full throttle just because they were under the same roof. It was pathetic.

She refused to let herself look inside the games room again and participated in the dinner conversation. After they shared a decadent chocolate dessert and drank their coffee, Grayson said, "Anyone up for a game? Darts? Pool? Or Broadgate has a very popular version of Clue, based in Coventry and using some of its more notorious citizens as suspects."

"Pool," Ivy said. "Unless you don't want to be on your feet, Keelie?"

"I don't mind," Keelie said, even though her mind was screaming at her to stay as far away from the games room as possible. The pool tables were on the opposite side of the room from the dart boards, however, so there was no reason to think she'd have any contact with Dr. Boone.

She stifled a smile as Ivy said, "Although I'm not very good at pool, Grayson. Are you?"

"Don't even try it," Grayson said. "Evan's warned me about you and Keelie."

"Damn it, Evan," Keelie said. "I have medical bills that Grayson could have been paying."

"You're not fleecing my boyfriend," Evan said. "You'll have to find your own hapless victim."

"Grayson being Evan's hapless victim," Ivy said.

As Grayson paid their bill, Keelie asked Ivy to go to the bathroom with her. While she fluffed out her hair and Ivy put on lipstick, their eyes met in the mirror.

"I really like Grayson," Keelie said.

"I really like the way he treats Evan," Ivy agreed. "The day Evan stole your Rulebreaker right out from under your nose was a good day."

"Yeah, you and Evan did all right with the men who

never loved me," Keelie said. "Don't think I haven't noticed that you've never one time talked about where you'll be living in New York."

"I can't believe how high rent is there," Ivy said, her gaze quickly moving back to her own reflection.

"It's probably a lot more manageable when you share a place," Keelie said. "Confess. You're moving in with Ted, aren't you?"

"Do you think I'm going too fast?" Ivy asked with a remorseful expression.

"You're old enough to know what you want," Keelie said. "Does your mother know?"

"Yeah. She hates it." Ivy shrugged. "But it would be silly to pretend sex is not part of our relationship. If we'd always end up in each other's beds anyway, living together simplifies things."

"Just tell me one thing," Keelie demanded in a stern tone.

"What?" Ivy asked.

"Does he make your teeth sweat?"

"You can't imagine," Ivy said. "So no lecture about taking my time? Getting to know him better? Remembering the disaster that Mark was? Being a strong, independent woman?"

"You couldn't be anyone else," Keelie said. "I hope poor Ted knows what he's getting into."

"Trust me, poor Ted knows," Ivy said and gave her a wicked smile.

When they walked into the games room, Keelie saw Grayson and Evan talking to Dr. Boone and his friends. She gripped Ivy's arm and said, "Let's grab a pool table and warm up. We have to live up to our reputation and kick Grayson's ass."

"Too easy," Ivy said. "You and Evan can play against Grayson and me."

"You may have taken my Remnant," Keelie said, "but I can still take you at pool."

"You can try," Ivy said.

Saying good-bye to Holly, her sons, and then Ivy had been emotionally draining, but Keelie held it together until she and Evan were on the road back to Coventry in Holly's Expedition. Her hope that Evan was unaware of the tears streaming down her cheeks ended when he pulled a few Kleenex from a box and handed them to her.

"Thanks. Sorry. I swear I'm happy for them," she mumbled.

"You remember hearing about my friend Raymond, right?"

Raymond had owned the first salon where Evan worked, and had died a few years before Keelie met Evan. "Yes, I remember who he is."

"Raymond was in and out of the hospital several times, and I thought I always had to be strong and cheerful for him. One afternoon when I went into his hospital room, he was asleep. I stood next to his bed, just looking at him, and I realized that he wouldn't be going home again. I didn't know I was crying until my tears splashed on his hand and woke him up. I apologized for crying, and Raymond said, 'It would make me so sad to think that nobody ever cried for me.' That may not sound like the kind of story to cheer you up, but it is. You cry because you'll miss them. Would you rather not care?"

"No."

"All right then. No more apologies."

They were quiet as they passed the exit for The Woodlands, then Conroe, until finally they were on a long stretch of interstate with nothing to break the monotony. Since it was dark, Keelie couldn't even stare at the landscape.

"Let me know if you need to stop," Evan said.

"I'm fine."

"Good. Anyway, I'm glad we're finally alone. I have a bone to pick with you."

"What'd I do?" Keelie asked.

"It's what you haven't done. You've been keeping a secret, and I think it's time to come clean."

"What are you talking about?"

"The man in your life," Evan said.

"Didn't we have this discussion before?" she asked nervously. "There is no man in my life."

"That's what you've been telling your friends. It surprised me that strangers know more about you than we do."

There's no way, she thought, racking her brain. She hadn't told anyone about Dr. Boone except Stephen. Stephen had met Ivy and Holly, but he wouldn't have repeated what she told him. Would he? She didn't know him well enough to answer her own question.

"Well?" Evan asked. "I'm waiting."

"I have no idea who you're talking about," Keelie insisted, thinking of Misty's mantra when she was a teenager: When all else fails, lie. Then lie some more.

"I'm all about privacy," Evan said, "but I don't get it. If it's just a fling, why does it have to be a secret? And if it's serious, why did you move away from him?"

"Who?" she asked.

"Stephen!"

"I'm not involved with Stephen," Keelie said. "Where

would you get that idea? I mean, he's nice. Cute. I like him. But we're barely even friends. Much less anything else."

"Here's the thing about small towns," Evan said. "Even without blogging grannies, people talk. They know if you drink Pepsi or Coke. They know which five days a month you need Midol. They know how often you change your sheets. You told a friend of Grayson's about Stephen. That person told Grayson and me."

"I must have been misunderstood," Keelie said, wondering if Dr. Boone had mentioned Stephen that night at the Broadgate Tavern. The veterinarian and his friends had stayed at the dart boards while she was playing pool with her friends, but she supposed it was possible that something had been said while she and Ivy were in the bathroom. "You've been in the hair business long enough to know that gossip is hardly ever accurate."

"That is incorrect," Evan said. "There's always a nugget of truth at the center of gossip. It's like a chocolate-covered nut that way."

"Thank you, Forrest Gump," Keelie said. "You would be the nut at the center of my life."

"You're really not keeping a secret?"

"There is nothing going on between Stephen and me," Keelie said.

After a few minutes of silence, Evan said, "If something was going on, which one of Ivy's 'R' men would Stephen be?"

"Hmmm. He's not the Rulebreaker, because he's free to date anyone that he wants. He's not the Romantic, because the most flattering thing he ever said was an awful 'you're the kind of girl who can meet Mom' comment.

He's not the Remnant, because he doesn't have to go changing to please me. What was the other one?"

"I have no idea. This was the Ivy theory of men, not the Evan theory of men."

Keelie racked her brain and finally said, "The Rake! That definitely doesn't fit Stephen. I guess he's some category that Ivy hasn't discovered yet. Or maybe because I'm *not involved with him,* I don't have a category for him. Got it?"

"You know you've considerably reduced your list of potential boyfriends by moving to Coventry, don't you?"

"That's fine by me," Keelie said. "It's been years since I auditioned boyfriends. I like my life the way it is."

"Boy, if this were a soap opera—"

"But it's not," Keelie said. "It's not a soap opera, a romantic comedy, or a romance novel. It's my real life. Could you stop at the next exit? Thanks to you, I'm craving chocolate."

"Is it Midol week already?" Evan asked.

"Maybe Grayson's friend can tell you," Keelie said and smacked his arm.

Chapter 17

Keelie's mother had once told her that it took six months to get comfortable in a new home or job, but only three weeks to form a new habit. She wasn't sure if that was true, but she was determined to develop a productive daily routine. She couldn't shake her tendency to wake early, and rather than idling away the mornings drinking coffee and watching CNN, she vowed that she'd act like she had to leave for an office job. She would shower, dress, and put on her makeup even if Hamlet was the only other living being who would see her. Of course, that was unlikely, since he was nocturnal.

Because her energy level was high in the mornings, she decided to alternate days between tackling her Wonderful Wife project and working on Destiny's story. No matter which, she would always stop for lunch, then take a walk around the square, maybe even stop in to see Evan for a few minutes, before returning home. Afternoons were always her sluggish time, so she could do some of the more mundane Wonderful Wife tasks then. At night, she would spend a couple of hours rereading what she'd been writing and making edits or adjustments.

It all sounded good in theory, but on the second day of what she'd established as her back-to-work week, she determined that it was too cold to be walking around town. On the third morning, she turned on the TV to check the weather and got sucked into back-to-back episodes of *Full House* on Nickelodeon. And when she found out that there would be a *Roseanne* marathon on Nick at Nite, she decided that she deserved a week to just lounge around. Officially, she was still on Buy The Book's payroll since she not only had another check coming, but also her vacation pay.

She did unpack all her books and arrange them on the shelves in her office, including the cookbooks from Gram. There was no point keeping them in her kitchen. It was silly to concoct an elaborate meal for one, especially when there was always cereal, soup, and microwave popcorn in the cabinets.

She also made her bed every day, no matter what. This was a long-respected rule among the women in her family. She'd heard it from Gram and her mother all her life, and she knew that Misty had insisted that her children join her in this daily ritual almost as soon as they moved from a baby bed to a youth bed. An unmade bed was a sign of slovenliness, a slow sliding down that would end with rusted cars in the yard, bad teeth, and frequent use of the word "ain't."

On the morning that she was making a peanut-butter-and-jelly sandwich for breakfast and heard herself rationalizing that one hour of e-mail for Wonderful Wife earned her a one-hour episode of *The Waltons,* she knew that her mother was wrong. It took a lot less than three weeks to develop *bad* habits.

She put the peanut butter away, took a shower, dressed warmly, and walked to the Lady Godiva fountain with a shiny quarter from her change jar. The air was icy, but she'd stopped believing in snow. That had been an empty promise of Ivy's to lure her to Coventry for Christmas.

"May I never spend another Christmas working in retail," she said, tossing the quarter in the pool of water.

She turned from the fountain to walk around the block to Evan's salon. As she was putting on her gloves, she saw a dog running across the square and paused. Surely there couldn't be another brindle greyhound in Coventry, and her heart thudded as she furtively looked around for Dr. Boone. But the only other person braving the cold was a lot shorter than the veterinarian, and Keelie smiled and started walking.

"Hi," she said, and Jennifer Boone turned around and regarded her with her amazing green eyes.

"Hi," Jennifer said. "I remember you. The hamster lady who doesn't like cats."

"It's easier to call me Keelie. If you don't tell everyone my cat secret, I won't tell them you're skipping school."

Jennifer smiled and said, "No school today. The teachers are having a meeting."

"Then I guess I have nothing to bargain with," Keelie said sadly.

"Not everybody can like cats," Jennifer reassured her. "I don't like . . ." She trailed off and seemed to be thinking it over. "Roaches?"

Keelie laughed and said, "Does your father see many crazy people with pet roaches?"

"No. I know a woman who has a pet boa constrictor,

but Dr. Townshend treats exotics. We mostly see horses and cows."

When Rip came over to Keelie, she bent, scratched his head, and said, "So what are you doing on your holiday from school?"

"I was on my way to Phillips Hardware," Jennifer said. She rattled a box she was holding. "Sometimes if he's not busy, Isaac plays dominos with me."

"I need a couple of things from the hardware store," Keelie said. "Mind if I walk along with you?"

Jennifer shook her head and kept her pace slow to allow for Keelie's bum ankle, while Rip ran ahead of them. "He's really not supposed to be off his lead. See? We both have a secret."

"I'll never tell," Keelie promised.

It was Keelie's first time inside the hardware store, and she stopped and stared around her with delight. She loved the smell of old wood and gardening chemicals, the rows of merchandise whose functions were a mystery, and the cushion of warm air that surrounded her. She located its source: a wood-burning stove near the back of the store. There were several chairs next to it, and a table, which was where Jennifer headed with her box of dominos.

"How's that hamster?" Isaac called when he came around a shelf and spotted her.

"He's great," Keelie said.

"That's good," Isaac said. "I heard that you'd moved into Rourke Apartments. It won't be long before people from Godiva Festival committees start knocking on your door. Someone will want to put you to work."

"Tell me which jobs to avoid," Keelie begged.

"Concessions and the dunking booth," Isaac said. "What can I help you find today?"

"I just want to look around," Keelie said.

He nodded, and she started walking along the rows of shelves, trying to figure out anything she needed that her mother hadn't already thought of. When she heard Isaac tell Jennifer that he had to place some orders but would play a game or two with her later, Keelie maneuvered through the store until she reached the stove.

"I'll play with you," she said. "Until Isaac is free."

Jennifer nodded, and Keelie took off her coat and gloves and sat across the table from her.

While they played their first game, Jennifer said, "Did I hear Isaac say that you moved here?"

"Uh-huh. From Houston."

"Why?" Jennifer asked, giving her a curious look.

"I needed a change, and I like your town," Keelie said.

"But there's nothing to do here. Don't you get bored?"

"I haven't been here long enough to get bored," Keelie said, inwardly wincing at the realization that nothing was exactly what she'd loved doing for days. She felt like a slacker.

"Do you work?" Jennifer asked.

Keelie explained about leaving her job at the bookstore to work for Wonderful Wife. Any time she paused, Jennifer fired off another question, and she finally realized that she was giving her a lot more information than she'd intended. No doubt it would be relayed to Dr. Boone over the dinner table, and soon Grayson would be sharing it with Evan.

Oh, please, she chided herself. Jennifer Boone would probably forget even seeing her today. And there was nothing so riveting about her life that it merited conversation at dinner or any other time.

"I would hate working at a bookstore," Jennifer commented.

"Why's that?" Keelie asked.

"I don't like to read," Jennifer said.

Keelie bit back an exclamation of dismay and said, "What do you like to do?"

"Cook," Jennifer said.

"I'm an awful cook," Keelie said. "My grandmother tells me that if I can read, I can cook. But even when I follow recipes, my meals never look like the pictures in the magazines and cookbooks. They probably don't taste like them, either."

"I couldn't learn to cook from a book, because I'm a bad reader. By the time I finished reading, something would be on fire."

Keelie laughed and said, "Then how do you learn to cook?"

"If someone makes a dish I like, I get them to let me make it with them. Plus I watch cooking shows, and I have a lot of DVDs of chefs who take me through cooking step-by-step. I'm going to culinary school one day to become a chef."

As they started another game of dominos, Keelie said, "Have you always disliked reading?"

"Not until third grade," Jennifer said. "I got behind at school that year, and I guess I never caught up. I've been tested for dyslexia and a bunch of other things. I can't remember all the names. But I don't have any of those problems." She shrugged. "I get bored, my mind wanders, and I forget what I read. I'm in a reading program at school. The stuff we read is so boring."

"If you're up for it, maybe we could help each other," Keelie said.

"How?"

"I'd like to learn enough about cooking to make a decent meal occasionally. If you were willing to teach me to cook, I'll bet I could find some things you'd enjoy reading. We could read them together and talk about them."

Jennifer's winged brows knitted with distaste, and she said, "Can't I just teach you to cook? We don't have to do the reading part."

"Then it wouldn't be a fair trade," Keelie said. "My best friend, who loves to read as much as I do, just moved to New York. We used to always share books or read them at the same time and talk about them. That makes it a lot more fun. I'm going to miss it. But maybe if I had another friend who could read with me . . ."

"Would we have to read books about horses? Everybody's always giving me books about horses. Since my father takes care of horses, people think, 'Oh, she must love horses!' I guess those people have never had to clean out stalls or exercise horses for their allowance. Ugh."

"Like coals to Newcastle," Keelie commented.

"What does that mean?"

"If you were a reader," Keelie said in a prim voice, "you'd know."

"Not fair," Jennifer said, but she returned Keelie's grin.

"I swear to choose books that I think you'll like," Keelie said in a wheedling tone. "You might actually find out that reading can be fun. And I won't end up poisoning myself with beef stroganoff or something. Do you know what gelato is?"

Jennifer giggled and said, "It's like ice cream. It has milk instead of cream, but it's dense because it has less air than ice milk."

"Who knew?" Keelie said. "Well, you did. See how much I need you? Why don't you talk to your parents and see if we can work something out?"

Jennifer's head jerked up, and she pinned her green eyes on Keelie. It took Keelie a few seconds to realize why she was uncomfortable. Jennifer's intensity and focus reminded her of the way Holly's cat Fernando stared at her.

"I guess I was wrong about you," Jennifer finally said.

"Wrong?"

"I thought you were being nice because you felt sorry for me."

Keelie was confused and said, "Not everybody likes to read, Jennifer. Why would that make me feel sorry for you?"

"Because of my mother," Jennifer said.

Keelie had a moment of sudden clarity. *Third grade . . . I got behind at school that year . . . I couldn't learn to cook from a book . . . If someone makes a dish I like, I get them to let me make it with them.* Of all the people in the world, she should have been able to read between the lines.

"Your mother died," she said softly. "When you were eight? Nine?"

"Five years ago. I was eight," Jennifer said.

"I didn't know," Keelie said. This was familiar territory to her, a place where she felt no awkwardness, so after a pause, she went on. "My father died when I was eight. He was a doctor who worked long hours. They said he fell asleep driving and ran off the road. What happened to your mother? Was she sick?"

Jennifer shook her head. "We went shopping in Dallas. Just Mom and me. When we were driving home, a man ran a red light and hit our car on her side. I don't remember it, and Daddy says she never knew what happened."

"Were you hurt?"

"I had a concussion and two broken ribs, and I was all banged up. I was out of school for nearly a month. But I don't have any scars or anything."

Just the ones that don't show, Keelie thought. She impulsively covered Jennifer's hand with hers and said, "I'm sorry you lost your mother."

"It seems like a long time ago. Sometimes I worry that I'm going to forget her," Jennifer said. "Do you have a lot of good memories of your father?"

"Not really," Keelie said, deciding it was better to be honest. "It isn't because I've forgotten as I got older. I didn't get to spend much time with him when I was a kid."

"Because he worked so much," Jennifer said.

"What I remember is good," Keelie said. "Sometimes he liked to smoke a pipe, and whenever I smell pipe tobacco, it makes me happy. And I remember when my sister—she's two years younger than I am—was four, she saw a TV show where people went Christmas caroling, and she wanted to do it. I don't know if anyone goes caroling in Coventry, but no one did it where I grew up. My parents took us caroling in our neighborhood, and my father laughed at people's expressions when they opened their doors and saw Dr. Cannon singing to them. Some people don't think doctors are human beings, I guess. What things do you like to remember about your mother?"

"She was pretty," Jennifer said. "She laughed a lot. Her grandfather raised hunting dogs when she was growing up, and she loved dogs. I always thought it was my mother who helped Rip find me."

"If you think it, I'm sure it's true," Keelie said. "I'll tell you a secret about Rip. I knew he was special as soon as I met him. I couldn't forget him, and he even inspired me to start writing a story."

"Really? You're writing a story about Rip?"

"The dog in my story looks like Rip, and I even named him Rip. But no other dog could actually be Rip," Keelie said. "He's one of a kind."

"Could I read the story?"

"Yes," Keelie said. "When it's finished, I would love for you to read it and see if I got it right."

"Hey, wait a minute," Jennifer said. "Did you just trick me into asking if I could read something?"

"Sort of," Keelie admitted.

"Just for that, I'll make you learn to cook something really hard," Jennifer said. "I mean, if my father says it's okay."

"It never hurts to ask," Keelie said.

She glanced up as Isaac walked over to them and said, "I'm sorry, Jennifer. I got tied up on the phone."

"It's okay," Jennifer said. "I beat Keelie four games."

"Three!" Keelie said. "We didn't finish this one."

"Yeah, but I'm winning," Jennifer said. She looked at her watch and said, "Oh. I have to meet my ride."

"Yeah, right," Keelie said. "You're afraid I'll make a comeback."

Jennifer shook her head as she put on her coat and said, "I think you play dominos like you cook."

"You are a dreadful young woman," Keelie said. "Maybe our first book will be *My Friend Flicka.*"

"Rack of lamb," Jennifer said in a threatening tone.

"Black Beauty."

"Spinach soufflé," Jennifer countered.

"You win."

"Just like dominos," Jennifer said and was out the door with Rip while Keelie laughed.

"Looks like you made a friend," Isaac said.

"She's something else," Keelie said. "Where's the pet section? I should take Hamlet a surprise."

The cold air made Keelie decide to skip a visit to Evan's salon, and she was almost home when the full impact of her conversation with Jennifer hit her.

Dr. Boone wasn't married. He was widowed. There had been no reason why he shouldn't have flirted with her in his clinic. No reason why he shouldn't have kissed her in Grayson's barn. Unless he was dating the woman she'd seen with him at the Early Bird Café.

Keelie gritted her teeth and wondered why she hadn't just asked Granny about him. Or Grayson.

"I hate Mark Page," she said to Hamlet when he deigned to wake up long enough to hide the chew toy she gave him. "Ivy's rotten ex made me suspicious of all men. And I told him I have a boyfriend! Dumb. I'm so dumb."

As if he agreed, Hamlet scurried into his most recent room that she'd made from a cardboard egg carton. She suspected that if the room had a door, he'd have shut it in her face.

Running into Jennifer—and finding out that Dr. Boone might not be as unavailable as she'd feared—had rekindled Keelie's enthusiasm for Destiny's story. She spent the mornings of the days afterward writing, forcing herself to stop for lunch. Afternoons were spent on Wonderful Wife business. She'd begun to enjoy the challenge now that she was getting more familiar with the massive volume of documents she'd been sent. She tried to vary her time between reading those, research-ing labor laws online, and typing the notes that would eventually become the standards and practices of the various franchises.

There were times she found it tedious though, espe-cially when the sun was shining and gave them an un-expected break from the cold weather. To clear her head, she walked to Evan's salon. She paused on the sidewalk, watching him through the window. His client had a head full of foil, which meant he'd be busy color-ing, cutting, drying, and styling her for a while. The woman was laughing hard at whatever Evan was saying, and Keelie decided against crashing her appointment. She knew from experience that sometimes moments with a good hairdresser like Evan were the only indul-gence a woman allowed herself.

She glanced inside the windows of the Godiva Inn as she walked by it. In its restaurant, which wasn't a very good one, she saw an elderly couple sitting at a table by the window. They reminded her a little of Gram and Major Byrnes in appearance, both of them dignified and crowned by white hair. The man was looking at his companion with open affection on his face, and Keelie smiled. Sometimes she thought that only the newly in love or lifelong couples understood the value of savor-ing their relationship as it was measured out in mo-ments. In between, people got too busy with their careers, their families, or the other million events of daily life.

The building next to the inn was a gift shop which hadn't been open any time Keelie passed it. Evan had told her that the owner always went to stay with her daughter on the West Coast after the Christmas holi-days. She'd be back in time to get her shop ready for tourist season, which supposedly kicked off around Easter, was busiest during the Godiva Festival, and stayed strong through the fall because of Coventry's appealing bed-and-breakfasts, the activities of other towns in the area, and the nearby river and state parks.

She continued walking past the site of the old school house, which was now a nursery school, and cut between the Early Bird Café and an office building to get to Godiva Street, which would take her back home. But as she crossed the street, she looked up at the sign that said "Independent Seven Toys" and decided to explore the historic houses of Independence Park.

The woman inside the Welcome Center knew her by name and introduced herself as Meredith. "We have guides during the season, but no one right now," she explained. "We stay staffed until Halloween, because we give a lot of student tours. The kids even get a little hands-on weaving experience. But we won't officially open again until—"

"Easter," Keelie said.

Meredith smiled and said, "You've moved here during Coventry's dormant season."

"That's exactly the way I wanted it," Keelie assured her.

"The houses are open, and if you take this guide, you can read a little about their original occupants and some of the items on display. Just don't touch anything."

"Thanks," Keelie said, taking the brochure. After a few minutes of small talk, mostly about the possibility of snow—Keelie was beginning to believe that everyone in town was in a conspiracy to dangle that hollow promise in front of her—she stepped back outside and walked to the most distant of the houses.

The brochure called it a weaver's cottage. If it had

ever been divided into rooms, it was now just one large space. Keelie pressed a button on the wall and period music began playing, with a fiddle being the dominant instrument. She read that the house had originally been the home of Jefferson and Mary Sprayberry and their five children. She looked around, trying to understand how a family of seven could coexist in such a small house. The walls were plaster and the floors were a rough wood. She learned from her brochure that the windows were large to allow ample light for the employees to do piece work at home. She assumed that meant even pregnancy and childbirth didn't give the women a break from their mill duties, and probably the children helped, too.

A sign in front of a loom explained that it was from the original mill. Keelie stayed on her side of the velvet rope as she walked around the room. Then she came to a child's desk. Dr. Boone had told her the same thing that was in the brochure about the establishment of the school for the workers' children. The small wooden desk was from that school, and Keelie leaned over the rope to get a better look at it. There was no explanation in the brochure for the little 'A' that was carved in one corner of the desk.

"Annie," she said out loud, reaching over the rope to trace the 'A' with a finger. "Or Addie. Amy. Ava."

She didn't realize that someone else had come into the house until a voice said, "It was Alice."

Keelie jumped, turned around, and looked at the woman who'd spoken. Keelie's first thought was that her eyes, although a different color from Jennifer's, were also as observant as cat's eyes. Like her skin, the woman's eyes were amber, and they crinkled with amusement as Keelie stammered out an apology for touching the desk.

"I do the same thing," the woman said. She held out her hand and said, "I'm Vanessa Bowen. You must be the hamster's mom."

"Keelie Cannon. It's so weird when people know who I am."

"My father told me about you," Vanessa said. "Isaac Phillips. I believe you also met my little girl, Rochelle."

"Oh, she's so adorable," Keelie said. "Very shy."

Vanessa smiled and said, "She told me all about the woman who had a hurt foot and a hamster. At home, the mouth never stops." She glanced at the desk. "We think it was Alice Sprayberry who carved her initial in the desk; that's why it was placed in this house. If it was, I'm sure she got a paddling from her teacher."

"I wonder what kind of life she had here. The house is so tiny. Do you know if she was already born when her family made that long trip from Alabama?"

"She was," Vanessa said. "You're right. The house is small. But can you imagine what it felt like to be the Sprayberrys? I'm sure work in the wool mill was hard, and life offered few comforts. But they were finally free people of color. This was their own house, and they were paid for the work they did."

"That's exactly what I was thinking about," Keelie said. "Annie or Addie born the child of slaves. Getting her freedom and not really sure what that meant. Making the journey here and starting over in a town that barely existed. All the things she must have been afraid of. New sounds and sights. Indians or wild animals. Even going to school must have been scary if no one in her family had done it before her."

Vanessa nodded and said, "My husband is descended

from those black settlers. We have their Bible, the first one they were allowed to own, with their names painstakingly written in it. I've always wondered if the children's parents learned to read out of it. Maybe they taught their parents as they learned in school."

"Your husband is Terry Bowen," Keelie said with a sudden realization. "Dr. Boone told me about him. He's one of the men who owns the toy factory, right?" Vanessa nodded. "I'd love to look at that Bible sometime. Hear any stories anyone knows about Alice and the other children."

"You should meet Terry's mother," Vanessa said. "She has a lot of stories that were passed to her. Of course, I'm sure they've been embellished over the generations, so I can't say they're all true."

"The best stories are a little true and a little invented," Keelie said. "I'm working on my first novel. Nothing may ever come of it, but I've already been wondering what I'll write next." She looked back at the desk. "Alice is the first bit of inspiration I've had, because what I'm writing is young adult fiction."

"Now that is interesting," Vanessa said mysteriously. "I don't suppose you'd like to have a cup of coffee with me at the Early Bird Café and talk more about this?"

"I'd love to," Keelie said.

"Let me just make a call," Vanessa said, taking out a cell phone. Keelie had to smile at how incongruous it seemed among the relics of the cottage. She walked away to look at a cane-bottomed chair, but she couldn't help overhearing Vanessa's conversation. "Faith, are you busy? There's someone I want you to meet. Okay, we'll be at the Bird in a few minutes."

Keelie turned around when Vanessa snapped her phone shut and said, "I'm ready whenever you are."

"We'll be meeting Faith Taylor. Her husband Carl is Terry's business partner."

They both put on their gloves before they stepped out of the cottage. Keelie looked at the sky, which had gone gray, and said, "I ask for only one thing. Please don't tell me it's going to snow."

"The forecast doesn't call for it," Vanessa said, looking up with a frown. "But when is the weatherman ever right?"

They were sitting in a booth, steaming mugs of coffee in front of them, when Faith joined them. Keelie recognized her immediately. She was the dark-haired woman who'd been with Dr. Boone in this same restaurant on the day Evan had moved into his apartment. So now she knew two things: Dr. Boone didn't have a wife, and he obviously wasn't dating Faith, since she was married to Carl Taylor.

Faith's hands were stained with something—ink or paint, Keelie couldn't tell. After Vanessa introduced them and Faith's coffee came, Vanessa repeated the conversation she and Keelie had just had. Faith glanced at Keelie from time to time, her eyes thoughtful.

"Inspiration always comes when I least expect it," she finally said. When she saw Keelie's puzzled expression, she laughed and held up her hands. "I'm an artist, if you couldn't tell. Although my hands look more like a mechanic's right now, because I've been using a lot of black."

"That's just one of the things she does," Vanessa said. "She's also the idea person behind some of the toys our husbands and their designers make. A few months ago, we were watching her daughter, Mia, and Rochelle pull the heads off their Barbies."

"Some things never change," Keelie said. "My

sister and I were always switching the heads on our Barbie dolls."

"I guess everyone who makes toys dreams of a success like Barbie," Faith said. "But as a modern woman, which Vanessa and I both are, you second-guess poor Barbie. Does she give our daughters unrealistic body images? Is she too into fashion and dream houses and Ken, and not enough into being her own woman?"

"I like to believe that Barbie helped me develop my imagination," Keelie said, thinking back to her childhood. "Misty and I concocted the most elaborate stories about our dolls and their lives. One of our favorites was the circus. Misty had a canopy bed that was our big top. Trapezes hung from the wood frame that held up the canopy. We used aluminum foil to make costumes for our Barbies. There was always Good Barbie—mine— and Ken-stealing Barbie—Misty's. Good Barbie inevitably plunged to the ground from her trapeze and was paralyzed, and Ken abandoned her for Bad Barbie. But in the end, Good Barbie always won. She was able to walk again, Ken came home, and Bad Barbie was left alone to contemplate her evil ways."

She blushed as she realized that both women were staring at her with big grins, and Vanessa said, "I love a good soap opera."

"I guess that was more information than you wanted," Keelie said. "And now I'm all disgruntled with myself because Good Barbie took Ken back. She should have stayed in the wheelchair, lobbied in Washington for people with disabilities, and hooked up with G.I. Joe after he returned from the war, and started a peace movement."

"Or she could have been our first woman president in a wheelchair," Faith said.

"The Godiva doll," Keelie said. "You're the two people who are trying to throw off the oppression of high heels and perfect little faces and create a more enlightened doll. I think my friend told me about President Godiva and CEO Godiva."

"Nothing is ever a secret in this town," Faith complained.

"But gossip never gets it right," Vanessa added. "We are, in fact, developing a doll, and you're right. We don't want a fashion doll, although, bless Mattel, even Barbie seems to have a multitude of possible careers now. But we look at our daughters and think Barbie's too much woman for them."

"And the Bratz dolls are teens, but they're all about fashion," Faith said. She looked around to make sure no one else was nearby and said, "This is all highly confidential."

"I won't repeat it," Keelie promised, "although I suppose you have no reason to trust me."

"Well, I do," Vanessa said. "You and I seem to be on the same wavelength."

"What do you mean?"

"Faith and I want our dolls to be based at least in part on girls who could have been real. Girls from different periods of time."

"Like the American Girl dolls," Keelie said.

"Exactly! Do you have children?" Faith asked.

"No," Keelie said. "But I used to manage a bookstore, and I know about the books that go along with American Girl dolls."

"Like Barbie," Faith said, "American Girl dolls and Bratz are very successful. But we don't want to just imitate any of them. What we want is dolls built on the scale of a fashion doll like Barbie, but with more realistic teen figures, and some of the historical accuracy of

American Girl dolls, which are much larger dolls and look like young girls."

"We want dolls that are more 'tween and young teen. The problem is, we can come up with a doll and give her a history. But we've been a little unsure how to present her background. Her story."

"Are you thinking maybe I could do research and write copy for you?" Keelie asked.

"Not exactly," Vanessa said. "Tell us more about this young adult novel you're working on now."

Keelie explained Destiny to them. Their excitement was palpable, but she wasn't really sure where they were going with all this. After she finished, the two women stared at each other for a few minutes, and it was almost like they were speaking a silent language.

"It's the perfect marketing tie-in," Faith finally said, and Vanessa nodded.

"What is?" Keelie asked.

"Your novel."

"I don't have a publisher," Keelie said. "I'm writing for the pleasure of it. But my friend Ivy wants to help me find an agent, so maybe one day—"

"What if you could approach an agent or a publisher with not only a completed novel, but a product that would help sell it, and a company that was ready to manufacture that product? And not just one novel, but ideas for other novels and a line of dolls that goes with those novels. We'd have to come up with a good name for your series and the toy line, but there would be a Destiny Doll to go with her book. An Alice Doll for another book. Dolls from all over the country dressed in the clothes of their time, whose most extraordinary feature is that they're ordinary girls who offer 'tweens a glimpse of history, but also the sense that they can overcome hardships, depend on themselves, be smart and strong. Now that is the kind of book and doll I'd want Rochelle to have."

"Even if Destiny does end up with Alice's head," Faith said and grinned. "Girls are always going to make up their own stories for their dolls, and that's the way it should be. But I agree that I'd be a lot happier with a doll who came with a well-written novel that Mia might actually read." She looked around with a guilty expression. "Not that I'm against all the electronic and computer games that Carl and Terry develop. But one thing I've learned about parenting. Kids will make the most of what's available to them."

"Like the Pencil Family," Vanessa said in a teasing tone, and Faith blushed.

"What's the Pencil Family?" Keelie asked.

"Vanessa, I think you're the reason there are no secrets in this town," Faith said. "I was a terrible student in math. Since I never could figure out what was going on, I used to take my pencils, which were various lengths, and have a daddy pencil, a mama pencil, and two kid pencils. And their dog, Eraser. I'd play with them during class."

"I'm sorry I'm laughing," Keelie finally said when she could breathe again. "But you can always use that against your children. 'When I was a kid, I had to play with pencils because we didn't have dolls!'"

"Well, it's true," Faith said. "Kids are inventive. You can refuse to give your five-year-old a toy gun, and you can teach him about Native Americans, but he'll just pick up a stick and pretend it's a gun to play cowboys and Indians. And there will always be girls who love dolls, no matter how many soccer balls or computer games you give them."

"But you can sneak in some educational stuff, too," Vanessa said.

Keelie nodded thoughtfully and said, "Merchandising. I can't even begin to tell you how many products go along with the Harry Potter books. Or for that matter, Winnie the Pooh books or Dr. Seuss books."

"Those products sell more books, and vice versa," Vanessa said. "And you know, this could all be turned into something even bigger if you tied it in with raising kids' awareness."

"Like how?" Keelie asked.

"Take Destiny, for example," Vanessa said. "You can create a Destiny novel and a Destiny doll. But one of the features that comes with the Destiny doll is Rip. What if kids can go to a Web site and join a chapter of other kids their age, or form a group among their friends and classmates, who raise money or sponsor a greyhound for adoption?"

"That's brilliant," Keelie said.

"Thank you," Vanessa said.

"It's bigger than anything I ever imagined," Keelie said.

"You just proved our point," Faith said. "Dolls and books can inspire girls to work together and do amazing things."

"How do you think G.I. Joe and Ken will feel about all this?" Keelie asked.

"G.I. Joe and Ken are the enlightened fathers of girls," Faith said.

"Not to mention that G.I. Joe and Ken admire creative women who make the bottom line look good," Vanessa said.

* * *

"You didn't sign anything, did you?" Ivy asked when Keelie called her that night to tell her about the conversation with Vanessa and Faith, after swearing her to secrecy.

"Of course not. We were just talking," Keelie said.

"This gives me an opening," Ivy said. "Ted and I are having dinner in a few nights with one of the agents I work with. Since this is one area in which I have absolutely no knowledge, I can ask him about merchandising rights for authors. If I'm clever enough, maybe I can lure him into agreeing to read your manuscript. Was that a yelp of excitement or fear?"

"Terror," Keelie said. "Are you sure—"

"Don't get all freaked out about it. Sooner or later, you'll have to let someone who doesn't know you read Destiny's story. I'm not saying he'll agree to represent you. But at the very least, maybe as a courtesy to me, he'll read it and give you suggestions or advice."

"I guess it wouldn't hurt to mention it to him," Keelie said.

"You know what? I'm not going to lecture you about having more confidence in yourself. It's actually kind of endearing that you're humble. Don't ever change. I'll be the evil, aggressive one. E-mail me an updated copy of the manuscript. I'll print it here, and you can put it out of your mind until you hear from me."

"Like I'll ever be able to do that," Keelie said.

"Focus on Wonderful Wife, and do whatever else it is you do with your days," Ivy said.

"I'm thinking of taking cooking lessons," Keelie said.
"Why?"

Keelie laughed and said, "You and Granny are the only two people I know who'd respond that way. I hope you never change, either."

Chapter 18

Jennifer had called with Keelie's first cooking assignment. Keelie was to find at least three recipes of dishes she liked and had no idea how to make. She hoped the rest of their lesson would be as easy, because she had no trouble coming up with things she couldn't cook.

She woke up even earlier than usual on Saturday morning, taking pains with her appearance. All the signs were good. Her hair was cooperative. She didn't stab herself in the eye with her mascara. Her favorite sweater, the same color blue as her eyes, was clean. And even though she wasn't inclined to praise herself, when she looked in the mirror at the rear view of her jeans, she was satisfied. When Dr. Boone dropped off his daughter, she would make sure he got a good look at Jennifer's student.

"I am not, absolutely am not, using the daughter to get to the father," Keelie said to the invisible Hamlet, who hadn't cared enough to emerge and check out her jeans with her. "I like Jennifer for herself, and I suggested trading lessons before I knew about her mother. And since her father said yes, he must trust my motives."

Unfortunately, it was Jennifer's aunt who brought her to Keelie's apartment. Jennifer introduced them by first name only, and although Laura seemed pleasant enough, she was obviously in a hurry.

"What time should I pick her up?" Laura asked.

Keelie looked at Jennifer, who shrugged and said, "I don't know what we're cooking, so I don't know how long it'll take."

"I'll be happy to drive Jennifer home," Keelie offered.

"That might be best," Laura said, then she was gone after a quick goodbye.

"Is Laura your father's sister or your mother's sister?" Keelie asked.

"My mother's," Jennifer said absently as she explored Keelie's kitchen and began a grocery list after she looked at Keelie's recipes. When that was finished, she said, "Can I see your apartment? I always wondered what they looked like inside."

"Sure," Keelie said. "Although you're already seeing most of it."

Jennifer pronounced the bathroom cool and paused at the photographs that were on Keelie's dresser, asking her who everyone was. Her examination of the office was quick, and Keelie suppressed a smile. Clearly, Jennifer was hoping that the book part of their deal had been forgotten.

She'd borrowed the car from Evan so she could drive them to Whole Foods in New Coventry. When they got to the grocery store, Keelie was a little daunted by Jennifer's long list and said, "My mother does cook, and she's the one who stocked my cabinets. But I guess she never thought I'd want more than the basics."

"I'm glad you don't have a lot of spices," Jennifer said. "I like cooking with fresh ingredients anyway."

"My grandmother would love you," Keelie said. "She was so disappointed when none of us turned out to be Martha Stewart."

"I'm not teaching you to make a tablecloth out of leaves," Jennifer said, and Keelie laughed.

The trip through the grocery store took longer than Keelie had expected, but she didn't mind the mini lessons Jennifer gave her in the produce and fish sections. They also lingered on the aisle that had personal care products, sniffing essential oils and helping Keelie find a good massage oil to use on her ankle.

"Does it hurt a lot?" Jennifer asked. "My broken ribs did."

"It's not so bad," Keelie said. "I think the cold weather makes it ache. I feel like an old woman who's complaining about my rheumatism."

"How old are you?" Jennifer asked.

"Twenty-eight."

"That's more than twice as old as me," Jennifer said, looking at her like she was as old as Granny.

"I see there's nothing wrong with your *math* skills," Keelie said, and Jennifer suddenly became interested in shopping again.

When they got back to the apartment, Jennifer unpacked the bags of groceries while Keelie put in a CD.

"What is that?" Jennifer asked as Keelie lowered the volume.

"Music that would have been popular in Regency England," Keelie said. "The last part of the eighteenth and beginning of the nineteenth centuries."

"Wow, you are old," Jennifer said solemnly, but the devilry in her eyes betrayed her.

"Hush, you. Did you ever see the movies *Sense and Sensibility* or *Emma?*"

"I think I saw *Emma.*"

"Those are set in Georgian England, or the Regency period," Keelie said. "They'd have danced to music like this at their balls. People were a lot more social then, since they didn't have TV or movies or computers."

"Who played the music?" Jennifer asked.

"Rich people hired musicians, but everyone owned a piano, or pianoforte. It was part of a woman's education to become accomplished at playing. But I'm not the teacher here. You are."

Somehow learning to cook from a thirteen-year-old wasn't quite as embarrassing as she'd feared. Jennifer definitely knew what she was doing, but she didn't make Keelie feel stupid. She was a girl who could laugh and cut up, but she had a serious approach to food, and she didn't make fun of Keelie's ignorance.

"Thank you for not laughing at me," Keelie said after Jennifer had to show her how to use her food processor, which was still in its box.

Jennifer shrugged and said, "Nobody likes to be laughed at. Except maybe clowns."

"Or comedians."

"Or boys who sit in the back of class and do stupid things on purpose," Jennifer said.

"Do you have a boyfriend?" Keelie asked.

"Mostly I have boys who are friends," Jennifer said. "My best friend is Jason. I'm going to the Valentine's Day dance with him, but he's not my boyfriend."

Keelie couldn't stop herself from laughing, and Jennifer gave her a funny look.

"It's the name Jason," Keelie explained. "I have an ex-boyfriend named Jason. So do two of my friends, and Ivy says we're never allowed to date Jasons again."

"It would be sad for all the boys named Jason if everybody felt that way," Jennifer said. "There are three of them in my class, but I only like Jason Bennett."

"Bennett," Keelie repeated. "That makes my decision for me."

"What decision?" Jennifer asked, keeping a close eye on Keelie as she arranged the ingredients of spinach lasagna in layers.

"I know which book we're reading first."

"I guess you didn't forget that part," Jennifer said with disappointment.

"Nope. A deal's a deal."

"Do *you* have a boyfriend?" Jennifer asked, as if hoping to distract her.

"Not since Jason," Keelie said. She concentrated on finishing the lasagna, but once it was in the oven, she said, "I know you don't like books about horses, but do you like to ride them?"

"It's okay," Jennifer said. "Do you ride?"

"I haven't since I was about your age. Where I grew up, horses weren't everywhere like they are here, so we had to rent them from a riding stable. Since we didn't have a lot of money, my sister and I only rode a few times."

"I learned when I was a kid," Jennifer said.

Keelie didn't let herself smile at the idea that Jennifer no longer thought of herself as a kid. "What did you like to do when you were a kid? Did you play with dolls?"

"No. I guess I'm a tomboy, because I always wanted to be outside. I liked playing with boys better than girls. What about you?"

"I'm one of those sissy girls," Keelie said. "I played

with dolls. Had crushes on boys, but my best friends were always girls. And I liked to read. A lot."

"That again," Jennifer said.

"How long does the lasagna have to cook?" Keelie asked, looking around but not seeing the recipe she'd printed.

"An hour and fifteen minutes."

"Perfect," Keelie said. "Let me get a book."

She came back from her office with *Pride and Prejudice,* but instead of making Jennifer start reading, she gave her a little more background on Georgian England and its views on the proper deportment of women and girls. Then, after they each ate a sandwich, they settled on Keelie's sofa, and she began reading aloud.

She looked up from time to time to see if Jennifer seemed bored, but she was listening to the story of the Bennet family with an intensity that reminded Keelie of Jennifer's father. Jennifer also laughed in all the right places, which Keelie found reassuring. She might not like to read, but Jennifer had no trouble grasping the subtleties of Jane Austen's wit.

She seemed almost surprised when Keelie closed the book and said, "Wait. Did she dance with him?"

Keelie gave her a wicked smile, handed her the novel, and said, "You can tell me next Saturday."

"You are a really sneaky person," Jennifer complained.

"I know. Let's check on that lasagna."

While they shared the duties of cutting and chopping vegetables for a salad, Keelie suggested that Jennifer come up with a cast for a movie version of *Pride and Prejudice.* It started out seriously, then they got silly and started naming actors from their favorite Nick at Nite sitcoms.

"I'm so addicted to that channel," Keelie said. "Do

you know how embarrassing it is that I cry over *Full House?*"

"Have mercy!" Jennifer said, and Keelie laughed. Jennifer added, "Seriously, you probably shouldn't tell that to just anyone."

"You know so many of my secrets already. What's one more?" Keelie asked.

When she drove Jennifer home, Keelie noticed with satisfaction that she held the book against her chest. She could definitely say that their first exchange of lessons had been a success.

"Look," Jennifer said, pointing from the window. Keelie glanced in the direction she indicated and saw two horses galloping across a field. "That's my dad and Grayson Murray."

Keelie slowed down and squinted, but she'd have never been able to identify them at that distance. "Do I need glasses? How can you tell?"

"I just know," Jennifer said. "I'm glad my dad's riding. He doesn't get to do it a lot."

When Keelie pulled into the Boones' driveway, she said, "I've always loved rock houses. It must be cool to live in a house with so much history."

"Our house is on the Godiva Tour of Homes," Jennifer said. "It's kind of weird when people come to look at it. At least they're only allowed on the first floor. Do you want to see it?"

"How can I refuse a chance to take the tour with an actual resident of the house?" Keelie asked. She hoped that when they got to the part of *Pride and Prejudice* when Elizabeth toured Darcy's ancestral home, Jennifer wouldn't remember this moment.

They went in through the kitchen so Jennifer could put her half of the lasagna and salad in the refrigerator.

The kitchen was large, and Keelie was impressed by the high ceilings with exposed beams and the back wall that was made of brick. She was also amused by Jennifer's summary of the best features of the kitchen: the expansive counter space, oversized pantry, Sub-Zero refrigerator, wide double oven, and rack over the island for hanging pots and pans.

"My dad had the kitchen redone for my thirteenth birthday," Jennifer said.

"Apparently he takes your culinary interests seriously," Keelie said.

"It was a bribe," Jennifer said. "I had to keep my grades up for my whole seventh grade year. My birthday is in June. After he got my last report card, work started on the kitchen. It took the whole summer."

Rip met them in the breakfast room, stretching after what appeared to have been a long nap, and accompanied them on their tour. As Keelie admired the house's features room by room, she found herself wondering how many of the furnishings had always been the way they were and which of them had been chosen by Lisa Boone. She had the sense that almost everything was probably much as it had been for the Boone parents and grandparents. Almost all of the furniture was antique, but it looked solid and strong. There were a number of old mirrors and prints on the walls, and she hoped that one day, she'd have the chance to really explore everything.

"This is the study," Jennifer said as she opened a door. She grinned at the way Keelie's eyes widened as she took in walls of nothing but books. "I guess you already know I don't spend much time in here."

"This would be like heaven for me," Keelie said. "I'd

do everything in here. Read by the fire. Eat by the fire. Sit with friends by the fire. It's a great room."

"Yeah, my dad spends most of his time here, too. He doesn't build that many fires, but he does read a lot. Like you." Keelie reluctantly followed her from the room. Jennifer opened a door on a small parlor and said, "This is my favorite room after the kitchen."

Keelie surveyed the worn furniture and faded rug. It was a comfortable room, but she wondered if its appeal might lie in the television and stereo she spotted. "Why is it your favorite?"

Jennifer led her to the windows and said, "In the spring and summer, it looks better out there. There are a lot of wildflowers, and nobody clears it out, so there are always birds and squirrels out there. And humming-birds. They're my favorite. Also, the walls hum."

"The walls? Why?"

"Bees get in the walls," Jennifer explained. "The buzzing sounds like humming. Do you want to go upstairs?"

"Maybe not this time," Keelie said with a sudden attack of conscience. She suspected that if any of the house had Lisa Boone's touch, it would be the upstairs rooms. She also felt weird about seeing Michael Boone's bedroom. "I'm a little tired, and I probably should get home and rest my ankle."

Jennifer and Rip walked her out through the kitchen. Jennifer told her that she'd call her again before the fol-lowing Saturday to set up their next lesson.

"You really don't mind spending your Saturdays with an old lady who doesn't know how to cook?" Keelie asked.

"I had fun today," Jennifer assured her.

Keelie had an urge to hug her but wasn't sure that was

acceptable to a teenager, so she just smiled and said, "I had fun, too. Thanks for the lesson."

She paused outside the door to pull her gloves from her coat pocket and put them on. When she glanced back through the door, she saw Jennifer talking to Rip. She was holding *Pride and Prejudice* to her chest again.

"A reader is born," Keelie whispered with satisfaction and walked to the car.

She slowed down when she got to the place in the road where she and Jennifer had seen Dr. Boone and Grayson, but there wasn't a horse or man in sight.

She went back to her apartment, picked up the rest of the lasagna, the salad, and her laundry, then drove to Granny's house. Granny and Fred were in the side yard doing something, and after she put the food in the kitchen and started a load of laundry, she went outside.

"Craziest notion I ever heard," Fred commented as she watched him take rocks from the back of his pickup and drop them on the lawn.

"What are you doing?" Keelie asked.

"I'm planting new flowers this spring and using the rocks for my landscaping," Granny said.

"She wants to use them to make a fountain, too," Fred said. "A lot of trouble. It'll draw mosquitoes in the summer and freeze up in the winter."

"You just wait and see," Granny said. She smiled at Keelie. "You look pretty today. That sweater matches your eyes. Did you bring your laundry?"

"I did," Keelie said. "But I also brought dinner to pay you back for letting me use your washer and dryer."

Granny looked surprised for a moment, then she said, "That's right. Today was your first cooking lesson from Jennifer Boone."

"At least I'll finally get a decent meal around here," Fred muttered.

"Let's leave him with the rocks and go inside," Granny suggested. "It's cold out here."

Granny poured cups of coffee for both of them, then she led Keelie to one of the house's side porches, which had been glassed in.

"What's this?" Keelie asked, looking at what appeared to be another of Granny's projects.

"This old wash stand has been in the attic forever," Granny said. "I'm stripping it."

"Can I help?"

"Sure. Let me get you an old shirt to put over your sweater."

When Granny came back with the shirt and a pair of gloves, the two of them sat on either side of the cabinet. "First you put on the stripping solution," Granny said. "Then you wait. Scrape with the scraper, and wait some more. There's a lot of waiting to this job. It goes better with someone to talk to."

"Good," Keelie said.

"Got something you want to talk about, do you?" Granny asked.

"Jennifer Boone," Keelie said. "She's an odd mixture of child and adult."

"It's that age," Granny said. "Plus I reckon she's grown up faster than most kids have to. She's quite the little lady of the house, isn't she?"

"She is," Keelie agreed. "One of the things I admire about my mother, looking back, is that she didn't let my father's death cheat Misty and me out of our childhood. I knew even then that she worried about things. Probably money. Trying to raise us on her own. But I had a lot of fun as a kid, too. Jennifer seems lonelier than I was."

"You had a sister," Granny pointed out. "And Jennifer's getting to an age where a mother is probably more help than a father."

"What about her aunt?"

"Laura?" Granny asked. Keelie nodded but kept quiet as Granny became lost in thought. Finally she said, "Maybe if you knew a little about the Fleming girls' background, it would explain Laura."

"Okay," Keelie said.

"I don't like to talk bad about people, and their grandparents were good folks. I grew up with them. They had three sons. Two of them moved away. The one who stayed was the father of Laura and Lisa. I don't know how Earl Fleming came out of that family. He was sorry as a kid and didn't get better when he grew up. Always looking to make a fast dollar, and he didn't care if it was legal or not. In and out of trouble. And his wife wasn't much better. Trashy, both of them. I think Laura got married to get out of their house. Her husband's a good man. They live in one of the New Coventry developments, but when they were first married, they rented a house in town. She brought Lisa to live with her, which was probably the best thing that ever happened to that girl."

"What was Lisa like?"

Granny sighed and said, "She was smart. And pretty. But there was always something about her . . . I don't know. I guess you'd call it calculating. Laura was the same. Not that I blame them for wanting to get away from their parents or trying to better themselves. But both girls were always aloof. You knew who they were and couldn't say anything bad about them, but you couldn't get close to them, either. I'm probably not making any sense."

They scraped in silence for a while, then Keelie stopped to drink her coffee, which was barely warm. She took both cups into the kitchen and topped them off, then came back, sat down, and put on her gloves again.

"Ambitious," Granny said, breaking the silence. "Maybe that's the word I'm looking for. No matter what Lisa did—whether it was making good grades or becoming a Daughter of Godiva or dating Michael Boone—you always got the idea that she wasn't enjoying the moment as much as trying to get one step farther away from her parents."

"They started dating in high school?" Keelie asked.

"Yep. And his parents didn't like it. Not that disapproval ever stopped hormones. They went away to A&M together. Both of them were planning to go to vet school and open a practice together. Then, out of the blue, Michael told his parents they'd gotten married. Lisa dropped out of school and worked until he was finished with vet school. By then, Michael's parents had decided to move to Galveston. He and Lisa moved into the Boone house, and she managed his practice. I'm sure those were lean years for them. It took time for ranchers to entrust their animals to a young vet. It was Grayson's business that helped Michael expand the clinic. He also referred other horse ranchers to Michael. Michael's always had good friends, and I suppose they were Lisa's friends, too. But just like when she was growing up, she never seemed that close to anybody."

Granny stopped talking, and the anxious look she gave Keelie made Keelie say, "What? Am I doing this wrong?"

"No. You're a lot of help. I feel like I shouldn't be saying bad things about her because she's dead. I'll tell you the only person who ever seemed to really know Lisa, and that was Dorothy. Dorothy wasn't the school principal then, she was a science teacher. She took a lot of interest in Lisa. It was Dorothy who made sure Lisa filled out her applications for college. Dorothy saw that Lisa got the financial aid she needed, including a scholarship. A scholarship also comes with being crowned a Daughter of Godiva, and Dorothy sponsored her in that. She went to a lot of trouble for Lisa, and once Lisa married Michael and dropped out of A&M, she avoided Dorothy. I don't know if she felt like she'd disappointed her or what, but I know it hurt Dorothy. I guess that's probably the biggest thing that colored my opinion of her, because Dorothy is a fine woman and deserved better. I don't know. Lisa always seemed more comfortable with animals than with people. But I do believe she loved her daughter, and it's sad for Jennifer that she died."

"But not for Michael," Keelie surmised.

"I think the world of Michael Boone," Granny said. "Maybe I sound like a judgmental, nosy old woman, but he deserved better than he got from Lisa. Not, to my knowledge, that anyone has ever heard him complain about her. But there was something missing. His parents knew it, too. They were always pleasant to Lisa—"

"But they couldn't get close to her, either," Keelie said.

"They're crazy about Jennifer," Granny said. "She usually spends a month with them in Galveston during the summer. Anyway, maybe I'm just full of it. After all, there are plenty of people who think Fred and I have a strange marriage, too."

"I don't," Keelie said. "All that bickering doesn't fool me for a second. You two adore each other."

"I just keep him around because nobody else will have him," Granny said. "Anyway, enough of all that. I'd rather talk about you. Lurleen over at the Bird told me you were putting your head together with Faith Taylor and Vanessa Bowen. What are you three up to?"

"I'm not here to give you material for your blog," Keelie said.

"I hope Faith hasn't roped you in to joining her Godiva committee. I've got first dibs."

"Why? What do you do at the festival?" Keelie asked suspiciously. "I've been warned to avoid the dunking booth and concessions."

"In your wildest dreams, can you imagine anyone letting me near food?" Granny asked.

"Does that mean it's the dunking booth?"

"I organize the dog show and pick its judges," Granny said.

"That doesn't sound so bad," Keelie said. "I like dogs."

"Good. I'll put you down for poop patrol."

"Wait. I thought I'd be judging them."

"You have to start at the bottom—literally—and work your way up."

By the time she got home that night, Keelie was exhausted. She didn't want to dwell on the things Granny had told her about Lisa Boone, but it was nearly impossible not to. She felt like she was grieving, but she wasn't sure for what. Maybe for someone who'd gotten married when he was only nineteen. To a woman who might not have adored or even appreciated him the way Keelie thought he deserved. Which was crazy. She couldn't know him on the basis of two meetings, and nobody knew what went on in a marriage but the two people who were in it.

But you can *tell,* she thought. All married couples argued and had problems, but even when their relationships mellowed after the falling-in-love stage, something visible remained. Like her mother and Huck. They had so much fun together, whether they were working or just hanging around the house. As squeamish as it might make her to think of them being romantic, she remembered what a kick he'd thought it was when her mother got her bellybutton pierced with Misty and her.

Or Misty and Holly. They were like a solid unit with their husbands. They might joke and complain about their snoring or how they left their clothes lying around, but anyone could tell they loved Matt and Dave. Carla and Scotty were going to be that way, too, just as Mrs. Johnson had been with Ivy, Holly, and Scotty's father.

That's what I'd want, she thought. *I wouldn't settle for less. It sounds like Michael did. But that was his choice. He must have had his reasons. He must have loved her.*

Anyway, if Granny was right, Lisa had been a good mother. She'd helped put Michael through school and worked in his practice with him. Maybe she'd had a hard time getting close to people because she was shy. Or maybe she felt insecure because she'd come from a bad home.

"Maybe in a way," she said, "Destiny's story is a little like Lisa's. What kind of adult will Destiny become, after her awful childhood? Will there be a Dorothy in her life, who helps pull her out of it?"

Even though she was tired, she went to her office, sat down at the computer, and opened her manuscript. She couldn't rewrite Lisa Fleming's life. She couldn't give her a happily ever after with her husband and daughter. And Destiny's book would end long before she grew up, but Keelie had to give her hope of a way out of her unhappy childhood.

She stared in front of her, seeing only what was in her head, until Lisa faded and Jennifer took over. Then gradually, Jennifer was gone, and Keelie's mind was full of Destiny. No matter how bad things got for Destiny, she always had Rip and the natural beauty around her. Keelie had a sudden image of the Boone house, then she smiled as she remembered Granny and Fred arguing over Granny's plans for a new garden with a fountain. She watched the monitor as her fingers flew over the keys.

They were just Alabama rocks, free for the taking from Mr. Joiner's farm, but when the sun shone on them, Destiny thought they looked like honey . . .

Chapter 19

"This is the third time you've wanted to eat at Broadgate Tavern," Evan said after they were seated. "I don't mind having dinner with you, but Grayson was right. This is not the best food to be had in Coventry, and I'm getting tired of bangers and mash."

"Order something else," Keelie said, pretending to study her menu while furtively checking out the games room. Of course Dr. Boone wasn't there, just as he hadn't been there on the other two occasions that she'd badgered Evan into coming to the tavern.

"I suppose I could get the shepherd's pie, but I don't know if it's made from real shepherds," Evan said.

"Uh-huh," Keelie grunted, looking toward the door at some new arrivals, none of whom was Dr. Boone.

"Maybe I should do the South Beach Diet," Evan said.

"What? Where? You're going to Miami?" she asked, turning her gaze back to him.

"South Beach *Diet*," he repeated.

"Why would you go on a diet? There's not an ounce of fat on your body."

"I was just confirming that you aren't listening to me," Evan said.

"I've heard every word you said. Why didn't you ask Grayson to join us tonight?"

"He's training a draft horse or something," Evan said. "That's all a mystery to me. And he probably doesn't want to play pool against you again."

"Chicken!" Keelie said.

Their waitress stopped on her way past their table and sounded a little huffy when she said, "As soon as I give them their drinks, I'll come back to take your order."

As she hurried off, Evan laughed at Keelie's abashed expression and said, "Making friends wherever you go."

"I can't believe she thinks I'm rude enough to yell my order at her," Keelie said. "Next thing you know, I'll be reading about myself on Granny's blog. Tell me a salon story."

"I don't know if I should," Evan said. "Back in the old days, the likelihood of you knowing any of my clients was slim. But now they're people you could meet any time. I can't be putting their business out there for everybody. I'm all about discretion."

She gave him a withering look just as the waitress returned for their orders. Keelie relayed hers in as sweet a tone as she could, but the waitress was clearly having none of her, especially when Keelie ordered grilled chicken. She was visibly nicer to Evan and recommended one of the restaurant's imported beers to go with his meal.

"At least I'm making *you* friends wherever I go," Keelie said sadly when they were alone again.

Evan showed his smile lines and said, "Everybody loves the hair god. I saw a new client today. She brought her dog with her. You know how they say people look like their dogs?"

"Uh-huh."

"Frighteningly true in this case."

"Why? What kind of dog does she have?"

"Pug. I swear, they could be mother and son. She was really sweet, though. She gave me a big tip. Probably because I had dog biscuits for Hoover."

"Her dog is named Hoover?" Keelie asked. He nodded, and she said, "Why did you have dog biscuits?"

"I bought a pack for Hamlet," Evan said. "But I'm not giving them to you. Who knows how many women may show up with a dog in tow?"

"Or a kid," Keelie said. "What kid doesn't love a delicious dog biscuit?" She winced when she realized that their waitress was back with Evan's pint. This time she didn't even glance at Keelie. When she was gone again, Keelie said, "That's it. I have to move."

"I'm not helping you," Evan said. "A friend only gets moving help every three years or so."

"You did nothing to help me," Keelie said. "My mother paid good money for that. Whereas I did move you. You owe me."

"As I recall," Evan said, "you were incapacitated then. You watched the rest of us take boxes up the stairs."

"I unpacked your bathroom stuff."

"You unpacked one suitcase that had products in it."

"Hello? It was a footlocker, and you have a lot of hair products," she said.

"Fine. If you move, I'll handle your kitchen stuff. I'm sure most of it is still in boxes anyway."

"Don't forget that I'm taking cooking lessons. You should be nicer if you want a dinner invitation."

"Having experienced a couple of your attempts in the past, I'll forego the pleasure," Evan said.

"You'll be sorry."

"I don't think so." He picked up a specialty drinks menu and studied it for a few minutes, then broke the silence. "What is so damned fascinating in the games room?"

"Nothing," she said.

"You're being strange," he said and tried not to smile at Keelie's expression when the waitress picked that moment to show up with their food. Fortunately she refrained from agreeing with him before she left.

"Do you ever think about how much our lives have changed in the past two months and freak out?" she asked.

He stared at her for a few seconds, then said, "Yes. You didn't think I'd say that, did you? But I do. We've changed jobs. Towns. Ivy's gone. Holly's gone. I'm in love. And you're learning to cook. The world has gone mad."

"Stop making fun of me."

"I'm not. It all happened so fast that you didn't have time to think about it. Now you do. Change is stressful, even when it's good change. Sometimes I wake up in the middle of the night and hear the Talking Heads."

"This is not your beautiful life?" she asked.

He nodded. "Your job may have been stale, but it was comfortable. Almost mindless. Sure you worked long hours at times, but it was basically go there, do it, leave, and dread going back the next day. Same with me. I went in, did my magic, and left. Somebody else stocked all the right products, dealt with sales reps, handled my appointments, made sure there were always stacks of clean towels, worried about liability insurance, paid the utility bills, dealt with tax withholding—"

"Stop!" she said. "Now I'm not only freaking out about me, I'm freaking out about you."

"But when I turn on the lights in the morning and reverse the sign to say 'Open,' or finish sweeping up at night and look around, it's all mine. Well, mine and Coventry Central Bank's. But you get what I mean. Maybe I deal with a bitchy client now and then, but I'm my own insane boss. When I look out the window, I see a little town where people are mostly pleasant. If I have a bad day, I can walk around the block and find you and a cup of coffee, or spend the evening with a man who treats me well, and life is good."

"Sometimes I get bogged down in my Wonderful Wife stuff and wonder what the hell my mother was thinking. What do I know about all that? I love working on my novel, then I watch CNN and the news is horrible, and I think, 'What difference would it make even if it was published? Who will care?' I love Coventry, but I find myself thinking about people from Buy The Book, or Mrs. Atwell's hair, or going out with you guys and watching the endless parade of Houston characters, and I feel like I've been dropped into somebody else's life."

"What do you do then?"

"I watch a *Facts of Life* marathon. Or clutch Hamlet and stare at the walls."

"You need to get laid."

"I totally do."

He paid the check and said, "You're coming home with me, missy."

"I don't think sex will work with us," Keelie said.

Her morose mood stayed with her during their drive. She couldn't understand why Dr. Boone had become the invisible man. She also couldn't understand why she didn't pick up the phone and call him. If she could think of a plausible reason, she would. Although she supposed opening a phone conversation with, "Dr. Boone, it's Keelie Cannon, and I need to get laid" would get a result. Like maybe a restraining order.

When they were inside Evan's shop, he pulled the shades and said, "No reason why anybody who drives by should see this."

"Have your way with me," she said, lifting her hands in a gesture of surrender.

"How many years have I waited to hear that from you?" he asked.

The only time he stopped was to take a call from Grayson. He explained that he couldn't come over because he was having a Keelie night.

"Wow, do I really need a whole night?" she asked.

"I want to take my time and do this right."

"Whatever."

Two hours later, he turned her chair around and smiled when her mouth fell open. "A shinier, even more adorable Keelie."

"I love it," she said, turning her head. He gave her a hand mirror and spun the chair so she could see the back of her head. "I can't believe I never let you give me highlights before. I always thought I'd look like a member of Vixen."

"Or like Freddie Prinze, Jr. in *Scooby-Doo*."

"If I looked like him, I'd never get out of my bed," she said.

"If you looked like Freddie Prinze, Jr., you'd never get *me* out of your bed," Evan said, "although I would correct your hair."

"You'll let me pay for this, won't you?"

"Are you nuts? Come on. I'll drive you home."

"I can walk," she insisted.

"I'm locking up and leaving anyway," he said. "I'm going to Grayson's. Unless you're still in a funk. I don't have to see him."

"I'm fine," she said. "Let's go."

As soon as she got inside her apartment, the phone began to ring, and she grabbed it.

"Keelie? Michael Boone."

"Hi," she said, hoping her voice didn't sound as squeaky to him as it did to her.

"I know it's late, but I'm about three minutes from your apartment. If it's okay, I'd like to talk to you."

"Can you give me five minutes?" she asked. "I just walked in the door, and I have to—honestly, I have to pee. I drank a lot of coffee at dinner."

"Can you multitask?"

"Why do you ask?"

"Pee and ponder this question: What's the difference between animals and people? See you in five."

She whipped through her apartment with Wonderful Wife efficiency, then made sure her makeup hadn't suffered too much damage from the shampooing Evan had given her. At least her hair looked amazing.

When she let Dr. Boone in, he must have thought so, too, because he barely said hello before he kissed her. After feeling stunned for perhaps a tenth of a second, Keelie kissed him back. With enthusiasm.

"That's what I thought," he said, pulling away. "Do you have an answer to my question?"

"Do you have attention deficit disorder?" she asked.

"Yes. Animals, unlike people, can't lie to you."

"That's true. In fact, it's probably truer than what I was thinking."

"Which was what?"

"They don't speak our language. They can't say what hurts or what they're afraid of or what happened to them."

"Would you like to take off your coat for this trip to *Animal Planet?*" she asked.

"When I examine an animal," he said, ignoring her question, "I have to watch and feel everything the animal does. How its eyes react. Whether I can feel muscles bunching up under the skin in response to my touch or some internal pain. The way it draws into itself. Anything irregular about gait, posture, or reflexes. I'm very good at what I do."

"I've seen you work," she said. "I believe you."

"That tends to happen with my human interaction, too. Sometimes I realize that I'm not listening to what someone's saying to me. Instead, I'm assessing their body language."

"Okay," she said, wondering why he couldn't see that her body was suggesting less talk, more kissing.

"When I walked into the exam room and saw you for the first time, this thing happened that's never happened to me before. I'm not exactly an inexperienced kid. I was married for ten years. I haven't been a monk in the five years since my wife died. But this was new. For example, I realized you had to be on medication or you'd have favored your bad ankle more. I knew you felt the attraction I felt by the way you shook my hand. And you liked it when I lifted you onto the gurney."

"Guilty," she said.

"The next time I saw you, at Grayson's, that thing between us was still there. You kissed me back. Just like you did tonight."

"Yes."

"But something made you back off that day, and you told me you had a boyfriend. Which surprised your friend Evan when I mentioned it, although he covered for you. Then my daughter told me it wasn't true. I couldn't figure out why you invented a boyfriend. But tonight, something Jennifer said might have given me my answer. You didn't know I was single, did you?" When she shook her head, he said, "So that's why you got mad at me for kissing you? Why you never e-mailed me Rip's story?"

"Yes."

"I wish you'd said something. It doesn't feel good to know you thought I'd be that disrespectful to you. Or to the wife you assumed I had."

"I'm sorry. You're right," she said. "I should have asked why you, as a married man, were kissing me. Now I want to know why you're not."

"Not what? Married?"

"Kissing me."

He laughed and said, "It's early calving season, and cows are notoriously indifferent to my private life. I have a seventy-mile drive ahead of me to the Ghost Springs Ranch, and by tomorrow morning, I'll have half a dozen more urgent calls to deal with. This will be my life for a few weeks. My techs will run my practice and call in other vets if they need one. I'll catch sleep wherever there's a spare room or in my truck. It's a bad time to start a romance."

"Where's Jennifer during all this?"

"At her Aunt Laura's."

"Can I go with you?"

"Tonight?"

She nodded and said, "I'll stay out of your way while you're working. Unless there's something I can do to help."

"You'll be cold and bored," he warned. "I have no idea what time we'll get back in the morning."

"I make my own schedule," she said. "And I can dress for the cold."

He stared at her a moment, then said, "Do you have a thermos?"

"Yes."

"Show me where the coffee is. I'll make it while you change clothes. Dress in layers. Clothes that can get dirty."

She dressed quickly, gave Hamlet fresh water and food, and thirty minutes later they were on the road. She programmed his numbers and Laura's into her cell phone, then programmed her cell number into his phone. She liked that he already had her home phone number. Apparently her imaginary boyfriend hadn't deterred him too much. Unless he'd just gotten the number because Jennifer would be at her place on Saturdays.

He lowered the volume on the radio and said, "Talk to me. Tell me about Keelie Cannon."

"What do you want to know?"

"Anything. Everything. Growing up. Your family. School. Religion. Politics. Boyfriends. The real ones."

She gave him the condensed story of her life, noticing again that he was an attentive listener, even though he couldn't watch her while she talked. He shook his head over her account of Rodney, smiled when she talked about her family and Hamlet, and looked thoughtful when she compared her loss of her father to Jennifer's loss of her mother.

"That about sums it up," she finally said.

After a pause, he said, "So this thing with Jennifer . . ."

"I made my deal with her before I knew your wife

had died," Keelie said. "I wasn't trying to get to you through your daughter."

"The thought never crossed my mind. In fact, if anybody's finessing this situation, it's Jennifer."

"Oh?"

"The day you brought Hamlet in, I made a feeble attempt to find out if you were single when I told Jen to let us know when your friend came back."

"The Miss or Mrs. Cannon thing?" Keelie asked.

"Jennifer got a lot of mileage out of it. All through Christmas, it was *Miss* Cannon this and *Miss* Cannon that. 'I'll bet *Miss* Cannon would like your new shirt, Daddy.' Or, 'You should get a haircut. *Miss* Cannon might not like it long.' She was a pest."

"Miss Cannon likes your hair just the way it is," Keelie said. "The first time I ran into her after I moved here, I didn't think she remembered me."

"She remembered. I heard all about Miss Cannon, the dominos, and the cooking lessons. If I hadn't been so busy, I'd have tried to see you and warn you that somebody was matchmaking. But the only day I actually had leisure time was Saturday, and she was with you."

Keelie smiled and said, "When my mother met Huck, my little sister and I concocted all kinds of schemes to throw them together. We liked him, and we were so afraid that he'd get away. It never mattered to us whether or not she liked him. Fortunately, she did."

He rested his hand on top of hers and said, "In case you're wondering, I like you. I should have asked Grayson to pass you a note through Evan. You could have told Vanessa and Faith that you liked me back."

"While we were making book covers from grocery bags," she said.

"You could have written my name on your tennis shoes."

"I could have longed for you to write a big 'I heart Keelie' on my cast."

"Our friends could have arranged to get us together at the pep rally. Actually, that's not far-fetched. They're always trying to set me up with somebody."

"Has there been anybody serious since Lisa died?"

"Nope." He was quiet for a while, but she felt no need to fill the silence. Finally he said, "You don't realize the millions of decisions and adjustments you make for a child until you're suddenly on your own. Jen always has to come first. Even though I've dated, there's been no one serious enough to bring into her life. If it didn't work out, Jen would lose her, too. She's lost enough."

"I understand," Keelie said. "I get the idea that Jennifer and her mother were close."

"Yes. You'll probably hear things about Lisa. I'm sure half the town already knows my truck was outside your apartment tonight and that you left with me. Tongues will wag, and a lot of them will wag to you."

"You could tell me first," she suggested.

She traced his fingers with hers and watched the road while he talked.

"I always knew who Lisa was," he said. "I never paid particular attention to her. Then in tenth grade, she was my biology lab partner. I liked her because she wasn't squeamish when we dissected things. I wanted to be a vet, but until I started talking about it to her, I don't think she ever thought about doing the same. We sort of stumbled into dating. You know those golden couples in teen movies that all the geeky kids hate? The star athlete and the popular girl?"

"Uh-huh."

"That wasn't us. We were just normal kids. Playing at

being in love. Thinking we were all grown up and could plan our lives."

"But you did do that, didn't you? You went away to college. You planned to open a practice together. Then you got married and had a baby, and she put her education on hold, right?"

"Not exactly."

She saw him glance at her, but it was too dark in the truck for her to read his expression. After a couple of minutes, he began talking again.

"Lisa and Laura had a bad home life. Laura got married to get away from her parents, and Lisa was determined not to do the same. She cared about me, and no matter what you hear, she wasn't using me to better her lot in life. In fact, after we went to College Station, we broke up. Lisa liked starting over in a place where no one knew her background. She reinvented herself."

"How did you feel about that?"

"I was eighteen," he said. "We had plenty of tension over it, but she'd always been my friend as much as my girlfriend, and we held on to that. Lisa got involved with one of her teachers. She ended up pregnant. He gave her money for an abortion and broke it off. She was crushed. Nineteen years old, scared to death, and alone. Except not alone, because I was there. She didn't want to have an abortion, so we got married."

Keelie frowned and said, "There's no way Jennifer isn't your daughter. She's a feminine version of you."

"Jennifer came later," he said. "Lisa miscarried her first child. Afterward, she just sank for a while. She dropped out of school. Saw a therapist for depression. There were times I wasn't sure she'd come out of it, but she did."

"It must have been hard on both of you," Keelie said,

thinking back to herself at that age. Her college years had been a breeze compared to his. She'd always known that no matter what happened, her mother and Huck would be there for her. She'd never felt alone the way Lisa must have. Or endured the parental disapproval that Granny had implied Michael went through because of Lisa. She'd gotten plenty of that from Gram, though. She knew what it felt like when love had conditions attached.

"Jennifer wasn't planned, and I felt a little overwhelmed. They say a child can't save a marriage. Maybe not if that's why you have the child, but our real marriage began after Jen was born. We fell in love with her, and because of her, we fell in love with each other. Adult love, not kids' love. As hard as those years were financially, with Lisa balancing work and childcare and me balancing family and school, we were happy. Lisa was a good mother. She hadn't had one, so she put a lot of thought into it." He paused. "Does it bother you to hear all this? I can shut up any time."

"It doesn't bother me," Keelie said.

"I wanted to talk to you after I heard about your deal with Jennifer because of the reading thing. Lisa, like me, always had a book in her hand. When she was pregnant, we used to read to her stomach."

"Aw," Keelie said, and her eyes filled with tears.

"Don't get all mushy on me. I was reading textbooks, so Lisa got to read the good stuff to her. After Jennifer was born, it was common to see either of us holding Jen in one arm and a book in the other. Reading out loud helped when she cried. When she was teething. When she fought sleep. It continued as she got older. She never went to bed without being read a story. After Lisa died, I read to Jen in the hospital. When she came home, she asked me to stop. She said she was old enough to read by herself. If I'd been thinking more clearly, I probably wouldn't have let that happen. That's when her dislike of reading began."

"She let me read to her," Keelie said.

"She's probably craved that for a long time. Since you didn't know it was a big deal, I guess it didn't feel like one to her." He slowed the truck, pulled off on the shoulder, put the emergency brake on, then turned to look at her. "Except for Grayson and a couple of my other friends, nobody knows some of the stuff I've just told you."

"I won't repeat it," Keelie said.

"I'm not worried about that. Lisa wasn't perfect. She was human. I'm not sure what people expected from her, and I don't care what they say as long as Jennifer has a balanced perspective of her mother."

"You're a good father," Keelie said. She squeezed his hand, then let it go. "Thank you for explaining things to me."

"I come with a child, a beat-up dog, a town full of nosy people, and a little bit of baggage," he said. "Do you still like me?"

She unfastened her seat belt, climbed across the seat to tuck herself between him and the steering wheel, and said, "What does my body tell you, Dr. Boone?"

Chapter 20

After Michael delivered a breech calf, he and some of the ranch hands had to look for cows who'd strayed to distant pastures to drop their calves in private. It had started to sleet. Since they'd be using flashlights to cover unfamiliar terrain and he didn't want her to risk reinjuring her ankle, Keelie stayed in the truck. Despite drinking two cups of coffee, she fell asleep. Just before dawn, he came back, and the blast of cold air from his open door woke her.

"Sorry," he said. He yawned and reached for the thermos.

"Why don't you let me drive back?" she suggested. "I'm rested, and you can sleep."

"You sure?"

She nodded and they switched places. She liked being with him inside the warm truck when it was so cold outside. She liked the way he slept next to her, as if he felt as comfortable as she did. It seemed strange to think of all the weeks she'd felt anxious or nervous about him, because now that she was with him, she was totally at ease. It was like they'd been together always.

People were beginning to be out and about by the time she got to Coventry. Instead of going back to her apartment, she drove to his house, where there was less chance of being observed and fueling gossip.

Michael woke up when she killed the engine, looked around, and said, "Good. I'll let you in the house while I check on my patients."

Rip met her inside the door, and she let him out so he could make a run around the yard. When he came back inside, she knelt to pet him. Then she used the bathroom, washed her face, and admired her hair. Evan truly was the hair god for giving her a cut that had survived several hours of sleep in the cab of a truck.

Rip kept her company in the kitchen. She could manage to cook a decent breakfast of eggs, bacon, and toast. She just hoped she wouldn't use some special pan of Jennifer's and ruin it.

Michael laughed when she told him that as they sat down to eat. "She keeps her favorites put away ever since I used her cornbread skillet to burn sausage. I generally stay out of her kitchen now. This is good. I thought you couldn't cook. I don't know who's the bigger con artist: you or Jen."

"I exaggerate my flaws," Keelie said. "Actually, breakfast is one of the only things I can cook. Except for grits and biscuits. I don't do those. My oatmeal is exquisite, however. I think it's wonderful that you encourage Jennifer's dream of being a chef. Especially that you renovated the kitchen for her."

"It needed it anyway. The appliances were my parents' 1970s stuff. Avocado green. There's a direct correlation between the life span of an appliance and how ugly it is."

"That's true," she said. "I owned a TV that was older

than Anna Nicole Smith's husband. It didn't have a remote. It wasn't cable friendly. The knobs were cracked, the veneer was chipped, and the damn thing wouldn't die."

"What finally killed it?"

"It's probably not dead yet. I donated it."

"Maybe old J. Howard Marshall didn't die either," Michael said. "He could be watching Anna Nicole's show on your TV."

They loaded the dishwasher together after they finished eating. Michael stared out the window for a minute, then said, "It's not going to be a good weekend for vets and newborn calves."

"Why not?"

"Snow."

She backed away from him, struck a pose out of *Invasion of the Body Snatchers,* and said, "You're one of them!"

"That's an interesting look for you," he said placidly. "One of whom?"

"The people who promise snow and never deliver."

"I don't control the weather, but I'm relatively confident we'll have snow by the weekend."

"Sure we will. What do you have to do now?"

He looked at the clock and said, "I have a sick horse to see at a farm in Mineral Wells. I could take you home. Or there are unopened toothbrushes in my bathroom, if you want to get cleaned up or take a nap. I should be back before noon."

"I don't know where your bathroom is," Keelie said. "I only saw the first floor on my grand tour."

He let Rip out again, then took her upstairs. When they walked into his bedroom, he said, "I had all the bedrooms redone last summer when they renovated the kitchen. Jennifer was ready to make the change from a kid's room to a teenager's room. This one still had my parents' stuff in it, because Lisa and I used the bedroom next to Jennifer's, which is now a guest room. I kept their furniture, but had the carpet pulled up, the floors redone, and the walls repainted. Faith picked out all this other stuff. I'd have been okay with a blanket and a pillow."

"She has a good eye," Keelie said, admiring the masculine appeal of the room.

"She is an artist," he said. "That's one of her paintings over the fireplace."

Keelie studied it for a moment and said, "I like abstracts. It's horses, right?"

"You have a good eye, too." He pointed. "Bathroom's through that door. Use anything you need. Sleep in my bed, or take the guest room if you'll be more comfortable. If you don't feel like sleeping, I've got lots of books in my study. And a computer. It's networked with the clinic's computers, and it has Internet access. Make yourself at home."

"Thanks," she said.

He kissed her again, then he was gone. She went into the bathroom and looked around, then picked up a bottle of his aftershave to sniff it. When she realized what she was doing, she set it down hard and said, "I will never admit to Ivy that I did that."

She opened drawers until she found a new toothbrush, and was brushing her teeth when Rip came in to check on her. She yawned while she petted him, then she undressed and turned on the shower.

"I guess he'll see what I look like without makeup," she said, studying her reflection after she got out of the shower. She wrapped herself in a towel while she dried her hair, then she neatly folded her clothes and laid them on the bed. He'd told her to make herself at home, so she took one of his shirts from the closet and put it on, then opened drawers in his dresser until she found a pair of thermal underwear. She shook her head as she looked at her reflection and said to Rip, "All hope of being sexy has just succumbed to death by cotton."

After she put on a pair of socks, she and Rip went downstairs to the study, where she found a Janet Evanovich mystery that Granny hadn't owned. When she went back upstairs, she hesitated, looked down the hall, then chose his room.

She read only a few pages before she fell asleep. When she woke up, she heard the shower running. Rip was on his back at the foot of the bed, all four legs in the air, and she said, "Not much of a guard dog, are you?" In answer, he twisted his body until his head hung off the bed. "You're an excellent contortionist, however." She climbed out of bed, took off the socks and thermal underwear, and said, "You can keep a secret, right?"

She pulled the shirt over her head, dropped it on the floor, and went to take her second shower of the day.

"Someday, I'll have to tell Faith how comfortable this bed is," Keelie said, scooting closer to Michael.

He kept his eyes closed, but he smiled. He ran one hand over her stomach until his fingers found her belly-button piercing.

"I don't know why that thing is so sexy," he said. "I didn't get a good look at the charm. What is it?"

"A peach," Keelie said.

"Right. Georgia."

"My sister's doesn't have a charm, but my mom's has

a little bulldog. Since Misty and I went to the University of Georgia, and that's the school mascot."

"Your mother's bellybutton is pierced?"

"Uh-huh. It was one of those girl things we all did together."

"I like girl things," he said.

"I noticed."

He laughed and opened his eyes. They stared at each other for a while with the wordless satisfaction of two people who'd discovered that everything worked between them in ways that were better than they'd hoped.

"I have an idea," Keelie said.

"I like your ideas," he said. "Lay it on me."

"While you're spending all these nights away, wouldn't Jennifer rather be home than at her Aunt Laura's?"

"I'm sure."

"Why don't I get Hamlet and stay here with her? I can sleep in the guest room."

"That won't stop people from talking."

"That doesn't bother me, if it doesn't bother you. I just think it would be better for your daughter if I don't take up residence in your bedroom. I can work at my apartment during the day and be here when she gets home from school. Get my cooking lessons every night. I could even bring my laptop here to work on my novel. Am I moving too fast?"

"I like the way you move," he said.

"I like the way you like things. Anyway, she has a Valentine's Day dance Friday night. I could take her shopping if she wants to buy something new to wear. Make sure she gets there and back. I can be here for whatever she needs. It'll give us a chance to get to know each other better. 'Cause I'm not one of those women who's going to walk out of your life. Or hers."

"I'm counting on that." He kissed her, then they were quiet for a while. "It's a lot to take on, Keelie."

"I know." She ran her thumb over his jaw, admiring it again. "My grandmother says I'm impulsive. Act first. Regret later. But this isn't a quick decision for me. From the first day I met you and Jennifer, I yearned to be right here. Even though I thought I couldn't be, because I didn't know about Lisa then. I took all my frustrated longing and put it in my writing. You and Jennifer and Rip inspired every page, even though the story is nothing like your lives."

"But this is real life," he said. "You can't control the characters or the plot. It's not always easy."

"Neither is writing," she said. "I've been where Jennifer has been. Like I told you, I lost a parent at the same age she did. I had a great mother the same way she has a great father. But I also know what it was like to have a good home get better because someone else showed up to love me and help take care of me. I believe I can give her that. I'm not saying that you're stuck with me. But no matter what happens between us, I can commit to Jennifer. I want to."

"Are you always this sweet?"

"Yes."

"Liar. I've watched you play pool," he said.

"You did? You watched me?"

"Terry and Carl told me I was pathetic. You and your indifference really put me off my dart game."

"I wasn't indifferent. Just keeping my distance from a man I thought was married. So the whole town knows you've been suffering, huh?"

"No," Michael said. "Elenore Storey hasn't blogged about it. Yet."

"Will you think about my idea?" she asked.

"No."

"No?"

"Yes. My answer is yes."

"I like it when you see things my way," she said.

"Is it wrong that I want to know details, when I never gave you any about Ted?" Ivy asked.

"Yes," Keelie said, propping the phone between her shoulder and her ear as she took cream from her refrigerator. She sniffed it to make sure it was okay, poured some in her coffee, and poured the rest down the drain. She'd have to make sure nothing was left to go bad while she was spending most of her time at Michael's.

"But at least you know Ted," Ivy said. "If I've met Dr. Boone, I don't remember him."

"He's tall. Lean. But he has good muscles. Work muscles, not gym muscles."

"Hair?"

"Brown. Falls over his collar. Parts it in the middle. But not in that 1970s way. He sort of pushes it back. I don't know who to compare him to, because all the men we know have shaved heads or that Evan look. Dr. Boone's hair is sexy. And he has incredible green eyes and long black eyelashes."

"I hate men. They always have better eyelashes, and they don't even care," Ivy complained.

"I know. There's so much injustice in the world. Poverty. Bigotry. Men's eyelashes."

"Bad movies made from TV shows—speaking of the

1970s," Ivy said. "How long do you plan to keep calling him Dr. Boone?"

"As long as it makes him laugh. He has a little tattoo on his upper right arm. The silhouette of a running horse."

"Do you like it?"

"Uh-huh." She took a sip of her coffee. "Oh, yeah. One other detail. Best. Sex. Ever."

"Now we're getting somewhere," Ivy said. "Are you sure you're not just crazed after your two-month version of foreplay?"

"Picture it: Houston. August. Sitting in a car with black vinyl seats on 45 North at five in the afternoon. Your air conditioner breaks. That's how much he makes my teeth sweat."

"I'm feeling the burn," Ivy said.

"And no complaints about using condoms."

"All this, and he's a doctor. It looks like I'm going to have to retire the 'R' list unless you can tell me a flaw."

Keelie gazed into her coffee. Maybe she should have had tea so she could try to get answers from her tea leaves. "Crap. I can't. That's bad, isn't it?"

"Yes. It means you're going to neglect your friends, start singing along to light rock on the radio, and ignore Destiny's story."

"I am absolutely not going to ignore Destiny's story," Keelie said. "In fact, I've already figured out the next chapter in my head."

"Good. Because I have an agent reading your first two-hundred pages."

"Oh, my God. Really?"

"Really. I told you that I'll get you a book deal, even if I have to beat every agent and editor in New York over the head with your manuscript. I'll need more pages for greater impact, so keep your butt out of bed and in front of the computer."

"Not a problem," Keelie said. "Because the thing about his being a doctor? Even a vet has lousy hours, especially during early calving season."

"I'll take your word for it," Ivy said. "There's his flaw, so you can relax now."

"If I were any more relaxed, I'd be under a head-stone."

Keelie decided to ignore the somewhat cool reception she got from Laura when she picked up Jennifer in New Coventry. She knew Michael had called his sister-in-law but had no idea what explanation he'd given her for the change in plans. Keelie could think of several reasons for Laura's attitude. On occasion, Keelie had felt put out when doing a favor for someone, then had felt equally put out when they didn't need her after all. It was human nature. And since by all accounts, Laura was hard to get close to, Keelie didn't take it personally. She was more concerned that Jennifer feel comfortable with the new arrangement.

As she pulled out of Laura's neighborhood of cookie-cutter ranch houses onto the highway, Keelie said, "I was thinking. I know you're a great cook, but I'd like to eat out tonight. I need to shop."

"What are you shopping for?" Jennifer asked.

"Clothes. I got a bunch of new clothes last month, but they were all for Houston weather. I need winter clothes. I need a better coat. Even though the Old Towne Shoppes are just down the street from me, they're a little pricey. I thought I might have better luck out here."

"New Coventry Mall has a Gap, The Limited, and

Foley's," Jennifer said. "There's an Old Navy across the street. And Target."

"Let's try the mall first," Keelie said.

She bought a coat, several sweaters, and some jeans at Foley's, surprised by Jennifer's patience while she tried on clothes and made her choices. She couldn't help but chide herself for spending so much money as an excuse to get Jennifer to the mall. After they ate at McDonald's—Jennifer's choice, because apparently even a gourmand could have a weakness for McDonald's french fries—Keelie suggested that they window shop.

"Doesn't your ankle hurt?" Jennifer asked.

"Nope. It's kind of fun to be a customer for a change."

They split her shopping bags between them and wandered through the mall. It seemed tiny in comparison to the Galleria, but Keelie imagined it had been a welcome addition for people who'd once had to drive to Fort Worth and Dallas to shop.

"I just thought of something," Keelie said. "You're going to a dance tomorrow night. Do you know what you're wearing?"

"If I had my way, I'd wear jeans and a hoodie," Jennifer said. "But I guess people are dressing up. I don't know why. It's not like it's prom or something."

"With your skin color and dark hair," Keelie said, "Valentine's Day should be your favorite holiday. You'll always look good in red."

"My dad gave me a red sweater at Christmas," Jennifer said. "I could wear that."

Keelie nudged her with her shoulder and said, "Can you not see that I'm trying to buy you something new? Take advantage of this moment!"

"Oh, well, if you're paying . . ."

They were passing a Hot Topic, so they went in. Jennifer tried on completely inappropriate clothes that made them giggle and joke about how her father would react. Then they went shopping in earnest, finally leaving the mall with a pleated plaid skirt from the Gap, accessories to double-belt it, a red tank that exposed a little of Jennifer's midriff if she stretched just the right way, and a short denim jacket from Aéropostale. When they got home, Jennifer modeled the clothes with different shoes and tights until they agreed on a complete outfit. She looked so adorable that Keelie wanted to be thirteen again.

Jennifer showed her where the wood was piled outside the house, and they built a fire in the study. Rip stretched out as close to the flames as he could get. Jennifer lay next to him and read out loud from *Pride and Prejudice* until they were both sleepy. While Jennifer closed the fire screen and turned out lights, Keelie took a walk outside with Rip. The sky was clear, and she had to smile. So much for Michael's prediction that it would snow.

As she curled up under the covers in the guest room, Keelie watched Hamlet run on his wheel for a few minutes before she turned off the light. She'd thought she might have trouble sleeping in an unfamiliar place, especially with the responsibility of a teenage girl in the next room. Instead, she slept hard until she felt a gentle pressure on her shoulder. She opened her eyes, but the room was dark.

"Shhh," Michael said, crawling under the covers. "I couldn't resist."

They curled up together, and she went back to sleep. The next time she woke up, the sky was gray and she was alone. She almost believed she'd imagined his late-night visit, especially when she looked out the window and his truck was gone. If she was lucky, he'd make it home that night while Jennifer was at the dance, and they could have some private time.

After Jennifer left for school, Keelie set up her laptop in the kitchen. She checked for the possibility of a wireless connection and smiled at the name "Boone's Farm." It was a secure network, though, so she'd need a password to connect. Instead of using Michael's computer, she took a shower, dressed, and went next door to the clinic.

A woman was misting some hanging plants. She looked at Keelie and said, "Hi. How can I help you?"

"I don't know if Dr. Boone told you that I'm staying with his daughter. I'm Keelie Cannon."

"Gracie Vargas," she said, holding out her hand. "I'm the office manager. Michael did say you'd be staying at the house for a while. If there's anything I can do for you, just let me know."

"Michael offered the use of his computer, but I have my laptop. I need a password to access his wireless network, though."

Gracie looked thoughtful and said, "I wonder where that is. Have you ever seen our facility? While I'm looking for the password, I could have someone give you a tour."

"I have seen it," Keelie said, gratified that for once, someone in Coventry didn't know everything about her. "I didn't meet any of the staff, though. Are you the one who was in the Bahamas at Christmas?"

"That's me," Gracie said. "You'll probably see my husband around, too. I manage the business side of things. Ricky manages the facility, including the grounds. We also have four vet techs and three animal handlers. And if all goes well, this spring, we'll have another vet to share Dr. Boone's caseload. He worries about Jennifer during his busy times, so you're an angel to look after her."

While she was talking, Gracie walked behind the counter and started looking through a file. Keelie wondered if anyone at the clinic suspected that she wasn't just Jennifer's babysitter.

The door behind Gracie opened, and Michael stuck his head out. When he saw Keelie, he smiled.

"Hi," she said. "I didn't think you were here."

"Just got back," he said. "Gracie, any emergencies?"

"None so far. A&M faxed those test results. I put them on your desk." Gracie watched as Michael gestured for Keelie to join him.

"I'll be in the office for a few minutes," he said. When they were on the other side of the closed door, he kissed her.

"Did I dream you got in bed with me last night?" she asked. "Or was that the ghost of Jeremiah Boone?"

"Depends," he said. "Did you have a good time?"

"I slept."

"Must have been Jeremiah then," he said.

"I wonder if he'll visit me tonight, when Jennifer's at her dance."

"Right. That's tonight. Does she need—"

"We went shopping last night," Keelie said. "You'll love the little black satin strapless number I picked out for her. It's hot."

"Oh, good. Be sure and get her hooked on drugs, too."

"Already taken care of."

"Keep a tab of what I owe you."

"You owe me nothing. I wanted to buy her an outfit.

She looks so cute in it. I'll pick up my digital camera today, just in case you don't get home in time to see her."

"It's been two days, and I'm already wondering what I did without you. Now if I can teach you how to mid-wife a cow without turning green—"

"I did not turn green," she said.

"You looked good green. I need to check that fax and get out of here. I'll try to make it back tonight before Jennifer leaves. Are you driving them to the school?"

"Jason's mother is."

He kissed her again, then she went back to the re-ception area.

"Found it," Gracie said, handing her a piece of paper. She now wore an amused but friendlier look. Appar-ently she'd figured out that Keelie was more than Jen-nifer's babysitter.

"Thanks," Keelie said. "Let me give you my cell phone number in case you need to call me for anything."

She wrote it down, said goodbye, and went back to the house. She smiled as she heard Michael's truck drive out, then she went to her laptop and spent the next three hours on Destiny's story. Just as she realized that her growling stomach couldn't be ignored, her cell phone rang.

"Hey, it's Huck. I figured you might not have checked your e-mail this morning. It may take a while to get the information about the Atlanta office to you. Your mother's in bed with bronchitis."

"Oh, no," Keelie said. "Has she seen a doctor?"

"I badgered her into it. How are you?"

"I'm great," she said.

"The rural life is agreeing with you?"

"Uh-huh." She paused, then said, "I'm glad you called. Are you busy?"

"Not too busy for you. What's up?"

"I met someone," she said. "A man. You can share this information as you see fit. In fact, it might be good to do it while Mom's in a weakened state. She won't be able to hound me with a lot of questions."

"Tell me about him," Huck said.

Keelie gave him the basics about Michael and Jennifer, then she said, "Was it hard dealing with a ready-made family? I'm only on my second day of this, so everything's going well. When can I expect reality to hit?"

"Since she's a teenager, be prepared for a roller coaster," Huck said. "One day you'll be her best friend. The next you'll be the embodiment of evil. Two hours later, she'll be nice again. Especially if she needs money for something."

"Were we that awful?" Keelie asked.

"Time has softened the horror," Huck said. "You know what was hardest on me?"

"What?"

"All those damn show tunes you girls listened to. I used to make up reasons to get out of the house so I could spend some time with Willie and Waylon and the boys."

"You poor thing," Keelie said. "I have no idea what kind of music Jennifer likes. I don't even know what kind of music Michael likes. I'm barely going to see him for the next few weeks. Is that any way to start a relationship? Am I crazy for doing this?"

"What does your gut tell you?"

"I'm where I want to be," Keelie said.

"Then crazy or not, ride it out. For what it's worth, I think you'll be a great stepmom."

"Let's not get ahead of ourselves," Keelie said. "It is only day two."

"I knew as soon as I met your mother that she was the one for me," Huck said. "It wouldn't have mattered if she'd had a dozen children. But the two she had just made things better."

"Thanks," Keelie said. "I hope you feel that way when you get my daily calls begging for advice."

Chapter 21

Keelie's sporadic sleep and hectic day caught up with her by mid-afternoon. Destiny's next chapter was only half-finished, but she'd felt guilty about neglecting Wonderful Wife. She'd made phone calls, sent e-mails, and rewritten an employee contract. She'd gone to her apartment to clean out the refrigerator, get more clothes, and pick up her camera and its accessories. She was almost at Michael's house when she remembered that Jennifer had given her a grocery list, so she had to go back to the grocery store, where she ran into Granny with her friend Lois.

"We thought maybe you'd come over last night," Lois said. When Keelie gave her a blank look, she said, "You missed *Sex* night."

Keelie knew her face was turning red, but before she could answer, Granny looked inside her shopping cart and said, "Is this for your cooking lesson tomorrow?"

"Tonight's dinner," Keelie said.

"Huh. You must be a fast learner."

"Actually, Jennifer's cooking dinner."

Lois frowned and said, "Isaac Phillips told me that Jennifer is staying at Laura's."

"No, she's back home," Nelson Rook said as he walked up. Keelie backed up her cart so he could get by, but he didn't seem to be in any hurry. "Ruthie Bennett and Jason are picking Jennifer up at the Boone house for the school dance tonight."

"Has Doc Boone already hired that new vet?" Granny asked.

"My Courtney wanted to ask Jennifer to spend the night after the dance, and Isaac told us she's staying at Laura's," Lois insisted.

"Is she cooking with you tonight instead of going to the dance?" Granny asked. "Maybe Jason got sick. That bug is going around—"

"Jennifer's still going to the dance with Jason," Keelie said. "She's cooking dinner for the two of us at her house. I'll be staying with Jennifer for a few nights until her father's workload eases up."

They all stared at her, then Granny said, "I believe we're finally going to get some snow."

"I think so, too," Lois said.

"That's good of you to help Doc Boone," Nelson said.

A third woman that Keelie didn't know joined them and said, "What's wrong with Dr. Boone? Don't tell me he caught that bug that's going around."

"Keelie!" Vanessa Bowen said as she came around a display and grabbed a huge box of Cheerios. She brandished it like a shield as she maneuvered her way through the carts. "I've been meaning to call you." She started pushing Keelie's cart away from the others. "If y'all don't mind, I need to have a word with Keelie."

Keelie gave the group a little wave and followed Vanessa and her shopping cart down the aisle. When they'd gotten out of earshot of the others, she said, "What's up?"

"Nothing," Vanessa said. "I was rescuing you." She looked at the Cheerios and frowned. "I don't eat cold cereal." She dropped the box in Keelie's cart. "You can't sneeze in this damn town without everybody offering you a tissue."

"And I suppose you have a Kleenex?" Keelie asked.

"I believe when and where you blow your nose is your own business." She winked at Keelie as she walked away and added, "Give Michael my best."

Keelie made it out of the grocery store without further incident. After she got to Michael's, she unloaded the groceries, then sat at her laptop to check Granny's blog, although she supposed even Granny couldn't have gotten home and on the computer that quickly.

She'd almost finished an e-mail to Holly when Jennifer came through the door with Rip on her heels.

"I hate the school bus," Jennifer said, taking an apple from a bowl and washing it.

"What happened?" Keelie asked.

"It's just Chuck Walters," Jennifer said. "He's so boring and arrogant and so—so—Mr. Collins."

"See what reading can do for you? I know exactly what you mean, and if you ever call Chuck Mr. Collins to his face, he probably won't know he's been insulted. Unless he's read *Pride and Prejudice,* too."

"He couldn't read a stop sign," Jennifer said. "Can I finish my homework at the table with you?"

"Of course," Keelie said. "But if it's math, I probably can't help you."

"It's math, but it's easy," Jennifer said.

Keelie reread her e-mail, smiled at her description of Michael—for once, the Johnson twins would know something before their grandmother did—and sent it. Then she started a similar e-mail to her mother and Misty. She and Jennifer occasionally spoke to each other, but mostly they concentrated on what they were doing. Keelie wondered if things could always stay this comfortable with them.

At four, Jennifer got up, washed her hands again, and began mixing up the ingredients for a meat loaf. When Keelie asked if she could help, Jennifer pointed to some potatoes and said she could wash them and wrap them in aluminum foil.

"All of these?" Keelie asked. "For just the two of us?"

"My dad might come home starving," Jennifer said. "But whatever we don't eat, I can always find a use for."

"All right," Keelie said doubtfully but did as she was told.

She made a salad, and Jennifer cleaned peppers and asparagus to roast in the oven. Keelie was sure she hadn't eaten asparagus until she was an adult and said so.

"I have to learn to cook anything," Jennifer said. "Even things I don't like. And if I don't try what I cook, I won't know if I'm doing it right. Usually I end up liking everything. Except Brussels sprouts. I'll never like them. Or beets."

"Me, either," Keelie said and shuddered.

She moved her laptop to Michael's study, and as she came back into the kitchen, there was a crashing noise outside. Jennifer noticed her look of concern and said, "You'll get used to stuff like that. Somebody's probably bringing in a sick cow or something. They use a chute to take an animal from a trailer into the clinic. A mad bull can make a lot of noise. By mad I mean angry. Not like mad cow disease."

"Good to know," Keelie said. "I saw bull riding

once at the rodeo. I wouldn't get anywhere near one of those things."

Jennifer shrugged and said, "They don't bother me as much as goats. Goats jump on me, and I hate that."

"Does your father treat goats, too?"

"Goats. Cows. Horses. Pigs. Sheep. I love lambs. One year, I got to bottle feed an orphaned lamb. But the best is bottle feeding a calf. The bottle is huge, and they look up at you with the sweetest expression while you're holding it."

"I want to do that," Keelie said.

"It's good that you like animals," Jennifer said.

While Keelie tried to figure out the implications of that statement, she heard someone use the knocker on the front door. Since Jennifer was busy, she said, "I'll see who it is."

"We come with the darkness," Evan said as she opened the door. He had a bag flung over his shoulder.

Grayson smiled at Keelie's confusion and said, "Fashion house call. Michael tells me that my godchild is going to a dance tonight, and Evan's prepared to turn her into a swan."

"Not like that'll take much effort," Evan said. "Are you going to let us in?"

"Does everyone know I'm here?" Keelie asked as they stepped inside.

"You were the talk of the Shop 'n Save today," Evan said. "It's just a few small steps from there to my salon. But we really are here at Michael's request. I'm all about privacy, and I'd never stick my nose into your business just because you neglected to tell me what all of Coventry knows."

"What does all of Coventry know?" Keelie asked with exasperation.

He whispered, "That Keelie Cannon is a child-snatching, vet-loving woman who's finally figuring out what it means to live in a small town. And you took Jennifer shopping last night."

"How do you know that?"

"Ignore him," Grayson said. "He's getting his information from me, and I got it from Michael. I'm sure there are people who don't know—or care—that you're spending time with Jennifer while her father's so busy."

"I heard it from Granny before I heard it from you," Evan said. His smile lines deepened as he looked past Keelie and said, "There's the dancing queen now."

Keelie tried not to look surprised when Jennifer said, "Hi, Gray. Hi, Evan. What's in the bag?"

"Beauty is in the bag," Evan said.

Jennifer smiled and said, "Dinner will be ready in about half an hour. Should I go ahead and wash my hair?"

"Yes," Evan said. He opened the leather bag and took out two bottles. "Shampoo, rinse, repeat. Then leave the conditioner on for three minutes, and rinse it out. Holler when you're decent, and I'll come up."

"I'll keep my eye on dinner," Grayson said.

"Thanks," Jennifer said. She took the bottles from Evan and went upstairs.

"Did I slip into another dimension?" Keelie asked. "You've met Jennifer one time, nearly two months ago—"

"I've met Jennifer several times," Evan said. "Sometimes she hangs out in my salon. She's made fun of me on horseback at Grayson's. We're pals."

Grayson nodded and said, "I'm sure Michael told her we were coming out tonight. I'm surprised she didn't mention it to you."

"It explains the potatoes," Keelie said. "I wonder why—" She broke off, narrowed her eyes at Evan, and slowly and with great deliberation said, "Is it at all possible that maybe the two of you might have talked about me before?"

"I'm sure your name's come up," Evan said. "You are my best friend. Even if you don't confide in me." He studied his fingernails a moment, then looked back at her. "I'm hoping that whoever made the first move, you or the good doctor, it means I won't have to eat at Broadgate Tavern again for a while."

"Count on it," Keelie said, "since a waitress there is probably telling people I feed the vet's daughter dog biscuits."

"Don't be ridiculous. Everyone knows Jennifer's the cook in this house."

After dinner, while Evan put the finishing touches on Jennifer's hair and outfit, Grayson built a fire in the study and sat in front of it with Keelie and Rip.

"All joking aside," he said, "I think it's good that Jennifer has been trying to set you up with her father for a while. If it's what you and Michael want, having Jennifer's blessing has to be a relief."

Keelie smiled and said, "I talked to my stepfather about this earlier today. Of course I'm glad that Jennifer's willing to make room for me in their lives. I guess you've known her since she was born."

"I never got to spend much time with her until I moved back here. I'd see her sometimes on holidays. They all came to my ranch in Wyoming a couple of times. She's a good kid."

"I'm sure it won't always be as easy as it is right

now—" She broke off with a noise of frustration. "I need to stop saying things like that. Everyone, including me, acts like it's a given that Michael and I are going to be together forever. Why? We barely know each other. By next month, he may have decided it's not working out. Or I may have. The only thing I know for sure is that I'll stay in Jennifer's life. Even if nothing comes of Michael and me, I'll be her friend."

"I don't think it's unusual to want something that feels right to last," Grayson said. "Or to feel it from the beginning. All love starts somewhere. First sight's as good a place as any. If you think about it, don't most people fall in love at first sight?"

"Lisa and Michael didn't."

"They neglected it for a while, but didn't it all begin when they noticed each other in high school? It's easy to say that circumstances forced them together, but what made them marry each other? What made him be the one she could count on? What made her turn to him? Why did they stay together once their supposed reason for getting married was gone? Jennifer wouldn't exist if they were just friends who were married. They struggled together during all those years, and when Michael opened his practice, Lisa was his partner there, too."

Keelie nodded and stared at the fire, realizing the truth of what he was saying.

"When Lisa died, he grieved her as deeply as anyone who's lost a life partner. He's never even come close to falling in love since then, and there were several women who'd have been more than happy if he had. If you weren't the right person for him, you wouldn't be here. And though I don't know you very well, Evan does, and he says the same thing about you."

"I don't understand how Evan knew I was keeping a

secret," Keelie said. "I never talked to him about any of this."

"It was the faux boyfriend. Even if Evan didn't know your reason for telling Michael that you had a boyfriend, it made him conscious that you two were talking about personal things. Then there was Jennifer. She met Evan the day the two of you took Hamlet to the clinic. Like the rest of the town, she knew Evan took over Molly's shop. It was only natural that since she wanted to play Cupid, she'd try to get the scoop on you from your friend. He didn't have to be a genius to figure out that she was talking him up to get information about you. Or to notice that Jen was coming to the salon with a dog named Rip. While you happened to be writing a story about a young girl with a dog named Rip."

"I guess it's a good thing that pool, and not poker, is my game," Keelie said.

"Not for me," Grayson said. "We've strayed from my point. The origin of love, whether it happens at first sight or not, is one of the great mysteries. Why shouldn't fate use a sick hamster or a near-collision between a car and a horse to bring two people together? It's no stranger than a million other beginnings."

"You are quite the philosopher," Keelie said. "Did you fall for Evan on that day when you were yelling at him?"

"I didn't fall. I was thrown. Which was quite a blow to the ego of a horseman like me."

Keelie was laughing when Evan and Jennifer came in. She checked out the outfit and said, "You look so good, Jennifer."

"Thanks. Maybe it's the lip gloss."

While Keelie took pictures of Jennifer, Evan said, "I warned her that if she ever puts makeup on that face, I'll dunk her head in a water trough. Her coloring is perfect. Nothing but clear gloss until she's over thirty."

Evan and Grayson left not long after Mrs. Bennett and Jason picked up Jennifer. Keelie thought Jason was adorable, but she was a little relieved that he was a boy who was a friend and not a boyfriend. Both he and Jennifer seemed much younger and innocent than she remembered herself being at that age.

"Which means that I'm probably being totally naïve about Jennifer," she told Hamlet when she fed him. "In this day and age, she probably knows a zillion times more than I knew when I was thirteen. Thank goodness I don't have to worry about *you* dating. A cardboard box, a leaf of lettuce, and you're content to stay home with me."

She went into Michael's bedroom to leave his Valentine's Day presents on his dresser. She'd bought him a plaid Ralph Lauren shirt at Foley's. The green in it matched his eyes. She'd also printed the partial manuscript of Destiny's story and tied it with a red ribbon.

"Am I being presumptuous to give him something on a lover's holiday?" she asked Rip, who watched her from the bed. "This is outstanding. Now I have a hamster and a dog to talk to. It's like I'm Keelie Freakin' Dolittle." She lay down on the bed next to him. "I'm exhausted. I should go to bed. Except I need to stay awake until Jennifer comes home. If I could just rest my eyes for a minute . . . If you were a better watchdog and would wake me up when she gets home . . . If I weren't so tired . . ."

When she opened her eyes, the lights were off but she could tell by the windows that it was early morning. That jolted her awake; she'd never heard Jennifer come in. She sat up and realized that Michael was crawling toward her from the foot of the bed, a wrapped condom between his teeth as he smiled at her. She giggled and he dropped it on the other pillow, then crawled on top of her, keeping his weight on his hands and knees.

"Good morning," he said.

Rip sat up and yawned, and Keelie said, "That is the most worthless animal I've ever known. He wasn't supposed to let me fall asleep. And he was told to let me know when Jennifer came home."

"Jennifer didn't come home," Michael said. "I asked Grayson to pick them up from the dance. After they took Jason home, Jennifer spent the night at the cabin. Because it's Valentine's Day, and I need some alone time with you."

Rip jumped from the bed and ran from the room as if he had an appointment elsewhere, which made Keelie laugh.

"It is Valentine's Day," she said. "Where's my present?"

"There are chocolate Kisses on the dresser next to my gifts," he said. "And a little something else."

She looked toward the dresser and saw a vase of roses. "They're beautiful. Are they yellow? I can't tell in this light."

"They're peach. Would I give Texas roses to a Georgia girl?"

"I honestly was only joking about a present," she said. "I didn't think you'd have time, and I would have understood."

"Just because cows have calves doesn't mean you don't deserve to be romanced," he said.

"Did you get that off a Hallmark card?"

"I thought it up myself. You're not the only writer in the family."

Family . . . He thinks I'm family. That's it. I'm done for. "I should brush my teeth," she said quickly. "I can't believe I fell asleep in my clothes."

"Parenthood can kick your ass," Michael said. "I don't care about your teeth. I've been looking forward to this moment for hours—"

"Only hours?"

"Weeks."

"It's not like we haven't done it before."

"It's been a couple of days, and we were rushed. Now I have more time to impress you," he said as he unzipped her jeans.

"No one's going to call and ask you to inoculate a sick pig or something?" she asked and unbuttoned his shirt.

"I have another vet on call for emergencies. I'm all yours," he assured her as he pulled her sweater over her head.

"Then by all means, impress me," she said and struggled with the zipper on his jeans.

"Bossy."

"Is that another of your not-so-subtle ways of comparing me to a cow?"

"Call me crazy, but I thought you found that charming the first time I did it."

"You're crazy."

When they were finally down to skin on skin, Keelie wasn't surprised by the way her flesh tingled, burned, and quivered wherever he touched it. It was natural that the electricity between them would be even stronger during sex.

Nothing she'd done before came close to making her feel the way she did with Michael. Their lovemaking flowed easily between gentle, passionate, funny, and tantalizing. She felt alternately teased and satisfied, but most of all, she felt like she was with a man who knew what he was doing and liked doing it.

Later, she pulled the covers over them and buried her face against his chest. She knew how tired he must be. Even though her thoughts were racing, she stayed still so he could fall asleep.

"You just heaved the deepest sigh," Michael said. "Is it too much?"

"What?"

"What I want. What Jennifer needs. Are you over-whelmed?"

"No. I'm feeling a little vulnerable," she admitted.

"Are you afraid this won't last?"

"I don't want you to feel like I'm rushing you."

He gently traced her jaw with his thumb and nudged her face until she was looking at him. "Life may be a little slower in Coventry, but love chooses its own speed." He smiled. "You could probably say that a whole lot better than I did."

She returned the smile and said, "Try it in fewer words."

"I love you."

"That's perfect," she said. He stared at her until she laughed and said, "Call me crazy, but I love you, too."

"You're crazy if you think you're staying in bed all day. We have somewhere to go." He pulled back the covers and she shivered. "Dress warmly, because it's really cold today."

"Where are we going?" she asked.

He shook his head and said, "Meet me downstairs."

She dressed quickly in her room, then found him waiting just inside the front door. He took her coat from the closet, put on his coat and gloves, and as she was putting on her gloves, he opened the door and said, "Surprise!"

She gasped and threw her arms around him. "I thought you didn't control the weather."

"Anything for you," he said and laughed when she ran outside. "Be careful on that ankle."

She reached down, scooped up a handful of snow, held it to her face to sniff it, then dropped it. Rip ran out the door, wasted no time finding a place to take care of business, and went back inside.

"That dog has more sense than people do," Michael said.

"You mean me," Keelie said. "But I didn't grow up with snow. Houston's only had ice storms since I moved to Texas. Coventry has finally lived up to its promise."

"Did you remember to pick up your camera yesterday?"

"Yes," she said.

"I'll get it. Where is it?"

She told him, and he went back inside the house. She didn't want to disturb the untouched surface of the snow, but she couldn't stay off of it. She loved the way it crunched under her feet. When Michael came back, they walked to the road and took pictures of each other and the house. They propped the camera on the mail box and set the timer so they could get a picture of the two of them together in front of the house, and she laughed as Michael half ran, half slid to get to her before the shutter clicked.

"This is heaven," she said after he retrieved the camera.

"You're not cold?"

"I'm cold, but I don't care."

"Hungry?"

"I care a little about that," she admitted.

"The snow will be here all day. Let's eat breakfast."

They cooked it together, except she kept stopping to take pictures of him and Rip. "I can e-mail them to my family," she explained. "I'm sure they're dying to know what you look like."

"I'll bet Jennifer is having a great time with Grayson and Evan," Michael said when they sat down to eat.

"Will the roads be cleared anytime soon?"

"Some of them, but everything's closed anyway. Just keep your fingers crossed that all hell doesn't break loose on anyone's ranch or farm. Because I've got four-wheel drive, and there's not enough snow to keep me home if I'm needed elsewhere."

After they ate, they called Grayson's cabin, but no one answered. Rip went for another dash outside, then settled on Michael's bed. Keelie and Michael bundled up again. He took his cell phone, and she picked up her camera.

She looked at his boots, which were rugged, and said, "Do you think my boots will be okay? They're not really hiking boots—"

"They'll be fine," he said. "Come on."

She stopped outside the back door and surveyed the snow-covered fields, then followed him as he walked toward the back of the clinic. He stopped abruptly, and she bumped into him.

"You already got your Valentine's Day present. But you also have a Christmas present the Storeys weren't able to give you in December. With Grayson and Evan's help, they've spent weeks restoring it."

"What is it?"

He rolled up the exterior door on the back of the clinic to reveal a red sleigh. She stared at it for a few seconds, then walked over to examine its upholstered cushions and run her hands over the different metal and wooden pieces of the rails, carriage, and shafts.

"It's wonderful."

"Apparently, you told Santa that you'd always wanted to ride in a horse-drawn sleigh."

"Is there enough snow?" she asked.

"Look between the runners. The sleigh uses those wheels if the snow isn't deep enough. And this," he said, walking to a stall, "is Logan, one of Grayson's sweetest draft horses." He led out a dapple gray Percheron and talked Keelie through the harnessing process. She loved the sound of the bells on the harness and was almost dancing with eagerness. She hurried ahead of Michael and took pictures as he led Logan and the sleigh from the building. While he closed the door to the clinic, she climbed in behind the horse.

"I can't believe this surprise has been in the works since Christmas," she said after Michael made sure the lap robe was tucked snugly around her.

He signaled Logan to go. "Can you imagine how tortured Elenore must have been because she couldn't blog about it? It was Jennifer's idea for them to bring the sleigh here."

"We need to keep an eye on her," Keelie said. "She's too good at keeping secrets. Last night, she told me a sick bull was being brought in. I never connected the sudden appearance of Evan and Grayson to all the noise I'd heard outside, but that's when they delivered the sleigh, isn't it?"

"And Logan," Michael said. "Are you warm enough?"

"I don't know if it's the lap robe or you, but I'm very warm."

"It's so quiet after a snowfall," Michael said, settling back while she took a few more pictures.

Finally she snuggled next to him, leaning her head against his shoulder with a satisfied sigh. She wanted to remember everything about this moment. The sound of Logan's hooves against the ground and the music of the sleigh bells. The smell of the air. The crunch of the snow. The hush of the blanketed countryside. The texture of the wool lap robe against her hands whenever she removed her gloves to take a picture. And especially being next to someone who loved her and understood that the simple pleasure of a ride in a horse-drawn sleigh meant more to her than anything that could be bought or owned.

Rip seemed to be laughing, too, as he rode next to Destiny in the sleigh behind Mr. Joiner's draft horse. Snow had turned her lonely Christmas morning into a fairy tale. Destiny knew that she would hold this moment within her always: as shelter, as truth, as promise, as love . . .

Epilogue

Michael's green eyes crinkled over his surgical mask, and Keelie returned his smile, even though he, too, could see only eyes.

"This isn't the day I promised you, is it?" he asked.

"I've had worse Christmases," she said.

Other times when she'd assisted him, she'd learned that she wouldn't get too squeamish as long as she didn't focus on his patients. But this morning's crisis was a little different from his usual emergencies involving calves, horses, or sheep.

As Michael finished suturing Elvis the cat, she saw him glance at the clock. Again their eyes met, and she shrugged and said, "We'll just book another flight. It's really okay. Except for the cat part."

"Which cat part?" he asked. "The gaping leg wound? The lacerated ear? The bloody—"

"Now you're just being mean," she said, and his eyes crinkled again.

"I did offer to call Sara Warren to handle this," he reminded her.

It was funny how everyone in Michael's practice

always called Sara by her first and last names. Keelie thought Sara was a godsend. After she'd become Michael's partner in August, their lives had gotten a lot less hectic.

"I just thought about how I felt twelve months ago," she said. "When you saved Hamlet's life at Christmas. Elvis needed you today the way we did then."

"It's been quite a year, hasn't it?" he asked.

She nodded, and while she watched Elvis and handed Michael whatever he asked for, she reflected on a year of memories. Meeting Michael at Christmas. Quitting her job at Buy The Book. Moving to Coventry. Becoming part of Michael's and Jennifer's lives in February. Getting an offer from a publisher for Destiny's book in April. Enjoying her first Godiva Festival in June. Staying in Michael's house the entire month of July while Jennifer was with her grandparents in Galveston. And somehow, because she was so busy finishing her novel at the end of summer, she and Hamlet had just never moved back into her apartment.

Then Sara had joined Michael's practice. Michael was able to take Keelie and Jennifer on the first real vacation he'd had in years. They spent a week with Evan and Grayson at Grayson's Wyoming ranch. The night before they came back to Coventry, with a million stars overhead, Michael had asked her to marry him and given her a ring.

She wondered what the coming year had in store for her. Destiny's book would be out in four months. She would probably have wrapped up the remainder of her Wonderful Wife projects by then and could start working on her second novel.

"Are you still with me?" Michael asked, and Keelie was jolted back to the sterile operating room. When she nodded, he said, "You make a great assistant, Mrs. Boone."

"Don't tell my husband," she said. "He'll put me to work all the time."

She watched how gently Michael moved the cat from the table to a post-op cage, hanging the IV and making sure everything else was in order. They scrubbed down the surgical area together, then stood side by side to take off their gloves and wash their hands. When she pulled her mask down, he leaned over and kissed her.

"Seriously, thanks for helping me."

She nodded and sat on a stool next to Elvis while Michael went outside to update the family.

"You know," she said, "I don't even like cats. And Michael's not a small animal vet. You should feel very special. I even postponed my honeymoon for you, Elvis. At least you waited until after my wedding day to have your crisis."

They'd married in a small ceremony on Christmas Eve morning, with only Jennifer, the Storeys, Michael's parents, and Evan and Grayson there. Then Jennifer bossed around a catering company for their open-house reception. It seemed like everyone in Coventry had attended. By the time their guests were gone, she and Michael were too exhausted to even think of making love for the first time as a married couple, although Jennifer, Rip, and Hamlet were tucked away at Grayson's, and her in-laws had tactfully stayed at a Coventry bed-and-breakfast.

She yawned at Elvis. They'd gotten up at four so they could drive to the Dallas airport to take a flight to New York City. They planned to combine their honeymoon with Keelie's first face-to-face meeting with her editor. They had a million plans with Ivy and Ted. Holly and her family would be flying into New York from Scotland and staying for a few days before they returned to Houston. Keelie and Ivy would get their first look at the new Johnson granddaughter. Then Keelie and Michael were meeting Keelie's family—including Gram and Major Byrnes—in Connecticut. Snow had been promised, but Keelie knew how those promises usually turned out. She'd warned Michael that if Connecticut was unseasonably warm, Major Byrnes might drag him to a golf course.

She hadn't expected any of their other honeymoon plans to go awry. But just as Michael had loaded the last of their suitcases into his truck before dawn, a frantic couple and their eight-year-old son showed up with Elvis.

"I hope you learned your lesson," she spoke softly to the cat. "Whatever you tangled with—raccoon, possum, Bigfoot—is best left alone." The cat opened one bleary eye, which gave him a drunken look, then he began to purr. "That doesn't work on me. I told you I don't like cats."

"He doesn't care," Michael said, his hands falling on her shoulders. "Your work here is done, and you're of no further use to him."

"He will be okay, won't he?" Keelie asked.

"You're a cat-loving fraud."

"No, I'm not. I don't like cats."

"Right." He dimmed the lights and pulled her to her feet. "The family has been reassured and sent home. Sara Warren's on her way in to keep an eye on Elvis until his release. And we can't get a flight before tomorrow."

"I can't believe a cat named Elvis ruined my honeymoon."

"You look really sexy in those scrubs," Michael said,

nuzzling her ear. "We could start our honeymoon here. Nobody except Sara Warren knows we're still in town."

"And Elvis."

"He won't tell."

They walked together from the clinic and squinted at the brilliant morning sun. She helped Michael take their luggage back inside. Then they stood in the kitchen and stared blankly at each other.

"We were supposed to be ice skating at Rockefeller Center in a few hours," Keelie said.

"I know. The house seems too quiet, doesn't it?"

"How pathetic are we? We just got married. We should be racing for the sheets. Instead, I'm wishing Jennifer was here to cook breakfast."

"I keep thinking I need to take Rip out for his tenth urgent walk of the morning."

"I forgot to have a talk with Hamlet about his new father."

"If you'll cook breakfast, I'll start taking down decorations," Michael said. "It won't matter to Jen, since she won't be back until after New Year's."

"Good. I've been traumatized by all this Christmas crap."

Keelie was leaning against the kitchen counter, yawning and trying to avoid bacon grease as it popped, when she happened to look up. She rolled her eyes when she saw the mistletoe over the door. Jennifer and Evan had certainly left out no Christmas cliché when they decorated.

She turned off the bacon and went into the pantry for a ladder. She hauled it across the kitchen and was on the third step, stretching toward the mistletoe, when Michael's hands slid around her waist.

"This," he said, "is how it all began. Keelie, on a ladder, in the bookstore."

"It sounds like the end of Clue."

"It sounds like the beginning of romance."

He lowered her to the floor. She looked up into his piercing green eyes and said, "I don't really care about Rockefeller Center."

"I don't really need breakfast."

"I'm sure Jennifer, Rip, and Hamlet are fine at the cabin."

He held the mistletoe over their heads, kissed her, and said, "I think it's time to start our honeymoon."

"Have I ever told you," Keelie said as they walked out of the kitchen and headed for the stairs, "that I love Christmas?"

ABOUT THE AUTHOR

A graduate of the University of Alabama, Becky Cochrane lives in Texas with her husband and two dogs. She coauthored the novels *It Had to Be You, He's the One, I'm Your Man, Someone Like You, The Deal,* and *Three Fortunes in One Cookie.* She has also published short fiction.

Visit her website at www.beckycochrane.com.